UNDER THE STAIRS

A totally addictive psychological thriller
with a shocking twist

STEENA HOLMES

Originally published as *Lies We Tell Ourselves*

Revised edition 2024
Joffe Books, London
www.joffebooks.com

First published in Great Britain in 2020
as *Lies We Tell Ourselves*

This paperback edition was first published in
Great Britain in 2024

This book is a work of fiction. Names, characters, businesses, organizations, places and events are either the product of the author's imagination or are used fictitiously. Any resemblance to actual persons, living or dead, events or locales is entirely coincidental. The spelling used is American English except where fidelity to the author's rendering of accent or dialect supersedes this.

Cover art by Nick Castle

ISBN: 978-1-83526-376-1

To my aunt,
Because you are brave, courageous, and amazing.
Keep doing what you are doing. Keep saving those
you can save. Keep loving those who need that love.
Thank you for being an inspiration.

TRIGGER WARNING

The following novel contains distressing content and subject matter. Reader discretion is advised.

A THOUGHT ON LIARS . . .

Some liars are so expert they deceive themselves.

—AUSTIN O'MALLEY, *Keystones of Thought*

PRESENT DAY

CHAPTER 1

PAISLEY VALLEY HOSPITAL
3:30 a.m.

Everyone lies: the doctors who say I'm safe, the nurses who promise I'm protected, the police who swear to find my abuser.

Everyone is lying — to themselves, to me.

No one can protect me. No one can keep me safe. No one will find the man who did this. Even though he's probably right here, in the middle of this mess, known by everyone.

I shiver as I lie in this bed, a thin gray blanket my only protection against the cold blast from the air conditioning. I could press the call button and ask for a new heated one, but that would mean having to reach the button that slipped from its placement on the bed.

I can't do that. I can't move. I can't talk. I can barely see. Every single bone in my body feels broken, my skin flayed, my nerve endings on fire.

It's a miracle I'm alive, they say.

I say miracles don't happen in today's world.

The pain, a cascading waterfall with a monstrous roar that's both deafening and destructive, slowly recedes until it's a dull throb, thanks to the morphine pumping through my system.

I know tears flow from my swollen eyes; they tickle against my skin and I wish I could whisk them away.

There's a commotion outside my hospital room. I know there's a police officer stationed by my door, a female. I don't recognize her, which is a good thing. I don't trust anyone. I can't. I've learned the hard way that those you think are on your side, the ones that should be protecting you . . . they're the ones to fear the most.

There's nothing quiet about this hospital. Not tonight, not at this hour. I hear everything: the squeak of a shoe, the whoosh from an opened door, the ding of the elevator, the ring of a phone.

And his voice.

Oh God . . . not here, not now. I'm supposed to be safe.

It's low, a murmur, but it's his.

I recognize that tone. I've listened to it for seven years. It's haunted my dreams, my nightmares, my every waking moment.

It's a tone full of danger. I've learned to be careful, to be wary. I've learned how to play his games. But here, with whoever is guarding me . . . I hear a hint of friendliness that has me shaking.

Don't be fooled, I try to yell out, but the sound is a muffled moan, a groan full of pain and fear.

At first, I think no one hears me, but then there's a pause and a creak from the door as it opens. Light from the hallway spills into my room, illuminating the dull walls and machines surrounding me.

There's a thud of a footstep and I feel his presence. He's watching me.

One machine, the one playing a consistent tune, is louder now, the beeps increasing. My breath hitches. My heart stops, then starts, blood rushes to my ears with the power of a tidal wave.

There's a chuckle. His chuckle. No. No-no-nonononono. He's here. He can't be here. They said I was safe. I'm not safe.

I'm in danger. More danger now even than before, when he beat me and left me for dead.

"My Angel." His whisper slithers over me, sealing me in a skin of cold sweat. I shiver. I shake. I want to scream, but my swollen throat won't cooperate.

It takes a mountain of strength, but I search for the call button. The pad of my index finger, the only one I can move, hits the bed, with a tap-tap-tap, until it hits something solid. I feel for the indent on the button as I stare at the man who scares me more then hell itself.

He's here. Just out of reach, a hovering shadow. I barely make him out, he's a blur, I know he's here. I know it's him.

"You think you've gotten away, that you're safe now, but that's not true. No one can protect you like I can. No one can keep your son safe, like I can."

I freeze. He keeps talking, his husky whispers wrapping me in chains, binding me to him.

"Stay quiet and he stays safe. That's all you need to do. Don't say a word and I'll return him to you." He hovers over me, close enough that I see the fire of truth shine bright in his eyes. He's a demon in disguise.

"Tell anyone about me, whisper my name even, and you'll never see your son alive again." He bends down, placing a kiss on my lips, searing himself into the open wounds he ministered earlier.

"Oh, my Angel." If his whisper is meant as a caress, then it's peeling my skin off in layers with its touch. "What will we do with you?"

TWELVE YEARS AGO

CHAPTER 2

PAIGE

According to my father, life lessons are never convenient and you can bet your fortune that they'll happen at the worst possible moments.

"Paige Fischer," he likes to say, "don't ever let your guard down. The moment you do, bam, the punch is gonna knock you out cold."

Well, I'm done with every single lesson life has to offer. Done. Finished. Complete. I've had enough with learning, enough with all the expectations . . . I just want to live my life.

Being the good girl, the smart girl, the responsible girl is so overrated. I'm sixteen. Six-freaking-teen and I should be treated like every other girl my age. So why aren't I? Because I'm better than the others? Because I'm smarter than the others? Because according to my parents, I should know better? Screw that.

Screw all of that.

Screw responsibility. Screw all the labels and expectations and . . . just screw it all.

It's quarter to four in the afternoon and my sister is making me late, again. I stomp my foot in acute frustration while

I wait for her to finish flirting with her pick-of-the-week boy. Everything about my twin sets me on edge today: from the flip of her strawberry-blonde hair to the give-me-a-break giggle and coy twist of her hips. My sister loves the game of chase, of setting her sights on someone unattainable and striking gold. Normally she casts her sights high, on the seniors at school, but today it's . . .

Actually, I have no clue who the guy my sister's flirting with is.

"Watch out for your sister," Dad always says. "She sees life through different lenses than you do."

Different lenses my foot. That's just what Jess wants our parents to think, that's all.

"Can we go already?" I call out, my voice pitched with hints of frustration.

Jess waves her hand, as if shooing me away. Oh no she didn't . . .

I should just leave her behind, that's what I should do. Serve her right too. See how she likes Dad tearing a new one up, instead of me. Even as I grumble, I know it's all a lie. I'd be the one getting ripped a strip or two, not Jess. Never Jess.

I clutch my schoolbag tighter against my chest, the bubble of anxiety that blooms against my rib cage growing as I watch my sister wrap another sex-crazed boy around her pinkie finger. If we don't head home soon, I'm going to be late.

Normally it doesn't matter. But today isn't a normal day. Today, I'm in a rush, thanks to one of my teachers being concerned about my less-than-perfect score on a recent assignment.

"Paige Fischer, I know you can do better than that. I'm worried about you. Are things okay at home? Friends bothering you here at school?" Mrs. Morrison had placed her hand on my shoulder, a gesture of concern, but it only made things worse. I like Mrs. Morrison, she's one of my favorite teachers, but to single me out like that, while everyone walked past in the hallways . . . thanks for nothing.

If it wasn't for my parents' number-one rule that they refuse to budge on — never walk home after school alone — I'd leave. In a heartbeat, without a second glance. I'm late for work again because of Jess. But does anyone care about that? About my life and how Jess always affects it? No.

If I'm late again, I'm fired. My boss says I've already been given too many chances.

I'm not sure what scares me more — my father finding out I'm about to be fired, or him finding out I'd left Jess alone to walk home by herself.

Either way, I'm screwed.

"Go ahead," Jess calls out, a hint of laughter in her voice. "I won't be long." Her dimples deepen with the tilt of her head. "I promise."

I was about to argue but stopped myself. Why bother? It's not like she'd listen anyway.

Besides, she just gave me an out.

"Fine. But you can be the one to tell Dad." I let that threat hang between us before turning my back on my sister and the boy, who were both clearly laughing at me.

I hate her. Hate how everyone thinks she's the prettier one, the popular one, the one who gets away with everything. Our parents have never really understood the animosity between us. Trust me, the feelings are not one-sided either. Jess hates me just as much and tells me every single day.

Mom thinks that because we're identical twins, we're supposed to be the bestest of friends. Like those twins in the Sweet Valley High books Mom read when she was our age.

Trust me, our relationship is nothing like those girls in the books.

Sure, we might look the same, but that's where the similarities end.

"Jessica Fischer, I hate you," I say, dragging the words out, my frustration-laced voice rising an octave with each step I take toward home.

I refuse to look back to see if she's following.

It's not until I'm about two blocks from home that the fear of ramifications from leaving her behind hits me.

My father is going to kill me.

Why, I have no idea. We live in the middle of freaking nowhere in the state of Minnesota. Small Town, USA. Safest place in the country, as my father likes to boast. Which makes his rule of never walking alone all the more absurd.

If I stop now and wait for Jess to catch up, then technically I'm not breaking his rule. But all it takes is a look at my watch to confirm I have maybe fifteen minutes to waste before I need to leave for work.

"You know, you do this every . . ." I turn to face my sister whom I fully believe is behind me. She has to be. She's just as scared of our father as I am.

Except she isn't behind me.

Jess isn't strolling down the sidewalk, arm in arm with that stupid boy she was flirting with. I pivot and look across the street, to see if she's walking on the other side, and a sick, twisted, gnarly knot sprouts in my stomach for a fraction of a second before growing into a flare of molten anger when the realization hits me.

My sister is nowhere to be seen.

Damn it.

Jess knows I'm in a rush; she knows if I'm late, I'll be fired. She knows this and obviously doesn't care. Out of the two of us, I'm the oldest by seven minutes, so technically, I'm in charge. Which isn't fair. Not in the slightest.

"Life is never fair, kiddo," my father likes to say. He likes to say a lot of other stupid stuff too. Like, *if wishes were dollar bills, we'd be rich*, and *since life is like a game of chess, we always play two steps ahead.*

If life is like a game of chess, then why aren't we all ahead already? If Dad lived what he spouted, we'd be ahead of the game, rather than knee-deep in debt. Ever since he changed jobs, life also changed, and not for the better. We rarely see him now, mainly only on weekends thanks to his shift-work. Mom had to find a part-time job that turned into full-time, which means I was also strongly encouraged to get an after-school job. If I want clothes, it's my responsibility now. But not Jess, oh no. Jessica isn't as book smart as I am, which means she needs more time to study during the week. She only has to work on weekends.

Life sucks and it sucks hard.

"I don't have time for this," I mutter as I scan the sidewalks, the yards, even the front porches for Jess. "Fine then," I finally call out, my voice a little raised in case she's trying to pull a prank on me. "I'll just tell Dad." I issue the same threat as before, hoping it's enough to light a fire beneath Jess's oh-so-perfect butt.

I don't wait around. Instead, I pick up my pace and basically run the rest of the way home. There's still no sign of Jess as I unlock the front door, but whatever. Not my problem. I repeat this over and over in my head. Maybe if I explain to Mom, Dad won't have to find out.

Sometimes Mom is a good buffer.

Sometimes.

I rush to change into my drab uniform for the local ice cream shop of black pants and a white polo shirt, pulling my hair back into a high ponytail, and gulp down a glass of milk, all the while keeping an eye on the clock. Work is only a few blocks away, mere minutes since I'm riding my bike . . . if I'm lucky.

Jess still isn't home.

Whatever. Not my problem. I keep that mantra going as I race to work with minutes to spare, and as I flip burgers and pour hot fudge over ice cream. I repeated it to my mom when she called earlier, asking if I knew where my sister was, and I keep that same train of thought as I take my time riding my bike home after my shift.

Why is it okay for me to bike to and from work alone, but not okay for Jess to walk home from school by herself? It's a double standard. We're the same freaking age.

Armed with a good half dozen arguments as to why I shouldn't get in trouble for breaking one of Dad's most important rules, I'm caught off guard when I notice a police car parked outside our house.

I skid my bike to a stop at the end of the driveway. Mom stands in the window of our front room, peering out the window, as if waiting for me. The light from the open windows shows Mom isn't alone.

Why are the police at the house? Is it Dad? Has something happened?

Mom motions for me to hurry.

My chest feels like it's about to explode from the instant pressure of anxiety that hits me. I drop my bike on the driveway, not bothering with the kickstand, and rush to the front door. Fear fuels my steps. Panic carries me across the paving stones and launches me into Mom's waiting arms.

Her arms aren't warm, welcoming, wrapped around me in protection.

Her arms are straight, strong, her stranglehold of a grip fastened around my shoulders.

"Where is your sister?" Mom asks, her voice carrying the weight of bricks despite the fact she's a clear mess.

The nauseating grasp that sweeps over me isn't because Mom's lips tremble with her question, nor because her eyes are saucer wide as she stares at me.

It's because Mom's voice buckles, breaks, bursts with a rawness I've never heard before as she repeats her question.

"Paige, where is Jessica?"

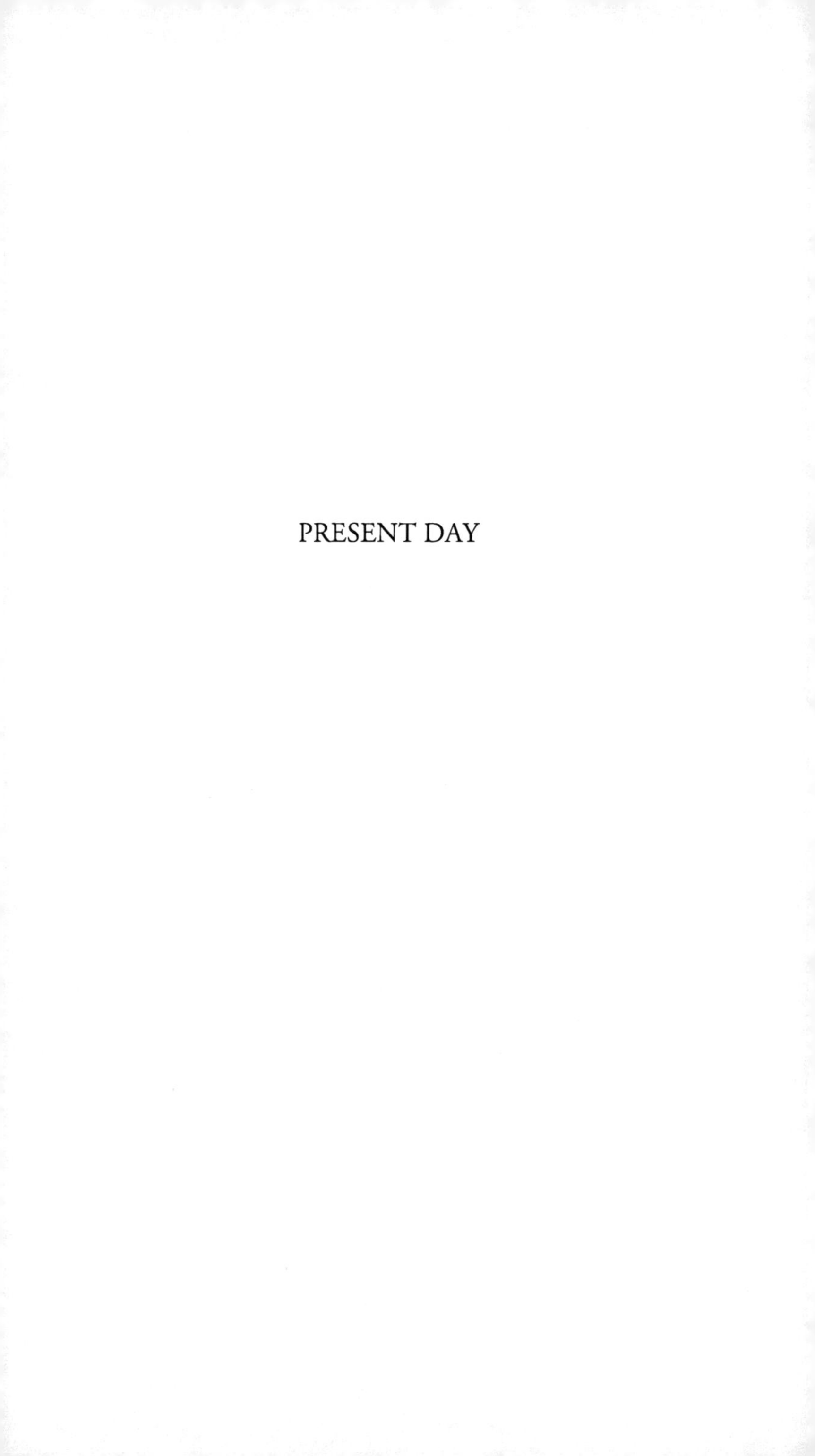

PRESENT DAY

CHAPTER 3

PAISLEY VALLEY HOSPITAL
8:00 a.m.

There's a clang that makes my arms jolt, and pain radiates across my shoulders, over my chest and settles in my breastbone.

The sound repeats, just as loud, but I don't jump this time.

My eyes blink open, the sleep breaking up until my vision is partially clear. I can see better today, I'm still viewing the walls of my room through slits, but I can see more, at least.

"Thank God. I thought you'd never wake up."

There's someone else here, sitting beside my bed. Her hair is fire, flaming against the backdrop of the sun pushing through the open window.

I can smell the air. It's crisp, clean, fresh and full of rain.

My lips are dry, cracked, and I taste blood as I force them open.

She moves, stands, the chair she's sitting on pushing back with a *screeeeeech*.

"Here," she says, "let me get you some water. The nurses say to take sips." She comes near and I see her face now. Pale skin covered in freckles, bright green eyes and a bowtie smile shaded in gloss. Her hands come closer, holding a cup with a straw.

I take sips. Several sips of lukewarm water, holding the liquid in my mouth, letting it coat my dry tongue. I'm half afraid to swallow, afraid of how it will feel.

Like glass shards, that's how it feels.

I wince as she pulls the straw from my lips and I can't hide the well of tears that pool in my eyes then slide down my cheeks. They're liquid fire, those teardrops, marking a trail on my skin that will never go away.

With a gentleness I don't deserve, the fire goddess is there with a tissue and slowly dots my skin, each touch a whisper.

"Here, we grabbed a few things from home," she says, withdrawing. She bends down and pulls a bag onto her lap. "I figured you would want this." She holds up a small container of something . . . I can't make it out.

My head pounds, a steady thump-thump-thump.

She twists the cap then glides what I assume is lip gloss, first on the bottom lip, then the top. The relief comes in waves and is slight, but it's there.

"Jamie ran home to grab some stuff, but he'll be back. He was here all night, by your side, as soon as Detective Lindsay called him. Girl, we were all so worried about you."

Jamie? Who is she talking about? Worried about me? I don't even know who this person is.

The smile on her face is soft, gentle, and she watches me in a way that suggests looking at me hurts her.

Who does she think I am?

I make a sound, a slight moan, but she's shaking her head.

"Shhh. The doctors said your trachea is fractured. They want you to remain as silent as you can, no moaning or talking for a minimum of two days, okay? There's a lot of damage to your throat and it needs to heal. They almost had to intubate you when you came in, something about being unable to breathe, but you're a fighter." Her eyes glisten as she stares at me. "Thank God you're a fighter." She looks away and wipes at the tears that slide down her cheeks.

What is she talking about? My heart quickens, picks up speed until it's pushing against my chest. Last night . . . I remember last night, and there was no one sitting by my side.

Other than HIM. I remember HIM. His words. His threats.

I glance around the room, overwhelmed with panic and anxiety, searching the corners, the shadows, for his presence.

"Shhh, honey, it's okay, everything's okay now. I promise." She's on her feet, bending over me, her hand inches from my fingers. "You're safe now. There are police outside your door. We're going to find whoever did this to you, I promise."

Okay? Everything is not okay. HE was here last night. If I'm being protected, if someone sat with me all night, how could HE have come in?

There's only one explanation. He spoke to the cop outside my door. They knew one another. Maybe he knew this Jamie too. Which means . . . oh God. It means I'm not safe.

I remember him walking in. I remember his chuckle. I remember him saying my name. I remember his threats. But I don't remember him leaving.

"I can't believe this happened. I still can't get over . . . One minute you were beside me as we visited with Gabrielle, then you left and I assumed you went home. Next thing I know I'm getting a call from Lindsay that you went off to find your sister, and he's yelling at me, asking why I didn't stop you. Why didn't you tell me?" She winces as she looks me over, taking in my broken body. "I'm so sorry."

I wish I could tell her I'm not who she thinks I am.

I wish I knew who she thought I was.

"When they brought you in . . . the swelling and bruising . . ." She looks away. "Thank God someone recognized you."

Wait. Someone recognized me? How? I haven't been *seen* in a long time, and not in any way someone would recognize me today.

HE made damn sure of that.

"I know this must be a lot to take in. I want you to know you're okay, you're safe and Lindsay has everyone searching for whoever did this to you." A fierce look enters her eyes.

I blink and try very hard not to swallow. I give myself a moment to take everything in: the machines around me, the intravenous lines attached to me, the bulky swath of bandages covering my body.

I'm alive. Yesterday, I didn't think I would survive.

The pounding in my chest notches up a volume, along with the beeping of one of those machines.

"I'm sorry," she says. "I know this must all seem scary. But you haven't been alone since you were brought in. Both Jamie and your mom have been here. Jamie will be back, and until then, you've got me. I hope that's okay?"

I breathe, in-out, in-out. Mom was here? My mom? No . . . that's not possible. My mom thinks I'm dead.

Besides, they don't know who I am. They obviously think I'm someone else.

I need to calm. I need to focus. I need to . . .

She's concerned; it's written all over her face.

I can't talk, my throat burns even just swallowing, but I move my lips to form one word. She's watching me. I mouth the word again.

"Where?" she says. "You want to know where you are?" She sounds confused, and I don't blame her.

"Honey, you're here at Paisley Valley Central Hospital." She pauses, searching my eyes for recognition.

My heart jolts, jumps, skips a few beats, refusing to settle.

Something in my eyes must catch her attention.

"What's wrong?"

Her gaze is intense, her focus laser sharp.

She's waiting for any minuscule movement from me, to indicate one way or another my answer.

No. I mouth the word and shake my head a little. I can't be here. Not here. This isn't right.

"No? What do you mean?"

This has to be a game or a test. Why is HE doing this to me? Why? He wouldn't bring me here. Not here. There has to be a reason. This is payback for what I did. It has to be.

"Honey, it's okay, I promise." Her voice is soft, with a tender cadence. Whoever she is, he brought her here to test me. I can't trust her. I can't trust anything she tells me.

If there's one thing I've learned since I was kidnapped at age sixteen it's this: No one is who they seem. Everyone wears a mask.

Everyone lies.

Breathe in. Hold my breath, count to three. Exhale. I do this over and over until I'm sure my face is a blank slate.

I have so many questions, but until I feel safe, I don't dare ask them.

There's a knock on the door. She finally looks away.

And that's when I let her words hit me, wash over me, flood me with their truth.

I know it can't be true, but for this brief moment, I'll pretend it is.

I'm in Paisley Valley.

I'm finally home.

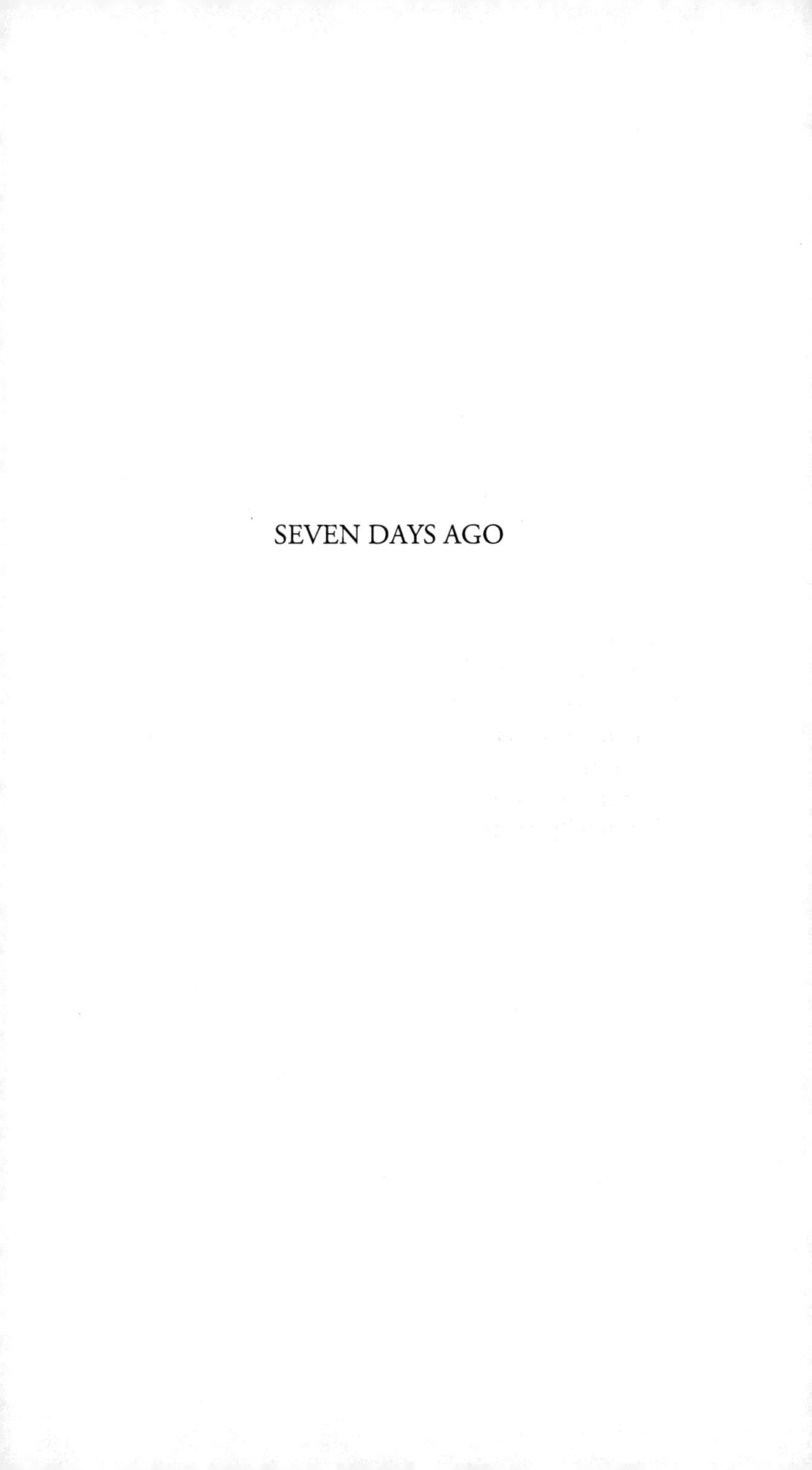

SEVEN DAYS AGO

CHAPTER 4

PAIGE

My cubicle isn't decorated with motivational posters, cute stuffed animals or a jar full of red licorices or bubblegum jellybeans, like others around me.

It doesn't scream customization or individuality or even hint at my personality.

It's never going to win one of the regular office cubicle-decorating contests either, for one simple reason.

Mine is covered in photos. And not the cute ones of smiling babies and adorable puppies in baskets.

The images I've clipped, taped and pinned to every available wall surface are of children, teens and young adults who have disappeared while on my watch. They belong to families I've made promises to help, promises I have every intention of keeping.

Working with CHILD — Children who are Hidden, Lost or Disappeared — helps me to keep these promises.

There are only two personal items on my desk: framed photos. One is of my son, Flynn, who just turned five years old. He's the love of my life. The other is of my twin sister, Jessica, forever frozen as a bright and beautiful sixteen-year-old.

Even now, twelve years later, it's hard for me to look at an image of my sister without the familiar weight of guilt and blame settling on my shoulders. You'd think I'd be used to it by now, but I'm not. The weight tends to get heavier with each passing year.

The person who said that time heals all wounds is a liar.

Ding-a-ling-ling.

The little bell hanging behind me rings. I'm not a fan of the bell, but the others in the office think it's cute. Apparently, I'm known for getting so absorbed in whatever I'm working on that I rarely hear my name being called. I swivel in my chair to find Anita, the full-time office manager-slash-receptionist, who also rules the staff with an iron fist and gentle heart, behind me.

"Hey, what's up?"

"You haven't heard?" Anita leans in close when I remain silent. "The cell? Detective Lindsay? Seriously . . . where have you been all morning?"

"Right here, working. Why?" She looks worried, which in turns worries me. Anita is never worried. Never off balance. Her eyebrows scrunch together and her lips turn into a frown.

"You seriously don't know? The whole office is talking about it. Didn't you check your email?"

The exasperation in her voice has me reaching for my phone to check my messages.

"Oh, read it later. I'll give you the bare bones," she says, swiping at the air, dismissing the fact I'm not up to date on the latest gossip.

She glances around and any heads turned our way are now looking elsewhere. I'm working in an office space with about thirteen other cubicles and normally there's a low-level hum that hovers over the room, but that hum is now a buzz which has me on my feet. People are grouped together, their voices hushed, their glances all seemingly in every direction but mine.

What is going on?

Anita gives her head a little shake and stamps her foot. "Little gossips, that's all they are."

"What are you talking about?"

Without answering, Anita grabs my sweater from the back of my chair, my purse from the hanger on my file cabinet, and then pulls at my arm until I'm following her out of the main office space and into the narrow hallway leading toward the front reception area.

"We have a Code Three," Anita says once we're alone.

I twist my arm from her hold and stop just before we hit the main office door. At CHILD, we have a five-code system. Three days ago, we had a Code One, which was an alert via social media on one of our missing persons files, and we were in the middle of exploring that. Most of the time, Code Ones rarely turn into anything, but when they do, they become a Code Two. A Code Two means there's been a possible sighting and when that happens, the whole office is on alert.

A Code Three is more serious. This is when a sex trafficking ring is located. The last time we were a part of a cell being located was a year ago.

Could the two be connected somehow?

"What do you need from me?"

We all have our roles when it comes to a Code Three. My role is of support. I'm there, part of the team, supporting the victims once we've been given access. Part of that support is helping to locate families and prepare them for reunion.

I'm expecting Anita to say that she has a list and wants me to go over the names of victims with her, but instead, she remains silent. She's angry, I see it, from the tightness of her lips, the way her shoulders are pushed back and even the raised chin. Angry and also jittery, her fingers tap-dancing along one thigh, and she's looking at everything, everywhere.

Anita is normally calm. Focused. The one to go to during an emergency.

"Come to my desk. I need to stay by the phone and I've been gone long enough." She opens the door and I'm hit with a series of flashes.

There's a mob outside our front office doors, a throng of reporters with their cameras focused on us, the flashes as they take photos blinding. There are two police officers standing guard in front of the doors, barricading anyone from entering.

"What the hell is going on, Anita?"

A new hire, Julianna, I think, gives out a small cry of relief as she sees us. She jumps out of the chair and rushes our way. "Thank God you're back. The phone won't stop and the people outside . . . please can I go back to my desk now?" Without Anita giving her the go-ahead, she pushes past us and escapes.

"She's not going to last long," Anita mutters. She ignores the throng outside the door and retreats to her desk. "I can't believe there's so many of them out there."

"Anita." I can't hide my frustration, despite how hard I'm trying to remain calm and not explode. While a Code Three is serious, with a ring being located and police being alerted, it means all hands on deck, time is tight, everyone focused. What it doesn't mean is that we have reporters outside our door, police standing guard, or phones ringing off the hook.

"Lindsay was there."

I instinctually nod. Of course he was there. Detective Lindsay runs the local task force.

"He was there, Paige. Before the police arrived on scene." Her tone is sharp, with an edge I don't want to touch.

I shake my head, not accepting what her tone means. She knows better than to even hint that there's anything shady about the man. Detective Lindsay is a friend. He comes over to the house for dinner, takes my son out to get milkshakes, drinks beer with my fiancé. He was the officer who took over my sister's missing person case, who has stood by my side all through the years as I've looked for her.

Detective Lindsay is a good guy. A solid man. An honorable man. He wouldn't be involved in a sex trafficking ring. He's the one trying to break them up and save the innocents.

There could be any number of reasons for him being there, but the main one seems pretty obvious to me.

"Right . . . because we were the ones who gave him the sighting information. I imagine he was following a lead."

She shakes her head. "From what I've read on his reports, this address was never on his radar. Plus, he's been completely focused on a different town."

That doesn't make sense at all. "Maybe someone passed him the message, then."

Anita remains silent. The fact she's not saying anything has me on high alert.

"He was not involved." The words spill out of my mouth on their own accord.

"Of course not," Anita says, but she hesitates.

She hesitates. Damn it.

I lean my head back and stare up at the blank ceiling, looking for answers, not from the tiles but from my own head that won't stop spinning.

Why was Lindsay there? What does that mean? What are the next steps?

First things first. We have procedures we follow for these incidents, procedures that help us navigate when the waters are muddied.

My role at CHILD is to facilitate relationships and communication between families and the authorities. I'm the middleman who barrages the police for updates, who hounds them to keep searching, leaving the families free to grieve, to grow and to keep believing in a better outcome. I'm also an advocate for the victims, there to listen, to make sure they are heard and protected.

It's not an easy role; sometimes it's mind numbing, monotonous and repetitive, while at other times it's heart-wrenching, exhausting and electrifying.

Today it's going to be a mixture of all those feelings.

My attention goes toward the crowd outside. I could swear there are more people out there now than even a few minutes ago. I don't understand why they're all here. Who tipped them off, and about what?

"Yeah, I know. Weird, right?" Anita says, as if reading my mind. "Lois is going to go out in a bit to talk with them. Until then, she says we're to ignore them and any comments are to be no comments."

Lois Fairfield is the CEO of CHILD and a battle-ax with the softest heart.

"But why are they here?" That's what I'm trying to wrap my head around.

"Isn't that obvious?" A voice to my right jolts me. Speak of the devil . . . She closes a door behind her. "The reporters are here because they're a pack of jackals at the whiff of decay. Someone let it slip that one of ours is involved in that sex ring." She turns her *don't dare tell me it was you* look toward Anita, who blanches.

"Anita?" I whisper her name, praying to God, if He was even listening, that it wasn't her.

"Definitely not," she says, her gaze focused on the wall opposite her. Her eyes are moving back and forth, as if processing a memory. "No, I haven't said anything. Maybe to Derek when we were talking, but I don't think anyone was here who could have overheard . . . Oh no . . ." She heaves a sigh that should have moved her desk with its heaviness. "Julianna, the new girl, was covering the phone for me for a minute or two. I told her to only redirect calls or take a message, and that if any call came from a reporter, she was to say no comment."

"I think, for the time being, either you are the one to answer the calls or you let them go to voice mail." Lois's voice is clipped, sharp and very clear with direction.

"Yes ma'am," Anita says, nodding her head, her cheeks flaming red.

"Paige, come join me for a moment, will you?" Lois gives me a slight nod and even slighter smile before turning in the direction of the executive wing. Without a backward glance toward Anita, I follow after Lois, walking past the director offices where the doors are all closed. Our footsteps are muffled on the carpet and it's only the dull thud of her office door closing that breaks the silence between us.

It doesn't break the tension, however.

Considering Lois is the CEO and that she has a corner office with large windows, her decor style is very minimal. Most of the decorations on her wall are of framed letters from families she's worked with, or drawings from children she's helped rescue.

I remember the first time I saw her office. It was on the day she offered me a position with the organization. I knew, from seeing what was on her walls, that I would like her and wanted to work with her.

My feelings have never changed.

"Paige, there's something you need to know," Lois says after she takes her seat and motions me to do the same. She shuffles all the papers on her desk into one pile and pushes them to the side. She takes the top one and sets it down in front of her.

"I'm sure Anita has already informed you that Detective Lindsay was at the location of the cell before the other officers arrived?" She pauses, looks at me, and I'm squirming in my seat. I'm not going to like what she has to say.

"He has nothing to do with that ring," I interject, unwilling to listen to her say otherwise.

"That remains to be seen, but until I know more, I'm inclined to believe you." The absoluteness that comes from her eases a knot that has settled inside me.

"There were two male adults in the house when they busted through the doors," she continues. "Unfortunately, as much as I hate to admit it, one of our own was in that house, a volunteer you work closely with."

I'm finding it hard to swallow. My throat is suddenly dry, my tongue stuck to the roof of my mouth. I want to ask who, who could be involved in something so horrific as a child sex ring, but I can't. Maybe it's fear. Maybe it's ignorance. Maybe it's because once that genie is out of the bottle, all the magic is gone.

Once I know, I'll never not know. But I need to know, and avoiding the issue is me avoiding reality.

She opens her mouth as if about to say something but then closes it again. There's this look in her eyes, like she's trying to figure out the best move in this scenario, before she leans back in her chair.

"Have we ever had someone from CHILD involved in . . ." I can't finish the sentence, the idea abhorrent. That one of our own would . . .

"No. Not a staff member, and certainly never a volunteer. We do extensive background checks. The fact this went unchecked, unnoticed . . ." Lois looks like she's going to vomit.

"Today, of all days . . ." Lois mumbles. "Twelve years for your sister, isn't it? Listen, go home. Your focus should be on your family. You should be with your family. Tomorrow is going to be crazy and I'm going to need you. I'm sure it's going to be a while before we're brought in for the victims of the raid that's still ongoing, if we're brought in at all."

Lois rubs her face, the weight of what's happening showing in the fine lines around her eyes.

"Who was it?"

"Bryan Powers."

I feel like I've been gut-kicked. Bryan? I can't wrap my head around that.

"I know. I feel the same, trust me."

"I vetted him. I approved him. I . . . How could I have missed it? This? I can't . . ." For a moment everything I'm thinking, feeling, disappears and I'm empty inside. Then the tsunami of anger hits, piercing my heart and spreading out until my hands fist, my leg bounces and I need to hit something.

"We all missed it, Paige. All of us." She looks down at a file on her desk, his file probably. "Pastor Jeremy's recommendation was the shining star in our acceptance. But we did everything by the book, everything is checked off. I don't know how this was missed, but it was." There's something in her voice that screams of self-incrimination. She's taking the blame, I know it.

She shouldn't. This wasn't her fault.

"Put it on me," I say, knowing exactly what will happen if she does. I'll be let go. I'll be the scapegoat. I'll have to step down but . . . this was my fault. Bryan is . . . was . . . on my team.

"Until we know more, no one is taking the blame but me. Is that understood? The timing is . . . unfortunate. But I'm going to need your team to step back until we can do an internal investigation, okay?"

"Me included?"

She shakes her head. "No, just our volunteer program. It's going to be halted for now. I'll have Anita take care of organizing that." She sighs. "I would, however, like you to go home. We both know what the upcoming days are going to look like. Take the time to grieve today, because I'll need your full attention come tomorrow."

Go home? Now? After this bombshell?

"What about Detective Lindsay?" How is he involved? I have so many questions, too many, they swirl in my head, jumbled together until nothing is making any sense.

"Until I know more, I'm not ready to make a decision on that."

The air in the room grows cold, heavy, weighted with everything not being said. Her desk phone rings and I stand. I can't even begin to imagine what it's like to carry this.

She ignores the call.

"Was that all you wanted to tell me?" I ask.

She weighs her answer.

"Detective Lindsay found photos. Of a lot of girls, ranging over years, he thinks. They haven't been released to the public — not until the families are contacted."

When she pauses, a thousand different ideas race through my mind, but there's one that screams so loud, the words leave my mouth before I can stop them.

"Was Jessica in any of those photos?" I want her to say no, but I pray she says yes.

Over the past twelve years I've come up with hundreds of scenarios of what could have happened to my sister. From all of the possibilities — being left in a ditch, buried in the desert, held hostage in a basement — sold to sex traffickers has always been my worst nightmare. I don't want there to be photos from this cell of my sister, because it means she's lived through hell. But at the same time, I need there to be photos, because it means she could be alive.

This could be the very first sighting of my sister since the day she disappeared while walking home from school.

There's a lot Lois doesn't say, but I can read between the lines, even though, right now, I wish I were illiterate.

CHAPTER 5

I take the long route back to my desk and find myself staring at my sister's photo.

All morning I've been trying to push the significance of today to the side. I've pretended it's a day like any other: made Flynn's breakfast, sipped coffee with Jamie out on the front porch, and then waved goodbye as we all went our separate ways — Mom to water the garden, Jamie to walk Flynn to school. Even though no one mentioned the anniversary, I hugged Flynn extra long before he left, and the gaze Mom and I shared said more than usual.

We didn't need to look at a calendar to remember.

Working here, I've become a master at compartmentalization. I've had to, or I would be a basket case.

But today . . . Jess doesn't deserve being pushed to the side, regardless of the reason. And especially because of the reason.

Lois is right, I don't need to be here.

"I miss you, Jess." I kiss the tips of my fingers then place them on Jess's photo. "I will find you, I promise."

My desk phone rings. For a second, I consider ignoring it and hiking out of the office, via the back door, before anyone notices I'm gone, but when I see it's the front desk, specifically Anita, I find myself picking the receiver up.

"Hey, I'm just about to leave."

"Paige, John and Elizabeth are here." Her voice is high, too high and there's a false cheerfulness that I know can mean only one thing.

"John's mad, isn't he?" John Mandera is a wonderful man with a heart of gold and the spirit of a male gorilla intent on protecting his family.

"Perfect. I'll place them in one of the rooms, does that work for you?" Completely ignoring my question, she doesn't give me time to respond, the line goes dead right away.

Well, there goes that idea of heading home.

I pull out the Mandera file from my cabinet and run through the most recent information. Gabrielle Mandera, missing since age sixteen, last seen outside a sandwich deli two years ago. Nothing since then. Her parents have been searching for her for ten years.

In my world, ten years can feel both like a lifetime and like no time has passed at all.

Gabrielle is now twenty-six. I hate to think what that means. Since she'd been seen only two years ago, a large part of me has hoped she's living on her own, not ready to reconnect with her family.

Three days ago we had a Code One — a tip that came from our social media page. Someone recognized Gabrielle's photo. We sent that tip to Detective Lindsay, who has been following up. Three days ago, John and Elizabeth were here, in the office, where we went over the possible steps taken from that sighting.

John wouldn't be here now if there wasn't a reason. If he's just checking in, he would have phoned me, wanting an update. The fact that they came into the office, today of all days, has to mean something.

Armed with Gabrielle's file clutched tight to my chest, I walk through the open office space of CHILD, past a dozen cubicles that are half full, then head down a long hallway full of framed photos of children and teens still missing. I've memorized each face, having studied their photos until I swear I would recognize any one of them in a crowded amusement park.

I hesitate in front of a door, glancing into the room through the window first. The Manderas have aged in the past three days. The loss they live with carries a weight, shows up as scars. I understand their pain, what it means to live with their lives on hold, never able to step forward without dragging the past along.

I know what that is like, because I live that life every single day.

Elizabeth sees me and gives me a slight nod. I swallow a groan. She's not smiling, not waving me in, not showing me any measure of the warmth that I've come to expect from her.

John has his back to me but I don't need to see his face to realize how wound up he is.

"John, Elizabeth, is everything okay?" I close the door behind me and take a seat beside Liz, who's wringing her hands.

"You tell us." John doesn't measure his words with forced calmness. Instead he blasts his frustration so there's no second-guessing exactly how he feels.

"We saw the news." His voice is clipped, tight, loaded with accusations.

I'm not ready. I'm not ready to answer any questions they are going to have about Bryan and his involvement in searching for Gabrielle. I'm unprepared and I hate feeling this way.

"First things first," John says. "We heard about Bryan and I have questions, but I — we — need to know about the photos."

"Photos?" How did they know about them?

"Don't give us any bullshit, Paige. We saw the photos and the boxes and know about the girls they rescued," John says. Despite the trembling in his hands, his gaze is firm as steel and twice as sharp. "We haven't heard from Detective Lindsay since he told us he was looking into the tip that came in. Did he find our daughter? Did he find Gabrielle?"

The look on John's face has me leaning back in my seat, wanting to create a bit of distance between us. I've never felt this way with John, ever. "We want the truth," he continues. "We saw the girls being led out of the house and to the ambulances. We watched as they carried boxes out of that place and had clear shots of stacks of photos." His tone is laced with disgust, distaste and dismay.

"I'm so sorry, John. They never should have shown those."

"Damn straight they shouldn't have."

"It was probably a mistake and a reporter used it to their advantage. It's not Paige's fault." Liz reaches a hand out toward her husband, but he ignores her.

She's right, none of this is my fault, but being on the receiving end is something I'm used to. I'm safe, like a vault people can deposit their anger, fear, frustration and worries into. It's not always easy. Oftentimes I end up feeling like a punching bag that's been hit with cement-filled gloves.

It takes John a second — a rather long second — until he gives me that deep nod of his to say he knows his wife is right and he's sorry.

I accept the non-verbal apology with what I hope is an understanding smile.

"Why hasn't anyone told us if Gabrielle was there?" John finally takes a seat, but he's antsy. His leg bounces despite trying to remain still.

"We just . . . we need an update. We need to know she's alive, that she's okay . . ." Liz's voice breaks and my heart goes out to her.

I place my palm on the file I carried into the room.

Honestly, I'm not sure how to tell them that I don't have the information they're wanting. Their lives are knotted, the tension increasing the more they're left out of the loop. They want me to untangle that knot, but unfortunately, I'm not sure I can. There are so many threads involved, the task is daunting.

"Let's start at the beginning. I'll share with you everything I know, but I need to warn you, it isn't much, and you probably know more from watching the news than I do about what's happening today." It's important I be as upfront as I can. When I start working with a family, I promise them I will always be honest, even when I know it will hurt.

"Three days ago, we received a tip from the CHILD Facebook account identifying Gabrielle from a photo that was recently updated on the page. As per protocol, the sighting was forwarded to Detective Lindsay who then followed up on the lead."

"Yes, yes, we know all this," John interrupts me. "We came in, spoke with the detective, who told us he was going to do some follow-up and get back to us. Except he hasn't. Why?"

"John, these things take time. It's not like one of those crime shows where everything happens one minute after the next, you know this."

"Right. And in the past, we've waited until there was more information. But not anymore. We have to hear about Bryan and this cell and see those photos from the news. You should have called us. You." The accusation is an arrow, its path straight, its target me.

"You're right, and I'm sorry." I don't tell him I've only just found out. I don't tell him that there's procedure for stuff like this. I don't tell him I have no clue what I'm doing at the moment.

All he wants to know, all he needs to know, is that we are doing everything we can to find his daughter.

"Not everything reported is accurate." This was one of the first things we try to share with families in the early stages when a child is declared missing. "What you hear or see on the news is rarely the full picture." Even as I say this, I realize it's a mistake. It sounds like I'm passing the buck, which I'm not.

"At least they have information." John pounds the table with his fist.

Liz jumps. I force myself not to react. He's angry, it's understandable.

"We think we saw a photo of our daughter in that box." Liz leans forward, a paltry attempt to block John from my view. She lays a hand on my arm and squeezes.

A lead wrench lodges in my stomach and it twists, tightens, and twitches until I'm about to heave. I swallow hard and hope I've somehow been able to cover the distress that's no doubt written across my face.

I think back to my earlier talk with Lois and her lack of response to my question about Jessica being in those photos.

"I saw her." John clarifies. "I want to know where she is and why no one has contacted us yet."

My mind races a mile a minute. I wish I had watched the news, seen what they saw, so I could give them something substantial.

"I promise, the minute we hear anything, I will call you." It's not what they want to hear, I see it in the fall of their shoulders, the downward turn of their gazes.

I feel like I'm about to step foot onto a tightrope strung over a bottomless pit. One wrong move, one false step, one unexpected twist, and I'll sink.

What if I were in their place? What if one of those photos is of Jessica? I would want to know and I'd want to know now.

"Will you give me a minute? Let me make some calls? See what I can find out?"

Liz tears her gaze from the file on the table and looks at me. Her face contains a mixture of hope and longing along with despair and confusion.

"I promise you I will get an answer." It's an easy promise to make, because I'm going to make sure I get one about my sister as well.

I can't just sit by and wait. I can't just go home and lose myself in memories. I've never been that type of person.

"I want to know why my daughter would be at that house. I want to know why her photo would be in that box of evidence taken from there. I want to know why she's never called us to help her."

John's list of demands sit between the three of us. I hear him. I understand his distress. If I had an answer to give, it's not one he's going to want to listen to.

I can think of two reasons Gabrielle would be in that home and why there would be a photo of her.

John's hands tremble as he quickly hides them beneath the table. Large drops of tears gather and fall along Elizabeth's cheeks and, as she wipes them away, her own hands shake.

"She's been so close . . . all this time." Liz's voice is fragile, like a china cup about to crack.

It's not hard to place myself in their shoes. Their hopes, beliefs, fears, concerns over Gabrielle are the same as mine for Jessica.

There's one difference. There's been a sighting of Gabrielle.

The fact that she may be alive is excellent news. The fact that she may be involved with this cell, not so much.

I leave the room and pause to breathe. Everything hits at once and it's overwhelming.

It's been twelve years today since Jessica disappeared.

A sex trafficking cell was discovered today. Victims were found. Along with one of my volunteers.

To top it off, somehow, someway, Detective Lindsay is involved, and I need it to be in a way I can understand and accept.

Then there's the fact Lois didn't answer my question.

What if my twin sister was there? In that house? A mere forty minutes away — away from me, her family, everyone who would have saved her, protected her, loved her.

No. She wasn't. I would know if she were that close. I'd have felt it. I'd have found her.

I'm a mess. Inside and out. I swipe at the tears streaming down my face and stifle the sobs that want to gush out in giant heaves. Footsteps come toward me, and I mentally slap myself. Get it together. This is not the time to lose it. I have to remain strong.

Just as the door from the front reception area opens, I turn.

"Oh good." Anita looks in. "Would you mind coming out for a minute?"

CHAPTER 6

DETECTIVE MERI AMBER

The minute I step out of my vehicle I wish I hadn't.

I didn't really have much of an expectation for Paisley Valley, other than believing it's a quaint town with a quiet vibe.

What I didn't expect to find was this throng of reporters.

CHILD. I know this agency well. It stands for Children who are Hidden, Lost or Disappeared. Not only have I spoken to the CEO, but I have a thread of messages between myself and one of the case workers there.

I never expected to be here in person. In fact, coming was a last-minute decision, and I'm still not sure if it was a smart one or not. I'm supposed to be on vacation, relaxing on the beach, enjoying the sun, the sea and a simple book, but instead, I changed my flight, repacked my suitcase and came here.

All because of a hunch and a suspicion.

I shove my way past the news vans, keep my head low, my profile small, a firm grip on my cross-body purse, and push my way toward the front doors.

I suck on the cherry Halls in my mouth, a bad habit of mine when I'm anxious. My partner back home got me to switch to the sugar-free ones and they're not too bad. Not as good, but they'll do. I'd dropped the habit about a year ago but recently picked it back up.

Two officers block my path as I reach the front doors.

"Do you have an appointment?" One asks me. That's his name — Officer One.

"I'm here to see Paige Fischer." I'm tempted to show my badge, but I hold off.

"Do you have an appointment, ma'am?" he asks again, his voice a little louder.

Maybe he didn't hear me.

The other cop widens his stance and pulls out a notepad.

Are you for real? I rummage through my purse and pull out my wallet, flipping it open so he can see my badge.

"I'm here about a case," I say, raising my voice. "Can you fellas let me through, please?"

Officer One steps aside.

"Just need your name, if you don't mind?"

I hold the badge out more and take a step forward. The last thing I want is one of the reporters to overhear me. "Detective Meri Amber."

"You mentioned a case, ma'am? If you don't mind me asking." He gives his partner a side look.

I sigh. "It has nothing to do with the bust I heard about on the news." That's all I heard about for the three-hour drive from Minneapolis. The case, my case, is personal, but they don't need to know that.

Officer One pulls open the door.

"Thanks, gentlemen."

Inside, the noise level in the room is the exact opposite of outside. There's a hush, weighted, broken only by the sound of the phone ringing.

"Hello, can I help you?" A small woman stands behind her desk, giving me a half smile.

Behind her is a large television screen where images of children, teenagers and young adults are shown, along with their names, dates of birth and when they were last seen. I can't tear my gaze from there, studying each of the faces, wondering . . .

"How can I help you?"

I step back slightly, needing some distance between myself and that screen, and focus on the woman instead.

"I'm here to see Paige Fischer." I learned a long time ago to keep any sort of question out of my voice if I hoped for affirmative action to my request. In fact, it was my father, a former detective, who taught me that, or should I say, showed me.

He wasn't known to be the asking type and I attempt to channel him now.

"Do you have an appointment?" She's looking down at her screen, her finger moving the mouse on its pad, probably trying to locate my name in Paige Fischer's calendar.

She won't find it.

"We've been in contact. Can you let her know Detective Amber is here, please?" My request is polite, my tone not so much. I drop the pretense of this being a pleasant conversation and hope she gets the message.

She stands, smooths her cardigan and mutters something along the line of I'll-be-just-a-minute.

I could go and sit, but that just shows I'm willing to wait. Another lesson from my father. I don't have to wait long, a few minutes maybe, and the receptionist walks out with another woman. I know from the CHILD website that this indeed is Paige Fischer.

Well, that was easier than I'd expected.

"Detective Amber?" Paige reaches out a hand and gives me a firm handshake. "How can I help you today?"

Her voice is pleasant, welcoming, but doesn't hide the fact that she has no clue who I am. She also looks like she's about to fall apart. Evidence of fresh tears remains on her cheeks and her eyes are bright, red-rimmed, and I may be wrong, but from the way she's holding her head straight, it looks like a headache is forming.

Doesn't look like I came at a good time.

"Is there some place that we could talk? Somewhere a bit more" — I look around at the empty space — "private?"

One brow rises, but she leads me to a room just off to the side. It's small, sparse, with just a table and chairs. Reminds me almost of an interrogation room, except there's no mirror, no camera and there's a nice picture on the wall.

She pulls out a chair for me, circles the table, and sits.

"You don't remember me, do you?" I stretch my lips into my I-swear-I'm-gentle smile, the one that disarms almost everyone I meet. But not Paige Fischer. Lovely. Just . . . lovely.

"Sorry, of course you don't," I say. "We've been emailing back and forth for a few years." My tone is apologetic and this appears to be all it takes to disarm her.

"Ah, I'm so sorry," she says, leaning forward, arms resting on the table. "Today has been . . . a day, and it's only noon." She rubs the back of her head and stifles a yawn.

She looks exhausted.

"Things look busy out there. I'm assuming the media is for the big case that's all over the news right now."

She looks like she's about to say something but stops. The look in her eye is measuring, like she's weighing how much to say to me. Eventually she gives a slight nod.

"Pretty hectic, but you're probably used to that. A sex trafficking cell in the town next over was discovered."

I nod, squashing my excitement. The whole drive here I kept thinking about the timing and how Dad would say there's no such thing as coincidences, just lucky timing.

She must catch the interest in my gaze. Her own eyes narrow as she leans back.

"So, Detective Amber, what can I help you with?"

I pull out my phone and flip through my photo app.

"I'm looking for this man and I believe he might be in the area."

"And you couldn't have phoned or emailed?" She sounds genuinely intrigued.

"Would you believe me if I said I was in the area?"

"In the middle of nowhere Minnesota? Unless you're visiting family, I'm not sure I buy that, sorry."

I like her honesty, appreciate it, actually.

"Fair enough." I breathe in deep, set my phone down on the table, screen down.

"I'm on vacation, supposed to be relaxing, some well-earned down time, or something. But my sister is missing, and when it comes to her, I really don't take days off."

I can see the wheels turning, dots connecting and I know the second she recalls our previous conversations.

"River. She's been missing for . . . nineteen years?"

I nod, impressed she remembers that much. My sister's case is now a cold case, to everyone but me.

"I understand that. Today's the anniversary of my own sister's disappearance. I'm supposed to be at home, but . . . How can I help?"

She let that bomb drop with a wallop and it takes me a second or two to navigate my way through that mini mine-field. It also explains why she looks like hell.

"I'm so sorry." The words slip past my lips and we share a look. We're part of a sisterhood, a society few understand.

I turn my phone over, refresh the screen and slide it closer to her.

"I'm wondering if you've ever seen this man before?"

She gives the screen a cursory glance.

The image she's looking at is a photo taken from a truck stop gas station video feed. It's old, grainy, but it's the only one I have.

"I know it's not the best." I wish it were. I wish it showed a clear facial profile. I wish it were more than enough to nab the man in question.

If wishes were pennies, I wouldn't be a cop. Another thing my father used to say. I miss him, or miss the man he used to be. He now lives in a nursing home and, thanks to Alzheimer's, has no idea who I am.

"I'm not sure what I'm looking at, to be honest," Paige admits.

"The only connection I have to my sister." I will her to look up, but she doesn't. She's intent on the image, as if she's trying to see past the pulled-down baseball cap, the bulky plaid shirt and shadows on the photo.

This image is burned into my brain like a brand on cattle.

The man I've been searching for stands in front of a four-wheeler, cigarette in one hand, take-out coffee in the other. A truck stop diner is in the background.

It's the only image I have, but we've met before. It was brief, I was sixteen, but I'll never forget him. Or his smell.

Smells are what I remember about people.

Paige, she smells like puzzles and Lysol, granola and wine. She's warm and driven and it wouldn't surprise me to learn she's an overprotective mother, or was raised by one.

I'm rarely off on my profiling.

"His name is Andy Rawlings. He's a truck driver, or was, and I believe he took my sister nineteen years ago."

She looks up then, her expression full of sympathy and understanding.

"I'm so sorry," she says. She doesn't say she doesn't recognize him. She doesn't say she's sorry for my loss. But I hear it. I hear it all.

I nod and take the phone back.

"I've kept my ear to the ground and periodically he pokes his head out of a hole. That last hole was here, at the truck stop outside of town. I don't know if my sister was his first victim or his tenth, but there's been more since her. I know it."

Paige perks up, shoulders taut. "I can look in our system, go through our files. See if anyone matches him. We have a good network of watchers, especially in this area. If he's around, someone would have seen him."

"I appreciate that. I've also been told he goes by Drew, too." I'm not sure why I feel the need to say this, but I put it out there.

I send the photo to her email and hear her phone ping. I've done what I need to do, for now.

"I'm going to see if that bed and breakfast I passed at the edge of town has room. I'll be around a few days. Will you give me a call?"

"Of course. I'll keep in touch regardless."

We both stand and she opens the door.

"I'm sorry for your loss," I say to her, remembering her words from earlier.

I walk through the still empty front reception area, push my way past the cops at the door, lower my head and make my way toward the rental.

My shoulder brushes against another shoulder.

"Sorry." The words are spoken in passing, the voice of the man, gentle and apologetic.

It's not until I'm at my car that I realize something.

He smells familiar.

I whip my head around, scan the area, but whoever I shouldered past is gone. I can't see through the shaded windows or the throng of reporters still gathered around. No one is looking back toward me, showing me any sort of interest, so I know it wasn't a reporter that I'd bumped into.

So who was it?

He smelled of grease, coffee and sweat.

Who did I know who smelled like that? I can only think of one.

CHAPTER 7

PAIGE

I got the call to head to the hospital came around an hour after Detective Meri Amber left. I was just about to walk out of the office and instead, I sent Jamie a text, letting him know I'll probably be late.

His reply: *Do what you need to do. I've got it here.*

I'd just sat in with Monique as she took a statement from one of the victims of today's raid. Rose Tanner, thirteen years of age. I had to step out, take a breather, because her story was too much.

Too much for today.

She'd been taken eight months ago, from a mall in Minneapolis. She'd been hanging with friends and was left alone, waiting for her mom to arrive to drive her home. Someone else had shown up, saying she was a friend of her mom's, even showing her a text message with the request to pick her up.

In eight months, Rose has been sold to multiple people, men and women combined, raped too many times to count. She'd lost considerable weight and a pregnancy test had come back positive.

Just shy of her fourteenth birthday. She's still just a baby.

Unfortunately, I've seen this way too many times. The pain is just as excruciating, the truth just as hard to accept, regardless of how many times I hear it.

"Here, you look like you need this." I look to my left and Detective Lindsay is there, holding out a take-out cup of coffee he no doubt got from the cafeteria.

"Thanks." It's nice to see him, to know he's here to help.

We lean against the wall, in solitary silence.

I have so many things I want to ask him, but seeing the haggard look on his face, I hold my tongue.

My phone buzzes with a text message.

Flowers arrived. A dozen . . . your mom says they're peonies.

My heart sinks.

"What's wrong?"

I show him the message. He swears.

"Is there a note this time too?"

I ask Jamie, my fingers shaking as I do so. I know the answer, it'll be no different than any other year.

There's a note. Jamie takes a photo and shares it.

The phone slips from my fingers. Lindsay grabs it in time, sees the image then types something back.

"I told him to keep the note for me. I'll stop by later to get it. I'll look into it." He hands my phone back.

This is the seventh year we've received flowers. My sister has been missing for twelve years, but for the past seven years, a delivery of flowers signifying how many years she's been gone has arrived at the front door.

Always with two words. *I'm sorry.*

"Maybe this time, the person messed up," Lindsay says, but I hear the doubt in his voice.

"Maybe." I'm not going to get my hopes up, though. Every year, Lindsay takes the note, contacts the local florist who delivered the flowers, and always comes up empty. The order came from one of those large website distributors where you can order flowers from anywhere. It's always paid for with a prepaid credit card, and the name and address used are always bogus.

Why would this year be any different?

I do a quick search for peonies and what they represent.

We've had purple hyacinths. We've had primrose, marigolds and even dark roses. They all represent the idea of forgiveness. Lindsay says it's their way of saying they're sorry, a personal apology.

A personal apology sent as flowers means the person knows us. I refuse to believe that. No one who knows us would have stolen my sister.

Mom believes the flowers are meant as a way to grieve. That they came when Jessica died. Why else would someone start sending us flowers seven years after she'd been kidnapped?

I refuse to believe that too.

"What do peonies mean?" Lindsay mutters.

"Shame," I tell him. The first thing that pops up on a search for the meaning behind the flower is shame, followed by a happy life and or a happy marriage.

Isn't that just lovely.

"Today just isn't getting any better, is it?" He draws out the words, not bothering to hide the exhaustion.

He tilts his head one way then another, the popping as he stretches ringing loud in the hallway.

He's not just talking about it being my sister's anniversary. He's talking about the rescue he did this morning.

"How many?" No matter the number, it won't be enough. It never is.

"Five girls. I should be happy that we rescued five, but we'd just missed out on a transport of at least a dozen more. A dozen more we could have saved, if I'd been there in time."

"Why weren't you?" I don't mean it accusingly; it's an honest question and I hope he takes it as such.

He shrugs. It's not an *I don't know* kind of shrug, but more of a *I wish I had a good answer* type of shrug. "I got a tip, spent way too much time validating it."

He's carrying the weight. It's heavy, and it'll bury him if he doesn't deal with it.

“Don’t bother,” he says, as if knowing what I’m about to say. “I followed protocol, but sometimes that’s not enough.” He rubs his face and suddenly he looks about a dozen years older than he is.

“Is it true about Bryan?” I keep wanting to believe there’s a good excuse for Bryan being involved in the cell. There has to be.

I drop that belief when I read the answer in Lindsay’s gaze.

“He was there. He was the one who answered the door when I arrived.”

Coffee splashes out over my hands as I squeeze the cup too tight.

“I thought you went early, ahead of the team?” I’m trying to piece everything together. I’m surprised he’s saying as much as he is to me.

“I did. His identity was part of the tip. I had to see his face, hear what he had to say, before the others arrived.” He closes his eyes. I imagine he’s replaying the scene in his head.

“Give the man credit. He didn’t try to bolt. He knew it was over, he was caught. I expected excuses, that he was there based on a tip, something ridiculous, but he said nothing. Nothing. I wanted to bash his face in.” The anger-laced words were softly spoken, his voice a low growl.

Bryan Powers. Late thirties. Married with two daughters. Religious. Even hosted a Bible study in his home every Thursday night.

This is going to destroy his wife and kids. They’re innocent, but most people won’t care. They’ll lump them in with what Bryan has done even though they probably had no idea.

To most people, that’s not an excuse.

Detective Lindsay looks like he’s about to say more when he straightens, shoulders pushed back into a stance that speaks of caution.

I peer down the hallway and find Pastor Jeremy staring at us. I give him a small wave, but he either ignores it or doesn’t notice it. We both arrived at the same time, and while

I went off to sit with the victims, Jeremy was there to offer support for both staff and families as they arrived.

Jeremy reminds me of a college boy, with all the charm and seemingly carefree attitude, and yet, he's a year or two older than me.

He's been a good friend these past few years, to both Jamie and myself. I didn't like him at first, felt he tried too hard, but the more I saw as he interacted with our families, the more I've come to realize he just has a really big, soft heart.

Of all the town ministers, he's the only one who has dedicated his time to helping the families with CHILD. The others come in if requested by one of their congregants, but Pastor Jeremy meets with probably eighty percent of the families.

The one thing I appreciate the most about him is that his intentions are never self-serving. He doesn't preach, or argue with those demanding to know why God would take their child from them. He's there to support, to uplift, to assist in any way he can.

His church base is made up of several small home groups where he goes and holds Bible studies throughout the week, rather than meeting in a dedicated building on Sundays.

Jeremy approaches, and that's when I notice Lindsay is like a coiled rattler, ready to strike at any moment. Is he angry at Jeremy? I want to ask, but I hold my tongue. Things have been strained between the two men for a while now. I wonder if Bryan is the cause.

If so, Jeremy is a mouse who has no idea what kind of trap he's walking into.

"How many?" Jeremy stares off to the side, hands in pockets.

"Perps or victims?" Lindsay asks.

There's no answer, which I find interesting. My first thought is always to the victims. What is going on between these two?

"Five girls," Lindsay finally says when Pastor Jeremy doesn't answer. "The youngest is seven. A thirteen-year-old just found out she's pregnant. And your boy—" Lindsay pokes Jeremy in the chest with his finger. "Your boy," he says again, spitting out the words like bullets, "tried to pretend he knew nothing about any of it."

This was news to me. He just told me Bryan had remained silent.

Jeremy's gaze is fixed on Lindsay's and, despite taking a step back after being jabbed, he holds his ground, taking the anger.

"He's lucky I didn't kill him. Him or the other asshole who was there."

The swearing catches me off guard. I've never heard Detective Lindsay swear. Ever.

"We don't determine the days of a man. Only God does."

Lindsay growls. A low, vibrating threat that Jeremy doesn't seem to catch.

"What he's done is wrong and he'll pay the price. But he has time to repent, to change his ways. Everyone deserves a second chance."

Up until now, Lindsay has contained his rage, his disgust, but at Jeremy's words, it's like he's an uncaged lion that's been prodded by an electric stick way too many times.

"Do not tell me God will forgive this. He's thumbed his nose at God, at all His dictates, His rules, knowing exactly what he was doing every second of every day. He has daughters, for fuck's sake."

It's a good thing I'm leaning against the wall, trying to remain invisible, because otherwise I'd have been stepping backward, getting as far away as I could.

"What Bryan has done is disgusting," Jeremy says, "but even he can be forgiven."

Lindsay throws a punch then, but it's aimed at the wall and not at the man in front of him. With another curse, he shakes his fist and stomps away, down the hallway.

I watch his retreating back, feeling the angry vibrations flowing off him even as the distance between us lengthens. Truth be told, I feel every word he's said. I believe it too.

A man who sexually abuses a child, who sells them to others who sexually abuse them, doesn't deserve forgiveness in my books.

He deserves hell. There are no second chances for predators like him. None.

CHAPTER 8

I missed dinner. I missed saying goodnight to my son. I missed focusing on Jessica like she deserves.

All day I've pushed aside the guilt that is always there, focusing on what's in front of me, those who need me, rather than becoming consumed with all my guilt-ridden *should haves*. I *should* be home, I *should* be with Mom, I *should* be making sure I don't miss dinner. All those *shoulds* become fuel for the fire, and despite how emotionally drained I feel, there's also a sense of tension settling in my shoulders, waiting for the inevitable anger Mom has in store for me.

My whole drive home was me thinking of reasons to counter her arguments. Yes, I could have been home, focusing on my sister, being there for Mom, helping her with dinner, but that's not where I was needed. I needed to be at the hospital with those girls, with girls like my sister, lost and needing rescue.

Those girls are going to need so much help and I'm determined to do whatever I can to make sure they get it.

I have a ritual for when I come home after days like today. I stand in front of the door and shake my arms, raising them slightly to the sides, increasing the shake until I feel a sense of freedom from the heaviness I've been carrying. I wait until my shoulders relax and my head lifts before I open the door.

The first thing I notice is how quiet the house is. My footsteps echo as I make my way into the clean kitchen that holds a lingering aroma of chicken potpie — Jessica's favorite dish. This is now the only day of the year Mom makes it, which I'm fine with, considering I can't stand the taste. Something about the cream sauce and whatever herbs Mom adds sets my stomach off each time.

As expected, there's no evidence of the flowers that were delivered today. Lindsay sent someone over for the flowers and note. If it's anything like past years, he's not going to get anything off of them, but he'll at least try.

There's a chocolate cupcake along with a note waiting for me on the counter. *Missed you. xoxo* in Jamie's handwriting. The house is quiet, with only the barest of lights being left on for me, and a part of me wonders if this is Mom's not-so-subtle way of telling me how pissed off she is.

Right now, at this time of night, after everything that's happened today, and especially considering what today is . . . caring about my mother's feelings is the last thing I'm in the mood to deal with, which only adds on another shovelful of guilt, adding more fuel to the already burning fire.

Venturing up the stairs, I bypass her closed door, not wanting to expend all my reserve energy on her emotions. Normally, when I'm late like this, I'm the good daughter who knocks, checks in to see how her day was, catch up on any Flynn news, and then go see my son.

Not tonight. My only focus right now is Flynn, holding him close, telling him just how much I love him.

I witnessed two reunions tonight. Both equally hard, both equally heartbreaking. The youngest victim of today's raid was a seven-year-old girl who has been missing for a month. The way her mother melted in the hallway before entering the room, it almost floored me. I saw all her emotions in that moment, the fear, the worry, the pain, the love. The moment she walked into her daughter's room, she needed to be strong. That was her last moment to take in what had happened, both the news her daughter was alive and the news her daughter had been harmed.

The other was a fifteen-year-old girl. Her father was the one who came and while all he wanted to do was hold her, she wanted nothing to do with his touch, recoiling as he reached out. The scars on both her body and heart were deep.

I hesitate before opening Flynn's door. I push away all the images burned into my head, push all the fears, worries, anger and ache into a box, clicking the lock closed. This moment is all about my son. He deserves my full attention.

I'm sure I'll find Flynn snuggled in bed, with Jamie reading him a book, but when I open my son's door, they're both lying on Flynn's bedroom floor, heads close together, neither one noticing me as I stand watching.

Flynn's room is cluttered with giant-sized bears, tiny toy cars, action figurines and a desk cluttered with crayons. His walls are decorated with his drawings we've framed and some signed pieces from his favorite comic book artists.

His favorite is a hand-drawn Superman. Flynn says it reminds him of his dad, right down to the glasses he wears. Jamie is a high school teacher by day, but when he comes home, he takes off his glasses and becomes Super Dad.

"Hey." I sneak into the room and bend, preparing myself for what's about to come.

Flynn scrambles around on the floor until he launches himself at me, forcing us backwards until we land in a pile in the middle of the hallway.

"You're home. Finally! Dad and I had the bestest day ever, but we missed you." Flynn's voice is full of excitement.

"Bestest day ever, huh?" I glance up at Jamie, who holds out his hand, helping me off the floor.

"We went on a hike and saw a lot of birds and even two foxes, Mom. Plus lots of rabbits. Dad says we're probably going to see a lot in town over the winter. I don't remember ever seeing a rabbit in our yard before. Then we went to the store to buy you gifts because Dad says it's a sad day for you, but I'm not allowed to tell you what we bought because it's a surprise. But I know you're going to love—" Flynn finally stops talking, but only because he has to take a breath.

"Whoa, buddy. Remember, it's a surprise." Jamie ruffles Flynn's hair, making it even messier than before.

"You didn't have to get me anything." I say this to Jamie, keeping my voice low so hopefully Flynn doesn't overhear.

"Flynn and I wanted to help you to remember to smile."

That explanation alone makes me smile. Not a *happy, laugh out loud* kind of smile, but rather a *you make me want to cry* kind.

"But your heart has to smile first, Mommy," Flynn says, wrapping his arms around my legs in a tight hug. "I want to help your heart smile."

My heart doesn't just smile at Flynn's words, it melts, straight into a puddle of goo that's full of sunshine and rainbows.

"My heart is smiling, love, I promise." I bend down to give Flynn a mama bear-sized hug before picking up his tiny body and holding him close.

For a four-year-old, he has an amazing concept of empathy.

He wiggles out of my hold and leads me by the hand into my bedroom, where a gift bag sits in the middle of my bed.

"You have to close your eyes, Mommy," Flynn insists as he jumps onto the bed and grabs the gift. "Close your eyes and hold out your hands."

It's hard not to smile when it comes to my son, and even Jamie doesn't try to contain his grin.

I close my eyes, hands held out, palms up, and listen as Flynn seems to wrestle with taking the gift out of the bag.

"Careful there," Jamie says. I'm not sure if he's helping or watching. If it were me, I'd be helping Flynn take whatever it is out of the bag, careful to make sure he doesn't drop or break the gift, whereas Jamie prefers to let Flynn request help if he feels he needs it.

Two different styles of parenting, but for us, it works.

Something heavy plops down in my palm, wrapped in something soft, similar to tissue paper. The item itself has a circular base and wobbles in my hands.

"Can I open my eyes now?" I attempt to speak, hoping he doesn't notice the emotion in my voice, but Flynn is right there, in my face, so close our noses almost touch.

"I love you, Mommy," he whispers, his warm breath brushing across my skin.

When I'm finally able to look at what I'm holding, my heart melts even more, something I wasn't sure was possible.

It's a coffee mug. A mug full of little chocolate kisses.

"I love you too, Flynn. This makes my heart so happy." I give him a nose kiss, my lips pulling into a smile to match the one in my heart.

"Is your heart happy?"

"My heart is so very happy, love."

The mug is soft pink in color with the words *No one makes my heart as happy as you* written on it.

It's perfect. Absolutely perfect.

"You missed dinner. Gramma is mad, but Dad says you were saving girls who were hurt and Auntie Jess would understand. Did you save those girls, Mommy? Were they hurt? I have bandages if you need some."

Jamie is watching me, gauging how I'm feeling. I give him a brief smile as I hug Flynn even tighter.

Today was hard, but here, my son in my arms, the stress from it all disappears.

Once Flynn is in bed, after reading him a story and telling him just how much I love him, I finally climb into my own and lean into Jamie's waiting embrace.

"Heart still happy?" he asks.

I don't reply because I don't want to lie. It's happy, but I can't hide my tears any longer. It all floods in, all the anger, the fear, the stress, the guilt, the sadness. It all bubbles to the surface and I don't know what emotion to focus on first.

Thankfully, Jamie senses this and helps me out.

"I saw the news," he says. "I can't believe what they're saying about Bryan."

I sigh, twist so I'm looking him directly in the face, a part of me thankful this is what we're facing first. "I've worked side by side with him for the last two years. How could I have missed he's a sexual predator?" That's a question that's been running through my head all day. I've thought over all the times we were alone together, discussing files, of when he interacted with families, of the care and attention he gave every single missing person case that crossed his desk. He's always the first one to volunteer to scout areas, to hike through fields, to be in a search party . . . I thought it was because he saw his own daughters in each of those cases, but apparently I was wrong.

"Do we ever truly know a person? You can't hold yourself responsible, Paige."

"Why not? I was responsible for him. He was on my team."

Jamie's lips tighten for a millisecond. "You aren't a trained professional. You didn't validate him. You didn't do his background check. You aren't a profiler who knows what to look for. Besides, I remember when Bryan joined your team. Don't you?"

I look away. Yes, of course I remember. That's another thing I keep thinking about.

"You knew something was off with him from day one, but you looked past your own instincts and decided to trust the word of others. It's not your fault."

Except, it was. It is. All it would have taken was one phone call, one email to Lois and Bryan would have been on the sidelines while they looked into him further. So what stopped me? For the exact reason Jamie stated. I'm not the professional and I trusted the words of others over my own gut feeling. On that, I can hold myself responsible, at least.

"Lindsay wants to kill him," I tell Jamie. "Pastor Jeremy says he deserves forgiveness."

Jamie snorts. "Are you surprised? One spends his life finding men like Bryan, who hurt kids, and the other tries to save them. Jeremy always tries to find the good in people, he even did that when he worked in some prison. I remember him telling me everyone deserves a second chance."

"What?" I twist back around. "He worked in a prison? When? Where? He never said anything to me about that, and that definitely never came up in his file."

"I don't know." Jamie yawns. "I think he mentioned it over beers or something. While he was in training, I think. It could have been a job, too, I actually don't remember." He yawns again. "There was this story, though, about a sex offender who repented and wanted to lead a Bible study on his ward. Apparently, that's when Jeremy realized small groups, whether they be house groups or prison groups, worked better than large church settings."

I don't remember him ever telling me he used to counsel sex offenders. In fact, one of his stipulations with working with CHILD was that he would only interact with the families and never the offenders. That doesn't make sense to me at all.

"Do you think he knew about Bryan?" I ask.

No answer. I feel the gentle heaviness of his arms sink, edge downward, until they almost fall off of me.

He's fallen asleep.

SIX DAYS AGO

CHAPTER 9

PAIGE

There's no police presence this morning, no crowd of reporters outside the office, but inside, the front lobby of CHILD headquarters is a madhouse.

Anita's on the phone, her attention on the computer as her fingers furiously type.

The waiting area in the lobby is full, every seat taken. The table of refreshments Anita likes to keep stocked up is empty. Doors open and close from our interview rooms, and Anita's phone continues to ring.

"What's going on?" I ask, looking over the crowded room.

Anita doesn't notice me at first, even though I'm standing directly in front of her. When she does finally pop her head up, she jumps, gasps and one hand covers her heaving chest.

"Oh my goodness, you startled me." She takes the headset off her head and runs her hands through her hair. "It's been a day, and we're only a few hours into it."

"What is going on?" I knew today would be busy, but not like this.

"Listen . . . something big just came in." She stops because her phone rings again. She picks up the headset, adjusts it, then hits a button on the phone.

She mumbles a few words after answering, her focus completely on her computer screen.

"Hey. Why are you calling? I just got off the phone with . . . oh, sorry, okay. Yeah, got it, I see them . . . oh my God . . ." Her eyes widen, nostrils flare, but it's the shaking of her hand . . . a hand that's normally steady, that has me on high alert.

"She's right here. No I haven't told her yet, she . . ." Anita shakes her head. "Just one second," she says, pressing the phone tight to her chest.

Her gaze goes from me to her screen and then back to me. "There's been an anonymous tip about another sighting," she says, her voice a low whisper. I lean closer, because she's so quiet, I almost can't hear. Her chest heaves a few times. "Paige, from the description, it could be—"

"Who's on the phone?" I interrupt Anita.

"Detective Lindsay."

A rush of blood shoots through my body like a runaway horse.

We have a protocol at CHILD in regard to every anonymous tip we receive: it gets logged and sent to the appropriate case worker as well as Detective Lindsay, who oversees most of the cases. He authenticates the tip and confirms if it's live or not.

If the tip doesn't come from us, but rather from Lindsay's team, then he's already done all that checking and by calling us, that's our cue to mobilize.

Families are going to need to be called.

Last night had been a late night. Tonight won't be any different and I'm already exhausted thinking about it.

And because of yesterday, every family with a child missing is already on high alert due to the news of a sex trafficking ring being located.

"Paige, it could be Jess." The words rush out of Anita's mouth, clear and concise, but all I hear is a jumble of emotions that begin with exasperation and end with hope.

Did she just . . . ? She didn't just say Jessica's name. Did she?

My hands shake as I reach for the second phone located off to the side of Anita's desk.

"Line four," she says.

My finger hovers over the button as I try to read her lips. They're moving but I can't hear past the rush in my ears. I think she's saying it . . . it could be Jess?

It could be Jess. It could be Jess. It could be Jess.

Those four words play over and over in my head until they're in rhythm with the beat of my heart.

Anita takes a sheet that's just come out of the printer and hands me the transcript from the anonymous tip. The one sheet contains all the necessary information, but the words are all jumbled into blurry sentences that my brain can't process.

"Paige, it's Detective Lindsay." Anita motions to the phone I have pressed to my ear. The one I'd totally forgotten about. She hits the button for me.

"This is Paige," I manage to mumble. I'm still trying to process the words on the sheet. A few are clear, like the physical description, but my brain is shouting IT COULD BE JESS so loudly that nothing else is getting through.

How could it be Jess? How? It's been twelve long years.

Miracles do happen, I've even seen them occur in front of me time after time, but they always happen for other families, to other parents and other sisters.

Never for me, for my family.

"I sent over the transcription to Anita. Have you seen it?" Lindsay's melted-chocolate-heated-to-perfection smooth voice is loud enough to grab my attention.

"I'm looking at it right now." The fact my voice isn't shaking surprises me. Maybe the truth of this hasn't really hit. "What's going on, Lindsay? Is this about the cell? Have we found the missing transport?"

"What? No. We're still searching. Listen, Paige . . . everyone is on high alert and our tip line is going crazy with sightings. But this tip, it's a live one." He drops that truth bomb without warning and all of my nerve endings stand at attention. A live one means the tip is real and in play — as in, it's happening right now. Right this very minute.

Breathe. I just need to breathe. Act as if Jess's name isn't on this list, like this is a regular sighting event. Distance myself, step away from the emotion . . . I've got this.

I once bought Mom a blooming tea set as a birthday gift. A blooming tea is like a dried flower bulb that blooms in hot water. As the water is poured over, the bulb transforms from a curled up tight wad of spices into an exotic flower emitting the most delicious aroma.

The same happens inside my heart right now . . . a ball of entwined hope I've kept buried, protected all these years, and all it takes is one photo listed on a sighting case and it all unwinds until there's a tiny strand of belief reaching up to embrace the spark of light brought by that news.

The words finally clear and I'm able to properly read the transcript that details the sighting of a female between ages twenty-two and twenty-eight, approximately 5' 6", dirty-blonde hair, with a slender build.

Anita hands me another sheet, this one with three missing poster images attached as possible identification. A single female was last seen being forced into a red pickup truck, Chevy, with tinted windows. Sighting occurred at a Walmart two counties over.

Missing posters attached were of Gabrielle Mandera, Susan Tinder and Jessica.

My sister.

Her face is there, printed out beside Gabrielle's and Susan's. Their photos are from a computer-generated image of what we believe the girls look like aged. The photo of Jessica is me, except my hair is darker, closer to auburn than strawberry-blonde like when we were kids, but it's my photo we're using since we're identical twins.

"What's happening?" I ask Lindsay as I hear some sort of noise in the background of our call. A signal clicker, slap of a hand against a wheel, static from the radio. Detective Lindsay is in his car.

"We have a tail on the truck. I'll keep you posted, but I wanted to let you know I'm on it," he confirms, without saying he's the one tailing the truck. But I know him. He's following up on this one personally.

I have one question that's bursting out of me, needing to ask, not just for myself but for the families involved. We are all going to want to know.

"I don't know who it is," Lindsay says, reading my mind.

"We haven't had a sighting on Jess since she disappeared."

"Doesn't mean it won't happen today."

Nothing else is said because nothing else needs to be said. We've had this talk a dozen times throughout the years.

There's a battle raging on inside me, between my mind and my heart. My heart refuses to give up on my sister, always believing that the next phone call, the next sighting, will be for Jess. But my head knows the reality of this happening is slim.

My head says to focus on the families, to be their support, to put them first.

Anita reads me like a book. She takes the phone from me. "Monique is still at the hospital, but I put in a call to Pastor Jeremy. He's on his way in."

"He doesn't need to come in. I'll be fine."

I swallow past the large lump where all of my emotions are rolled tight inside — hope, anticipation, fear — and push it down inside my soul until I'm able to talk. I appreciate the concern, both from Detective Lindsay and from Anita, but I'll be okay. Until we have a positive identification, there's really nothing I can do.

Anita's silence balloons, filling the air between us, and the downward tilt of her lips conveys a rebuttal worthy of the Supreme Court.

"My families always come first," I tell Anita, hoping, wishing, needing her to believe me.

I can see in her eyes she does.

"Of course they do." Lois's voice is there behind me. My eyelids sink closed, realizing she's probably heard everything.

Why, today of all days, does she have to keep sneaking up on me?

"It's not that I don't trust you, Paige. It's because I know how traumatic your sister's disappearance has been for you. Things come up, they always do, when we least expect it."

I slowly turn and try to hide every single thought filtering through my head, from my face.

I'm not very successful.

"Monique or Jeremy is there to support you," Lois continues, "in case you ever need it."

I study her, attempt to read her, but she's closed off.

"Today, however," she says, just as the front door opens with a whoosh, "in light of yesterday being your sister's anniversary and everything that is going on, it's only fair to yourself and to the other families that someone else lead. Plus, there's no sense in you being here today anyway. We have a team coming in to start looking over all your files."

"My files?"

"More specifically, the ones Bryan was part of. They need to be audited, in light of the situation. Who knows how many leads he buried or how he influenced cases?" Her lips thin into an angry white line.

Someone coughs from behind Lois and I know right away it's Pastor Jeremy. His hands are buried deep in his pockets, with a scarf wrapped around his neck which helps to highlight the dark bags beneath his eyes, and tousled hair from the wind outside.

Lois blocks my view of him, making sure I both see and hear her clearly.

"It's not a request, Paige. I hope you realize that." Despite how low her voice is, there's no hiding the power behind every single word she speaks.

I nod because that's the only response I can give.

CHAPTER 10

I've seen John Mandera happy, sad, angry and mad. But I've never seen him furious.

For the past few minutes, Pastor Jeremy and I have stood off in the corner, our backs to the crowded room as we discussed a plan of action. I'd blocked out the noise but noticed Jeremy's attention was glued to Anita's desk.

It's not until I start to turn that I'm able to actively recognize John's voice. He's standing at Anita's desk, arms on the front counter, body leaning forward, face almost over the top of Anita's computer monitor.

"We saw the post on Facebook," John says, his voice clipped with emotion. "Before you took it down. We saw it."

"John," I call out, hoping to grab his attention. He whips around and points a finger toward me. "You can't keep this from us. I don't care if there's not further information, I want to know if it's Gabrielle."

Elizabeth stands slightly behind him, her hands clutched tight around her purse. She's not saying anything, just standing there, eyes downcast.

"I understand that." I cast a glance toward Anita, who mouths *I'm sorry*.

"Hey, John," Jeremy says as he approaches the couple. "How about we head into one of the meeting rooms? Do you want a coffee?"

Nothing else is said as Pastor Jeremy leads them into a room while I head into the kitchen to grab us all refreshments. That's when Anita corners me.

"I'm so sorry. I've been having issues with our Facebook page today. Normally all posts are monitored and have to be approved, but that one slipped through before I could take it off. I swear it wasn't up there more than five minutes."

"It's not your fault, Anita." My mind is scrambling about how to handle this. I'm always one to place honesty first, but there's a reason we have a policy in place for not telling families about possible sightings until we have confirmed identification.

What if it's not Gabrielle? What if it's not Jess? It's bad enough I'm having to temper my own hopes. John and Liz shouldn't have to as well.

"Before you ask, yes, the post did mention the three girls. The poster must have gone through our photos first before saying anything." Anita sucks her lips in and bites them, a habit she has when she's frustrated. "I'm so sorry," she repeats.

She starts to twist her hands together and I almost beg her to stop. "Are you going to tell them?" she asks.

I nod. What choice do I have now? They'll know if I'm lying or hedging and they deserve better than that from me.

She sighs. "I wonder if they called the Tinders?"

That hadn't even occurred to me. I hope not, but . . . Elizabeth and Susan Tinder are close. She might have sent Susan a text.

"I think it's something we need to be prepared for." I place some cups on a tray while Anita fills a coffee carafe.

"Before you go in there, there's something I need to know." Anita cocks her head. She's going to ask me about Bryan and my files, I know it. Now isn't a good time. I need time to wrap my head around everything that is happening.

"Are you going to tell your mother?"

This is not what I expected to be asked and it throws me for a bit of a loop. Am I going to tell Mom? Eventually. "I'll talk to her."

From the slight slant to Anita's eyes, I gather that isn't the answer she wanted. I get it, but I know my mother and this isn't something she's going to want to know. As far as she's concerned, Mom is ready to carve Jess's name in a headstone and have it rest beside my father's grave. If I thought yesterday was emotionally taxing on her, getting this information, without validating if it's Jess or not . . . that would toss her over the edge.

"Paige . . ." Anita draws out my name with a shake of her head.

"If the identification comes back that it is Jess, I'll call her. I promise."

It takes a bit, but she eventually accepts my promise.

Armed with fresh coffee, I head to the room where Jeremy is waiting with John and Elizabeth. The moment I enter the room there's an abrupt stillness, as if the three of them were in the middle of a conversation that I'm interrupting.

"Coffee is fresh." I attempt some lightness, blasting a smile on my face, hoping to see some smiles in return.

Jeremy attempts one. Elizabeth stares at the table. John pushes his chair back and stands.

"Why didn't anyone contact us? Why do we have to see it on social media first? Between that and Powers, I'm not very happy with how things are being run right now." John crosses his arms, his voice sharper than a blade. "I want some answers, Paige."

I swallow. Of course he wants answers. I don't blame him. But the answers he wants, I don't have. Not about why they saw the news on social media first, especially when they shouldn't have, or information about Bryan Powers. A third party is going to be going through every file he may have touched. There is no way to know if he influenced any of our cases or harmed any other children we are actively seeking.

But I can't say that.

Both John and Elizabeth are waiting for me to give them the only answer I have to give. "There's been a sighting." My voice contains none of the strength I know I need to convey. It also holds none of the conviction they need to hear.

I should have let Pastor Jeremy take this on.

Elizabeth cries out in shock, her hand covering her mouth seconds later, while John's gaze doesn't leave me, it's almost militant as I take my seat.

"Is it Gabrielle?"

I look to Jeremy, hoping he'll take the lead, realizing I need to step back.

"They're not sure," he says. He hesitates for a second, and I can see him struggling with what his next steps should be. Eventually, he places the sheets on the table and slides them toward the Manderas so they can see the drawings themselves. "Three images were identified: Gabrielle, Susan Tinder and" — he looks up at me — "Jessica."

My gaze slides to the file in Jeremy's hands and I catch my image — Jess's image — peeking out. My heart jerks, with pain radiating from the center of my chest to sit in the muscles on my shoulders as I let her name sink in.

It could be Jess.

"Paige!" Elizabeth reaches out to squeeze my hand as I sit. "Oh, honey." There's a mixture of hope and despair in her voice, a mixture that I'm sure tastes almost sour on her tongue.

I'm sure because I have the same taste.

"I feel sick." Elizabeth leans back, swallowing hard. Her lashes are coated in tear droplets.

As she struggles with the news, I realize I need to step up and be the support they need me to be. So I lean forward, fighting back my own tears, and force myself to focus on the family in front of me. "Don't you dare apologize. It could be any of the girls on that sheet, or it could be someone else entirely. Those were the three that were pointed out as possible similarities." I look to Jeremy, hoping he'll say something, but he's like a blank slate and I have no idea what he's thinking right now.

"I . . . I wish I had a better answer." I hope they won't take that as a cop-out. "We're all in this together, wishing for the exact same thing, aren't we?"

Liz continues to sniffle. John stares down at his clenched hands.

Jeremy clears his throat, looking like he's come to a decision. "Detective Lindsay will let us know as soon as he finds out," he says. "In the meantime, why don't we do what we always do when there is a possible sighting?"

"I'm not in the mood for a *kumbaya* session, PJ. Sorry." John pushes his chair back, his legs jack-hammering with tension.

"To be honest, neither am I." Pastor Jeremy lets the sarcasm in his voice slip out. "I was thinking we'd head to the group session room and wait for the Tinders to arrive. I'm assuming you told them?"

"I did," Liz says. "They deserved to know."

Jeremy nods then turns to me. "Perhaps your mom and Jamie will be joining us too?"

I lift my shoulder in a very non-committal shrug.

"They need to know." He leans closer to me, his voice low.

I don't answer. His sigh tells me exactly how he feels about that.

"If it is Jessica, your mother will never forgive you," Elizabeth speaks up.

Mom still hasn't forgiven me for the day Jess went missing, so this whole I'll-never-be-forgiven vibe, I'm a pro at living with it.

I'm stuck in a *damned if I do, damned if I don't* scenario. Mom has managed to place the loss of my sister in a padlocked box that only ever gets opened on holidays or the anniversary of her kidnapping.

She stopped coming to the group sessions years ago, stopped inquiring about updates. In fact, she even brought up the idea of holding a funeral for Jessica shortly after Dad died.

When we talk about forgiveness, I'm not sure I can forgive her for that one.

No. I'll wait till we have more news.

Making this decision isn't easy. Not sharing the news, pushing it aside and trying to remain emotionally detached, it hurts. Hurts more than I want to admit. It's a betrayal, not letting myself hope for Jess's return. Because I do . . . I do hope it's her, with all of my heart. I would give anything and everything for it to be my sister today.

But, by taking a step back, by attempting to look at it through realistic lenses, I have to accept that it's probably Gabrielle. We've had more sightings of her over the years than anyone else. More close calls, more hopes for a reunion than anyone else on our list of missing family members.

In the past twelve years, we've never had a sighting of Jessica. Sure, early on, her photo would often be included with the tips because her features would be similar to others, but lately, in the past five years or so, my sister's photo has never been included. Not until today.

Twelve years ago, my sister disappeared without a trace. The possibility of her coming home, while it's something I'll never stop hoping for, is slim.

It kills me a little more every time I admit that.

"There's something I think we need to discuss." Jeremy places both hands on the table and folds them together. He doesn't say any more and I'm not sure if it's because he doesn't want to utter the words no one wants to hear, or if he's hoping I'll jump in and finish it for him.

"No. Don't say it." Liz closes her eyes, as she knows exactly what Jeremy is about to say.

I don't blame her. Truth is ugly. It's never easy, even when sugar-coated. Truth strips us of all our ignorance, wishful dreams, and dredges up pain we've all tried to hide.

The truth is never as clear as people make it out to be.

"What if it is Gabrielle, you mean?" John says what Jeremy didn't. "What does it mean if it is our daughter? Our daughter who could have come home, could have reached out and didn't?" John's voice is brusque and loaded with a mixture of distress and disappointment. He leans back in his chair, and everything about his posture shouts anger and denial all in one.

"Please don't," Elizabeth begs, but it falls on deaf ears.

"If that is our daughter, if she's not dead and has willingly stayed with whoever took her all those years ago . . . I guess that's something we're going to have to live with, isn't it? She's a grown adult, able to make her own decisions. She could have left these guys at any time."

I wince when he says that, because what he claims isn't necessarily true. That's his frustration speaking and not his true belief. I've known him for far too long. He may sound angry, but he can't hide the sheen of tears either.

"John." I look him straight on. "What we need to do right now is focus on the positive." I try to encourage him because I know it's what he needs to hear. "From what we know, she's alive and she looks . . . healthy." It doesn't sound like much, but those two facts are more than what most families have to hold onto.

I reach for a photo from Gabrielle's file and bring it out into the open.

It was taken outside a sandwich shop just last year. She's wearing tight jeans and a pink spaghetti-strap tank top and carries a child on her hip. She's stick thin, but there are no obvious bruises or cuts on her skin, and the smile on her face as she looks down at the child . . . it tells me a lot.

It's because of this photo that John spent seven months driving to that sandwich shop forty minutes away, every single day, in hopes of seeing his daughter.

He never did.

"If . . . if she was there, in that house, or if . . . if she's still with whoever took her . . . is she still being sold for sex?" Elizabeth's voice wobbles as she stares at the photo of her daughter.

I can't answer. My throat has completely dried up, like I inhaled sand and every single swallow grates my skin into tattered strips.

I look to Jeremy for help.

"Until we find her, we're just speculating," he says.

"That's why you brought it up though, isn't it?" John says. "To prepare us for the *what-if*?"

Jeremy nods. I can tell he's weighing his next words. I would be doing the same. "It's possible she's helping to take care of the girls under her. She might be in a relationship with one of the Romeos, and she might be staying because it means keeping her child safe. We won't know until we find her again and can ask."

Elizabeth's eyes close as she lets out a sigh full of sorrow and heartache. "Of course she's protecting him," she says. "Gabrielle always protected those around her. She was such a mother hen, even at a young age."

"Do we know if the child is a boy? Was . . . is he actually hers?" John's voice is blunt.

This is hurting them — not knowing about the boy, not knowing about their daughter, all of it.

I lean toward Liz and reach out to grab her hand. "There's no way to tell from that photo, and no one has seen the child since, but you recognize that look on her face, don't you?" I wait for Liz to give me her attention. "Only a mother could smile like that."

There's love in her eyes, in her smile. That's the first thing I noticed.

The relief that covers Liz can't be masked. She needed someone else to confirm the hope already growing in her heart.

"Shouldn't there be hospital records?"

Good question. I flip through the pages to find the one that answers it. For some reason I feel like I should know the answer to this. "There would be if we knew the name she went by and if she had gone to a hospital. Often, these groups will have nurses on call to come and do home births."

"He's her anchor baby," Elizabeth whispers.

Anchor baby is a term used to describe the child a trafficker will allow as a hold over the women. They make promises they never intend to keep or use the child as a hostage to keep the women compliant and docile. It's a term Monique, the social worker I work with daily, introduced to one of our group meetings about a year ago.

"So what do we do now?"

John is a doer. It's why he drove to that sandwich shop every day, last year. It's why he's always at our fundraisers and why he hands out fliers with his daughter's face on them.

He's doing everything he can to try to find Gabrielle.

I understand that drive.

I used to go and wait at the corner of our school, where I'd last seen Jess, hoping, praying that she'd come back, twirling her hair around her fingers, as if nothing bad had happened.

But Jess never came back and I eventually grew tired of waiting for someone else to find her.

That's why I work with CHILD. With the training I've received, I know I'll eventually find my sister, to right my wrong.

I was the one who lost Jess. I'm going to be the one who finds her.

CHAPTER 11

DETECTIVE MERI AMBER

This is my third truck stop.

The guy in my photo is a trucker. Over the years, the detectives involved in my sister's case told me they checked out every possible truck stop along the routes they figured the guy would have taken.

Over the years, I've gone to each of those stops, too.

Truck stops are frequently utilized by traffickers, either used as a marketplace, a means to transport human cargo from one city to another, or as a place for prostitution.

I can see the impact CHILD has had on the area and it's great. Every stop I've been to so far has been plastered with signs, offers of help and instructions on what to look for.

It feels good to be doing something.

I search out an older woman in the dining area. I don't know her name, I have no idea how long she's been here and she certainly isn't expecting me. But no matter where I go, she's the one I search for. Nine times out of ten, the older they are, the longer they've been there, and the more secrets they know.

"Looking for a seat?" a voice behind me calls out as I walk along the outer rows of the dining room.

"How can I help you, hon?" Gladys, her name in bright red on her uniform, carries a few menus in one hand and a cleaning rag in the other.

"Do you have a minute to talk?"

She snorts, brows raised high. "Do I look like I have a minute? There's a dozen hungry drivers in the room and I'm here alone. Either you sit in a booth and order, or you come back another day."

I take the offered menu and find myself sitting in a booth.

The tabletop is clean, silverware wrapped in napkins in a wood container against the wall. The menu offers everything you'd expect at a diner and more.

It takes her a solid seven minutes before she reappears. She pours me a coffee, even though I didn't ask for one.

"How hungry are you?"

"Not overly."

"Then try the chicken sesame salad." Her pen hovers over her notepad. "Now, ask away. You've got two minutes before Johnny starts yapping about his pie."

I pull out the photo from my purse and slide it across the table. "Ever seen this guy?"

She laughs. "Oh honey, you've got to do better than that." She picks up the photo, brings it close to her nose and gives it a good once-over. "The guy could be anyone, but that truck . . . it's local." She tosses the image back down to the table and writes something down on her notepad.

"I'll get the salad to go, how about that?" she says. She tears paper from her pad and leaves it with me.

ALLS Transport was underlined with two hard lines.

A quick map search on my phone shows me it's just out of town, in the industrial area. Clicking on their link brings me to a website. Their *About Us* section says they've been in business for close to thirty years.

I go deep into their website, looking over their personnel, routes they generally take and transport they specialize in.

On the bottom of the page there are photos of their trucks and logo over the years. I compare this with the image in the photo and, sure enough, there are similarities.

There's a claim that they have lifetime employees and that they support CHILD, making sex trafficking industry training mandatory for all new employees.

At first, I find myself impressed that they're so open with this information. But I've seen too much, heard too much, been involved with too many crime scenes not to know better.

"What exactly are you looking for?" Gladys is there with my bagged salad.

"I'm looking for someone."

"Well, no guff. Figured that when you showed me the photo." One brow cocked upward. "Have a name?"

"Andy Rawlings."

She quirks her lips into a frown. "What did he do? Steal cargo? Behind on child support? I just serve the guys food, I'm not their bloody advisor."

Her comment is interesting. Either she knows the guy I'm looking for, or a lot of people come through asking similar questions.

There's a lot of ways I could go with this, but I decide honesty is the best. I don't have time to play the long game here.

"I think he took my sister."

The sarcastic smile on Gladys's face disappears. "Oh honey, I'm sorry to hear. Head over to CHILD, you can't miss the signs once you get into town. They can help. You don't need to be doing all the legwork yourself."

"I'm a little more invested than they are, and they seem a little . . . busy right now."

Gladys holds her hands tight to her chest. "It's a shame. But listen, none of my regulars are involved in that stuff." She points to the walls. "You see those signs? We all know what to look for, we all have that number on speed dial."

I see the signs.

I also see the way everyone looks over at us, keeping watch.

I notice Gladys hasn't outright answered my question, though.

"Thanks for your help." I hand her a twenty. "Keep the change."

I feel eyes on my back as I walk out. It's not long before I hear their footsteps. I'm being followed. I head past the slots, the shower area, and down the steps to the store. A glance over my shoulder shows me two men trailing me.

I slow my steps, pretend to be interested in the selection of chips. They stand, legs spread, in the doorway.

Are you freakin' kidding me?

"Anything I can help you with?" I keep my arms loose, down at my sides; lips turned into a friendly smile. I could show my badge, but why bother?

Neither one says a word. Tough guys, huh? One has the beginnings of a potbelly. The other is bald with tats all over his arms.

I pull out the photo from my purse and hold it in front of me. "Either one of you recognize this man?"

Both look at the photo, then each other, then back to me.

"What about the name Andy Rawlings? Know him?"

Again, no words.

What's with the silent treatment? Don't people realize they reveal so much when they say nothing?

It doesn't take a profiler to notice the signs. The bald guy's lips tighten. The potbelly one looks to his friend then to the floor before looking back to me. Their stance isn't as solid, either.

So, they do know him.

A quick walk through the store, a nod to the cashier, then I'm out in the hot afternoon sun. The lot is half full of parked trucks, the gas pumps have a lineup and the boys are now standing at the doors I just exited.

I count at least three ALLS Transport trucks. Are they tied to the guys at the door?

I give them a wave once I'm in the rental, slowly drive by those trucks. Two are empty. One has a shade covering the front windshield. If the outfit is local, why is a guy sleeping here, at a truck stop, rather than at home?

I write down their license plates then unwrap a sugar-free cherry Halls and stick it in my mouth. I'm close. I can feel it. I won't get excited, not on something so small, but little by little I'm getting closer to finding out what happened to my sister.

Next on the agenda: visiting ALLS and seeing if Andy works for them. If my dad were here, we'd bet on the outcome.

CHAPTER 12

PAIGE

Anita's performed another miracle. In the short amount of time we've been in the small conference room, she's managed to set up a table with cookies, sandwiches and another fresh pot of coffee in the group room.

The first thing I do is head to the coffee.

The room we are in is a multipurpose room. The walls are painted cornflower blue, covered in handmade painted signs offering hope and love. There's a small coffee table with a vase of fresh flowers surrounded by four armchairs, and a bookshelf that's a free-for-all. There's even a sign on one of the shelves: Take One, Donate One . . . and surprisingly, those shelves are always full of new books.

Normally the feel in this room is one of openness, but today, the air within the four walls vibrates with pent-up emotions no one is uttering but everyone feels.

John and Liz each sit in one of the armchairs, hands breaching the space between them, their fingers clasped tightly together.

I've always been amazed at how strong the Manderas have remained throughout the years. Families I work with often fall apart, the stress being too much. We have several counselors on staff, and their services are always available to family members. Some take it. Some don't.

My parents never did, not as a couple at least. It wasn't until a few years ago I found out, by accident, that Dad would meet up with one of the men at a bar for drinks, a once-a-month check-in that he always kept under wraps.

Pastor Jeremy takes the seat beside John and places two half-heaped plates of food on the small table in front of them. "I know food isn't going to help, but it gives your hands something to do as we wait." He smiles as he notices their joined fingers. "Although, that doesn't seem like an issue for you right now."

"John is my rock." Liz's gaze is full of love as she stares into John's eyes.

It's hard to watch them, and yet, I can't look away either. A twinge of guilt settles in my stomach. I should call Jamie. I should ask him to be here. I want what they have . . . the way they support each other, lean on one another . . . I want that. And yet, there's something always stopping me from taking that action.

My relationship with Jamie is complicated. He's always available, offering silent support, never forcing me to step into a situation that makes me uncomfortable, never challenging me to be more than who I am.

He's the strong, silent type. His love is the same too. Strong, silent, secure. I love him and I've never questioned that.

But we don't have what the Manderas have, and I wish we did.

"How have you two managed to keep so strong, if you don't mind me asking?" Jeremy sits on the edge of his seat as he gives the couple his complete focus.

I have a feeling I know why he's asked, especially considering there was no one else in the room that could benefit from the conversation. No one other than me.

"Communication and acceptance," John says. "We are both allowed to feel what we feel, no questions, no guilt."

Liz nods. "Realizing this probably saved our marriage. We both deal with missing Gabrielle differently, and that is okay. It took me a while to understand that, though. For years I couldn't understand why John could be so angry when all I wanted to do was cry." She pats her husband's hand with tenderness.

I have to squash back a boiling mass of emotions that rises as her words hit a nerve. She just described what my life was like after Jess went missing.

I always knew Dad loved me, but his anger was tied to a hair-trigger switch that could go off at the slightest touch. And Mom . . . for years, all she did was cry. They never separated, but their marriage changed after Jess's disappearance. Dad started sleeping in the spare bedroom around the fourth-year anniversary, claiming he kept Mom up with his snoring, but I knew the truth.

The love lost between my two parental figures scarred me more than I'd ever admit. Probably as much as losing my twin did. I learned a lot of really hard lessons: the main one was, the only person I could rely on for emotional stability was myself.

Which explains a lot when it comes to my relationship with Jamie.

"Don't forget the counseling," Liz continues. "That woman you connected us to, Pastor Jeremy, has been a godsend. There were plenty of dark spots she pulled us out from."

Jeremy nods to them, but he looks at me. I can't read what's in his gaze, which is unusual because I've always been able to read him. What you see is what you get. Ask him a question and he'll always give you an honest answer.

The longer he looks at me, though, the more I start to understand his unspoken message, and I don't really like it.

I pull out my phone and send off a text to Jamie.

There's been a sighting. Female. I hesitate, contemplating if I should say it could be Jessica. In the end, I decide not to. *Could be any number of girls* is what I text instead.

When I look up, three sets of gazes are focused on me, like those tiny red lasers people use to tease cats.

I give a somewhat sheepish grin.

"I hope you're texting either your mother or that handsome man of yours." Liz leans her body slightly forward. "You shouldn't be carrying this by yourself. Your shoulders already bear too much weight from trying to carry the rest of us."

My heart melts. I appreciate her concern, it touches me, but carrying that burden, as Liz put it, is my job.

"I was telling Jamie," I explain. "Mom . . . with Dad passing away . . ." I'm really struggling with my words, how to explain it. I rub my face, rethinking my thought pattern. I can't admit Mom is ready to say goodbye to Jess, that in fact, she's already said goodbye in her heart and wants to make it official by holding a small memorial service.

Over my dead body.

"I'll let Mom know once we have more details," I say instead.

"Of course, of course," Liz whispers with understood grief.

My phone vibrates and I don't even need to look to know who is texting me.

Do you need me?

I'm not surprised that Jamie would read between the lines and ask this. A smile creeps along my face as the force of his love washes through me.

What I love most about him, right in this very moment, is the fact that he asked if I needed him, rather than assuming I did. He once told me that one of the things that attracted him to me was my inner strength.

Because of that, I try to never let him down.

Do I need him? Yes and no. With him here, it would make things all the more real, and I'm not sure if I can hold on to the strength needed to get through the next few hours.

The phone vibrates with another message: *Do they think it could be Jess?*

My fingers hover over the screen, hesitating before pressing the tiny buttons. If I say yes, Jamie will come, no questions asked.

He'd also insist Mom be told.

Waiting on more information.

Technically, I'm not lying, but that does nothing for the pebble of deceit lodged in my soul. Dad used to say that enough of those pebbles could drown a person.

It's not so much that they drown a person, but rather they destroy the ability to hope.

Say the word and I'm there, Jamie texts. *Keep me updated please.*

Rather than reply, I send him a thumbs-up emoji.

Knock-knock. The door edges open and in walks Anita, escorting Susan Tinder's mother into the room.

Liz jumps up from her seat and smothers Carol Tinder in a hug.

"Could . . . could it be true?" Carol's voice is mouselike: timid, squeaky and hard to hear in loud places.

"It could be any of them." Liz pulls back, her voice infused with tears.

Carol glances around and notices me. "Jessica too?"

My smile wobbles. "She was included based on the description, but Susan and Gabrielle have actually been spotted in the past, so . . ."

A flash flood of relief mixed with fear flies across Carol's face before Pastor Jeremy joins the mix and gives her a hug.

"How are you, Carol?" he asks. "It's been a while since we've had a chance to catch up."

Carol Tinder rubs her hands together, as if trying to get warm.

I notice and fill a cup with coffee. Carol likes hers black, if memory serves.

The smile is a sweet one as I hand the woman the hot cup. Her hands immediately wrap around the mug as Liz leads her to one of the corner chairs. While Carol sits, shoulders hunched inward, Liz places one of the throw quilts folded in a basket across Carol's lap, tucking the edges in around her legs.

There's something about Carol that brings out the mother hen in others.

"I called Mike about the sighting, right after you told me." She directs this to Elizabeth. "He's on his way home," Carol says, her voice so low it's hard to hear.

"Was he nearby?" Pastor Jeremy asks.

"No. He's down in Nevada. He'll be back tomorrow."

Michael Tinder drives truck for a local transport carrier.

"How are you? Is there anything you need until he gets home?" Pastor Jeremy asks.

A small dip of her head, gaze focused on the mug in her hands, her whisper soft as she says, "I'm okay. I'm afraid to hope that Susan's been found, after all this time, you know?"

"We're all afraid, love, we're all afraid." Liz pats her knee in a motherly gesture.

"That fear is normal." Pastor Jeremy stands to the side, close by my chair. I'm starting to feel a little claustrophobic. I need some space between me and the others, away from the deep swell of emotions that swirls between the two families.

"What happens if it is your daughter?" Jeremy speaks up. "What happens if it's not? That fear, disappointment, hope . . . it's okay to allow yourself to experience the range of emotions flooding you right now. There's no right or wrong response."

No one says anything as his words settle in the air.

Minutes drag until they become hours. Those hours inch past, one second at a time, filling the room until it feels like my skin is covered in ants. Anita came in a while ago to say Monique was held up at the hospital, which was completely fine. But now I'm tempted to leave, to head back to my desk and attempt to focus on something other than the upcoming possible disappointment. But it's like Jeremy senses my thoughts and he hovers, reading my flight response with clarity.

These moments of waiting, of not knowing, of watering a seed of hope only to know it might be trampled on at any moment, they are the worst.

When speaking with families new to CHILD and our services, I try to warn them about moments such as this one right now. I want them to be aware that the road they're on, trying to find their child, to rescue them from a possible sex trafficking ring, it's not an easy path.

A few years ago, the United States was considered one of the top-three worst places in the world for human trafficking. In the past fifteen years, the practice has grown until it's everywhere, in every state, city, town. Still, even today, there are people who believe human trafficking only happens in third world countries, or somewhere other than here, at home.

The trafficking effects are similar to a spider's web, and more and more children and teens are being sold into the slave trade than are found.

I'm not going to remind these two families in the room of that, though. That burden of knowledge is all my own. Despite knowing the statistics, I still believe all three of these women are alive. I have to believe that. I want to believe that.

These families need me to believe that.

That's my role. My job. It's also a good reminder of why I have to keep believing that Jessica is still alive, and that maybe, just maybe, she was the one to be spotted in that vehicle today.

Mom may believe she's dead, but I won't. I can't. The bond twins hold, the bond we held as children and then teens, it's still there, still as strong.

I would know in my heart if my sister were dead.

And yet, there's that pebble of doubt deep in my soul that I'm living a lie with that belief.

CHAPTER 13

By the time Detective Lindsay walks into the room, everyone breathes a sigh of relief, myself included.

Lindsay is a man most people step back from when he approaches. His shaded jawline and weather-lined face rarely display a smile, unless it's warranted. He carries a hard edge about him, a shield he seldom lets down.

Lindsay transferred to our small, middle of nowhere town close to thirteen years ago for one reason: to lead a task force against the sex trafficking rings in the area. He'd been a younger version of himself then, not as hard, as rough around the edges, like now.

He's different with me, though. We have more of an older brother/younger sister relationship, bordering on father figure, if I'm going to be honest.

Lindsay was the one who helped me get my first job here at CHILD, working the phone lines fresh out of high school.

"I'm sorry for keeping you all waiting for so long." He looks around the room, giving each person time with his gaze. That shield he holds in front of him, the wall not many get past, he lowers it now, for these families in front of him.

For me.

And I'm thankful. This is what we all need.

"Did you find the truck? Was it . . . ?" Carol is the one who speaks up, her hand a fist in front of her mouth, stopping her from saying more.

Damn it. I know that look he's wearing. It's his one-two punch: disappointment followed by hope.

Not only was the girl seen not Jessica, but it's not Susan or Gabrielle either.

I feel so sick.

There's been a rotten feeling eating my stomach lining for the past few hours and it's all I can do to keep from gagging.

Breathe, Paige.

In through the nose, out through the mouth, over and over until I can swallow back the shared disappointment we're all feeling.

"It wasn't any of our girls, was it?" John's voice is matter-of-fact, void of all the hope he'd held earlier. He's holding Liz's hand in his own.

Pastor Jeremy is back behind my chair. His hand is on my shoulder and I can feel the heat from his skin. It's like he's red hot, on fire, and I appreciate the warmth.

I need to get it together. I need to step away from the edge of disappointment that's crumbling beneath me and stand strong. I should be speaking up, offering words of encouragement, but those words, the ones that normally come easy, are bricks on my tongue, weighing it down.

"I'm sorry." Detective Lindsay clears his throat. "It ended up being a false lead. Just an elderly couple who loaned out their vehicle to their granddaughter. The girl came off a bender, so she was a little rough looking when she'd been spotted this morning."

John straightens and looks toward his crying wife, whose head is down, a tissue clenched tight in her fists.

Carol swipes at tears that fall down her cheeks. Pastor Jeremy heads to her side, squatting beside her chair, and rests his hand lightly on her knee.

The air is heavy, saturated with loss and heartache.

"The good news" — my voice squeaks like a captured mouse in a trap — "is that we obviously have an active community on the lookout for your daughters and my sister." I try to infuse those words with a smile and confidence.

I'm not sure I'm all that successful, not until John lifts his head and gives me the briefest smile.

"Yes," he says. "The support is what's helped us the past few years. It hasn't always been there, as you know." He looks at me while saying this. "Imagine if it was."

I've imagined that scenario for years. It's always hard to look back on the past and wonder *what if*.

What if CHILD had been established in our town then? *What if* the community had stood together, strong, shoulder to shoulder, and searched for Jessica, like we do now?

Don't trip over your feet by looking behind you all the time, another one of Dad's sayings.

Liz rests her head on John's shoulder. "It's going to be okay," he says, his voice lowers lovingly.

A pang pierces my heart and I regret not asking Jamie to come and sit with me.

"I just wish whoever posted it online today had been sure," Carol whispers. She looks smaller than before, like she's visibly shrinking into herself.

I glance at Pastor Jeremy. I know the two have a good relationship, they've been able to bond, and he's often been at her side following her husband leaving.

He catches what I'm trying to convey in my glance.

"The good thing is that people are so familiar with the girls that they've become recognizable." His voice is filled to the brim with hope, and it starts to drip out in a force that saturates the rest of us. "The fact that people aren't turning a blind eye, that says so much."

My head bobs in a nod along with everyone else's. Even Lindsay's.

"That tells me that the work CHILD is doing" — Lindsay speaks up, and all our gazes turn toward him — "all the school talks Paige and her team have been doing, all the fundraising and public speaking you do for your daughters, all the training seminars for local businesses . . . it's working." The gruffness in his voice breaks a little.

"And yet, the number of our children being stolen from us hasn't decreased, has it?" The level of accusation in John's voice has even me reeling back.

"Sadly, no," Lindsay answers him point blank. "It's a multi-billion-dollar industry now, so it's an uphill battle. But no one is giving up this fight. Not you, not this organization, and not this woman." He points to me. I'm not able to smile or even acknowledge him. I hate being singled out like this.

John stands, holding his hand out for his wife. "Carol, Liz and I have a standing invitation for puppy therapy after every setback. Why don't you come join us?"

Carol's face holds the same question everyone else is dying to ask; I know I sure am.

"John and I go to the local animal shelter and ask to play with the pups. There's a huge play area and you get slathered in wet kisses and cuddles. It helps . . . which is what matters, right?" Liz explains.

"I love that idea," I say, making a mental note to add this to my ever-growing list of ideas and even possible upcoming events. Who doesn't love puppies? I could even organize a CHILD-sponsored adoption event.

"I . . ." Carol is about to turn them down, it's there in her voice, a *thanks but no thanks.*

"I think I'll come along too," Pastor Jeremy interrupts. "Carol, how about you and I ride together? Then maybe we can grab a bite to eat later on? I could use the company, if you don't mind me foisting myself on you." His arm wraps around her shoulders in a side hug.

With a blush and nod, Carol is led from the room. The moment he looks back to say goodbye, I mouth *thank you* to him. Carol shouldn't be alone today, not after this. It's not the first false sighting for Susan, but that doesn't mean it hurts any less.

Soon, Detective Lindsay and I are the only two left in the room.

"Sorry about today." His voice is rough, hoarse, and the toll of his job spreads across his weathered face.

"Don't ever apologize," I say, giving him a brief hug, sensing he needed one. "No one has fought harder for my sister, and for their daughters, than you."

His cheeks blaze with embarrassment.

"Did you tell Sarah?"

I shake my head.

"Figured. Well, she knows, regardless."

"What?" The word pushes out of my mouth without thought. "How? Why?" Jamie wouldn't have told Mom. I would know if he had, my phone would be going off with all Mom's text messages.

Please don't tell me Anita called her. Anita's supposed to be on my side . . . Inside, I'm groaning. I already wasn't looking forward to tonight, but now, it's going to be even worse.

"She called and invited me to dinner this weekend, something about making sure I have at least one good meal by week's end. Figured she ought to know." The look in his eyes, the hint of shade in his voice, his disappointment in me comes across rather strong.

That's not fair.

"Isn't that my call to make? Not yours? And what good would telling her have done?" I ask. His eyes narrow at my question and I shrug. The challenge was intended. "She doesn't want to know, Lindsay, and you know that. She doesn't want to have hope anymore. She wants to move on, to say goodbye to Jess, and I . . ." My voice breaks as another sweeping tidal wave of hurt, fear and unmet hope washes over me.

I turn. I don't need to see the pity or even sympathy in his eyes.

"You can't blame her for wanting to move on." The depth in his voice is what breaks me. Tears pool, stream, gather on the edge of my chin and drop, one at a time, onto my sweater. I quickly swipe them away.

"You realize she's not saying it for her benefit but for yours, right?"

No, I don't realize that, because it's not true. How can it be? How can saying goodbye to my twin, giving up hope of ever finding her, be beneficial?

Sounds like Mom's trying to excuse away her need for closure and placing the blame on me.

"I can't believe you'd fall for that." I roll my neck, hearing the satisfying pop-pop-pop, and let out a small groan, all the while avoiding Lindsay's gaze.

He heaves a heavy, weighted sigh. "One day the two of you will see how stubborn you're both being."

I rub the pad of my thumb against a spot on my forehead, where a headache has bloomed into something voracious. I should head to the house, cuddle with Flynn, get a hug from Jamie, but . . .

"Well, that day isn't going to be today."

CHAPTER 14

Like when I was a schoolgirl caught sneaking in hours past curfew, Mom waits at the front door, arms crossed, giving me the fiercest of frowns.

Crap.

"Paige Elizabeth Fischer." My full name, which tells me just how upset with me she is. *Damn you, Lindsay.* My curse may be silent, but it's full of contempt.

I want to blurt out an explanation, I want to tell her I did it to protect her, to protect myself, that I understood why she wouldn't want to come to the office . . . but I find I can't say any of that.

There is so much pain radiating from Mom. It's in her gaze, in the way she's holding herself, the way her lips wobble as she stares at me, like she's trying to remain strong but is barely holding it together.

Everything I was going to say disappears. I rush forward, wrap my arms around her bony frame and whisper *I'm sorry, I'm sorry, I'm sorry* over and over.

Mom's hug is warm, homey, like a thick hand-knitted wool sweater on a cold Christmas day. "Hush now, Paige . . . shhh, it's okay." Mom eventually pulls away. "Why are you apologizing? You were protecting me, like you always do. Silly girl. Just like your father." Mom glances away, out toward the door behind me, but not quickly enough to hide the pain that's settled in her face at the mention of Dad.

"Your father made me promise him that I wouldn't let you continue to do this, and yet here I am, breaking that promise. Again. You're not alone . . ."

It almost sounds like she's going to say something else, like I'm not alone, she's here with me, she loves me . . . or maybe she's waiting for me to jump in and tell her that it's okay, that I understand.

But I don't. I can't. The muscles in my throat tighten until I'm breathing through an opening the size of a straw and all the tears I'd managed to hold back spring forth in a rush, flowing down my cheeks with the power of a waterspout.

I'm so tired of crying.

"Oh, honey."

Mom pulls me in tight again, gently rubbing circles on my back, the healing power of her hug doing wonders to my wounded heart. It's been a long time since I've been hugged like this by Mom, a longer time since I've had her comfort me, be there for me like this.

"Today was a hard one, wasn't it? I knew the moment Lindsay told me about the sighting."

I pull away, my arms dropping to my sides. "If you knew, then why didn't you come down?"

I should have known better. A vise grips my lungs, twisting, turning, tangling them into a knot that won't ease. It won't ease because I won't let it.

She knew. I forgot about that. She knew about the sighting. Knew I was there, alone, with the other families. Knew and didn't care.

I shouldn't be surprised.

Mom walks away, ignoring my question and heads into the kitchen. I wait until I'm able to relax my fists, following.

She's wiping down the already spotless kitchen counters. Her motions are stiff, her arms outstretched, lips taut, shoulders set back, creating a rigid pose.

She's angry. I'm angry. This is not going to go well.

The table's been set. I can smell dinner in the oven, the aroma of lasagna filling the air.

"You're right," Mom finally says. "I should have dropped everything and driven down to join you, but . . ." She's standing in front of the kitchen window now, staring outside. "Well, I figured if there was news, you'd tell me."

On the inside, I'm screaming. Shouting, swearing, screeching words of hurt and anger, giving breath to wounds that will never heal.

On the outside, I wear a mask of indifference, one I've perfected over the years. One I wear quite often around my mother.

Pastor Jeremy says everyone handles their emotions differently. Some people run from situations they can't control. Others prefer to surround themselves with those in the same emotional place as them.

Mom is the avoidant type. She always has been and that won't change, no matter how much I want it to.

I'm the opposite. At least, I think I am. If there's an issue, I want to face it, fix it and move forward.

"Liz and Carol were there." I push a button Mom would rather I leave alone and wait to see how she's going to react. "They asked about you."

Mom winces. "That's not fair, and you know it."

I toss a wet Kleenex clenched in my hand into the garbage. "Fair? Do you really want to go there, Mom?"

Her lips tighten. Yeah, I didn't think so.

"Then don't tell me I shouldn't carry this alone." There's so much more I can say, so much more I wish I could say . . . like, if you knew, why didn't you come and wait with me? If you knew, then why didn't you call or even check in with me? I don't say any of this because I know it won't make any sort of difference.

There are boundaries that have been set between me and Mom, boundaries Mom put into place years ago. Every so often, I push against them, hoping, praying she's ready to let down her guard and be the mom I've needed for so long.

But that day isn't going to be today.

"Mom, I—" I stop at the closed look in Mom's gaze just before she turns her back on me, giving me the cold, indifferent shoulder.

That hurts more than anything else right now. When will I stop thinking Mom will be there . . . for me?

"You know my feelings on this." The note of finality in her voice has me swallowing my reply.

I head upstairs to change while Jamie is outside playing with Flynn. I stick my head out the window and wave hello. Flynn shows off his football-throwing skills, then I hear Mom calling the two in for dinner.

By the time I make it back down the stairs, Flynn meets me at the landing.

"Dad is upset with Gramma," he whispers.

Jamie rarely gets upset. He's the calmest, most stoic and levelheaded person I know.

The tension in the kitchen is thick and divisive. Jamie's arms at his sides, hands stuck in his front pockets, shoulders ruler straight. My mother's arms are wrapped around her body in a tight hug. Her chin is raised and her eyes are saucer wide.

"What's going on?"

No one says a word, but everyone is saying something through their gaze: Mom's is narrow, and Jamie won't look at me. He's staring at my mother.

This won't be good.

"Dad and Gramma are having words." Flynn speaks up, his little voice full of sarcasm. He's too young to pick up on the tension, which tells me there's too much of it lately.

"I think it's more than just words," Jamie clarifies, his tone low and monitored. "She owes you an apology."

"Me? Why does she owe me an apology?"

In retrospect, I can probably list a whole slew of reasons an apology is warranted.

My gaze goes from Jamie to my mother before I throw my hands up in the air in obvious frustration.

"Today has already been a hellish day and we still have a few hours to go before it's over. Regardless of what's happening here, can we just agree to disagree and eat dinner?"

Mom's reply is to pull the dinner out of the oven.

Jamie won't stop glaring at her.

"Jamie and I happen to have different opinions about expectations," Mom says as she brushes by me with the lasagna in hand. She fiddles with placing the dish in the center of the table then wipes her hands on the apron around her waist. "No apology is needed, especially since you and I already spoke about what happened today."

Flynn sidles up to me and nestles in tight to my leg. I wrap an arm around his shoulders and hold tight, giving him what I hope is a reassuring smile.

He's one of those souls who carry the emotions of others.

"Go wash up for dinner, okay?" I gently push him in the direction of the downstairs washroom and wait till he's left before I give my mother my full attention.

"Anything you want to share now that Flynn is out of the room?" Yes, there's a heavy layer of sarcasm in my tone, and yes, it's intentional.

Mom's lips move, but no sounds come out.

"Would you like me to tell her, then?" Jamie offers, his tone biting.

Silence reigns as we all take a seat and Mom dishes out the meal. Tonight is Flynn's turn to say the blessing.

"Dear Jesus, thank you for this food. Bless Gramma's hand for making it, even though she swore like a trucker earlier today. She's really sorry."

My eyes pop open. What a little cheeky . . . I catch Jamie's smirk and we send each other a wink.

"Jesus, let us have a good night with no one fighting," Flynn continues. "Gramma is sorry for saying it was Mommy's fault and Daddy's sorry for yelling at Gramma and for telling her it's time to start being a parent, because, Jesus, she's a good gramma and he didn't mean that. Oh . . . and thank you that Mommy helps kids like me. Amen."

Whether intentional or not, Flynn just tossed a lighted flare onto the table, illuminating the cracks between Mom and me.

It takes me a few to force out the words lodged in my throat like a pair of spiked balls.

"My fault, Mother?" Everything in my voice issues a challenge, forcing Mom to look up. I feel like that's all I'm doing lately . . . challenging her on her words, on her actions, and it's exhausting.

Five long seconds pass, leaving ample opportunity for Mom to backtrack, to explain, to do what Jamie demanded earlier, apologize.

My mother either doesn't hear the challenge or she's choosing to ignore it.

"I'll take your silence," I say, my voice full of fury and pain, "as confirmation that you're blaming Jessica being taken from us on me . . . Am I right?" I swallow the spheres of hellish hurt down. "You'll never forgive me, will you?"

CHAPTER 15

There is nothing about today that I love. I always wish that I could run away, escape, slip away without anyone noticing. I used to think about heading to a quaint B&B in some small oceanside town where no one knew me or knew the significance of the day. In this small town, I'd sit on the beach, let the ocean waves drown out the drilling accusations in my brain.

The ones that blame me for Jessica disappearing.

It tears at me knowing Mom still blames me.

It's bad enough I carry that condemnation. It's bad enough to know in my heart Mom holds me accountable . . . but to hear it, to realize, even after all these years, that she still holds me liable . . . I'm not sure there's a way to get past that.

For twelve years, I've carried that weight without complaint. Sure, it's heavy and comes with a fear that one day it'll be too much, that I'll break, but I try very hard not to complain.

How can I? It is my fault Jessica is missing. I broke the number-one rule in our home . . . I left my sister alone. There's no excuse. I knew it was wrong, I knew I'd get in trouble once Dad found out, and I'd still done it. Didn't matter that I was a teenager. Didn't matter that I figured we were old enough to walk home by ourselves. There's no excuse.

I lost my twin sister. My parents lost their daughter.

We all lost a piece of our hearts, our souls, that day.

I'm still hollowed out. Half a person. That will never change.

After dinner, Mom locks herself in her bedroom with a bottle of wine. Jamie takes Flynn to the park to burn off some energy, which means I'm left to do what I do best: clean up the mess left behind.

I stand outside of Mom's room and tap my knuckles against the door. "Hey, Mom? Jamie took Flynn to the park. Why don't you come join me for a drink downstairs?"

No sound.

"Mom?" I double tap the door again. Still nothing. Short of begging, I'm not sure what else to do, considering she's locked her door, so I can't just pop my head in to make sure she's okay.

I make my way back down the stairs, pour myself a glass of wine and sit in the front room, curled up in a chair, staring out the window, waiting for my family to return.

Not much about this room has changed in the twelve years since Jessica left.

Sure, the chairs in front of the window are new, but the same style and in the same place as they've always been. My parents used to sit here and wait for us to come home in the evenings, when we were out with friends. Mom would watch us from these chairs in the winter when we built snowmen in our front yard.

I miss her. Jessica. I miss her with a fiery passion that burns away, day and night, until there are times I feel like there's no part of me left. My twin. These twelve years without her have been hell. Years of living life, growing up, going to school, getting a degree, falling in love, having a baby, burying our father . . . I was never supposed to do these things without her.

Knock. Knock.

So lost in thought, I didn't notice anyone walking up the front drive.

Wine glass in hand, I uncurl myself from the chair, peer through the curtains and see Pastor Jeremy standing on our welcome mat, a basket in hand.

"Hope I'm not disturbing everyone," he says once I open the door. He looks a tad uncomfortable, like he knows it might not be a good time to drop in but he's doing it anyway.

I sidestep so he can walk past me into the house.

"Not at all." I don't bother to mask anything on my face. He has a way of seeing past it anyway.

"Did I come at a bad time?"

I lift my shoulder in a shrug. "Just nursing this glass of wine and wondering what my sister is doing."

Jeremy gives me this long look and I know he sees past the alcohol in my hand, catches the stain on my cheeks from crying and even the wobble of my smile as I pretend everything is fine.

"Care for company?" He hands me the basket he's holding. "I meant to bring this by yesterday." Inside is a small succulent garden. I swallow back a tidal wave of tears that bunches at the base of my neck.

"Dad was the gardener." The words slip out, soft, unbidden. Dad loved to garden. He said it was his quiet time, when he could think over issues and figure out solutions.

"Maybe you could take it up," Jeremy suggests.

I snort. I have a black thumb. The garden is now Flynn's. This summer he wants to set up a little fairy garden among the plants and Mom's offered to help with it.

"Hey, don't mock it. I've got my own little garden at my place. You'd be surprised at how peaceful it can be to spend time with your hands in the dirt."

The fact that he gardens doesn't surprise me. The idea he thought I might enjoy it too does.

"You know me better than that. Mom took over Dad's gardens, though, so I'm sure she'll take care of those. She's even been teaching Flynn a bit about it. He's still learning what's a weed and what's a flower, but he'll get there."

Rather than wine, I pour Jeremy a tall glass of ice water, knowing he doesn't drink. He joins me back in the front room, where I take up sentry, watching for the guys to return.

All I want in this moment is to hold my son, hear his laugh and tell him a story about Jess.

"What do you think your sister is doing right now?" Jeremy asks.

I sigh, the feeling deep and heavy in my bones. I pinch some skin on my arm, tightening my grip until the sting intensifies, buzzes, and my brain jolts from the pain.

"I think she's rubbing this space on her arm," I say as I rub the same spot. "I think, wherever she is, she knows she's not alone because of this pinch." It's small, the idea, the action, but it was all I have.

Jeremy has this look on his face, like the idea has never occurred to him about our closeness as twins.

"Is that legit? A real thing, between twins?"

"For us, yes." Regardless of how much time passes, the connection between my sister and me, even something as simple as a pinch, will always be there, as long as my sister is alive.

"Do you ever feel a pinch, from her?" He leans forward, anticipation drooling from his lips.

He has the same look on his face now as countless others.

Every time someone finds out I am a twin, it's like a magical world opens up for them and all the unimaginable secrets they've always wondered about are soon to be theirs.

"I do. All the time. It's how I know she's thinking of me. We used to do it as kids. At first it was in fun, then we'd do it when we were annoyed with each other." The smile that forms on my face warms me. I used to hate whenever she'd do it because it always came at the worst possible moments.

Like when Dad was yelling at us over something she'd done. Or in class when I was answering a question. Or when I was deep in thought and she knew how annoyed I'd be.

God, I miss that. I miss her.

I jump just then as a bolt of electricity fizzles through my veins and I almost spill a bit of my wine in the process.

"Whoa!" Jeremy almost jumps out of the chair. "You okay?"

"I just got a pinch." I choke on the words, my body flooding with so many emotions. Tears well and it takes me a moment to compose myself.

"Serious? Where?"

I close my eyes real tight and hold my breath, wanting, wishing, needing this moment to last as long as possible. The pinch is on the back of my thigh, where I'm sure I'll soon have a faint bruise. A balloon of anxiety, anticipation, hope and shock grows in my chest until my skin hurts from the pressure. My hands shake, tiny tremors at first, but they increase until they resemble earthquake-like tremors and wine spills on my leg.

"Breathe, Paige, come on, just breathe." Jeremy takes my glass then enfolds my hands between his. His touch is warm. "Open your eyes, it's going to be okay."

I don't want to open my eyes. I don't want to talk or even listen to him right now. I just want silence. Silence where I can feel safe to just . . . feel. To feel the burn, the tightness of my skin, the flare of heat that is cooling. I yank my hand from his and pinch myself again, harder this time.

Come on, Jess, I'm here. Pinch again. Tell me you're still here too.

No matter how hard I pray, wish, believe, hope . . . she doesn't respond.

But I know I didn't imagine that first one. I know I didn't.

"Why haven't we found her yet?" I open my eyes and let the tears that gathered beneath my lashes cascade down my face. All I've done is cry today. "No sightings. Not one shred of hope in all these years. She vanished without a trace twelve years ago!" I swallow hard and take back my almost empty glass of wine, downing the remaining liquid in one swallow. He hands me a tissue, which I use to dab up the liquid on my pants.

"All those stories we hear of people being kept in basements, boxes beneath floorboards, locked in little garden sheds in a backyard . . . what if that's her? What if she's here, in town, for all these years, and we—" I can't continue, there's no words to describe the agony of my heart.

For the longest time, Pastor Jeremy doesn't say anything.

At first, I want to rail at him, demand an answer, but I remain silent and stare into his eyes, mirroring his breathing. It doesn't take long for the balloon in my chest to deflate, for the anxiety to dissipate and the pain to leave.

"Mom still blames me." I barely whisper the words. "She tries to hide it, tries to pretend she doesn't, but it's there, still, after all these years." I push my lungs outward as I inhale, needing all the fresh air I can get.

"Pain has a habit of bringing the worst out of people," Jeremy says. "Today, especially, that pain has a heartbeat."

Pain has a heartbeat. He's right.

"I don't know how to do it."

"Do what?"

"Accept that a part of me will always be this way, empty."

He nods. "Like there's something inside you unfulfilled? Wanting? Waiting to be complete again? I get it. And there's no real answer to that, Paige. You just . . . do. One moment at a time, one hour at a time, one day at a time. It's the only way to get through."

He looks away then, out the window, staring at nothing, but everything, at the same time.

"You sound like you know by experience."

He doesn't reply, not at first. Sensing he might need some space, knowing that I certainly do, I return to the kitchen to refill my glass. The sun starts to drop from the sky, painting it with rich oranges, blues and reds.

Jamie should be home soon with Flynn.

"Living with regret and shame, it's a hard weight to bear." Jeremy's voice is full of echoes.

"Regret and shame? What would you know about that?"

He gives me the saddest smile I've ever seen from him.

"We all live with regrets, Paige. All of us." The air coming out of his lungs whispers secrets his voice can't give breath to. "We're all on the same journey of life, each down a different path, but we all face the same struggles, one way or another. Just because I'm a minister, just because I try to live the best life I can for the God I serve, doesn't mean I'm perfect."

A shadow of a different man crosses over his face. He looks haunted with a past I can't even comprehend.

What secrets haunt him?

"I'm still just a sinner in need of someone's forgiveness. It's a battle I face every single day of my life, and it's a battle I'll never win."

He pushes himself to his feet.

"You make it sound hopeless," I say as I stand alongside him.

He laughs. The sound is hollow at first, but then the man I know, the one I'm more familiar with as a confidant and co-worker, appears.

"How can it be hopeless, Paige? We get a gift — to live each day as best we can, to right wrongs, to forge new paths. It's a blessing."

"Would my sister consider it a blessing?"

The hand now on my arm gives me a soft squeeze. "Life is a blessing, and considering she's your sister, I'm sure she would."

At the door, just as he's about to step away, I stop him with a question that's always been there but never asked. I'm not sure why. Maybe I didn't want to pry or assume anything. Regardless, I ask it now.

"Are you lonely?"

He's an enigma, a chameleon, and I've often wondered about the man behind the smile, the caring eyes and sympathetic ear.

"What an odd question," he says, not quite answering. "I live a full life, Paige. I might not have someone to share that life with as a partner, but I have families who are there for me, welcoming me into their homes, into their lives."

"Your church members, you mean? I don't think I've ever heard you talk about parents or siblings."

His eyes light up with fierceness. "My church family is my family. I'm who they call in the middle of the night when someone's being rushed to the hospital, or when they receive bad news. I'm the one they trust with their secrets, with their problems. I pray for each person on a daily basis, and I'm just as much a part of their family as they are mine. As for siblings, I'm an only child. And my parents . . ." He looks off into the distance. "They've been gone for a long time now."

"I'm sorry, Jeremy."

"Don't be. Dad never . . . understood my vocation. He thought I'd follow him into the family trade. When I didn't . . . well, we didn't talk much to begin with."

Still, losing a family member, intentional or not, is hard.

But there's something about his answer that's off, like he's trying too hard to convince me he's fine. I don't buy it. The life he just described means he's busy, and those family members are time-consuming, exhausting, on the best of days.

"But who do *you* go to, Jeremy? Who knows your secrets? Your fears? Who do you share your problems with? Who do you call up, in the middle of the night, when you can't sleep and just need to hear another voice?"

I know where he lives. It's a small bungalow, one bedroom, a small yard in the back, in a part of town that needs more upkeep than other neighborhoods. He likes to sit on his front porch and invite those he sees to join him for a fresh cup of coffee and a chat. He lives alone with no dog, cat, or even fish to take care of.

I've always thought he lives a lonely life full of minutes he's desperate to fill with busywork. Like coming over here, to check in on us.

He surprises me with a hug. "Thank you for caring. That means so much to me."

There's a softness in his face, a boyish appeal that no doubt has all the mother types in his small groups wanting to smother him with home-cooked meals and handknit sweaters.

My mother included, even though she doesn't attend any of his Bible studies or meetings.

"To answer your question, I'm not lonely," he finally says. "How could I be when I have friends like you, making sure that I'm okay?"

As he climbs down the front porch steps, I sit down, wine in hand, waiting for my boys to return.

My question had been a slip of the tongue, one that probably could have waited for another day, another time.

Maybe it's because my sister is at the forefront of my thoughts.

Maybe it's because I'm worried she's lonely, afraid . . .

I rub at the spot on my thigh where I felt the pinch.

"I miss you, Jess. I hope you know that. I'm not giving up on you, not now, not ever." I whisper the words into the breeze, hoping, praying that they're carried along the currents to wherever my sister is being held.

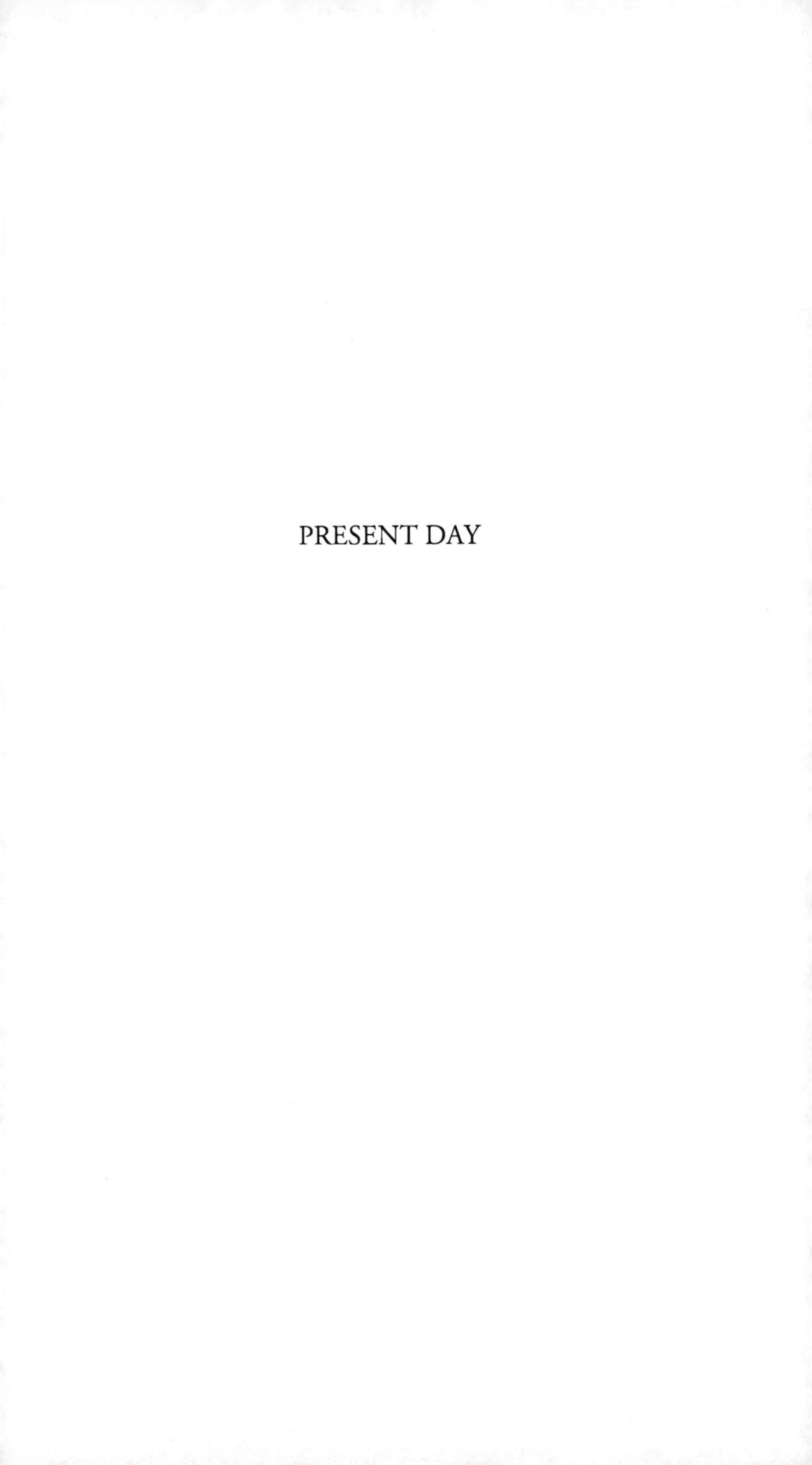

PRESENT DAY

CHAPTER 16

PAISLEY VALLEY HOSPITAL
9:00 a.m.

There's a commotion outside my room. Feet pounding against the tiled floor, carts being rolled, some sort of alarm going off.

I look around and realize I'm alone.

The woman here earlier, I hear her voice along with another outside the door.

Who is she?

I'd nodded off, fallen asleep, but I'm wide awake now. Awake and on edge.

I need to leave, I need to escape. I need to . . . I need to stop. Keep quiet. I remember the threat: if I want my son to stay safe, stay alive, I need to keep my mouth shut.

The heaviness in my arms and legs reminds me there's nothing I can do, nowhere I can go.

I've been beaten before, bad enough to leave me with a permanent limp, but never like this.

In the past, a doctor or some type of medical professional would be brought in. I'd be given a few bandages, have some limbs wrapped, and they'd dole out medication as they pleased . . . but never enough to erase the pain.

Depending on how serious my injuries were, I might be left alone for an evening. Or a day. Sometimes even a full weekend. Those were rare. Those were welcomed.

I doubt I have any skin unharmed or untouched by gauze or a sling or cast right now. Even my toes hurt.

My eyes drift, but I refuse to relax. Things happen when you relax, things you can never control.

Knock-knock.

The woman walks back into the room. Her footstep is light, like her smile.

"Sorry about that. We have an officer stationed outside your door, but it's shift change, so I was just filling in the replacement."

Officers outside my door?

"They're there for your protection," she says, being able to read my thoughts. "Remember? I mentioned this earlier."

I shake my head. No, I don't remember, so many things are foggy.

"Are you okay? Is there anything you need? I know this must be stressful for you, not being able to talk. Can you nod? Does it hurt?"

Who are you? I mouth the words, but she looks away. Did she do that on purpose?

"Would you like another drink of water?" Without waiting for a response, she brings the cup and straw close to my lips again. "Slowly," she says. I take tiny sips, let the water sit in my mouth until I've enough courage to swallow.

Hurts just as much as last time.

"There's a button here for your medication. If the pain is too much, press it, please." She shows me the button and places it beneath my fingers.

I'm tempted. Truly tempted. But the pain is manageable and I've had worse.

Much, much worse.

"Paige, Jamie sent a text — he'll be here as soon as visiting hours open."

Paige?

I haven't heard that name in years. I close my eyes, remembering a girl with reddish-blonde hair. She was fierce and protective and so smart. I loved her and hated her.

I shake my head and repeat my earlier question. This time she notices.

"Who am I?" She leans forward. "Paige, you don't recognize me?"

Hearing that name again, an arrow pierces my heart.

I'm not Paige. I wish I were. I wish . . .

She stands and leans across the bed, reaching for my right hand. It's wrapped in bandages, unlike my left hand, which is covered in a cast that goes from the palm of my hand up to my shoulder.

She gently nudges some of the wrapping out of the way, like she's looking for something.

I know what she's looking for, or rather, what she's looking at.

My tattoo.

She slowly leans away and sits down again. Her mouth gapes open and I read the questions on her face.

I'm not who she thought I was, and that realization hits her.

First, it's shock. Then surprise. Followed by fear.

"You're not . . . Paige, are you?" I can barely hear her voice, but it doesn't sound like a question. More like an accusation. "Who are you?"

Who am I? I want to tell her . . . but then I remember HIM.

His face from last night. His taunts. His threats.

He likes to play games and this is one of them. It has to be. Will I tell? Will I seek help? Will I try to out him?

If I do, and it's all for naught, he'll kill me.

If I don't, and this isn't a game . . . then he's won because he finally managed to break me.

Who are you? It's the only safe question I can ask right now.

"Oh God." She closes her eyes. "Oh God, what have we done?" She jumps up and rushes out the room, her voice high, fast, insistent as she talks to whoever is out there.

I force a moan to escape, making it as loud as I can, the pain feeling like it's tearing my vocal cords to shreds, but it's not loud enough to stop her.

I don't know how long she's gone, but it feels like forever.

When she returns, her chest is heaving, she's out of breath and she's pocketing her phone.

"Okay, how about we start over?" she says to me. She pulls a notebook out of her purse and opens it. "You can't talk, but how about you answer questions with a yes or no blink? One for yes, two for no? It's not the best, but it's a start. Does that sound okay?" She pauses and waits.

Blink.

"Okay." The words comes out on her breath. "Your name is not Paige, is it?"

Blink.

Her head dips in a nod.

"Do you know where you are?"

Blink. According to her, I'm home. In Paisley Valley. I want to believe her, I really do. I remember waking up in this room last night. But how did I get here? Why here of all places?

I've lived in palatial hotel rooms. I've slept in grungy storage rooms with a bare mattress and a pot to pee in. I've hidden in trucks taken cross-country.

But I've never been close to home. Never close enough to wind up in its hospital.

"My name is Monique Haskill and I'm a counselor with CHILD. Have you heard of the organization? You might have seen posters in bathrooms at truck stops, diners, or grocery stores?"

Blink. Heard, seen, I'm aware of it.

"I'm sorry for the confusion earlier. We . . . I thought you were a friend of mine. She went missing last night. When you were brought into the hospital, we thought you were her."

I can see she's telling the truth, it's there in her eyes.

"You were found yesterday, in an abandoned farmhouse about an hour from here. You were brought in by helicopter. I'm not sure if you remember that?"

An hour away? I've been an hour from my hometown?

Did HE know this?

I doubt it. He liked to spout how he'd saved me from life worse than death, how he brought me to the farmhouse to protect me, how he kept me out of sight because if people knew he had me, we'd both end up dead.

He just wanted me to himself. Eventually he started believing his own lies.

"We received a tip that helped lead us to you." Her voice is hypnotic, so gentle, so unassuming.

What's she hiding? There has to be something. What isn't she telling me?

"You were unresponsive when you first came in and you were taken directly into surgery. You're badly banged up, a lot of internal bleeding, broken bones." She stops, giving me space to take in her words.

HE did a number on me, then. He was in a murderous rage with the intent to kill me. So what stopped him?

"It was the tattoo on your wrist that made us believe you were someone else. She has a similar tattoo and my . . . associate was the one who noticed it. Your hair was slick with blood, so no one really noticed if the color . . . We were so focused on what we saw and who we thought you were, and then they had to shave your head . . . I'm so sorry . . ." She looks away, her voice thick with emotion.

I believe her. There's a need inside me to believe what she's telling me is true.

There's a huge part of me that wishes I were Paige. If I were her, my life would be so different. It would mean I was wanted, that someone still missed me.

I know that's not true. HE says no one is looking for me because they believe I'm dead.

"Could you tell me your name? Maybe mouth it? I'm not good at lipreading, but I can try."

My name? I don't have one. Not anymore.

I stare at the edge of my tattoo that can be seen from the opening at my wrist. She has one too? What are the odds?

"Is . . . is your name Angel?"

Startled, I make a sound I quickly regret thanks to the pain intensity. On a scale of one to ten, this is a thousand times worse than anyone could imagine. I can feel my throat muscles rip apart with my unexpected moan, the tears edged with razor teeth.

"Shhh, it's okay. I'm so sorry this is happening. Can we call you Angel? Just blink if that's okay."

Angel. That's what HE calls me. His angel, the one he saved from hell.

Blink. Why not. That's who I am, who I've become. The girl I was is dead.

"Angel, you are safe, I promise. The organization I work with, CHILD, we rescue girls, teens, women like you, from sexual predators. Is that what happened to you?"

Happened? Like it was a chance thing that I was kidnapped off my street, close to my home? It wasn't chance. The men who took me, they'd been watching me, introduced themselves to me. I knew them. I was their mark and they rubbed that in my face all the time in that first year.

I close my eyes, not wanting to see the pity in hers.

There's a knock on my door. Monique goes to answer. Her voice is strained, thick, and she keeps looking back toward me.

She says I'm safe, but I know otherwise.

FIVE DAYS AGO

CHAPTER 17

PAIGE

I cherish the mornings when I walk Flynn to school. It's the only *us* time I get with my son, when it's just the two of us and no one else. I don't have to share him, and as selfish as that makes me sound, I don't really care.

I try to leave a little early so we have time to stop at a park.

If given the choice, out of all the playgrounds in Paisley Valley that we could walk to on our way to school, Flynn always chooses to play at the Hillsong Playground, right smack dab in the middle of town.

It has everything a kid his age can dream of, complete with a pirate ship jungle gym. I think that's why he loves it so much. Many mornings, he'll play pirate up there with other kids from school.

I wave to the other mothers who have the same idea as me. They're sitting on the park benches, chatting away with a neighbor, a friend, while their child plays.

Once upon a time, they'd invite me to join them. I've declined enough that they don't anymore.

Today, of all days, I'm glad for that. The last thing I want is to be fodder for the gossip mill. The immediate backlash over Bryan Powers is inflammatory. I'm doing my best to leave it at work, to ignore the news, the constant email inquiries, and just focus on my son.

It's not easy. Especially knowing I'll be heading into the office and will have to deal with this. Today, tomorrow . . . for who knows how long.

I'm here to spend time with Flynn, to create lasting memories, to give him space to be a child. If I wanted to build relationships with the other mothers, I'd join them for coffee once the school bell rings.

"Mom, watch!" Flynn calls out. He's hanging upside down on one of the monkey bars, both legs curled around the bar.

He's too high. I rush over, hands reaching out to catch him if he falls.

It's not an if, more like a when.

"You've got to be careful, Flynn." I stand beneath him, hands on his shoulders, my arms holding his weight. The last thing I want is for him to slip off that bar and land on the ground, his head taking the brunt of his weight before his neck bends.

There are so many ways for a child to get hurt while playing.

It's why I watch him closely, why I don't sit on the bench and play on my phone or gossip with the other mothers.

"Mom, I've got this." Flynn attempts to wriggle out of my grasp, but I won't let him.

"How did you get up there by yourself?"

"I climbed."

"Well of course you climbed," I say, trying really hard to remain calm. "You have to be careful, Flynn. What if you had fallen off? You could have gotten hurt."

"Moooommmm." Flynn drawls out my name, complete with an eye roll, before reaching his hands up, grabbing hold of the bars, unhooking his legs and dropping to the rubber mulch.

"I'm a kid. I'm supposed to explore." His shoulders hang low and he doesn't look me in the eye. "Dad says I won't know how to do things unless I try it first."

I breathe in deep through my nose, the air filling my lungs, trying to remain calm, but it's doing nothing for my mindset.

Jamie would say that. He's also a boy and grew up riding his bike until the streetlights came on each night. He has no idea what can happen to kids nowadays.

Why do men think every bandage and bruise is proof of being a boy?

"I'm all for you trying things, Flynn. But can you give me a heads-up next time?" I might as well have spoken into the wind. My son is off toward the climbing-rope section of the pirate ship.

Let the boy run, he's going to be fine.

My father's voice nudges me to slow down my own spurt as I race after him. While Dad was alive and able, he would join us on our morning walks to school.

He said it was to spend more time with me and Flynn. I always figured it was his way of teaching me a valuable lesson on parenting the strong-willed.

Some days, you've just got to let go . . . and let God. That was one of his favorite sayings and one that still annoys me to no end.

What did *let God* even mean? Let God do what, specifically? Teach life lessons? Stop Flynn from breaking an arm, twisting an ankle? Keep him safe?

I lost trust in God a long time ago when it comes to that. Sure, I trust Him with a lot . . . but not with the safety of my son. If He couldn't protect Jessica, why would I trust Him to protect Flynn?

This is a repeat topic I tend to bring up with Pastor Jeremy. Mainly because he's always telling me to loosen the reins a little and it pisses me off. He's not a father. He doesn't have a family. What right does he have to tell me how to parent Flynn?

When I ask him, he gives me a pat answer, a ready answer that no doubt works for a lot of those in his small group, but let's be real . . . those scripted answers never work for me.

Faith without action is dead, isn't that what scripture says?

"Hey, Mom?" Flynn calls out as he's halfway up the rope wall.

"Yes, Flynn?" I'm there now, at his back, ready to grab him if his grip slips.

"Did you ever try things, you know, when you were a kid?" He looks over his shoulder at me, his foot slipping from the foot hold in the wood.

"Careful." He's not up too high, thank God, but any higher and he'd turn his ankle if he fell.

"Did you?"

It takes me a full minute to remember his question. "Of course I tried things. I tried a lot of new things," I say. Where is he going with this?

"Gramma let you?" He sounds shocked, surprised.

I laugh. "Yes, she let me. Remember, I had my sister with me all the time, so I was never alone."

"So maybe I need a brother or sister too, then?" His hands continue to climb up the rope, his feet firm against the wood, one step at a time, until he reaches the top with a triumphant smile.

Oh, sweet Jesus . . .

"I'd be a great big brother, Mom. I'd do a good job protecting them, too. Just like you do me."

I didn't think it possible for my heart to swell even larger than it is, but somehow, with his words, it's near bursting.

"You'd be an amazing big brother, Flynn."

Where's this coming from? Jamie's brought it up a few times here and there, that he's ready for another baby if I am, but Flynn never has.

Am I ready? Hell no. Flynn is enough for me.

He wasn't planned. I wouldn't say he was a mistake, but he'd been a surprise, that's for sure.

Having another baby . . . It's a struggle to wrap my head around the idea. It would be one more life experience without Jessica, and I'm not sure I can do that.

Not on purpose.

It's the same reason I haven't been able to set a wedding date yet.

"So we can get one? Can I have a sister, please? I'd be the best, Mom. I promise."

I push away every single thought but one. "Oh, Flynn." I force a laugh. "We can't just go and pick one out. That's what you do when you get a puppy, not a baby brother or sister."

With one giant leap, Flynn's down on the ground, beside me, before I have a chance to tell him to be careful.

"Can we?" He has the most hopeful gaze I've ever seen. "Get a puppy? Please? Dad says it's up to you, and Gramma says she's fine with it, as long as I promise to play with it and clean up any dribbles and pick up the yucky poop outside."

"A puppy? What?" I wrap my arms around Flynn and hold him close. Where did this come from? How did we get from a baby to a puppy?

He did this on purpose, didn't he?

"Dad said you might say no to a baby but yes to a puppy." The look on Flynn's face has my heart squeezing with motherly love despite knowing I've just been played.

How am I supposed to say no to those eyes?

There are moments, rare moments, when I see my sister in Flynn, and now is one of those moments. His grin, those dimples, the twinkle when he knows he's caught me off guard . . .

"He did, did he?"

Flynn nods, his lips tight together as if trying to stop himself from saying more.

Leave it to Jamie . . .

"I think this is a talk I need to have with your dad before I say yes or no," I say, taking his hand in mine. "But right now, it's time we head to school. Otherwise you're going to be late."

The topic of a puppy is all Flynn talks about as we walk. How he'll take care of it, how it will sleep with him in his bed, how they'll play together and go for walks together and be the bestest of friends.

And all I can think about is my sister.

Getting a dog wouldn't be a betrayal toward Jessica, right? Even though, as children, we'd begged for a puppy, a kitten, a hamster and even a budgie. My parents always said no for one reason or another. So we made plans, one day we'd move out, live together and fill our apartment with pets.

Jessica even talked about working in an animal shelter and starting one of her own.

We had so many plans, so many dreams . . .

What would Jessica say if she knew I didn't let Flynn get a puppy, a potential best friend, all because of her and a promise we'd made way back when?

Jessica would smack me on the ass and tell me that it's not my son's fault and that I should stop forcing my own issues on him.

Jessica would also be the first person to take Flynn to the local animal shelter and help him pick out a dog. She might even bring an extra one home, because then they wouldn't be lonely.

Realizing that, I find there's only one answer. I pull out my phone and send my lovely fiancé a text.

So . . . a puppy, huh?

CHAPTER 18

ANGEL

There's only one thing she loved about her life.

One motive that kept her going, day after day, hour after hour.

One reason she'd done the impossible and hadn't given in, given up or taken her life.

Her son.

Samuel played in the corner of the kitchen, close to the radiator where she nursed some seedlings into life.

"Remember, don't touch them. Okay, Sam?" She massaged the curve of her back, a sad attempt at comfort. "If we want to grow cucumbers, we need to be extra careful with these ones."

Her son looked up with an expression of understanding. His beautiful brown eyes, perfectly round, perfectly his, held a light she swore she'd never take advantage of. He was her blessing and after the life she'd lived, she didn't understand why he was hers.

He left the seedlings and ran to the back door, hands and nose plastered on the glass portion of the screen door.

"Are you wanting to go out and play, Sam?" Angel dropped her feet from the chair she'd been using as a footstool and grabbed the edge of the table for support as a wave of dizziness rushed through her.

It had been days since she'd had anything of substance to eat. Their meager supply of food had dwindled to almost nothing, which meant tonight's dinner was their last can of tuna on stale buns she'd made from the last bit of flour she had left.

It had been three weeks since Drew last came home.

Three weeks of bliss. Three weeks of peace for Sam. Three weeks for her body to heal from his last visit.

Sam looked over his shoulder at her, then returned his nose and hands back to the glass, completely focused on the paradise outside.

She didn't blame him. Anything was better than the prison they lived in.

The only home Sam had known was a dump. A falling-down, ramshackle farmhouse that should have been torn down years ago. The main floor consisted of four rooms: a kitchen, bathroom, closet and a room that served as both a living room and a bedroom for Angel and her son. The upstairs had two bedrooms, a small closet and a bathroom with the only shower in the place.

The heat rarely worked and the only reason they made it through the winter was thanks to an old corner fireplace. The walls held newspapers and old clothes for insulation and were full of more holes than windows. She'd tried her best to stuff the holes with odd pieces of fabric, but she was limited with supplies.

Once she wrangled her five-year-old into his sweater and rain boots, he bolted across the makeshift porch, jumped past the broken step and ran for the small storage shed that contained his most prized possession . . . his soccer ball.

While he kicked the ball, she took the little remaining wood and brought it into the house. If she moved the bed closer to the fireplace, that, along with the extra blankets, should keep them warm for the night.

Tomorrow, well, that would be a different story. Unless Drew managed to magically appear.

She had no way of getting ahold of him. No phone. No computer. Not even a radio. The only electronics she had in the house was an iPod, an old thing that Drew would add audio books and songs to whenever he showed up.

She tidied up the table, placing Sam's books in a pile, all the while keeping an eye on him through the door.

Drew used to bring her books to read, but after she used the books for firewood one winter, he stopped. He'd bring Sam books occasionally but always made her promise never to destroy those books, saying it was important for Sam to learn to read. He couldn't — or wouldn't — speak, but he was a bright boy.

It was a rare moment of praise from Drew for the child. His child.

Back at the door, Angel looked out, but her son was nowhere to be found.

"Sam?" She opened the door and called out, "Sam, where are you, honey?"

She stepped outside for a better view. She wasn't too nervous; they were in the middle of nowhere, at the end of a dirt road long forgotten about. The only one ever to drive to the house was Drew.

He was a long-haul truck driver. It'd be a miracle if his route led him close to home.

When he first . . . found . . . her, she'd assumed he'd take her on the road with him. She'd met a lot of girls stolen and sold into the sex trade industry who'd lived on the road, chained, drugged, beaten into submission.

Instead of taking him with her, he brought her here, to this hellhole.

He said he was saving her. That if it weren't for him, she'd be dead.

He was probably right. But who made him God?

"Sam?" Voice raised, Angel stepped as far from the house as she could, which was never far enough, and finally caught sight of Sam.

He was out in the side yard.

"Sam!" This time she came close to screaming his name, which had his head snapping up.

She didn't like him beyond her view or voice, especially since he would never respond to her calls with a yell of his own.

"Come on, honey, stay close, okay?" She gave him the brightest of her smiles as he ran toward her, his eyes full of questions and concerns.

He kicked the ball to her in reply.

She kicked it back, turning her foot sideways, a habit she remembered from when she'd played soccer as a child.

Without thought, she glanced toward the road, breath held for the barest of moments. No blooming dust indicating a car. Once her mind registered they were still safe, her lungs relaxed and the air escaped in a singular sigh.

"We can play for a little bit," Angel said to her son, "but then it'll be time for dinner, okay?"

He, too, was looking toward the road.

She hated that he'd picked up on her habit. Hated that it had become one of his own.

For the next half hour, they kicked the ball. Angel had to sit on the steps behind her a few times, her body weary from the exertion.

Eventually they headed into the house. While Sam washed his hands and face for dinner, Angel prepared the tuna sandwiches, making sure to leave one bun aside for Sam's breakfast.

"Sam, do you remember which pot has the celery growing?" They had one stalk that was ready to be picked. She'd shown Sam the container on the deck a few days ago.

He scrambled off his seat and raced across the kitchen to the door.

Within seconds, the screen door banged again and he stood there, wide eyed, hands shaking.

The knife in her hand dropped. She knew that look, that shake.

Dinner forgotten, Angel rushed out the door and stood on the back deck, her attention solely focused on the road.

Sure enough, plumes of dust billowed off in the distance. It was faint, but there.

"Shit."

She rushed back into the house and grabbed a bag off a hook. One quick glance inside confirmed her pullover was still in there, along with a few books, flashlight and Sam's favorite stuffed lion.

Sam was already pulling on his sweater and grabbed socks off the radiator.

Angel threw the sandwiches she'd already made into the bag and quickly filled a water bottle for him. They had roughly two minutes till Drew turned into their driveway.

"You remember what to do?" She bent down and looked Sam in the eyes.

He nodded. The fear was still there, shining bright in his eyes.

"Remember the blankets you put in there? Make yourself a bed, okay? It'll get cold." Her fingers trembled as she zipped up his thick sweater, wishing he had a proper winter coat to use. "Put my sweater on, the one that's in the bag. It'll help keep you warm. There's sandwiches in here, plus some books. When all the lights are off, sneak back in the house and curl up in bed, okay?"

She hugged him as long as she dared to. "Close the door tight behind you, but remember to keep an eye on that hole we made. If it's safe for you to come in early, I'll call you from the door." With a kiss on the forehead, one meant to last a lifetime, she watched as he ran out of the house, jumped down the steps and beelined it to the shed.

He made it in, with the door closed, just as Drew's truck appeared. She struggled to control her breathing, self-regulating the panic coursing through her with the speed of a tornado.

Sam was safe. That's what mattered.

CHAPTER 19

The screen door slammed behind Drew as he walked in, arms full of bags.

Angel tore her gaze from the swollen bags of food he carried, and armed herself with a mask of a smile.

If her focus was on what he'd brought rather than on himself, there'd be hell to pay.

"Happy anniversary, Angel," he said, when she finally dragged her gaze to his.

Flecks of gold sparkled in his eyes, and the dimples he believed to be his most attractive feature were on full display.

Anniversary? She swallowed back the bile snaking through her and forced her lips into something that resembled a smile.

"I wasn't sure if you'd make it home in time or not." *In time* had everything to do with needing more food for Sam and nothing to do with him and their anniversary. Would he notice? She hoped not.

If he noticed her lying through her teeth, he didn't let it show.

He dropped the bags he carried on the floor.

"I would have been here sooner, but I stopped at the store first." She was tugged tight to his body, where he smothered her face in kisses from his thin lips.

Angel pushed every single thought in her head away. She ran to the place in her mind where safety beckoned. Her safe place resembled a lake, one so far off in the distance no one else knew about its existence.

It beckoned her into its black, bottomless depth, the water heavy as it covered every inch of her skin. The heaviness protected her, warmed her, distanced her from what happened to her body in that moment.

Drew kissed her with a fever that left imprints of fire and pain with his touch. He walked her backwards until the back of her thigh bumped against the table, his intention clear and direct. Her body was his playground, his clay to massage at will. Her body was malleable, formless, an empty shell, just as he liked. He took her then, her cheek smashed against a placemat, his thrusts quick and forceful.

She swam in her lake, diving deeper into the depths, the darkness calling out, its song weaving a story she'd written years ago, a story without an ending.

When he was done, he gave her space, his apology unspoken.

Drew headed back out to his truck, saying he'd retrieve the rest of the bags, while she cleaned herself up. Her underwear, ripped beyond repair this time, was tossed into a bag in the closet. Nothing ever went unused. Once it was cleaned, it would be used to stuff a new hole she'd found in the living room wall.

She held the screen door for him as he worked his way up the stairs, sidestepping the broken one. "I'll take care of that tomorrow," he said as he brushed past. "Should have fixed that last time."

Angel flashed the man a thankful smile, not even bothering to attempt to cover the look of gratitude he read with obvious pleasure.

"I left you alone for too long. I won't do that again." He glanced over at her, a look of expectation on his face as he unpacked the bags he'd brought in.

"I always miss you when you're not here." Lies. Lies. Lies.

"I take care of you, don't I?"

Her stomach grumbled loudly as she took in the boxes of cereal, cans of soup, pasta and sauce.

"Good, you're hungry," he said, giving her a wink. "I brought home something special for dinner. It should be in that brown paper bag."

Angel peered into the bag full of take-out containers and opened one of the lids . . . chicken fried rice. Her stomach growled even louder.

"See, I know you," he said. The smile on his face turned once he opened the cupboards. "Where's all the food?"

Angel tensed. She recognized that look, that tone. He was going to blame her, call her a fat pig, say she fed their son too much, that she needed to do better with what he provided for her . . . his accusations would be followed by a slap, a kick, a punch . . .

Her hands went to cover her belly. She struggled to relax her muscles, starting from the shoulders and working her way down to her thighs. The looser she was, the less it would hurt.

One item at a time, he filled the cupboard, never looking her way.

He did that on purpose. Everything he did was done on purpose.

The longer he stood there, the harder it was to remain calm. Her stomach tensed, bunched together, the need to protect the child she carried was instinctual.

"Angel, I was away too long, I'm sorry." When he finally turned, she struggled to remain calm. She didn't recognize the emotions in his gaze and that scared her.

It almost looked like his apology was . . . sincere.

He looked from her to one of the kitchen chairs. "Why don't you sit?"

"I . . ." She struggled for the words. "I forgot to give you a list of things we needed last time." She slowly lowered herself onto the kitchen chair, feeling caught off guard. "I'm sorry, it was my fault." Carrying that blame was habitual. She was always at fault. Never him.

Never him. Until today. She wasn't sure what to do with that.

All of a sudden, he was in front of her, pulling her up out of the chair, holding her close. "The fault is on me. Three weeks was too long." He cupped her face in the palm of his hands. "How can I make it up to you?"

Angel kept the image of her lake as her focal point, needing the calm, the water to wash away every expectation and expression she carried on her face.

Something was wrong. He was being too nice. Too soft. He was never like this.

It was a trick. It had to be.

"Angel? I'm serious. How can I make it up to you?"

She knew this was a trick. A test. One she was going to fail.

She had a list of ways, none that he would accept. So she picked one out of the plethora that filtered through her mind. It was a longshot, a reach, it'd be a miracle if he agreed.

"Take me shopping? That way I wouldn't have to make a list?" She whispered the request, certain he'd say no.

She could count on one hand the number of times he'd taken her shopping since he'd brought her here. Less than five and never to the same store or even the same town.

And especially never to the town she'd grown up in.

He took his time to respond, his stare hard, intense.

He stepped back from her without saying a word. She'd gone too far, asked too much. She was sure of it.

She'd been right — it had been a test and she'd failed miserably.

"Where's the boy?" Drew took the bag with their special dinner and set it on the counter. "I bought him some pants, guessing at the size. Figured if they're too long, you can roll them or something. Also got him some running shoes and a new coloring book."

It took Angel a minute to follow his words.

"Thank you." She was surprised at the gesture. She'd asked for new jogging pants and shoes months ago. Sam had torn a hole through his last remaining pair of pants last week and she was prepared to cut away a section of her sweater to cover that hole if necessary.

"So . . . where is he?"

"He's in the . . . his . . . playhouse," Angel said, clearing her throat.

She'd once told Sam about a tree fort her dad had built for her when she was a kid. While he never vocally begged for his own fort, she could see it in his eyes, every time he'd look at the large maple tree in their yard.

"Kid still likes that?" Drew sounded surprised. "Isn't it too cold out there for him?"

"He bundles up with my thick hoodie and his sweaters." Of course it was too cold for him out there, Angel wanted to say, to shout right in Drew's face, but she didn't. She couldn't.

A raised voice for sure got his hand. She'd had enough slaps to last her a lifetime.

He took off a lid from the fried rice and stuck his finger in the center. "The food is cold," he muttered.

"That's an easy fix," Angel said, pasting a smile on her face. "I'll put it in a casserole dish and reheat it in the oven. Won't take but a few minutes."

"While you do that, I'll go grab Sam. He should be here with us, celebrating. Oh, and I got you some new hair dye. Noticed your roots were showing last time. I'd like you to do your hair tonight. I don't like the color." The door slammed behind Drew as he left. She stood there and watched, hands gripped tight in front.

Something was up, off, and that scared her. She couldn't read him, and after all this time, she could always read him, anticipate his actions, his moods.

Except for tonight.

If this was a new game he was playing, she was going to lose. It was the fear of what she'd lose that scared her the most.

CHAPTER 20

By the time the boys had made it back to the house, the table was set, and the remaining bags Drew brought in were placed to the side.

She knew better than to go through them.

Nothing was hers. Everything was his. Not respecting that distinction always brought painful consequences.

Angel wore a mask of bravery and contentment throughout dinner, pretending their nuclear family dynamic was normal. Drew told stories of his trips, the people he'd seen, the dogs he'd met that kept other truck drivers company.

Sam's eyes lit up like fireflies at the mention of dogs. Drew often told Sam stories of his own childhood pet, and characters in a few of the books he'd bought Sam had dogs as pets. It was no wonder Sam wanted one.

Silently, Angel wanted one too. One that would make for a good guard dog, perhaps protect Sam, because the day would come, she was certain, when there would be a time she wouldn't be able to.

"Tell you what. Once your mama tells me that you've started to talk, that's when I'll think about getting you a dog of your own, okay, squirt?"

Instead of the excitement of a promise made filling Sam's face, he looked downward, the sparkle gone from every facial feature.

Angel's heart broke for him.

She wasn't sure why Sam remained mute. He'd only ever seen a doctor twice. The first time, Drew had taken her to see a "doctor friend" who understood their "situation." The second was when Sam was really sick and Angel had feared he'd die. That same doctor had given Sam some booster shots, handed Drew medicine and warned them that Sam had an irregular heartbeat.

He'd also warned them it could take time for Sam to learn to verbally communicate due to being born with Down syndrome.

Angel hadn't been surprised. Drew still hadn't accepted the truth. Or, if he had, he placed the blame on Angel, saying that was God's punishment for her wicked ways.

The irony wasn't lost on her.

"Since today is such a special day," Drew said, ignoring the disappointment hanging in the air, "I have an extra special gift still for you." He took Angel's hand in his.

"More gifts?"

"You're not complaining, are you? This one is for you." Drew pulled a silver chain that hung around his neck out of his shirt and unfastened it.

The air in Angel's lungs snagged as he placed the key in her hand.

He lifted her right leg and set her foot on his lap.

His fingers trailed the sensitive skin around her ankle. It was swollen, red and full of partially healed cuts.

"Your skin is so delicate," he said with a gentleness that roiled her stomach. "I'm getting a special cuff made for you to wear all the time. The underside will be soft and it's padded, so no more cuts like this." He rimmed those cuts with his finger, pressing down hard enough for the pain to shoot up her leg. She flinched.

His smile grew wider. “Of course, if you’re good, the cuff won’t be attached to the chain. But, that’s up to you, now, isn’t it? You know the rules.” He tore his gaze from her ankle. The message in his eyes told her he wanted her to break the rules, that he liked her chained up.

She hated him for that look. Hated him for that look and for a million other reasons too.

Her leg quivered with anticipation. Drew took his time. With a flick of his finger, he unlocked the metal cuff that had been wrapped around her ankle for the past three months.

She wanted to lift her leg off his lap and place it on the floor. She wanted to feel what it was like to not have that leg burdened by a twenty-foot chain where the end was bolted in cement. She wanted to never hear the clink-clank-thunk of the chain hitting the floor, or the swish-swash as she dragged it behind her with each step she made.

Not having that on her ankle meant she could run with Sam, they could go out into the field and catch fireflies at night, she could teach him to climb a tree.

Not having that binding on her ankle meant she wasn’t captive to the confines of that twenty-foot chain, that she could go upstairs and have a shower, she could go in Sam’s fort and play games with him . . .

Tears gathered at the corners of her eyes. Drew preened.

“I told you earlier you could have asked for anything. I expected you to ask for this . . . but you didn’t. Instead, you asked for something that would make my life easier. That” — he leaned forward, taking her hands in his — “means a lot. It tells me more than you probably intended.”

Angel forced her lips to turn upwards, to give him a smile that spoke of fondness and hinted at embarrassment.

If he were a smart man, he’d be able to look past that mask, he’d see the hatred that boiled her blood, the humiliation of having to pretend something she didn’t feel in front of her son.

That putrid emotion she felt for this man barely skimmed the surface of her true feelings. He disgusted her.

His every vile touch, the sound of his voice, the smell of his presence, repulsed her.

He had made the mistake once to tell her all he wanted was her love.

How could she love a man who held her hostage, used her, abused her?

How could he believe she'd ever fall in love with him?

She'd rather kill him, stain her soul with his blood, than love him.

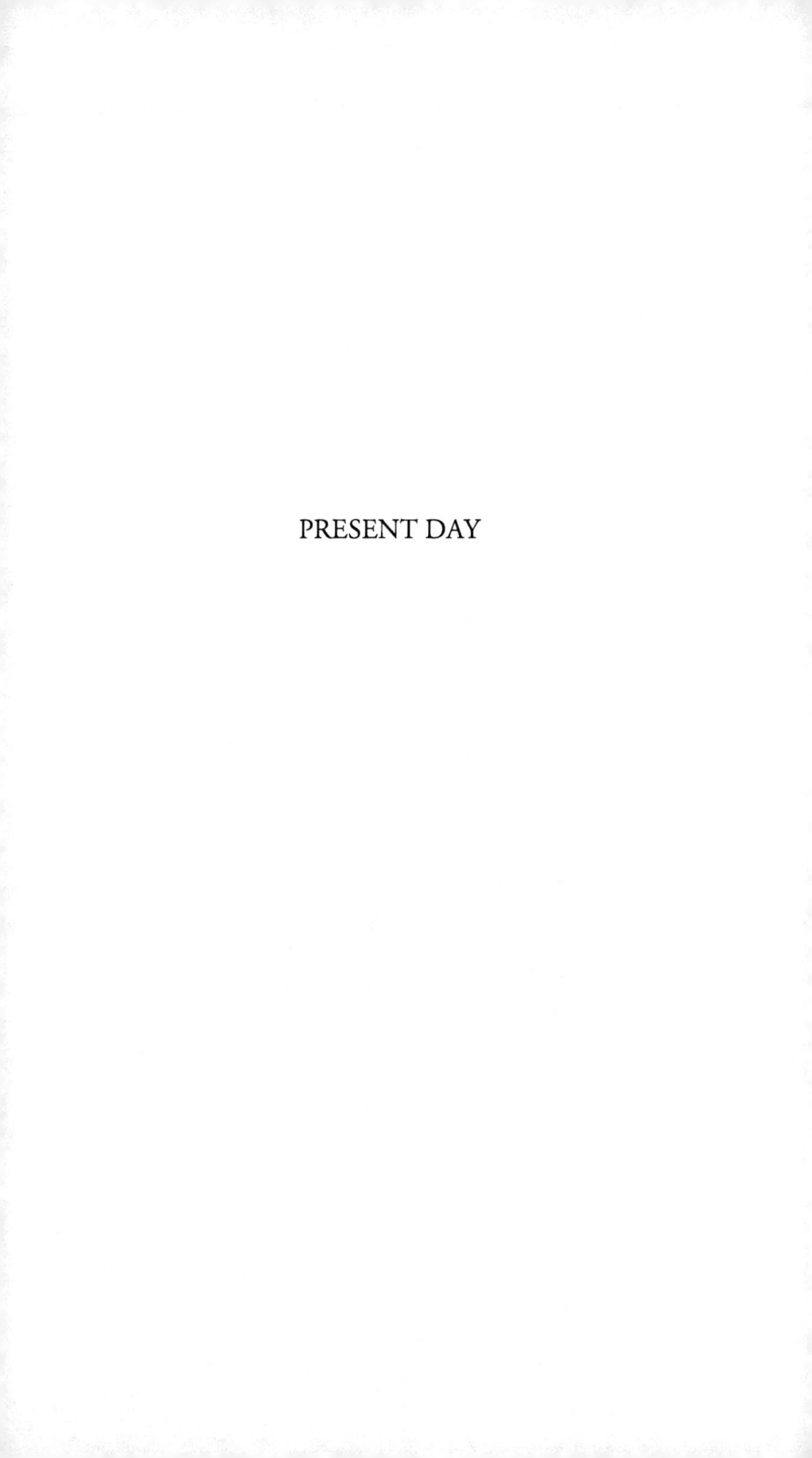

PRESENT DAY

CHAPTER 21

PAISLEY VALLEY HOSPITAL
NOON

The sun slashes through the curtain slit and warms my feet beneath my blanket. That warmth somehow slides its way up my legs and I'm feeling cozy and sleepy.

Monique's phone rings, and I can't help but stare at it as she holds it in her hands. I notice they shake a little as she takes the call.

"Jeremy, is everything okay? No, we haven't found her yet . . . Yes, I know, I'm sick with worry too. It's okay . . . it's not your fault . . . we all thought she was her . . . Have you talked with Lindsay yet? He's looking for you. He wants to know why you called Paige and not . . . Oh, all right." A frown appears as she listens before hanging up.

"Sorry, about that. I thought maybe they'd found my friend, but . . ." She looks away, an attempt to hide her pain, but it's there in her voice. She's worried.

"I used to be a social worker in Minneapolis, right from college. All I wanted to do was help children, protect them, keep them safe. I dealt with parental abduction all too often, so I know what happens and how this works. It's never like the TV shows, where everything gets wrapped in a nice bow at the end of each episode. She's . . . Paige, she's been missing for fifteen hours now. I just . . ." She stops and stares off into the distance.

"My eyes were opened early. I came from a normal home, both parents still together, a golden lab, a cat, had good grades . . . I didn't understand what life is like for most kids. I thought the ones I'd be saving, protecting, were with men and women who shouldn't be parents, that I'd be giving them a better life by helping find families who would love them." She inhales and blinks away tears that shine in her eyes.

"After twenty years, I came to CHILD. Helping to save children who have gone missing, are kidnapped, sold into sex trafficking . . . It's a different heartbreak now."

Her phone dings again.

She waits a second before looking at it. "Oh . . . Angel, do you mind if I step out for a bit? I'm needed downstairs."

I lift my lips into a small smile which she reads as acceptance.

Of course I don't mind. She has no idea how much I prefer being alone. That's the only time I can relax, not be on guard.

Monique leaves with a promise she'll be back.

I'm not sure if that's a promise or a threat. She seems harmless, but I've been burned by harmless guises in the past. Drew seemed harmless too, at first.

When Monique was here, the quiet was weighted, the space full. Now there's room for me to breathe, to think, to remember.

Drew's presence suffocates me, even now. I can smell him; his scent is permanently burned into my being until it's always there.

He's still here, hiding, waiting, I know it.

I'm not safe. Not from him.

He was my savior, my Jesus in disguise. He saved me from a monster, a demon from hell.

I'd been chained in a basement. I slept on a stained mattress, bound to a pipe that came out of the ground. I shared a bowl of food and water with mice who scurried in from the dark corners.

Senior said I was his hidden vice, a secret addiction. There was one window in my prison cell, my view blocked by the metal of a window well. He'd barricaded and nailed the window shut so it never opened.

I lived on that mattress for three years. Always with one or both ankles broken. Senior did that to make sure I never ran.

Until Drew. He found me, carried me to safety, promising I'd never be used like that again. He offered me the world and promised he'd find my family and take me back.

I believed him.

I slept on a real mattress, on a real bed, one with four legs and a headboard. One that had fresh sheets and extra blankets. He never touched me, not while I recovered, not while the bruises disappeared and as my roots grew.

I stayed in that bed while my bones healed. The first time I walked on the floor on my own was to the window. I wanted to open it, feel the breeze of fresh air on my face.

It was nailed shut.

That's when I knew. I'd been fooled by another demon in disguise.

Monique's last words to me were to urge me to get some sleep. My chest hurts, the pressure of not being able to breathe pushing me down into the mattress until I swear I'm about to be swallowed. I'm not sure sleep is possible, not on my own. All it would take is a push of the button and a sweet elixir of nothingness would be ministered.

But I need to think. I need to remember how I got here, and how I can get out once I've healed enough. Until then, I'm helpless, powerless, and utterly destitute.

Can I trust Monique? Can I trust the nurses and doctors and police officer outside my door?

Remembering how easily Drew walked into the room doesn't give me much hope.

My eyes close and I welcome the stillness sleep provides until there's a hand on my arm, squeezing.

Someone stands over me.

Her sandy-blonde hair is pulled back into a bun and her brown eyes are covered in glasses, but they do nothing to hide who she really is.

I recognize her.

There's a wheezing sound, of someone inhaling through a straw, struggling for air, and I realize it's me.

I try to withdraw farther into the mattress, try to pull away, demand my muscles listen, but her grip is strong and I'm being held prisoner.

I know her.

I know those eyes. That grimace. Those fingers. I remember that grip from long ago. That snark. Her scent.

"Isn't this a pickle." Her head is bowed, her voice low, but it's strong, steady and full of dangerous promises. "Imagine my surprise when I got a call last night and was informed who the Jane Doe on my floor is." She chuckles and shivers rise along my skin.

"Despite not being able to talk, you've made a mess, I hope you know that. Your mess is now my problem and I'm supposed to clean it up."

Tiny goosebumps race across my skin.

"I'm sure you've heard rumors of what happens to girls like you, who think they can be rescued? The rumors are true, but I can protect you, if you want. Stay silent, and you'll stay alive. Have I made myself clear?" She looks at me then, direct, and that's when I know I'm not safe.

I'll never be safe again.

"Consider me . . . your guardian angel." She pulls out a needle from her pocket and inserts it into the tube that runs down into my arm.

"Sleep tight." She stands there, hovering, guarding, waiting until my eyes close and I succumb to sleep.

Her shoes squeak as she leaves the room, and the last thing I hear is a dull thud as my door closes.

FOUR DAYS AGO

CHAPTER 22

DETECTIVE MERI AMBER

From what I've been told, Andy Rawlings was last seen in this area. I get word about sightings every few years, and every few years I do my best to chase down the leads.

I always come up empty.

I have feelers out with some drivers I've met since joining the police force. They're the ones who point me in the various directions. Sometimes they tell me they saw Andy at a stop. Sometimes they hear his name or call sign on the radio.

In the handful of times one of my contacts sat with Andy at a diner, no one has thought to take a photo.

Not sure if it's a trucker code or the guys just don't think of it, but one of these days, I really wish they'd figure it out.

ALLS Transport was a bust. Sure, they have records of an Andy Rawlings working here but no, without a warrant, they refuse to tell me more.

I thought maybe I'd wait them out, sneak up on a driver as he pulled into their lot, see if they had any news about Rawlings.

Eventually a cop car rolls in, stopping right in front of my rental car.

A big hunk of a man steps out. He fills out his suit in a nice way, a good way, but there's nothing nice or good about the expression on his face.

"Can I help you?" I lower my window and give what I hope is a nice, I'll-play-this-your-way-for-now kind of smile.

He's completely expressionless.

He takes off his sunglasses and bends down, just ever so slightly, leaning one forearm on the top of my car.

"You're making folks inside that business a bit uncomfortable," he says.

I look out and see someone in the window and give them a wave.

"That so? Not harming anyone, am I? Just sitting here in my car, minding my own business." Okay, that much is a lie. Every time I see someone pull in, I rush out of my car and knock like a crazy woman on their truck door. I admit it.

"I'm Detective Lindsay. I hear you are" — he pulls out his notebook and scans it quickly — "Detective Meri Amber?"

"That's me."

"On a case I missed the memo about?"

If that's his not-so-subtle way of reprimanding me, he's got to do better than that. Despite his deadpan expression, slight disappointment in his voice, he doesn't scare me.

"Nope."

He looks at me. I look back. He wants me to say more, but . . . that's not going to happen. He can ask nicely.

"Why don't you follow me? We'll head down to a coffee shop a few blocks over and have a chat over coffee. Marco should be pulling out a fresh tray of fritters."

"You know, I'm not really the donut type."

That gets a reaction. One brow raises. "They've got fruit cups and salads."

He doesn't really give me a chance to respond. He assumes I'll follow and he's assumed right.

He pulls up to a really quaint café called The Mug Shop, complete with chalkboard signage and a French-style patio set up in the front. Almost reminds me of home and my favorite coffee shop. Doubt the coffee is as good, though.

Like a gentleman, he holds the door for me then proceeds to the counter.

"Right on time." Marco, according to his name tag, pops out of the back. "Fritters are cooling and I made an extra large one for you." He looks my way. "I'll make that two?"

"No thanks." Who wants a fritter when there are huge scones in the display case? "I will, however, take the largest chocolate chip scone you've got. Make that two . . . I'll take one to go." My mouth is already drooling, just thinking about that first bite.

"I'll heat it up, yes?"

I can't nod fast enough. I'm already regretting not stopping here first when I drove into town.

"Two coffees," Detective Lindsay says. "How do you want yours? I don't see you being a straight-up black type. Probably one of those French press, coconut milk type of drinkers, aren't you?"

Oh, he's snarky. This could be fun.

"Whatever coffee you've got, but room for extra cream. I only like a hint of coffee taste, please."

"Go grab seats," Marco says. "I'll be right there."

The detective is already ahead of him, heading to a table by the window. He takes the seat that gives him the optimal view of the street and his vehicle.

"So . . . Amber." His drawl has a slight twang to it, just a hint, but that's not what I notice first. It's his smell. Fresh cut grass, strong black coffee, with a hint of sweat. Reminding me of the past, of an early Saturday morning back home with Dad.

When he doesn't say more, I give it a few seconds. "So . . . Lindsay."

He's looking at my rental, trying to size up the kind of cop who drives a sedan.

It was the cheapest option and I didn't want to stand out. But . . . considering the only vehicles I've seen are pickup trucks and SUVs, it's obvious I failed.

"You're not visiting family, you're not here for a job, not here about a case and you're harassing one of our largest businesses . . . Want to tell me what's up?" Lindsay leans back in his chair and gives me what I can only call *the stare.*

"Would you believe me if I said it was personal?"

Nothing. I get nothing from him. No change in expression. No hint of acceptance. Nothing.

"Not a lie. Honest." I copy his stance, leaning back in my chair, but I keep my arms loose, hands relaxed in my lap.

Marco arrives with our coffee and food. My coffee is almost the color I like and before I have a chance to ask for more creamer, he produces a little milk cup. "Figured I was close, but you never know."

I add a splash or two of cream, give it a swirl and take a sip. "Perfect."

I'm not really fussy when it comes to coffee. I can't be, considering I drink the crap at work all the time.

I have two options. I can tell Lindsay the truth, which, in all honesty, is probably the only way to go. Or I can give a half truth and then beg forgiveness once he figures out I lied.

"I'm following up on a lead to a cold case."

He sips his coffee and tears off a piece of pastry, shoving it in his mouth.

"My sister was abducted nineteen years ago by, I believe, a truck driver. He was last seen here, in Paisley Valley, a little over two weeks ago."

He shoves another piece into his mouth, chews, then wipes his fingers on a napkin.

"Sorry to hear. Are you working this through CHILD?"

As awesome as CHILD is, the only one really interested in this case is me.

"I met with Paige Fischer when I got into town. Haven't heard back from her, though," I say as I cut open my scone. This thing smells delicious. I take a small bite and groan.

"Marco is an award-winning pastry chef, used to work in those swanky hotels over in Europe. Came home to take care of his ailing father and opened up this place." Lindsay raises his coffee cup toward Marco as he wipes down his counter.

"I'm going to need to put in an order for these," I say just before I take another bite. I'll order a dozen or more and freeze them.

"So who exactly are you looking for?"

"Andy Rawlings."

I study Lindsay for a reaction, but I'm not sure why I bothered. This guy is a blank slate, has the expression-free look down pat.

"What does he have to do with ALLS Transport?"

I pull out the photograph I have. "I believe he used to work for them. Not sure what outfit he's with now."

"Could be on his own and subcontracts out," Lindsay suggests.

I thought of that too.

"I get word about him every few years. This guy is a ghost. Either he keeps to himself, works a few months a year or . . ." It's as frustrating as hell trying to locate him.

"I know a few like that. Those are the months they hunt." His lips press together. "Why don't you send me what you have and I'll look into it?"

This surprises me. "Why?" The question slips out, unintended.

"It's what I do. Locating drivers is something of a specialty for me." He takes another sip of his coffee. "I head a task force that works with CHILD. Left Washington to come here and do this."

Note to self, look up Detective Lindsay and figure out why I haven't heard of him before.

"Two eyes are better than one."

He nods.

"How long you here for?"

"Another few days. Took some personal time."

His look says he knows I'm holding back. We sit in silence, listen in on the conversations of others who slowly fill in the seats around us.

"Let me see what I can come up with, okay?"

"In between what hours? Don't you have enough on your plate with that cell you broke?"

"I've got a good team."

I understand what he means without him having to explain further.

"Appreciate the help. I'd like to lay my sister to rest, where she belongs, you know?"

His head dips in a slow, understanding nod.

"If you've got a photo of her, I'd appreciate a copy. I like to see all the faces of the kids I try to save."

This request hits me hard. I pull out my phone, wait for his name to come up as an airdrop and send him the best photo of my sister I have.

"Appreciate that." I swallow back the swell of unexpected emotion.

"Do me a favor? Leave the guys at ALLS Transport alone?"

And do what . . . twiddle my thumbs? I think not.

"Will do."

If he catches the lie, he keeps that info to himself.

CHAPTER 23

PAIGE

With my eye on the time, I putter around the small group room at CHILD, moving chairs to create a circle, checking that the coffee pot is on, that the cream and sugar containers are full.

It's five minutes until my weekly group meeting starts and so far, I'm all alone.

It happens . . . sometimes. Considering this is the first meeting since the Bryan Powers fallout, I'm honestly surprised no one is here.

Today's group is called Real Parenting, and we focus on what life looks like after a child has gone missing, especially if there are other children still at home. It's hard to be present and active when all we want to do is grieve.

I finally hear a gaggle of voices coming from down the hall and smile in relief. Women enter the room, their faces aglow with shared laughter.

Thank you, Jesus. Maybe today won't be as bad as I thought it was going to be.

"You need to tell Paige that story," Margaret, one of the older ladies of the group, says. "Having a boy herself, she's probably lived it."

Iryna, one of the younger moms, closer to my age than any of the others, grabs a white mug and fills it with coffee. Iryna is new to Paisley Valley. She immigrated from Ukraine less than ten years ago and moved here with her husband, who works as a trucker for a local transport company. They have twin boys, aged four.

She's been a part of the CHILD family for almost three years now. Her fourteen-year-old stepdaughter went missing after walking home alone from soccer practice on a Sunday afternoon.

"Oh, yes? Your boy, he also walks around the house in your bra, with oranges stuffed inside the cups?" Iryna wiggles her brows as the room fills with laughter, my own included.

"Oh, he hasn't done that, not yet at least."

"Declan was so funny. Then Jacob had to do it too. Here, I take photos." She pulls out her phone and passes it around.

The easy laughter and camaraderie continue as everyone grabs their coffee and fresh cookies Mom made this morning and takes a seat.

"For some reason, I thought Pastor Jeremy would be joining us today? He said he'd see me here when I saw him last," Margaret says, just as Monique enters the room.

"We figured we'd leave the real parenting talks to the parents and give him a breather from all the meetings he attends." Monique closes the door behind her. "Sorry for being late."

There's a hush in the room, the jovial atmosphere dissipates, with Monique's presence.

"He is a busy man." One of the other ladies speaks up. "I think he's one of those souls who feel they have to fill up every hour of every day or they're being lazy."

"And yet, as busy as he is, he's always available if you need him," another says. "One phone call, text message or email and he's there."

The praise for Pastor Jeremy continues until even I can't handle it anymore. I cough and look at Monique. We'd discussed earlier how to handle today's group session.

"How is everyone doing since our last meeting?" Monique asks. "I know a few of our families have" — she turns to me — "I don't even know what to call that experience. False hope? Stress-induced hours?"

"Living hell." Cassie, another member, speaks up, her voice full of pain. "I hate those days." She glances toward me. "No offense. I mean, I'd rather have hope that there's been a sighting rather than not know at all, but . . . it's hard."

I nod, understanding all too well what Cassie's alluding to.

"Hard isn't quite the word yet, is it?" Margaret says, as the mother hen of the group. "It's demoralizing, exhausting, stressful, and like Cassie said, it's a living hell. You want to hope, you need to hope and yet . . ." Her voice trails off as she gives me a worried glance. "Are you guys okay?"

"Is it hard, that hope, keeping it alive?" Iryna asks.

This is not how I anticipated the beginning of this session. I thought for sure we'd be discussing the cell, the victims and of course . . . Bryan.

But rather than focus on what's happening outside of our group, they do what we do best . . . focus inward and do what we can to protect our own.

Being a part of the CHILD family isn't something I'd wish for anyone, and yet, I can't imagine what my life would look like without this family in it.

"Keeping hope, it's a journey," I say in response. "In the beginning, that's all you have, hope. Hope that they'll be found, that they're okay, that they're alive. Then fear kicks in and it's easy for that faith you've developed to die a silent death. Is it hard, keeping hope alive?" I repeat Iryna's question, and look everyone in the eye, one at a time.

"Absolutely," I say. "I work at it every single day, believing that one day we'll find Jessica, even though we've never had a single sighting of her, not once in the past twelve years. I often fail at keeping that hope alive, though. It doesn't come easy."

There's a hush in the room until Cassie gets up and walks, something she does often during our sessions. She's not one to stay still, not for any period of time.

"How is your mom doing?" Cassie grabs her purse and roots inside, pulling out a Tylenol bottle, popping the lid and dropping two in her hand. She holds the bottle out, as if asking if anyone wants some. No one does.

I try to hide the sigh that I'm sure echoes around the room. Things are . . . difficult with Mom right now.

"How about we let Sarah speak for herself, the next time she's here, okay?" Monique tries to steer the conversation away from my mom. "We'll stick with our motto of only speaking for ourselves, if that's okay with everyone?"

While I appreciate what she's attempting to do, I promised these ladies transparency and honesty, and not answering this question breaks that promise.

"Mom and I handle the idea of hope and keeping it alive differently," I say, looking at Cassie directly. "Which . . . hasn't been easy since Jamie and I moved in with her after Dad's passing."

Moving back home has been a huge adjustment.

"Does Flynn ever get confused?" Cassie addresses an issue I've often thought of bringing up in one of our sessions.

"Funny you should mention Flynn. I think he finds it hard, for sure. I tell him about Jessica all the time, I try to keep her alive for him, but every time her name is mentioned to Mom, you see the pain. He knows talking about her makes me happy but her sad . . . so he's caught in the middle."

I hate that. Hate that he questions himself whenever he mentions Aunt Jessica.

It's the same whenever I try to bring Dad up. He's been gone for six months, but Mom still isn't ready to have him brought up in casual conversation. It's like she needs to prepare herself, build up walls around her heart before she can remember their life together.

I understand . . . to a point.

"And that's not fair, not to him," Monique adds, bringing me back to the topic at hand.

Despite the words Monique uses, I don't feel reprimanded or censored. Just . . . understood.

"It's not just that, though," I continue. "I find I'm struggling, as a parent, to teach Flynn about hope. Does that make sense? You'd think hope would be the easiest thing to teach to a child, since they're full of so much wonderment and joy."

Others around the room murmur their agreement.

"No, I don't get it." Iryna's the only one to voice an opinion. "How do you struggle to teach hope?" She honestly sounds confused.

I take a moment to let my jumbled thoughts come together into something resembling cohesiveness.

"I think it's safe to say we all know I'm a helicopter parent." I let my smile shine through. My parenting style has come up time and time again over the years. It's a struggle for me.

"Part of the reason I'm like that, well, I think it's obvious."

"Fear." A few of the women speak in unison.

I make a show of rolling my eyes. "Right, fear. I'm afraid to let him out of my sight, or give him alone time, or trust him with anyone, even his own father. And I'm working on that, I really am, but . . ." I lift my shoulder in a shrug.

I've spent hours in counseling sessions, multiple talks with Jamie about our different parenting styles, and it all boils down to the same conclusion: my fear and guilt colors every aspect of my life.

"So." I focus back to Iryna. "To answer your question, it's hard to teach about hope when I'm constantly living in fear that something will happen to my son."

"Ahh, yes, I have this fear too. Good." Iryna breathes a sigh of relief.

"What do you mean by good?" Monique asks.

Iryna glances around the room, obvious confusion on her face. She picks at the cookie from her plate, and her brows scrunch together until she looks up, her face less pensive.

"My language, it's not always so good, you know? I mean, it's good to not be alone in this fear. I have it too. All the time. Robert . . . he says I smother our kids too much.

But what if they go missing too? They'll need that smothering to remember, to get through."

Her lips tremble as she speaks about her twin boys. She loves them with a fierce passion, while her husband rules with a firm hand.

Margaret, who sits beside Iryna, reaches out to hold her hand. "You are the best mother those little ones could ask for and don't you forget it."

"We won't let you." Cassie gets up to give Iryna a hug.

The next half hour, each mother speaks about trying to keep the hope alive. A lot of tears are shed, but they're followed by laughter and hugs too.

At the end, Margaret asks about Bryan.

"I'm sure everyone here has read the official emails sent out," she says, "and we've all shared our feelings about Bryan to Lois directly and agreed that we don't want to give him any time in our group. But . . . we have to ask . . . how are you guys doing?"

I look to Monique, who looks to me. I think we're both taken aback by that.

"Wow, I honestly . . ." Monique is struggling for words, which is rare. "Thank you, I honestly mean that. Every group I've been in, he's been the focus and we thought for sure . . ." She gives her head a shake and then leans back in her chair.

"We thought for sure you'd want to talk about him too," I say for her. "I'm glad you've shared your feelings with Lois, that's important. As for us . . . it hasn't been easy. He was on my team, which means we now have investigators who are going through every file he's touched to see if he's influenced cases when he shouldn't have. Personally, I'm broken up and haven't really had time to focus on him and what it means."

"Lois," Monique says, interrupting me, "has this in hand, which means we don't have to worry about it too much."

Nothing else needs to be said and everyone seems to be aware of that.

After the session, Monique stays behind to help me clean. I have a feeling she has something she needs to get off her chest, and while I want to ask her about it, I decide to wait. Thankfully, I don't have to wait too long.

"I appreciated you speaking up."

I dip my head in acknowledgment. That can't be all she wants to say.

"I have a phone call I need to make," Monique continues, "but I thought maybe we could sneak away for coffee afterward? It's been a while since we've caught up."

"And you'd like to check in on me and make sure I'm okay." I say what she didn't. "Am I reading between the lines correctly?"

Monique's eyes twinkle just a moment before she laughs. "Yes," she says, "you read that right."

I gather the tray of dirty dishes. "I'll take these to the kitchen and then meet you outside?"

Monique checks her watch. "Sure, that's plenty of time."

Dishes taken care of, I head to the front where Anita sits at the front desk. The screen behind her flashes with photos of missing children and just as I walk by, my face comes up on the screen and pauses for a total of four seconds.

A red banner, beneath the image, displays the words HAVE YOU SEEN JESSICA FISCHER?

My stomach does a flip-flop, a gut-kick reaction to that banner beneath my own photo, except it's not meant to be me. It's meant to be my sister.

That gut reaction proves one thing. No matter how many people, therapists, strangers, tell me it's not my fault Jess is missing, I alone know the truth.

CHAPTER 24

Marco, the barista-slash-owner-slash-everyone's friend of The Mug Shot, waves as we enter the quiet coffee shop. It's my favorite café in town, and with it being the closest one to our office, it's also the most convenient.

Which also means we are known by both name and drink request.

"Sit down and I'll have your coffees out in a moment," Marco calls out.

"Thanks, Marco," Monique and I say in unison.

I beeline to the corner table where two comfy armchairs are situated. I love coming here either super early in the morning or midday, when I need to recharge and regroup. Sometimes I'll sit here and listen to my queued podcasts while sipping a large flat white.

Today, we're the only ones here and the quiet atmosphere is exactly what I crave.

"How was the anniversary dinner?" Monique asks, rooting through her bag and pulling out her phone. "With all that's happened the last few days, this thing hasn't stopped ringing. I'm turning it off," she explains before returning the phone to her purse.

"Whoa, nothing like getting right to the issue." I'm a little startled and uncentered. I'd expected the question, just not in the beginning of our conversation.

"We've known each other how long?" Monique's brows rise toward her hairline. "You know me better than that."

I stare out the window, watching the world pass by. Out of habit, I give the skin on the top of my hand a pinch.

I'm done talking, thinking, remembering the anniversary.

"Just like any other year. Mom made chicken potpie, which I missed since I was at the hospital, and when I get home, she ignored me." I keep my attention outside, to the real world, the world that continues to move forward regardless of the chaos around it.

"Your mom understood, though, I hope, why you were at the hospital?"

I snort. "You're kidding me, right? According to Mom, I give three hundred and sixty-four days a year to my job; the least Jess deserves is one day."

Technically she's not wrong.

I give so much to my job, but that's by choice.

Marco appears, carrying a tray with two mugs and two plates. "I made some pastry today that . . . well, it doesn't look the best, but it's delicious, I promise." He looks slightly embarrassed.

"What are they?"

"Hazelnut bear claws." He wrinkles his nose. "They taste good, but . . . I can't really sell them like this. So they're on the house. Enjoy."

"That man is crazy," Monique mutters through a mouthful of pastry once Marco leaves.

He isn't crazy, not to me. He just has high expectations of himself. That's present in every detail around us, from the way he set up the café to exude comfort, to the food he makes, to how he dresses our coffee.

I feel Monique's silent questions despite her not saying anything.

"Spit it out," I say, mumbling around the food in my mouth.

"Things seem unusually tense between you and your mom."

Unusually tense? Yeah, there's a reason for that.

"Mom is pushing to say goodbye to Jessica."

"I don't think she's exactly pushing to say goodbye," Monique says, her words more of a question than an answer. "Maybe she's just ready to move past waiting."

I'm really struggling to hold back the words sitting on the edge of my tongue, demanding to burst out, come what may.

I don't want to say something I'll end up regretting. Once it's out there, in the universe, you can't take it back.

Monique, of all people, should understand that there's no difference between wanting to *move past* or to *move on*.

If we had confirmation of Jessica's death, then fine, I get the need to move on. I would have no choice but to.

Except, we don't. She could still be alive and I have to believe that.

I need to.

"Waiting is hard, Paige. You know that."

Yes, waiting is hard.

"It's exhausting and demanding," Monique continues, "and you're in a perpetual state of never moving forward with your life." There's something in her voice that bothers me. It holds a hint of . . . blame? That can't be right.

"Waiting also means never giving up," I counter. "That's what Mom is doing. Giving up on ever finding Jessica. What happens when Jessica is found? When she comes home? When she sees her gravestone . . . How do we explain that?"

I pinch the skin on my hand again, over and over and over. The fresh pain barely equals the torment inside me, though. I would need to cut off a body part, refuse all pain medication, live with the phantom pain for the rest of my life, for it to equal how I feel inside.

"No. I'm not giving up." The words push past the spiked mallet head lodged in my throat. "Not until I have to, and we're . . . we're not there."

"You aren't there," Monique clarifies, and right then, in that moment, I feel a measure of anger toward her. She should be siding with me, not my mother.

"Mom shouldn't be there either. She's still saying goodbye to my father . . . how can she add Jessica to that? That's something I can't get past. I'm not . . ." I hesitate, unsure if I want to be one hundred percent honest. Honest responses mean never being able to take back the words spoken in haste.

"You're not . . . what?" Leave it to Monique to not give up, to not let me backtrack.

"I'm not sure I could forgive her if we did that." My voice, whisper thin, hurts with the admission.

What does that say about me? Being unable or unwilling to forgive so easily?

"Doesn't sound like there's a 'we' in that," Monique says. "Sounds more like it's something your mom might need to do. But Paige" — she leans over and lightly touches my arm — "just because she stops waiting doesn't mean you have to."

An electric shock courses through me at Monique's words. I haven't thought of that, haven't processed the distinction, and why not?

She's right. Just because Mom wants to say goodbye doesn't mean I have to.

I never will. That's a promise I made in the very beginning, a prayer I've uttered over and over and over again.

I will never give up on my sister.

"Mom wants to hold a funeral. Just a small one, family only, and place Jessica's grave beside Dad's."

Monique stays silent.

"Going to the funeral, accepting the plot beside Dad is being used . . . having to visit her when I visit Dad . . . I can't do it."

"Then don't." Monique says that so matter of fact, like it bears no consequence.

"Mom will never forgive me."

Monique sips her coffee and just looks at me.

Too often, her silences say more than enough.

I let out a very long, very tired sigh.

"Let me ask you a question." Monique sets her coffee back down on the table. "What kind of example do you want to be for Flynn?"

My confusion must be evident because Monique starts to chuckle.

"It's a simple question, Paige. What's the example you want to set for Flynn? Do you want him to know that no matter what, regardless of whatever happens to him, you will always be there, always waiting for him? Or do you want him to know that you're exhausted with life, leaving him unsure of how to react or respond to you?" Her pointed look is a knife straight to the heart.

"Children mimic not what they're told, but what they're shown."

What am I showing Flynn? What's my example?

"Did you ever let go of any of your kids?" The question flies out of my mouth without thought. I don't even know where it came from. "The ones you worked with? You must have."

A curtain drops over Monique's countenance. It's a subject neither one of us has approached throughout the years we've known each other.

All I know about Monique's previous career is that it's taken its toll on her, and she rarely talks about it.

That doesn't mean I'm letting her off easy. She's not the only one with a sharpened knife.

"Oh no you don't." I lean forward, my gaze intent. "You don't get to hide from me, especially not today."

Monique turns her gaze out the window.

I give her time to reclaim herself, her thoughts, to work through the myriad of emotions that are fluttering across her face.

"Being a children's aid worker is hard." Monique's voice is barely loud enough to be heard. "You're warned, in the beginning, not to get attached, but you do anyway." She pauses. "Sometimes you're the one taking a child from the only home they've ever known, becoming the enemy for them to throw their hurt, hatred and rage at. And sometimes . . . sometimes you're their savior, swooping in to save them from the one hurting them."

There are so many things I want to say, but they're all platitudes, phrases put out into the universe because nothing else can be said.

It's in those moments that, sometimes, the best thing to say is nothing at all.

"Did I ever let any of those kids go? No. I should have, but I couldn't. They're always with me, still. Some send me Christmas cards. Some hate me for tearing their worlds apart. But they're all here." Monique touches her chest, her hand covering her heart in a vow.

"So you get it." It's hard to push those words out.

Monique pulls her attention from the window to me. "Get it?" Her brows knit together in a you've-got-to-be-kidding-me look. "I get needing to find a reason to move forward." Her voice drops. "I get what it's like to feel mired in grief, desperate for a way out."

I feel like I missed something, some important message that has meaning to Monique.

"There is no right or wrong response here, Paige. I wish it were cut and dried, where you can pick a side, but life is messy and unfair and no one makes it out unscathed."

CHAPTER 25

DETECTIVE MERI AMBER

I'm spinning my wheels and hate the feeling. I want to call Lindsay and demand he tell me what he knows, because I know he has to know something.

But it's only been a day.

In this line of work, a day can feel like a lifetime or like life is speeding by. A day can reveal horrific, unforgettable details that haunt your nightmares. A day can also turn into another year a cold case remains unsolved.

I'm running out of time.

This morning I woke to my phone blowing up with text messages, phone calls and even Facebook messages from my work family back home wanting to know how my beach vacation is going.

If I leave now, I'm sure I can find a flight and enjoy the last few days of my time off on a beach somewhere. I could leave this in other capable hands, admitting I've done all I can with this last update. My sister's case is a cold case for a reason.

But I won't. I've traded soft, sifting sand beneath my toes for a small town in the middle of nowhere and I have no regrets.

Especially with the best baker this side of France just down the street from my B&B. After yesterday's scone, I'm now craving another. I'm going to put in an order, so I can take them home. The icing on the cake would be if he ships his product as well.

Just as I'm about to open the door to the café, it opens for me and out come two women, one of them being Paige Fischer.

She sees me and it's clear she's taken aback.

"Detective . . . Amber?" She searches her memory for my name and I'm pleased she remembers it.

"Still here. Still waiting for that email." My not-so-subtle reminder hits its mark because at first she pales, then her mouth opens before her cheeks bloom a cherry pink shade.

She totally forgot about me.

I'd be offended except I can only imagine how busy she must be.

"I'm so sorry," she says, pulling out her phone. I stand there with some kind of look that's supposed to be friendly, but from the way the other woman is watching me, it's not coming across that way.

"What am I missing?" the woman finally asks.

"Oh, Monique, this is Detective Meri Amber. She's from out of state and here looking for her sister."

Monique's eyes flare open with sudden interest.

"She's been gone for nineteen years," I tell her.

The rush of adrenaline forming all over Monique's face disappears in a flash. She then drops her shoulders. "I'm so sorry."

"I just sent Anita the photo," Paige tells me. "Again, I'm very sorry."

"What photo?" Monique leans over to look at the image Paige shows her.

"It's old and grainy, but it's the only photo of Andy Rawlings I have."

"Who?" Monique immediately looks up, which has me suddenly interested in who this woman is.

I study the woman's face. I have no idea who she is or why she's interested in what's happening, but she recognizes Rawlings' name.

"That's not Andy," she says, taking the phone from Paige and peering at it closely.

"I can guarantee you it is," I say. "It's old, though, taken the day he took my sister, but it's him."

She shakes her head. "No, I know Andy."

I'm now on full alert, my whole system blazing red, emergency sirens screaming in my ears.

"I'm sorry, who are you?" Slow down, back up, take stock from the beginning. That's what Dad would say.

"This is Monique," Paige answers, her voice full of confusion. "She works with me at CHILD."

Like that explains anything to me.

"Rawlings is retired, or semi-retired, I guess. He's a trucker and an informant from when I first started with CHILD." She hands the phone back to Paige but is looking at me. "He wouldn't take your sister. I'm afraid you've been following the wrong lead."

"Do you have a file on him?"

Monique's shoulders square back. "Not one I can show you."

My left brow rises to meet my hairline.

"I've already spoken to Detective Lindsay."

She stares me down. What the hell is wrong with this woman?

"Monique?" Paige's voice drops.

"Listen, I'm sorry. I really am. But Rawlings isn't who you are looking for." She leans her head back and stares up into the bright blue sky. "Is he your only lead?"

He's been the only lead since day one. My sister was last seen talking to him at the gas station. It's believed she climbed into his truck, for whatever reason, and that's the last she was ever seen.

Rawlings is the monster I'm looking for and if this woman thinks she's not going to help me locate him, she's delusional.

"Does he live in the area?"

Her lips thin. "No."

"Monique." Paige pulls her to the side, both their backs to me. That's fine, I'll wait. "What is going on? What would it hurt to help her? She's looking for her sister. You'd think, especially after Bryan, you'd want to help."

"She's going after the wrong man. Rawlings . . . trust me, Paige, he wouldn't take her sister. I've known him for too long and he's done too much for me. Sharing his information just makes things . . . messy."

"Messier than things are right now? But what would it hurt?" Paige casts a glance back toward me.

I can see the second Monique capitulates.

"Let me talk to Lindsay first, okay?" This she says to me. "Then I'll share his file."

My back goes up. I should be happy. I should be thrilled that I have another lead, a solid lead, but I'm angry. Who does this woman think she is to withhold information like this from me?

Why is she protecting him?

I stay where I am even after they leave me. I'm not sure if they're aware, but their voices are carried in the wind and while I can't make out full sentences, I hear enough.

"What is going on?" Paige asks.

"Rawlings . . . custody . . . Tinders." The farther they walk, the less I can make out. But I've got enough.

I've got another name.

CHAPTER 26

PAIGE

The audit team has taken over the office. They sectioned off two conference rooms and my filing cabinet is empty. I feel like every eye is on me as I stand in my cubicle.

My phone buzzes with a text. It's Jamie.

At the park with Flynn. Can you join us?

Can I join? Absolutely.

The ability to shrug off an emotionally difficult day and play with Flynn at the park holds way more appeal than staying here.

It's a beautiful afternoon. The sun is high in the sky, the billowing clouds barely move and the air is full of the singsong cadence of birds flying from one branch to another.

The closer I walk to the park, the clearer the playful screams, shrills and shouting from children playing becomes. I can't even hide my smile as I speed up my pace.

I don't recognize Flynn's voice through the chaos, nor can I see him, but I'm not too worried. There are a total of four different playgrounds, along with multiple walking paths, green spaces to throw balls, and even a dog park. Jamie and Flynn could be anywhere.

The smart thing to do would have been to text Jamie for his location. Eventually, though, I'll find them. If they aren't throwing a ball, then they are probably at either the third or the fourth playground. We like to rotate through the play areas with Flynn and we'd just been at the second play area the other day.

Sure enough, that's where I catch sight of Jamie, at the second last area, full of swings, slides and play structures.

He's on a park bench, partially angled so I only see his back, but I know it's him from the school bag at his side. It's Flynn's. Once again, this is just another way of how we parent so differently. If I'd been the one to pick up Flynn from school today, I'd be right at his side, enjoying the afternoon, rather than sitting life out, waiting on a bench.

No, that's too harsh. After being surrounded by teenagers all day, Jamie is probably enjoying a few moments of quiet, of being alone, as alone as you can be in a play area surrounded by a dozen or more screaming kids.

I scan for Flynn, sure I'll find him on one of the swings or in a group waiting their turn to climb the rings of the slide . . . but he's not there.

Nor can I find him standing on top of any of the play structures or hanging like a monkey or crawling through the bottom holes like an Army cadet.

In fact, I don't see him anywhere.

What I do see, imprinted on my mind the moment Jamie looks over at me, is the phone in his hand.

"Where's Flynn?" I rush over, purse slung over my shoulder, one hand gripping the handle tight so it doesn't fly off my arm.

My fiancé, the father of my child, stares at me with the blankest of expressions.

I want to slap that look straight off his face.

"Jamie, where is Flynn? I can't see him anywhere!" I turn, mentally cataloging every child, every adult in the area.

Twelve. Eight boys, four girls. Seven adults, most of them female. Three of them male. One stands by the swings, hands in pockets. Another leans against a tree, baseball hat covering his eyes, black hoodie, jeans and black running shoes.

The other male is Jamie.

The females are either playing with their children, or huddled together with other women, their focus on their children. One holds onto the handle of a stroller, pushing it back and forth.

I still don't see Flynn.

I. Don't. See. Flynn.

Until that moment, I'd been calm.

Now I'm a storm. A tumultuous tornado raging through a valley where nothing is protected and everything is in my pathway.

My phone is in my hand and I'm videoing the surroundings, capturing every single child and adult that's visible. I then focus on the vehicles in the parking lot, checking that no adult is dragging my son toward a vehicle.

Remain calm. That's the first rule. Don't panic. Catalog everything. Notice everyone.

Remain. Calm.

I can't breathe. I'm trying to. I inhale, push my lungs out with effort, but there's no air — nothing coming in, nothing going out.

"Flynn?" I call out, my voice calmer than the thunderstorm brewing inside.

I check the play structures, bending down to peer inside, noticing one child after the other, but never Flynn.

I force my feet to not run as I walk from one area to the other, calling, coaxing, cajoling . . . masking the panic.

I pull his photo up on my screen. "Have you seen my son?"

The group of mothers shake their heads, calling out to their own children, *marcos* calling *polos*.

Jamie is already heading toward the men. The one who stands by the tree, he follows Jamie, calling Flynn's name. The other remains where he is.

"Paige, he was just here." Jamie's at my side now, his phone tucked away in his back pocket, one hand providing shade over his eyes and he looks out over the playground once again.

"He's not here now. Where did he go? Did he tell you he was heading to a different park? Who was he playing with?" I shoot him one question after the other, no pause, no room for him to reply.

"You were on your phone." The accusation laced in my voice comes nowhere near the anger in my gaze.

It's either be angry at him or go into full-blown panic at the thought of losing my son.

I will not panic.

My fingers move across my phone screen, hitting the buttons for nine-one-one. Every second my son isn't found is an hour he could be missing. Away from me. From us. In someone's car, stuffed in a trunk, scared, screaming . . .

I swallow hard, forcing the vision, the nightmare from my mind.

"Nine-one-one, what's your emergency?"

I catch Jamie's shocked expression. "You called the police? He's around here, Paige. We'll find him."

A part of my brain turns a lock on listening to Jamie. His mouth moves but I'm only focused on one thing: my son is missing.

"Yes, yes, my name is Paige Fischer and my son is missing. We are at the Hillsong Playground, the third playground, the puppy parking lot." There's the bright neon yellow sign ahead with the graphic of a dog, high on one of the light posts.

"I can't believe you called." Jamie shakes his head and leaves my side. He searches, calling Flynn's name over and over.

He'd better find him.

"Paige, when was the last time you saw your son?"

"I . . . this morning. But his father brought him here, to the park. When I came, our son wasn't here, he's missing. Jamie, my fiancé, he was . . . distracted."

"Is Jamie your son's father?"

"Yes."

"Okay, Paige, here's what we're going to do. Help is on its way and will be there in three minutes. In the meantime, keep searching for Flynn. Could he have gone to one of the other playgrounds? What is he wearing?"

"Jamie?" I run over to where he stands, talking to the men. "What's Flynn wearing? Did he have his sweater on? The one he wore this morning? It's gray with bright green, remember?"

"What? Yes, yes. That's what he wore. I'm going to head to one of the other parks, see if he's there." Jamie brushes past me and runs in the direction of the last park in the area. It's just over a slight hill, not too far.

"Paige, I have a message for you from a Detective Lindsay. He just pulled into the parking lot. Can you see him?" The operator's voice is smooth, solid and offers a strong foundation for my chaotic mind.

I turn toward the parking lot. Lindsay's here. He's here.

"Yes, yes, I see him."

Without thought, I hang up, stuffing my phone into a pocket, and grab onto Lindsay's arms, my grip firm.

"Flynn's missing. Jamie wasn't paying attention and he's missing." Hysteria laces my voice, runs through my blood. I'm living a nightmare in the making, one set on repeat.

"I will not lose my son." My whisper is more promise, less prayer.

"We'll find him, Paige. I promise." Detective Lindsay's gaze never wavers.

I trust him. I believe him.

He's everything I'm not. Calm. Strong. Even-tempered.

"Where is Jamie?" Lindsay glances around the grounds.

"He went over to the fourth park, just in case, but he wouldn't—" I stop myself. I'm on the edge of a precipice that leads into a very dark hole, one I'd never crawl out from if Flynn isn't found.

"Paige, I need you to remain calm, can you do that? Breathe . . . come on, Paige. Breathe with me." Lindsay's calm voice is the complete opposite of how I'm feeling.

I do as he asks, inhale, then exhale . . . one breath, two breaths . . .

"Good, good." A slight smile appears on his face. "Other units will be here soon." He points toward the parking lot entrance. "In fact, they're pulling up. We'll find him, okay? I promise."

I swallow hard. "He's wearing his gray sweater, the one with the green pinstripe down the arm. And jeans. And dark running shoes. Jamie has his backpack. No hat." I repeat the words I'd given the nine-one-one operator.

"And where is Jamie again?" Lindsay writes my words down in his notebook.

"He headed to the other park, to see if Flynn would have gone over there, but he wouldn't have. He knows better. He knows to never leave our sight, to always be within speaking distance, to tell me when he's heading to another play area."

Detective Lindsay waves over the two policemen as they exit their vehicles. I don't recognize them. "Go see if you can find him, okay? I'll talk with these men and we'll start searching the park."

"But what—"

He touches my arm, stopping me.

"You did the right thing calling the emergency line. Everyone is on the lookout, I promise."

All it takes is one slight nudge, a push, toward the direction where Jamie had gone and I run, calling for Flynn, begging others to find him, call for him.

Jamie stands at the top of a hill, eyes once again shaded, as he searches around the space.

"Have you seen him?" I grab hold of his arm, holding tight. "Where is he? Where has he gone?"

Jamie goes to touch my hand, but I jerk away. I don't want his touch, not now, not while Flynn is missing.

Where is my son?

Off in the near distance is the last play area in the park. It's also the smallest one, with tire gravel, swings and two swirly slide structures. Beside it is a green area where a small group of boys kick the ball to each other.

"He's over there," Jamie says, after giving me an unreadable look.

I follow the direction of his finger, where he points to three small boys who stand off to the side, watching the others kick the ball around.

Flynn. He's there. He's one of the three.

My heart, which has been racing, skids to a stop, knee-jerking my body into a downward motion. If it wasn't for Jamie grabbing hold of me, I'd have landed on my knees.

As if sensing what I'm about to do, Jamie pulls me tight to his side. "Shhh," he says. "Just leave him be."

I drink in the sight of my son as my heart finds a much calmer, steadier beat. I breathe in, fresh air filling my lungs, and even dare to give a small wave as Flynn glances back over his shoulder and notices us watching him.

"Ahh, you found him." Detective Lindsay comes up behind us.

I almost expect his voice to be full of censure, of judgment, even a little bit of laughter, all at my expense.

I'm overreacting. I'm in full parental panic mode. I called emergency services, pulling Lindsay and other officers away from actual duties to come and soothe my overprotective heart.

"I'm sorry," I say.

My gaze remains fixated on my son.

"For what? For being a mom? Don't think twice about it. I needed to stretch my legs and I happen to know those other two were sitting at a local café, drinking coffee. There's nothing to apologize for."

I sneak a look at Jamie, whose face is unreadable. "I'm going to go down there," I whisper, untangling myself from his lax hold.

I keep my steps small, careful, mindful I shouldn't run even though I want to, I want to rush down the hill, but I don't.

Instead, I paste the bravest of smiles on my face and call Flynn's name.

I don't engulf him in a hug. I don't nag him about our rules. I don't do anything to signify the terror I'd felt only minutes ago.

"Hey, Bud," I say, standing behind him. "So . . . I'm thinking we should head home to make dinner, what do you think?" One hand on his shoulder, a gentle squeeze. I'm proud of myself for not losing it.

He glances up, then over at Jamie. His hand goes up in a wave until it drops back down to his side. "What . . . what is Detective Lindsay doing here?"

Do I tell him the truth? Do I admit my fear? My overreaction? I hate lying to my son.

"Well now, that's a funny story. See, I came here to meet you and Dad after work, but kiddo . . . we couldn't find you. And you know how we've talked about you going off on your own and stranger danger, right?"

Flynn nods.

"So . . . being the mom I am, and because I love you so much . . . I thought maybe you'd gone missing." I rub a spot in the middle of my forehead. It takes everything in me to act as if everything is kosher.

Flynn's eyes widen until they're saucers. "Oh."

My nose wrinkles. "Yeah. Say goodbye to your friends, okay?"

Somehow, I manage a feat that can only be labeled heroic. I step away from my son and head up the hill, never once turning back to see if he follows.

Those were the hardest steps I've ever taken.

CHAPTER 27

ANGEL

She had a hate-indifference relationship with Drew.

Most days she hated him. Hated his touch, his presence, his voice . . . hated every single thing about him. Hated that he bought her, used her, hurt her.

But he'd saved her from a monster worse than him. He gave her Samuel. He kept her alive. And he gave her companionship.

Like today.

"Do you get lonely?" Drew asked as they sat side by side on the steps. Sam played in the yard, building a stick fort, a task he could spend hours on with no complaint.

It was a gorgeous day out, with a warm breeze that played with the ruffle on Angel's dress. One hand rested on the swell of her stomach. The other was in Drew's hand, his fingers gripping hers.

"Angel? Did you hear me?" His free hand played with her hair, twisting and twirling, at times tugging.

She tore her gaze from her son to her captor.

He wanted her to think of him as her partner. Her husband. Her spouse.

She refused to think of him as anything other than her captor. Her tormentor. Her rapist.

"Smile, sunshine. It's a beautiful day and I'm here taking care of you. You're not chained, doesn't that make you smile?"

She held out her bare leg and stared at the scabs circling her ankle, lifting her lips into the smile Drew expected to see.

She thought about his question. As a child, she'd been an extrovert; the need to be surrounded by friends, to always be with someone, it was a driving force for her.

Later, after she'd been taken, she surrounded herself with other girls like herself. There was safety in numbers, more protection. Eventually she became a leader, a den mother to those who passed through the doors.

"I like the quiet," she told him, removing all inflection in her tone. He only knew the side of her she wanted him to know. To him, she was Angel. His angel. That's all he cared about.

He searched her gaze. For what, she wasn't sure.

A flutter of fear, panic and anxiety grew in her chest, expanding until the pressure made it difficult to breathe.

So many thoughts skidded through her head, like a skipped rock, each bounce against the water creating a ripple effect she couldn't stop.

He held her over a cliff, one that ended in separation from her son and possible death. All it would take was one push, one wrong word, pausing too long to answer . . . She was never safe, never secure when he was around.

"Stop." Drew's hand landed on her knee, his squeeze hard and hurtful. "I can see the questions you're trying to hide from me."

She dropped her head, her hair falling forward as cover. His grip hurt and he knew it.

"I'm sorry," she eventually said. His hold loosened.

"I'm not getting rid of you," he said, "if that's what you're worried about."

She forced the air out of her lungs, causing her shoulders to drop. He began to knead the bunched-up muscles.

"Do you honestly think I'd ever let you go?" He lifted her arm and kissed the tattoo on her wrist. Angel wings. "We're bound for life, you and me. I know I saved you from that basement, but the truth is, you also saved me."

If he expected a response, she wasn't going to give him one.

"Do you remember the day I first saw you? I knew you'd be mine, one day. It didn't happen then, but I never stopped searching for you. No other girl mattered to me. None but you."

Growing up, life had been all black and white. Her parents were clear about the rules as well as their consequences. There had been no gray area, no in-between where the guidebook allowed for murky answers.

It didn't take her long to learn that her parents had been wrong.

She'd been kidnapped as a teenager, something her parents had said only happened to *those girls. Those girls* who didn't listen to their parents, who flirted too much, wore revealing clothing, thought they could get away with whatever they wanted.

Except, she'd been kidnapped and she hadn't been one of *those girls.* She'd been a good girl. Sure, she liked to push the boundaries a little, see how far she could bend her parents before they'd break, but she didn't ask to be taken, to be forced to have sex against her will. She'd been kept in a room where days blended together, where she'd been so hyped on drugs she couldn't have attempted to escape even if she'd wanted to.

Eventually they brought her out to parties. Then, when she proved herself, she was often someone's *reward.* More like damaged goods. She'd been bought, borrowed and sold too many times to count.

Then she went to church.

It was a Sunday afternoon, in the community room, where she and five other girls were on display on the pretext that they'd been runaways helped by a non-existent charity.

While all the do-gooders and Jesus-lovers ate their pot-pies and sipped at their tepid teas, she put on an act worthy of an Oscar, sharing her sob story in order to open wallets.

The truth was, they were there, on display, for special guests, personally invited to the fundraising event, guests who sat at those tables and pretended to be people they weren't.

That's when Drew had first seen her. Standing on a platform, wearing a soft white summer dress. He said a halo appeared around her, a glow from the stained-glass window behind her.

He'd been an invited guest.

"You were so beautiful that day, but I could see in your eyes how much you hurt. I thought I'd lost you that day. I searched for years, always hoping I'd see you again. All I've wanted to do was protect you." He pulled her close, arm wrapped around her body, his hand covering hers on her belly. "I've done that, haven't I? Protected you?"

Angel hated that question, how he placed his own insecurities on her.

"You've always been kind." She forced the knife-carved words out of her mouth. He must have heard something in her voice because his hand dropped from her belly and he pulled away from her.

"Kind? That's what you say to the man who rescued you from that basement? You have no idea what he had in store for you after he was tired of you, do you? Who provided you a house to live in, food to eat, and let you keep your child? Not many would, you realize that, right? Kids like Sam . . ."

He didn't need to finish his threat. She knew what happened to most children born to someone like her. They were either aborted or sold.

"Sam is my world," she whispered.

"So you love me, is that what I'm hearing?"

On cue, Sam looked up and waved, his bright, beautiful and full smile beamed his happiness.

"Our children need parents who love each other," Drew said, the tone of his voice changing when she didn't reply.

She kept her gaze focused on her son. On the trust in his eyes.

To be here, to remain here, she needed to play Drew's game.

"Yes," she said, her voice stronger than she expected it to be.

"Yes . . . what?" Drew grabbed hold of her face, his fingers pushed deep into her cheek muscles. "Yes, you love me? Yes, our children need parents who love each other? Yes . . . what?" He demanded an answer from her.

"Yes, our children—" She tried to wrap her hands around his, to relieve the pressure from her face, to avoid bruise marks. Somehow she managed to get him to release her. She took his hand and brought it back down to her stomach, and placed it there, palm flat. "Our children," she repeated, her voice stronger than it had been all day, "need to be raised in a home full of love."

She prayed he couldn't read between the lines. That he didn't look past the words she'd spoken to the message behind them.

She didn't say this home, their home. She thought about her family, what it had been like growing up surrounded by parents who loved not only their children, but each other.

Her children would never have that. Not while she was held captive here, with him.

CHAPTER 28

The barest of light filtered through the gap between the door and the floor.

Angel kept her focus on that light, how it changed, darkened, disappeared. Disappearing was okay. Disappearing meant she wasn't alone.

Sam's tiny fingers, just the tips, appeared beneath the door.

"Leave Mommy alone," Drew barked. His gruff voice issued an order not to be ignored.

A tear slipped down Angel's face as Sam's fingers left the small area, leaving her alone, once again.

Her head bowed, the pressure of failure hurting more than anything else.

"I thought I told you to go play outside?" Drew's voice was a little louder, a little harsher, and a lot more menacing.

A shudder ran through Angel's frame. She wanted to shout out, to comfort her son, to say it was okay, but she couldn't do any of that.

She was locked in the closet, in the smallest of spaces, wrists bound and chained to a bracket high above her.

The closet of shame. Of punishment. Her consequence.

"Mo . . . mmy?" Her son, her bright, beautiful and bold son, spoke his first word and it was for her.

She gasped a sob, unable to stuff it back, knowing she'd just made things worse.

Her son spoke his first word and all her heart could do was break.

The silence that came after that beautiful, broken word was too much.

Drew waited for her to come to her son's defense, to speak up and assure him she was okay, that he should go out and play, like Daddy said.

Drew waited for her to break another rule.

But she wouldn't. She couldn't. The longer she remained in the closet, the longer the game played out, and in the end, it was always her son who paid the harshest price.

"Do I need to repeat myself?"

Angel had to bite back a cry, her mind screaming the words she needed Samuel to hear.

Go. Run. Listen. Please go. Be a good boy.

The moment she heard the thud of her son's heavy steps, the slam of the door as it closed behind him and the thump-thump-thump of him stomping on the wood stairs, relief tore through Angel, the unwelcome catalyst for the torn sobs that she struggled to conceal.

Drew's good moods never lasted. After that first night, she'd remained alert, ready, cautious with every word she spoke because she never knew what would set him off.

Some days, all it took was for her to give their son more attention than him. Other days, it was because she'd burned his toast, left his bed before he gave permission, had the audacity to say no.

Today, there'd been no reason.

He'd been antsy all morning. Brusque, abrupt, his words laced with criticism and heavy with anger.

Sam had wanted to play outside, begged her to join him, but seeing the glower on Drew's face, she made up some excuse to stay inside. She'd colored her hair, like he'd told her to, hoping it would help his mood.

It didn't matter. Nothing she'd done or could have done would have changed anything.

Drew had already decided on her punishment.

Her arms ached. Her back spasmed. Her shoulders burned with the pain of a million needles stuck in her skin.

She'd only been in the closet for less than an hour, but it felt like an eternity.

Knock. Knock.

His knuckle pounded on the door, first with simple taps.

Her head lifted. Her lips tightened. She would not utter a sound, no matter how much he taunted, teased or played with her mind.

"Still alive in there?" Drew asked, his voice deceptively sweet.

She pictured him, only a few feet away. If he opened the door, he was close enough to reach in and grab her throat.

"All this could be over, you know. All you have to do is say the right words. Can you do that, my Angel? Give me what I want?" The voice belonged to the man who had sat outside with her, only yesterday. The man who said he loved her, their family.

But the moment that door opened, she'd find a completely different man waiting on the other side.

Thud-thud.

His fists hit the door, the power vibrating through the wood, rattling the cans surrounding her.

"Say it, Angel. Say it, or Sam's next."

A strangled cry rose from inside her, escaping as a gasp. No. Nonononono. She would never let Sam take her place, and he knew that.

He played dirty, but then, she shouldn't be surprised.

"I'm . . ." — Angel hung her head, stretching the taut muscles screaming with pain — "sorry." The words were whispered but loud enough to matter.

"What's that?" His voice was closer, clearer, softer. It taunted, teased, throwing her panic into overdrive.

"Please, Drew," she begged, knowing that's what he wanted to hear. "I'm sorry." Her eyes closed, her spirit broken, embracing the torrent of fear for her son. "I'm sorry, I'm sorry, I'm sorry."

Her apologies were met with silence.

Her chest tightened, swelled, armored balls of dread lodged in her throat, filled her dry mouth, settled in her heart with a thwack.

Then she heard it. The twist-click bait of freedom. His hand on the door handle, the slight turn, as if he had every intention of opening the door.

Another game he liked to play.

Eyes open, she waited. Waited for that first hint of light, for the idea of release from her tiny prison.

She waited, only to hear the sound of his laughter and the scuff of his shoes on the floor as he walked away.

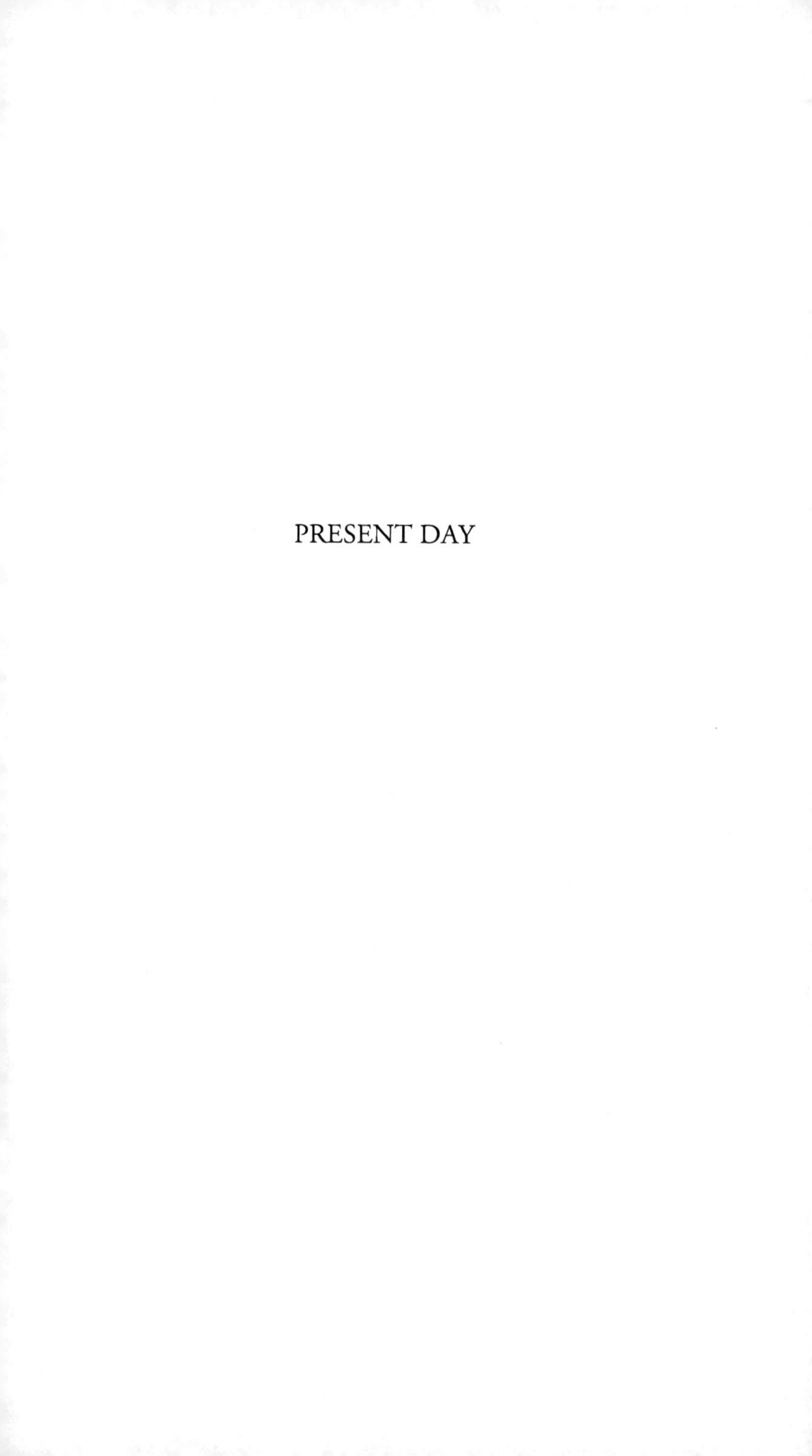

PRESENT DAY

CHAPTER 29

PAISLEY VALLEY HOSPITAL
2:00 p.m.

I always assumed hospitals were like libraries. Muted sounds with hushed whispers, the thud of books as they hit the wood tables, the swoosh of the doors opening and closing. I was wrong.

Hospitals are more like malls, and the hospital rooms are the stores. They're noisy with alarms going off, sirens blaring from the street outside, voices being yelled down the corridors. There's no rest, no privacy, no sense of security.

I'd give anything to be where it's quiet.

As a teen, whenever I told Dad I was studying in the library, his face would beam. Like he was proud of me, like taking time to study was the greatest thing I could have done.

The guilt that radiates off Monique is smothering. She keeps asking if I want her to call my family, as if there's a way to let her know who they are.

I don't. I don't want them to see me like this. To know me like this.

I hope my family thinks I'm dead.

The girl they knew . . . she is dead. She died three days after she'd been kidnapped. For three days I'd been sedated, drugged. I remember bits and pieces, faces, smells, sounds, but that's all. Until three days later.

I woke up in a room with four other girls. Four other girls, like me. Drugged, dirty, scared. A woman came into the room and explained what was happening. She told us we'd been transported across country, that our families didn't want us. She said she was accepting members into her new family, but there were rules.

Rule number one: if we wanted to cry, we might as well die.

Rule number two: if we wanted to live, we had to give.

Rule number three: if we wanted to survive, we said goodbye.

I said goodbye to the girl I was and became someone else. Someone strong enough to survive.

I hear sounds coming from the hallway, beyond my room door. It's a cry, a child's cry.

Sam!

I want to cry out, to call out, to say I'm here. I struggle against the bed, thrashing my shoulders against the pillows, wanting to sit up.

"Angel, stop. What's wrong?" Monique is there, her hands hovering over my shoulders, as if trying to push me down.

"Sam." My broken voice is unrecognizable. The effort grates, and I taste blood as I swallow.

If Drew intended to silence me one way or another, he did a good job.

"Don't talk, you'll do more damage." She looks toward the door. "I'll go see what's going on, okay?"

My gaze never leaves her back as she heads to the door, opens it, barely enough for me to see past her. She stands there, talking to someone, maybe the cop outside the door, then turns to me.

"It's nothing. Just a little girl running down the hall," she says, closing the door behind her.

"Sam." I say his name again. Tears stream down my face, and I'm not sure what hurts more, the pain or the guilt.

Where is my son? I need to know he's safe, that Drew doesn't have him.

My gaze goes from Monique's face to my stomach and I want to disappear.

She hasn't said anything, but I know. I know.

There was no way my baby could have survived Drew's anger.

None of that matters, not now. I want to yell this, to shout the words until she hears me. All that matters is my son. I need him. I need to know he's safe. I need to know Drew hasn't harmed him.

My chest heaves, my breath increases, my nostrils flare as I suck in air, my mind racing as I struggle to remember my last moments with Sam before I lost consciousness.

My arms were wrapped around him. He was curled up against my body. I remember telling him it would be okay, that we were okay. I remember thinking I'd saved him, protected him from Drew and that I just needed to rest.

Then I woke up here.

"How . . . ?"

"Shhh, please, Angel. Please don't speak. Not yet."

I wish I could move. I wish I could yell. I wish I could tell this woman to leave me the hell alone. But all I can do is cry.

"Angel, did you say Sam? Was that the word? Just blink yes or no."

Blink. Yes.

"Is Sam . . . your son? Is that why you reacted when you heard the child out in the hall?"

Blink.

"You . . . you came in alone." She says this with hints of apology.

Noooooo. I groan, trying to say the words, indicate how wrong she is.

I would not have come in alone. I couldn't have.

"When the police arrived, you were alone in the farmhouse."

It hurts so much, but I moan again. I was not alone. She's mistaken.

The machines to my left start screaming, their beeps drowning out my moans.

The door to my room opens.

"What's going on in here?" The nurse from earlier walks in, stethoscope around her neck, frown visible on her face.

I look away.

"Monique, if you being here is too much for her, I'm going to need you to leave."

"Angel, do you want me to leave?"

Do I?

"She was trying to talk," Monique says.

The nurse is over by my side. "Let me make myself clear." She waits for me to look her in the eyes. "If you want to heal, you need to not speak. Doctor's order for forty-eight hours. There's extreme trauma to your vocal cords and esophagus."

I see the challenge in her eyes.

I slowly close mine.

"Here, press this button if the pain is too much, okay? This will help. Why don't you try to sleep, that's what your body needs right now."

I feel the button beneath my finger and the pressure on my index finger as she pushes it down on the button.

It seems I don't have a choice.

"Angel." A hand touches me. I open my eyes to find Monique there. "I'm going to go see what I can find out about Sam, okay?"

Blink. Thank you. Thank you-thank you-thank you.

"Sam?" The nurse looks from Monique to me.

I close my eyes, turn my head. Keeping silent might be my only safe place right now.

Footsteps across the floor, the swoosh of the door opening wide, then a heaviness in the room when it's just the nurse and myself.

"Who is Sam?" She hovers, threatening, but she's too late.

The rush of sweet oblivion hits me.

Who is Sam? She doesn't know. That tells me Drew didn't warn her about our son. It could mean anything . . . he has him, or Sam hid, like we'd talked about.

But the fact she doesn't know about him, that gives me hope.

THREE DAYS AGO

CHAPTER 30

PAIGE

My eyes burn as I stare at the computer screen, scrolling through emails, notes, recordings, files I'd kept that are tagged with Bryan Powers. I spent the morning sequestered in one of the workrooms, answering question after question, feeling like I had to justify myself and my actions.

Last night, Jamie reminded me this isn't about me. It's about Bryan and the damage he's done.

That's the only thing that's getting me through this today without losing my cool.

It's been three days since the cell was discovered and Bryan was arrested.

Three days for those girls to be reunited with their families.

I should be there with them, standing watch, helping the families, offering advice. Not being there is hard, harder than I thought it would be.

Yes, this feels like a punishment.

So far, I have no idea what the internal audit has found. I pray to God that Bryan didn't hinder any of our cases, that he didn't stop us from rescuing anyone.

I close my eyes and count to five. I need eye drops, they're so dry. I've tried to institute a twenty minute, twenty second rule, even setting up reminders on my phone. For every twenty minutes I stare at a computer screen, I need to look off in the distance, focus on something else for twenty seconds.

But blinking while being on the computer would be a good idea too.

"Here, looks like you can use this." A small bottle lands in front of me. I look up to see Anita standing there.

I take the offered bottle, tilt my head back and sigh as the liquid provides the necessary relief.

"That feels so good."

"If you don't take better eye care, you'll be wearing glasses sooner than later," Anita scolds. "Now, how about you take a break from the computer and come with me? You have visitors."

"Visitors? Who?" I blink several times, thankful that the gritty feel in my eyes has disappeared.

"John and Elizabeth." Anita's blank face doesn't offer any insights as to why the Manderas have shown up. "She made you a banana loaf."

Hmmm. That's interesting. Liz only makes banana loaf in the middle of the night when she can't sleep. John often likes to tease that he knows to be careful when he wakes up to the smell of banana bread.

When I enter the room to greet John and Liz, they barely notice my arrival.

John's leaning forward, elbows on the table, whereas Liz sits in the chair, back rigid, purse resting on her thighs, the straps clutched tight in her hands.

"Hey guys, everything okay?" I keep my voice soft, gentle, as I close the door behind me.

Both heads shoot up like rockets. Liz attempts something resembling a smile, while John's face doesn't change. He looks tired. Exhausted. A man with the weight of the world on his shoulders. Too tired, too weak for the weight.

Liz glances toward her husband.

"Liz hasn't been sleeping," John finally mutters.

"I can't," Liz says. "All I can think about is that little child, boy or girl, but our grandchild. I'm worried about the living conditions, whether Gabrielle is healthy, what that little one is seeing day in, day out—"

"She's going crazy with worry," John interrupts.

Liz breathes in, filling her chest with her sharp inhale.

"We're both worried and realize we can't sit idly by anymore," he says. "We need to do more."

The fear they both carry, the worry, the concern, I see it. I hear it in the almost apologetic tone of their voices and I want to tell them that this is a normal reaction for an abnormal situation.

"I hear you," I say to them. "You need to feel like you're doing something. Tell me, do you have any ideas?"

The need to be proactive in the search for a missing child is something CHILD has focused on for years. It's important for parents, for families, to be involved, as much as they want, without becoming a nuisance or hindering any efforts of the authorities. Years ago, I put together a simple pamphlet outlining ways loved ones can get involved.

Liz pulls out that same pamphlet from her purse. "We've made some posters and can place them around stores in neighboring towns and post things on social media too."

Those are both great ideas.

"The main goal," I say, "is to get Gabrielle's face back into the public eye. We want her to see it and know you love her and want her back home."

"Do you think she will?" John asks.

He's asking if she'd want to come home, if she believes they love her. It's a hard one to answer.

When victims of sex trafficking are rescued, one question that comes up time after time is the question of whether they are still lovable. To them, the things they've done in order to survive are unforgivable. They aren't the perfect child anymore, or even close to the child their parents remember.

How could someone love them when they don't even love themselves?

I take both John's and Elizabeth's hands in mine. "I think anything we do is a help." It's not the answer John wants, as his face so clearly shows, but it's the best one I can give.

"My schedule for the next few weeks is heavy with school assemblies. I'm adding Gabrielle's photo and her story. Sometimes, especially in high schools, there are kids who might recognize her. It's happened in the past."

Liz lets go of my hand and leans back in her chair. "What do you mean, recognize her? Why would they? They're in school, at home with their families, aren't they?"

John's lips purse together, the lines across his forehead deepen. He knows what I'm about to say.

Elizabeth knows too, she just doesn't want to accept it.

"She means our daughter could be helping to . . ." John purses his lips once again, stopping himself from saying more.

Elizabeth shakes her head. "No. Our Gabby wouldn't do that. Not our Angel."

John winces. I'm not sure if it's from the nicknames or from Liz's refusal to accept the truth.

"She could be grooming other girls to have them join their" — I pause — "their family. We've talked about this, remember?"

Elizabeth won't budge. Her knuckles whiten as she pushes her shoulders back. "My Gabrielle would not befriend other girls in order to sell them."

Those words hang in the room between the three of us.

It's a belief most parents need to hold onto, and I get it. I wish it weren't so, that none of the girls I try to find would do that — groom other girls to take their place or join their twisted sense of family. But the men who sell them, abuse them, treat them so horribly, most of them demand the girls do this. Or else.

"I'm sorry, Liz. I really am."

"Thank you for including her in your presentations." John coughs to clear his throat, the words no doubt hard to say. "We realized, after the false sighting, that we need to do more." He sighs, reaches for his wife's hand. "We want our girl to come home, to know that home is a safe place for her and her child."

His chair scrapes against the floor as he pushes it back. "If there's anything else we can do, please . . . will you let us know? If you need us to come and speak at one of your presentations or . . ."

Elizabeth's face is set in stone. She won't look at me as she stands. I try not to take it personally.

I follow them out, stopping at Anita's desk along the way, with promises to be in touch.

"Why is Liz so upset?" Anita waits until the Manderas leave before she asks.

My attention is focused on the video screen behind Anita. "Can we update a few of those photos on there?"

"Already on it. We should have some sketches in the next few weeks. Now, answer my question." Anita wears her *don't-mess-with-me* frown.

"She's just . . . being a mom who needs to believe the best." I stare out the windows and watch them walk down the street. "I mentioned I was going to add Gabrielle's photo and story to my high school presentations." From the *gotcha* look on Anita's face, she understands.

It's a sad truth and one I'd even heard Mom mutter to Dad when they thought they were alone.

Maybe that's another reason Mom's been so adamant about moving on, saying goodbye — she doesn't want to believe the alternative.

Not me. It doesn't matter what my sister has done or what she's been forced to do in the past. I just want her home.

CHAPTER 31

PAIGE

My fingers brush against fabric as they trail from one dress to another in the closet.

I've stood here for fifteen minutes, doing nothing but touching each item of clothing, my mind blank, empty, wasting precious time.

"Hey, beautiful, close to being rea . . . dy?" The excitement in Jamie's voice edges toward disappointment as he walks into our bedroom.

I turn, my fingers clutching the damp bath towel over my chest. "What time was the reservation again?"

Skepticism fills his gaze as he glances down at the watch on his wrist. "In fifteen minutes."

Going out for dinner, even one that's been booked for weeks, is not on my list of things-to-do-on-a-Friday-night. Especially tonight.

Ever since the incident at the park, things have been . . . tense, between the two of us.

Truth be told, I'm the one who's tense, on edge, bordering between anger and fear. Jamie on the other hand has been his usual self: loving, considerate, providing ample space for me to deal with my issues.

He has his moments, little cracks he tries to hide. Like now.

"Would you rather I reschedule?" Jamie offers.

A myriad of thoughts and feelings flows across his face. Hope, disappointment, patience, understanding.

I don't deserve him. I really don't.

I brave a smile. It's one of those *I'm trying, honest* smiles.

"I just can't decide what to wear," I say, turning back to the closet.

He comes behind me, one arm snaking across my waist, the other taking hold of a hanger and holding it out.

"How about this?" he whispers into my ear. "I had a dream last night that you wore this for our date."

The dress he pulls out is a navy-blue, short-sleeved dress. It highlights my blue eyes, which look like the deep blue of the ocean right now.

It's a special dress for special occasions. Like the night he proposed.

"Can you call them and mention we'll be a few minutes late?" I grab hold of the hanger and brush a kiss across his cheek.

The way his eyes light up like stardust confirms that rescheduling, not to mention canceling, would have been a mistake.

I'm not sure what my issue about tonight is. I feel like I'm being forced to attend a bachelorette party when I haven't spoken to the soon-to-be-bride in years. Except, it's nothing like that. It's a night out with Jamie, the man I love. What is my problem?

I rush through getting ready, using only the barest of makeup, strap on some heels and take a moment to breathe.

"Smile," I say to the woman in the mirror. "Smile, relax and enjoy tonight. You need this," I continue. "Jamie needs this."

The woman in the mirror, she doesn't smile back.

I force the edges of my lips to turn up, relax my shoulders, straighten my spine and wait for my smile to become a little more . . . natural.

Jamie deserves tonight. He deserves a night when it's just the two of us, when everything else in our lives is pushed aside and we focus only on ourselves.

By the time I make it down the stairs, my whole family waits.

"Wow, Mom," Flynn says the moment he sees me.

"Ahh, you look beautiful, honey." Mom gives me a hug. "Flynn and I are going to have our own date night, while you two are gone, aren't we?" She pulls Flynn close and squeezes his shoulders.

"Gramma says we can order take-out and rent a movie." Flynn wiggles out from Mom's grasp.

I ruffle my son's hair. "Well, aren't you lucky! Maybe Dad and I should stay home and join you guys on that date. It sounds like fun."

I wink at Jamie, to let him know I'm only joking, but from the frown on his face, he doesn't believe me.

"No way." Flynn crosses his arms over his chest. "You should go. Go, go, go . . ." He places his hands on my hips and pushes me away.

"Whoa there, sport." Jamie grabs hold of Flynn's hands and takes them off my body. "That's not how you treat your mom."

"But . . ." Flynn pouts. "You said you'd talk to her about . . ." He looks up at me, then cups his hands over his mouth and whispers something into Jamie's ear.

"Yeah, I know, buddy, I know. Relax . . . I've got this."

Got . . . what? I look to Mom to see if she knows what's going on. My mother's face is swathed in a secretive smile that tells me way too much.

Pretending to ignore the looks and whispers, I grip my purse tight to my stomach. "You'll be home all night?" I address this question to Mom.

Yes, I'm struggling with leaving Flynn alone. I'm a helicopter parent with boundary issues.

"I'm not going anywhere, promise."

"Mooooommmm . . ." Flynn drawls out my name while rolling his eyes.

Even Jamie looks a bit impatient.

"Go have fun," Mom says. "Live a little." Her smile is a little too bright, a little too . . . suspicious.

My brow rises a notch. *Live a little?*

"Don't worry about coming home early either," Mom continues. "We've got several movies planned, so you'll still be able to put this ragamuffin to bed."

Jamie coughs. Riiiighhht.

Game-day smile plastered on my face, I wait as Jamie opens the door for me.

I'm really regretting not canceling our date tonight.

* * *

"Have I mentioned how beautiful you look?" Jamie holds up his glass of red wine and clinks it against my glass of rosé.

"A few times, but who's counting?" My eyes twinkle as a blush rushes across his face.

Jamie booked dinner at a new Italian restaurant that's been open for about six months. The atmosphere is elegant, romantic and totally out of our price range, but Jamie received a gift certificate from a parent of one of his students.

We're on our second glass of wine and have already agreed to walk home, leaving our vehicle parked for the night.

"I know you didn't want to come out tonight." Jamie reaches across the table for my hand. His thumb draws circles against my skin, his eyes staring at the engagement ring on my finger.

"It wasn't that I didn't want to come out . . ."

He shakes his head. "No, it's okay. You don't have to explain. I screwed up the other day at the park." He lets out a long sigh. "You've been . . . distant . . . since then, and I get it."

I pull my hand away, suddenly uncomfortable.

"Jamie, I . . ." Words I want to say, words I need to say, disappear, leaving me at a loss.

"You have every right to be upset with me, Paige. I should have been present, at all times, while at the park. It doesn't matter that I hadn't been on my phone for long, or why I was even on it . . . my attention should have been one hundred percent focused on Flynn. I messed up. If something had happened . . ." He fiddles with his glass, swirling the remaining liquid. "I would never be able to forgive myself, so I get why you've been upset."

Something Pastor Jeremy said once gnaws at me now. Forgiveness isn't something anyone earns, it's something we give, willingly. But the key is to accept and embrace the act of forgiveness.

Accept and embrace. That's definitely something I struggle with. Not just accepting forgiveness but living with what it means. Until Jess is found, I'll never be able to forgive myself for leaving her behind. If I'm not able to forgive myself, then how can I truly know how to forgive others?

At least, that's what Jeremy says. He also warned that the inability is like a virus, infecting others and affecting their own ability to accept and embrace forgiveness. I thought maybe he meant Flynn, but now I wonder if I've tainted Jamie too.

"But nothing did happen." I take hold of the hand I'd let go and wind my fingers through his. "I overreacted and haven't been able to let that go. You have nothing to apologize for, Jamie. I mean that."

My stomach knots up as I realize just how unfair all of this is to him . . . keeping him on the hook, teasing him with the promise of a future, a future I keep placing on hold.

"I'm the one who should be apologizing." I reach for my glass of wine and take a sip. A very long sip. Oh God, I'm not going to do this, am I?

"It's not fair of me to—"

Jamie squeezes my hand. "Stop," he interrupts me. "We've had this talk more than enough times for me to get it, Paige. Yes, we parent Flynn differently, but there's nothing wrong with that. We all have lines we don't cross, and I'm well aware of where your lines are when it comes to our son. I get it."

"That's the issue." My voice is soft, certain and strong, despite how much my heart is breaking right now. "I shouldn't judge you based on the lines I keep for myself. But I do, I have, and that's wrong. You're right, we parent differently and the way I parent is based on fear, which isn't healthy. Not for Flynn, not for me, not for us as a family." My hand shakes as I lift my glass and drink the rest of my wine.

Jamie notices.

"What are you saying, Paige?"

What am I saying? I'm not even sure. The day in the park rocked me, like an earthquake set on destroying any solidity in my life.

"Paige?" Jamie pulls back, leaning away, distancing himself as much as possible. His face is a mask, his classic teacher face: chin down, brows hunched over his eyes. He rubs his nose, a habit, from wearing glasses all day.

"I don't know what I'm saying," I say, my voice small, barely loud enough to be heard.

His shoulders drop. When he finally does lift his gaze, there's something there, something that swooshes across the air, across the distance between us and nestles in my heart, like an arrow.

"Fear-based anything isn't healthy, we both know that. But it hasn't damaged us, not as a family, not as a couple, nor will it." He sounds so sure, sure enough for both of us.

That arrow burrows even deeper, the tip anchoring in until it's lodged in tight.

I want to say something, whether it's to agree or argue, I'm not sure. He seems to sense that, my uncertainty, and leans in, closing the distance between us.

"When we found out you were pregnant with Flynn, do you remember the promise I made?"

I nod. Of course I do.

"That promise holds true, even now, even after all this time, even though we haven't set a date for our wedding. I promised you I would never leave you, that I would remain at your side, and we'd raise our son, together. I'm still here. Still at your side, and I have no plans on leaving or being pushed away." He emphasizes those last words, as if understanding what I'm doing, even if I don't realize it.

Tears swell, pooling, gathering together until they're too many, and then diving down, springboarding off my lashes and forging their own lanes along my cheeks.

I take a napkin and attempt to stop the flow, soaking the cloth as I do so.

"I don't mean to," I manage to say.

"I know." There's no smile on his face, just compassion and complete transparency.

I wait until we've almost finished our meals before I feel like I can continue without losing it.

"Jamie, I meant what I said earlier, that I don't mean to push you away."

Jamie finishes swirling his fork with pasta noodles and holds it in midair. He says nothing, but the tension between us is full of expectation and readiness.

"You deserve so much more than what I offer you. You've always been there for me, with me, by my side, never pushing, never forcing me to change . . . You've accepted me and all my faults, all my baggage from day one. You moved in with my parents after Dad fell sick and never complained about losing your own space. You wait . . ." I stare up toward the ceiling, struggling with my thoughts, needing my words to be clear and understood.

"I wait for you to pick a date," Jamie finishes my sentence. "I'll keep waiting too, Paige. As long as it takes."

"But you shouldn't have to." I rub the center of my forehead, my finger pressing in deep where a headache forms. "That's the point."

"You make me sound like a saint, and I'm anything but." He looks down, knots his hands together. I can see how he's struggling.

God, I hate this.

"Setting a date . . . that's not what's important to me," he finally says. "I want to marry you, Paige, that hasn't changed. But signing a paper, saying our vows . . . that's just a formality for a life we already have. When I proposed and you said yes, when I slid that ring on your finger . . ." Jamie pauses and reaches for my hand.

He plays with the ring on my finger, rubbing against the diamond, the smile on his face telling me he's replaying that day over in his head.

"You became mine on that day. I'll wait, however long it takes, as long as I know one day, I'll see you walk down that aisle."

My mind, my heart, they're too full for words. Everything I want to say, everything I thought I needed to say, disappears as Jamie's words flow through me, filling all the crevices, all the empty spots that have appeared thanks to my fear and doubt. His words awaken something in me, something that's been cocooned for years.

But they don't completely erase the scars. Those scars are too settled, a permanent fixture on my soul.

I'd made a promise, a promise that can never be broken — not by me. It was a promise made in the dead of night, where pinkies joined and blood from a pin-prick blended. A promise, no matter how childish, that cemented an already unbreakable bond.

The promise made had been a simple one: neither Jess nor myself would marry without the other by our side.

"Jamie, I love you, with everything in me. That will never change." I pause, stare down at the ring he's still playing with and struggle with the words I know will break his heart.

"I love you," I continue. "But I will never marry you."

The smile on his face doesn't waver. It doesn't falter or fade. But the smile in his eyes, that real, authentic, honest smile I've always been able to trust and count on: it dies.

I shouldn't have ended my sentence there. I shouldn't have stopped, waited, paused to gather my thoughts in a measly attempt to explain myself.

But I did. Those words, those *I will never marry you* words, will always be there, scorched in his memory, and no matter what I say, how I explain or beg for forgiveness, they are always going to be burned into his subconscious.

"I love you," I try again, my voice full of tears, "but until I know what's happened to my sister, I can't marry you, you understand that, right?" I pull the words out of me and like errant strands of yarn, they unwind something that had once been secure between us.

CHAPTER 32

The lights blaze a welcoming beacon as we walk up the pathway, silent, hands to ourselves.

Jamie holds the door for me, helps as I shrug out of my light jacket and then heads to the kitchen without a word said between us.

I'm pulled in two directions. I want to follow him and fix what I broke, but I also need to check on Flynn.

My son wins my attention. He's on the couch, oblivious, knees tight to his chest, popcorn bowl balancing on top.

I stand in the doorway, something stopping me from calling his name, and watch him.

Mom is soon at my side, glass of water in hand, and gives me a look. One of her *how-did-you-mess-up-this-time* looks.

I hate that look.

"What's going on? Jamie's pouring whiskey and barely said hi."

"Why do you assume something is going on?" I hedge. One of the downfalls of living with my mother is the lack of privacy.

Mom crosses her arms and one of her brows rises like a steeple.

"We're fine," I say.

That steeple rises even higher. "Really?" Mom says. "Because neither one of you look *fine.* Word of advice? Figure it out before your son notices. He had high hopes for tonight."

High hopes for tonight? What does that mean?

Jamie's earlier comment to Flynn, just before we'd left, something like *I've got this*, pops up in my head and I sigh.

I have no idea what that meant, but obviously there'd been a plan for tonight and I screwed it all up.

Great. Just . . . great.

Jamie walks out of the kitchen, glass in hand. "I'll get Flynn ready for bed, okay?" He gives Mom a quick little head shake before giving me one of those *barely-there* kisses on the cheek. "It'll give you time to change before you tuck him in. I poured you a glass of wine, left it on the counter."

Seconds later, Flynn's tired voice meets Jamie's low one.

I listen in, taking in the familial sounds, holding them tight to my heart before I go in search of that wine.

He poured one for Mom, too.

"Do you want to talk about it?" Mom asks after a few minutes.

I struggle not to snort. Talk with Mom about what happened tonight? I don't think so.

"I forget sometimes that complete honesty isn't always the best policy."

Mom winces. "You get that honestly," she says. "Your father used to complain all the time that I had no filter either."

"Any chance you want to fill me in on what everyone else seemed ready for?" I trail behind Mom as she heads into the front room. Mom takes one seat, I take the other.

"That's between you and those men upstairs, honey."

That's what I thought.

I'm not sure Jamie will tell me, at least, not tonight. After I'd said what I did, the remainder of the evening felt . . . contrived? I kept trying to make things better, to pretend like I hadn't ruined it. Jamie did the same — he even ordered us dessert. It didn't matter.

I screwed up, big time, and I have no idea of how I can fix it.

Flynn's pounding footsteps leading from his room to the bathroom have me glancing upward toward the stairs. Jamie's there, leaning against the railing, his gaze on me.

I give him a small, tepid smile.

He smiles back.

"That man loves you," Mom says after Jamie leaves his post.

"I know."

"Do you? Sometimes I wonder . . ." Mom's voice trails off as she turns her attention from me to whatever is outside the front window. "I try not to interfere between you two, but that doesn't mean I don't see things. He shows you, every day, how much he loves you." She shakes her head, still focused out the window. "In the beginning, it made your father and me so happy, to see you being loved like that."

"And now?" I'm not sure I like where this is headed. I wonder if Mom hears that in my voice. There are hints of annoyance, of anger and of caution. Caution for Mom to be careful with not only what she says, but how she's about to say it.

"Oh, it still makes me happy." Mom finally turns her attention from the window. Her gaze is full of honesty. "You deserve to be loved like that. But he deserves it in return, too."

There are so many ways I want to respond. So many things I want to say that wait on the tip of my tongue, pushing against my clamped lips. Words to defend myself, to justify whatever Mom is about to condemn me for.

Instead, I hold my tongue, pushing everything back. I'm surprised at myself, truth be told.

Mom is right. Jamie deserves so much more from me.

"I'm trying."

This time, the message in Mom's gaze contains a mixture of gentle pity and harsh discernment. I shift in my seat, uncomfortable with how well she reads me.

"What was it your father used to say about trying?" Mom says, her voice about as soft as a newly sharpened blade.

I don't even have to think about which phrase suits this situation.

"When you say you're trying, it means you need an excuse. How about leaving that excuse behind and just doing it?"

Mom nods. "Yep, that was it. I hated when he said that. Almost as bad as when you'd try to apologize and he'd say—"

"Sorry means nothing. Change. That's the only apology you need," I finish. "Yep, hated that one too."

We share a look, one full of history and memories and heartbreak.

"I miss that man, every single moment of every day. He wasn't supposed to go first." Mom's voice is gentler, brimming with unshed tears. "I regret so many things, Paige, when it comes to your father and our relationship. I took him for granted. Took his love, patience, understanding . . . I grew to expect it, stopped appreciating it like I should have, like he deserved . . ."

I wait, knowing there's more.

"He never complained. He stood by my side, even when we both knew I overreacted or was wrong. He loved me, even when I was emotionally withdrawn, unstable and unable to let go of my grief. After your sister . . ." Mom can't look at me. "After your sister disappeared, I got lost, you know? Inside me. I stopped being a good mother. Stopped being a good wife." Tears drip down her cheeks. "He never complained. He filled in the gaps with you, and don't try to tell me otherwise." She lets out a long, airy breath. "And when I found myself again, he never threw that back in my face."

A door upstairs slams. Another set of pounding feet as Flynn runs from the bathroom to his bedroom.

I gulp the last of my wine and set the glass on the table between us, those steps my cue to get ready.

"I regret not loving your father better, Paige. When it comes to regrets, that's a hard one to live with."

I let all of that — all of Mom's honest, raw admission — sink in. It's the closest thing to an apology I'll ever get from her.

"I love you, Mom." I give Mom's shoulder a slight squeeze as I leave my seat. A part of me wants to give her a hug, but that touch would open the floodgates to tears that could go on forever.

Neither one of us is ready for that. Not tonight.

Mom's chin dips toward her chest. The aching smile on her face relaxes at my touch.

* * *

Forty minutes later, with Flynn tucked tight in bed, his nightlight glowing in the corner, I take my place beside his bed, a notebook on my lap, and stare at the innocence resting on his face.

He's my cherub, an undeserved miracle from God.

Every night, after he falls asleep, I sit by his side, in a reading chair Jamie brought from our old house, and I stare at Flynn. Every lash, every sigh, every wiggle from the corner of his lips is preserved in my memory.

The notebook on my lap is almost full. Years ago, Dad built me a memory chest. It's full of things I keep hoping to one day share with my sister: high school yearbooks, photographs, newspaper clippings of events, Dad's obituary, Flynn's sonogram and baby blanket, ten birthday gifts wrapped and waiting for Jess to open them.

It's also where I keep my notebooks. So far, I've filled eight notebooks for my sister to one day read.

Sometimes I draw Flynn — the shape of his nose, his smile, the flyaway wisps of hair, how he'd hold his stuffed lion tight in his sleep.

Sometimes I write a story, a retelling of my day.

Most of the time, I use the journal as my way of sharing my heart, a daily cathartic exercise so I don't feel so alone.

Words are hard to come by tonight. They sit heavy on my heart, the weight of a mountain, burying me one boulder at a time.

"Hey, beautiful."

I clamp my hand over my mouth to muffle my gasp. He scared me.

"Sorry, I thought you heard me open the door." Jamie stands to the side, hands buried in his jean pockets. "I'm headed to bed, and wondered if you were ready to join me?"

I look at the time on my watch and realize I've been here longer than normal.

"Sorry, I lost track of time, I guess." Jamie reaches for my hand and pulls me to my feet. There's a question tattooed across his face as he glances at the notebook in my hand. I wait for him to ask it, to state the obvious, but he doesn't.

I give Flynn a kiss goodnight, breathing in the clean scent of his freshly washed hair and set my notebook on the top of Flynn's bookshelf, where it remains out of sight. I don't think Flynn knows about its location, but if he does, he's good at keeping secrets.

"I'm sorry about earlier." I've waited until we're both in bed, side by side, before I address the elephant in the room.

"Which part?" His tone tells me I have a lot to apologize for, but his teasing grin reassures me none of it is necessary.

"How about all of it?" I entwine my fingers through his. "For ruining whatever you'd had planned for tonight. For taking so long in Flynn's room after he'd fallen asleep. For . . . avoiding you?" That last one might have come out as a question, but I never meant it that way.

"You didn't write much in the journal." Jamie ignores every point I make, like it doesn't matter.

My nose twitches. "What I needed to say wasn't meant for Jess."

"You don't need to keep apologizing, Paige. Not to me. Besides, the evening isn't over, so technically, whatever I had planned hasn't been ruined." He shifts in place, turning so we're facing each other.

Like earlier, he plays with the ring on my finger. A ring I never want to take off.

"So, there's a plan, is that what you're saying?" I attempt to lighten the mood. I'm not sure if it works or not. "One that both our son and my mother seem to know about?" My brows lift as high as the corners of my lips.

"Technically, it's your son's plan. I'm just the middleman."

Now this is intriguing. I tilt my head as I search for any hints on Jamie's face. He gives none, other than a grin that tells me it's a good plan.

I can only think of one thing.

"If it's about him being the bestest big brother ever," I say, adding some laughter to my voice, "he already tried that one with me. He went from baby to puppy faster than expected . . . Unless . . ." My eyes narrow as Jamie's shit-eating grin widens. "Someone put him up to that."

"He might have mentioned something . . ." Jamie reaches for his phone and scrolls a bit before holding it out to me.

I'm looking at photos of Flynn sitting on the floor, covered in puppies. It's the cutest photo, with so much joy plastered across our son's face.

"Swipe through, there's a few. We stopped by a house that had a sign about a new puppy litter."

I swipe, I enlarge, I focus on the happiness on Flynn's face. There are more than just a few photos, too. There's one of Flynn lying on the ground, being swarmed by little puppy bodies, one where three are licking his face, one with two who'd fallen asleep in his lap.

The last photo, however, has me handing back the phone. I just can't . . .

It's Jamie holding a little cream-colored pup in his arms. The look on his face reminds me of when he'd hold Flynn as a baby.

"That one's a boy. The litter is a Pomeranian-Shih Tzu mix, seven puppies in total. Four male, three female. They might grow to be about ten to fifteen pounds, don't shed much and they're really great family pets." He sounds like a salesman.

"A boy, huh?"

Jamie scrolls to a photo where Flynn holds the same puppy Jamie had in his arms. "Flynn called him Charlie. All the little guy wanted to do was cuddle. It was almost as if he knew Flynn was his . . ."

I don't bother to hide my eye roll. "Lay it on a little thicker, will you? Geesh."

"Puppy is better than a baby, don't you think? Unless . . ." Jamie leans in. "Unless you think it's time we expand our family?" His lips hover close to mine, his smile contagious.

I give him a nice long kiss, one that teases, before placing some distance between us. I mirror his grin. I can't help it.

"How about we go check out those puppies tomorrow?"

In response, Jamie puffs his pillow before dropping down, his head cushioned. "They're expecting us around ten," he says, struggling hard not to laugh, before turning off his bedside light.

CHAPTER 33

ANGEL

The day had started like any other, but something was different.

She could tell.

Drew was going to leave soon. Nothing had been said, not yet, but the signs were there.

He'd fixed the hole in the living room wall, worked on the upstairs bathroom so Sam could finally have a proper bath in the tub, hung lamp fixtures that had sat in the closet for over a year.

He was antsy, irritable and she did everything she could to keep Sam out of his way.

She stood at the kitchen counter, Sam at her side, as they mixed together flour, yeast and salt. Sam loved to help make bread, and she'd been making a loaf a day since Drew brought home groceries. Once this was done, it would be time for Sam to head to bed.

"Should probably do another food run soon." Drew sat at the kitchen table, bent over a notebook he'd been writing in all day.

Wiping her flour-dusted hands on her apron, she half turned and waited to see if he'd say anything else.

"I could make a list," she said, taking a step toward him. "Or, we could come with you?"

It was a risky request, she realized that.

The pen in his hand dropped to the table. He twisted his head to look up at her before kicking one of the table chairs out.

She sat.

"It's been a while," she said, shocked at how steady her voice remained.

His lips quirked, his head tilted, but he remained silent.

She wasn't sure if he was considering her request or waiting for her to start begging.

When it came to getting out of the house and going into town, she had no problem begging.

These trips were gifts. They only happened once a year, if she were lucky. It was the only time Drew ever let her leave the property.

"It's been a while for a reason, or don't you remember?"

Angel wanted to keep eye contact, to lift her chin in defiance, to argue her case and demand he take them. She wanted to fight, defy, challenge the man who wielded power over her with a single glance.

She dropped her head and didn't need to feign submission. He'd beaten her rebellious spirit out of her years ago. There was still a glimmer, a vague memory of defiance buried deep inside her, but it only reared its head when Sam was threatened.

"I remember," she said, her voice whisper soft. One hand rested on her belly, fingers splayed against the roundness. "But things are different now."

His gaze trailed down her body. "Because of the baby? So, if you weren't pregnant, you would still be trying to leave me?"

Her lips pursed. The real answer was yes, of course she would try to leave, run away, any chance she had. But the only answer she could give was the lie he would believe.

"I made a mistake," she said, peering up at him from beneath her lashes. "I haven't tried to run since then. It's been over a year." She licked her dry, chapped lips, trying desperately to forget the memories of that day.

Drew looked toward Sam, then back at her. She couldn't read his expression at all.

"You tried to take my son away from me." The inflection in his tone sent a bevy of goosebumps to trail along her skin.

"I'm sorry." Her mouth parched in an instant, making it hard to swallow.

His head dipped in a nod. "I'm sure you are, *now*," he said.

"I've been good, Drew, just like I promised I would." She rubbed her belly. "I think that's why I've been able to carry this child as long as I have, because I've been good."

His lips tightened, his focus on her belly.

"I've been praying," he said. "Praying God would protect this one . . . maybe you're right. Maybe all those other miscarriages were because of your sin."

She flinched. She wasn't sure she believed in God anymore. How could she? The God she'd been raised to believe in had been a loving Father, someone who was supposed to protect her . . . not turn a blind eye when she needed Him the most.

To Drew, anything that happened was always her fault. Her sin. Never his.

"Not sure if I can trust you, though," he continued. "I want to . . . but you've betrayed me too many times already. It's why I chain you up whenever I leave. Or have you forgotten?"

"I haven't." She wasn't sure if he heard her, if she'd spoken loud enough for her voice to carry the short distance between them.

How could she forget? He reminded her every single time he wrapped that chain around her ankle. He was no better than Senior, keeping her chained up, but she'd never say that. He said he did it because he needed to ensure she stayed put, that she didn't put him or Sam at risk, that being bound to the house was the only way to keep his family safe.

She saw through him, though. She read the excitement in his gaze, heard the hitch in his voice, saw the tremble of his hands and the bulge in his pants every time he held that cuff in his hand.

An ache started in her chest and rose to her throat, lodging in her mouth until the weight was heavy enough to crush her. She should have kept quiet. She should have made a list for him and left it at that. Why, why did she speak up?

"You wouldn't force me to chain our son, would you?" He leaned forward. "You wouldn't make me wrap that chain around his ankle, keep him from going outside, knowing the freedom a child should experience? Is that what it would take to keep you here?"

Her head moved, sudden quick shakes, a silent scream of NO.

He leaned back, rubbed his chin and smiled. Not an *I've-got-you* kind of smile but more like *I-have-an-idea-you-aren't-going-to-like* smile.

She shivered.

"If I take you, maybe I should insist he wear the chain for once. Until I come home again."

No. Nonononono.

"It's okay," she said, "we don't have to go. I'll . . . I'll just make you a list." She would do anything, anything, to protect her son and not have him wear the chain.

Drew tore a piece of paper from his notebook and pushed it toward her. "Make the list, then."

He got up, rubbed Sam's hair and went outside.

The moment the screen door slammed behind him, all the air Angel held in her chest released with a swoosh. Her shoulders bowed and sobs ripped wounds inside her.

Sam came over and wrapped his skinny arms around her, holding her tight.

She forced herself to stop crying, wiped the tears from her face and kissed his face, every inch of his sweet skin until he giggled. His laughter, his light, his smile. They were the only things that helped her get through each day.

"How about we finish making that bread, okay? And then I have a surprise for you." His eyes lit up and he looked at her with heady expectation.

"I can't tell you, silly," she said. "That's why it's going to be a surprise." She took the dough out of the bowl and dropped it onto the counter. Sam's hands immediately wrapped around the bread and began to knead, just as she'd taught him. Push with the heel of the palm, fold with the fingers, push again. Over and over until his little arms shook with effort.

"I think that's good," she said, coating the dough with flour before placing it back in the bowl. "Now, are you ready for my surprise?" She looked out toward the door but couldn't see Drew.

"Daddy fixed up the bathtub today. Do you know what that means?"

It took less than three seconds for Sam to charge out of the kitchen and run up the stairs. He was struggling to step out of his pants before she even made it into the bathroom.

If there was one thing her son loved more than playing soccer, it was bath time. She filled the tub with bubbles and while Sam enjoyed moving his boats through the suds, she sat on the floor and kept an ear open for the slam of the kitchen door, but thankfully it never came.

Every so often, Sam would stop playing and tilt his head, as if he too were listening. Seeing him do that was like having her heart carved out with a dull spoon. He shouldn't know what fear was like, what it meant to be afraid, to always be on edge. She tried to take all that on for him, to hide just how wrong their life was.

It killed her that she wasn't protecting him like he deserved, like he should be. She would do anything and everything to keep a smile on his face, peace in his eyes, ease in his soul.

Anything.

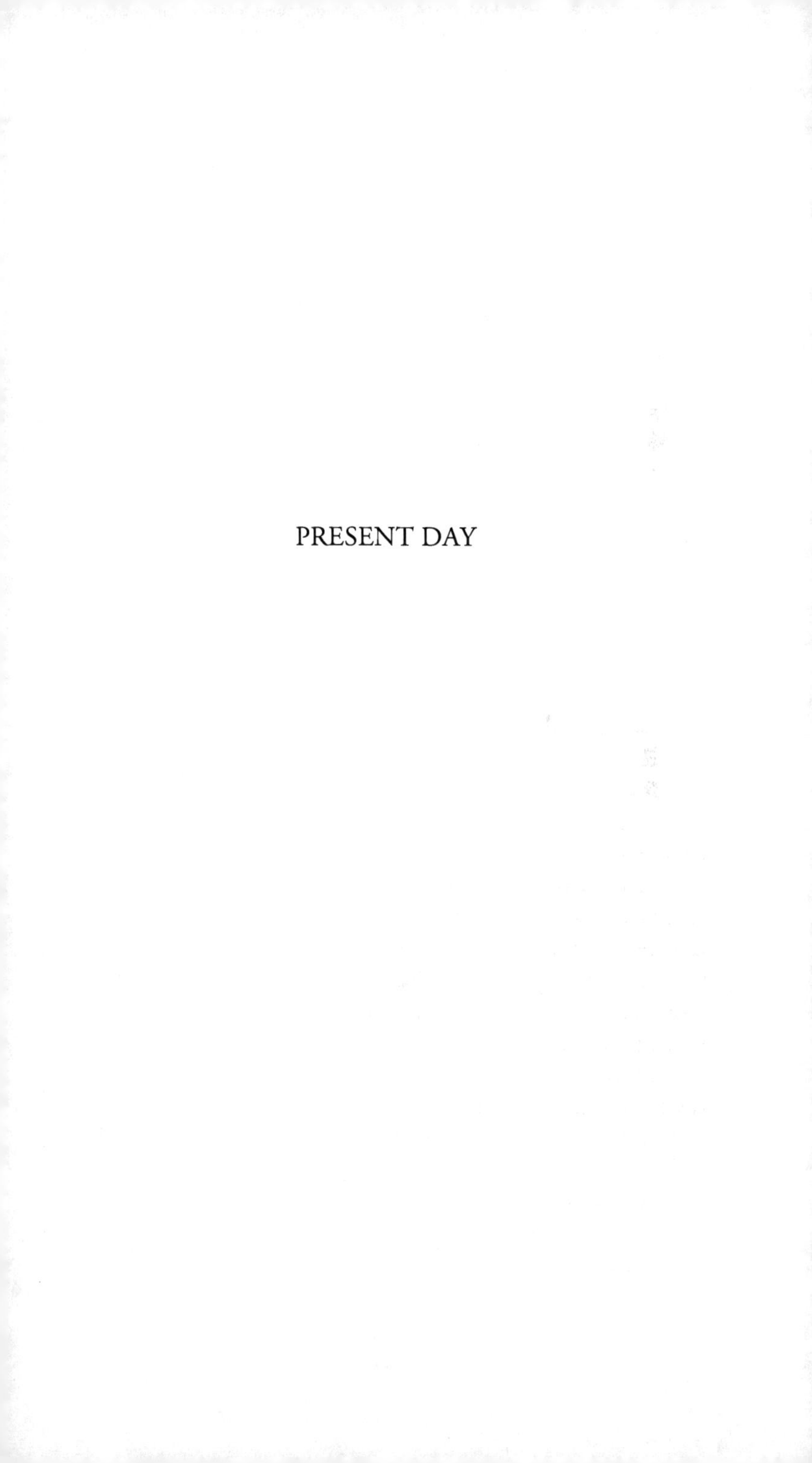

PRESENT DAY

CHAPTER 34

PAISLEY VALLEY HOSPITAL
1:30 p.m.

Hushed voices fill the room as I struggle to open my eyes. Everything is blurred, watered down, like I'm swimming in a lake with fogged-up goggles.

There's so much noise surrounding me. Voices. Machines. Squeaky wheels of carts as they go past my room. The door must be open.

"Angel?"

It's her voice. Soft, full of concern and hesitation.

Monique is always here, my constant companion.

"Angel?" She's at my side now, bending close to me so I can see her clearer.

"Sam." My voice is barely there, but even that much effort feels like I've swallowed sandpaper.

"Shhh, don't talk," she reminds me.

Where is my son? I stare at her, challenging her to understand me, to have answers for me.

"Angel? I'm Doctor Peterson. It's really important you don't talk." A loud, authoritative voice commands me to look at him.

I tear my gaze from Monique's to see this doctor standing at the foot of my bed. He's wearing a white lab coat, one hand shoved in a pocket, the other holding a clipboard nestled to his chest.

I blink several times to get the sleep out of my eyes. Do I recognize him? I need to know.

Dark hair. Glasses. Scar leading from his chin to his right cheekbone. No, I don't recognize him at all.

There's a heaviness that is inside my bones. I ache everywhere, a dull, pulsing throb that starts at my collarbones and ends at my ankles.

"Your vitals are good, other than some understandable spikes throughout the day. I know this must all be hard for you to take in, the pain, not being able to talk or move, but it's only for a few days, okay? We have you on morphine, is that helping with the pain? Are you feeling any nausea or dizziness?"

I blink twice.

"That means no," Monique says. "Since I've been here, I know she's hit the button once. And then the nurse . . ."

The doctor nods. "I see that on the chart here. If the pain is too much, don't hesitate to use the morphine, all right? It's there to help."

He turns toward someone who is standing off to the side. A man.

I look at him and I want to run, hide, get as far from here as I can.

He's tall, lethal, carries a face of anger and I don't feel safe.

I don't recognize him, but I recognize his type.

This is too much, it's all too much. In the background, my lake beckons, it calls to me, reminding me it's the only safe place I know.

"Stay with me, Angel, please?"

There's a pressure on my arm. It's light, gentle, but the weight catches me off guard, stops me from diving into the gentle waters of my safe place.

"I know this must all be hard for you, so much happening, so much out of your control. We want to help you, as best we can."

I look over at the man off to the side, then back to Monique, hoping she reads the question in my eyes.

I need to know who the man is.

It feels like forever before the doctor leaves and the man approaches.

"Angel?" He pauses, as if waiting for me to acknowledge my name.

I don't.

"I'm Detective Lindsay and I run a task force dealing with sex trafficking." He pauses again.

He's a cop. Do I trust him?

I trust no one.

"Angel, I have some questions for you, and I'll try to keep them as simple as I can so you can answer by blinking. Okay?"

One blink.

"Thank you. I know Monique has filled you in a little about how you were brought in, but would you mind if I start at the beginning?"

I don't blink yes or no. I really don't think he's asking for my permission.

"You were brought in last night after a tip came in following a possible sighting. You were airlifted from an abandoned farmhouse and rushed into surgery. We would like to contact your family for you, but we need to confirm a few things first. Is that okay?"

I look away. My family? No. I don't want them contacted. Let them continue to mourn my death. All I want is my son.

I keep my focus on the picture that's across from me. It's a country scene, an old white farmhouse in the distance, surrounded by flowing wheat and cornfields. A driveway, edged in a white fence, leads from the house to a road.

It reminds me of Drew's farmhouse, where he kept me prisoner. Will he take me back there? Will he find someplace else for me? In a box in his truck, like he's threatened for years? Or maybe in a basement, similar to where he found me?

What about Sam? What will he do to our son?

"Angel? Is it all right to call you that? I want you to know you're safe here."

Blink. Blink. I am not safe. I already know that.

The nurse will return. Drew will be back tonight as well, I'm sure of it.

No, I'm not safe.

"Is Angel not your name?"

This time I turn my attention to Monique. I don't blink. I don't make a sound.

"Do you not feel safe?" She leans in close, her voice soft. "Angel, I promise, no one is going to harm you here. We have an officer outside your door and I'm here. No one is ever going to hurt you again."

"Angel, I need you to confirm your identity for me, please. It's important." The detective's voice is insistent. Not harsh. But there's persistence in his voice, like what happens next depends on my answer.

"It may be about Sam." I almost don't hear Monique's words, she says them so quietly.

I inhale, my breath like razors, sharp, deadly. I force myself to swallow my shout and my heart races, the machine beside me beeping faster.

Sam. Could they have news on Sam? Is that why he needs to know my name?

Sam knows me as Mommy. And Angel.

Blink.

Pause.

Blink.

Yes. Yes. Yes. Call me Angel. Call me whatever you want. Just bring me my son.

The weight of a hand on my arm grounds me.

"It's okay," Monique says. "I told Detective Lindsay about what happened earlier, with the child, and how you were asking for Sam."

"Is your name Angel?" Detective Lindsay asks. The insistence in his voice is stronger. He's sitting on the edge of his seat now.

Blink.

Oh God, please . . .

"A little boy was just brought into emergency about an hour ago. He was found hiding in a shed at the farmhouse where you were found. He's not saying much. In fact, he's not saying anything. Is this" — he goes to turn the phone in his hand around — "is this your son?"

Sam! He's sitting on a hospital bed, knees tight to his chest. There's a tray beside him, with an apple juice box and a bag of popcorn. He's wearing my sweater and he's been crying.

I try to lift my arm, needing to hold his photo in my hand. I struggle to sit up, moaning as tears well in my eyes.

"Sam." His name is torn from my throat, ripped from the deepest recesses of my soul. The pain doesn't register, it doesn't matter. I just need my son. I need to see him, hold him, know that he's okay.

Detective Lindsay rises, a big lumbering ox, the chair scraping against the linoleum floor.

"Why don't I go see what I can do about bringing him up here, okay? The doctor said they can put him in the bed here, bring your beds closer together." He gives me this smile, a smile that completely alters his face.

His smile makes me want to trust him, to believe I can.

"When I come back, let's work on finding your family, okay? I'm sure you'd like to have them here with you."

Some sort of communication passes in a single look between him and Monique. I should care what it means, but I don't. All I'm focused on is my son and having him here.

Then it hits me.

The nurse knows about him. Drew will see him when he returns. I've just placed my son in danger.

What have I done?

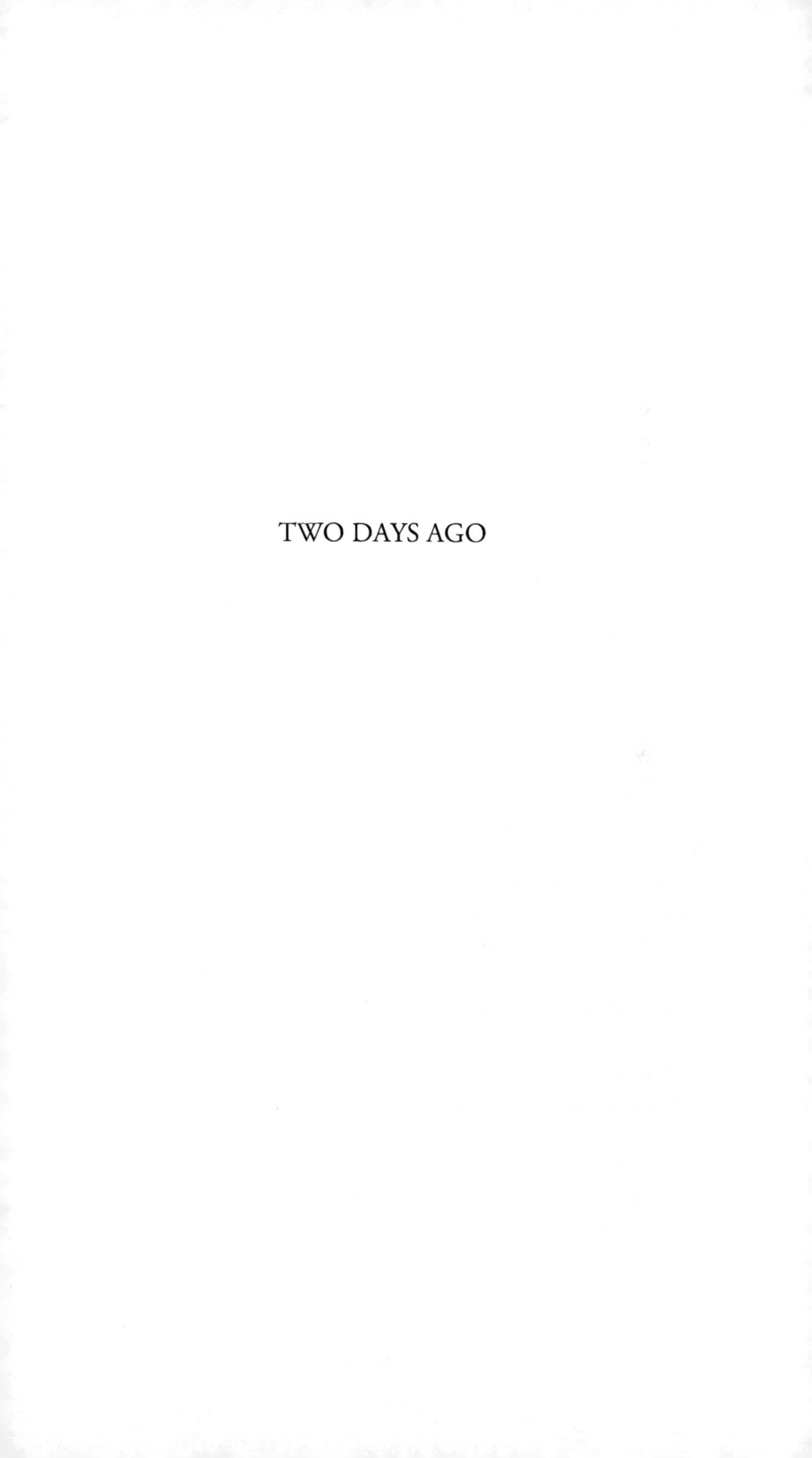

TWO DAYS AGO

CHAPTER 35

PAIGE

Today's group session, Mom Talk, is full. Every chair in the circle has an occupant, to the point where we had to bring in more chairs for a few latecomers.

Sometimes there are overlaps between the group members, like today. Cassie and Iryna, from the Real Parenting group, are among the late arrivals.

As the group starts, I keep track of issues that pop up during early conversations, jotting them down in my notebook so I don't forget. So far, it's not much, things Monique says we'll look into, some possible topics for future sessions, and then a few things that I think should be passed on to Detective Lindsay.

I have almost two full pages.

"Nicole," Monique says to the woman sitting three chairs down from us. "How are you doing? I noticed you've been a bit quiet today."

Nicole's hand covers the slight bulge of her growing belly. Missing from her face is the glow of pregnancy, the smile of contentment or even happiness.

Nicole glances around the room, as if measuring how her words may affect everyone else.

"Sarah's only been gone a year. It was a year last month that she went missing from her high school dance. A year of . . ." A shudder runs through her body. "Of being sold for sex, tortured, drugged and who knows what else, if she's still alive." She swallows hard, then glances my way. "I know it's only been a year, a year that to some of you is nothing, but . . ." Her hand continues to rub circles on her belly, but I catch the gleam of tears in her eyes before she lowers her face to hide them.

"Even one day is too long." I keep my voice soft, gentle, without any judgment.

Nicole draws in a shuddered breath. "This baby is unexpected, unplanned and . . ." Her tears fall faster, her body shaking from the emotion wracking her body.

"Unwanted?" Monique says, finishing her sentence. "It's okay to admit that, Nicole. No one is going to condemn, criticize or censure you for a feeling."

Everyone nods. Margaret, who sits beside Nicole, reaches over and holds her hand.

"I miss my daughter so much," Nicole's finally able to say. "I miss her laughter at stupid videos. I miss how she'd help cook with me in the kitchen. I even" — she lifts her face then, and a hesitant smile appears — "I even miss arguing with her when she didn't do her chores."

Her hand continues to rub her belly.

"I still wait for her, every night, to come home. I leave the light on in the living room, in case . . ."

"In case she tries to sneak in after curfew?" Iryna says. "I do that too. Still."

"Mark . . . he's excited for this baby. He's always wanted a large family, but after so many years and then the miscarriages, we just kind of gave up. Sarah was enough, our family was complete. But now . . ." Nicole's voice wavers a little. "Now it's all he focuses on. It's like he's given up trying to find our daughter. How could he have moved on so fast?"

I share a look with Monique. That same question comes up time and time again.

"Men and women deal with things differently," Monique says. "Remember that talk we had a few months ago, about how easy it is for men to compartmentalize? My husband phrased it as his mind was full of boxes. Each issue went into a box and once that lid was closed, he moved on." She shrugs. "Not the perfect example, and of course, it's generalized, but it gives an idea. I don't think Mark has forgotten about Sarah. In fact, I know he hasn't because he sends Paige weekly emails asking for updates, doesn't he?"

I mirror the laughter in Monique's voice. "He does." My grin is wide and true. "Every week he asks if there has been any news, if Detective Lindsay has provided an update and if there is anything he could be doing that you both haven't done already."

Nicole's eyes widen in surprise. "He does? I didn't know that."

"See, honey," Margaret speaks up. "He hasn't moved on."

"Something that often comes up," Monique says, speaking to the group, "is the guilt we moms tend to carry. We worry we're focusing on our missing child so much that we ignore the other children we have, or our marriage, or anything else in our life that used to be important. As a new mom" — she focuses on Nicole — "it's normal to worry about loving a new child while grieving for your missing one. I can promise you, though, as one who has had several children, the love you have for one child doesn't diminish when you have another one. It just grows, matures, becomes something more than you ever thought possible."

Nicole seems to take all that in. "I guess I'm worried that when Sarah does come home, she'll think we tried to replace her."

This time I'm the one to speak up. "Catherine," I say, directing my attention to the woman beside me, a woman who has been extremely quiet so far. "I'm sorry if this is too personal, but I'm thinking about a conversation we had after you . . ."

Catherine gives a brief wave. "After I lost Trina during childbirth?" she says, finishing my sentence. "And how I'd felt exactly like Nicole, that she was a replacement baby for Joshua, and how I was afraid I wouldn't be able to bond with her."

Joshua, who would have been close to thirteen years of age now, reported missing at age nine. Four years ago he'd been snatched by an active sex ring. Three years and six months ago, his body had been found, broken and beaten, in a ditch on a country road.

Officially his death was labeled as an overdose.

I was with Catherine when she identified his body, saw the small ring tag burned into his thigh, confirmation of the group who had stolen him from his parents.

I was left with nightmares for weeks after that, worried the same thing could happen with Flynn.

There's a reason I'm a helicopter parent.

Catherine leans forward in her chair, elbows resting on her knees. She speaks to the group, but her attention is one hundred percent on Nicole.

"From the time I found out I was pregnant to the day I went into labor, I resented my baby. She was an oops, unplanned and definitely unwanted. I blamed her for hindering me in searching for Joshua, for all the morning sickness, the exhaustion, the baby brain. I was angry at everyone — myself for letting this happen to me, my husband for not having his condom stash restocked, for everyone around me who was thrilled when I couldn't hide my pregnancy any longer."

Catherine pauses, one finger tapping against her lips, as if gathering focus, strength, to continue.

There's not a sound in the room. No one coughs, moves, speaks. Nothing.

"I wasn't just angry," she says. "I was scared. Scared at the emotional damage I was inflicting on my baby because she had to know she wasn't wanted. Scared that I wouldn't be able to bond with her once she was born because of my anger. Scared that she'd steal the love in my heart for my son

. . . and that I'd lose focus on what was really important — finding him.

"The day he was found . . . that's the day I went into early labor." Her skin pales at the memory, while her hands start to shake.

I reach over to give comfort. I'm so proud of her, for being able to share what she has.

"It was hard and if it hadn't been for Paige, who was there with me when I saw Joshua's face . . . I lost both of my children that day — I lost the hope of holding them in my arms, seeing their smiles, knowing they were okay . . ." Her voice catches, snares on a thread of tangled heartache. "When I gave birth to Trina, when I held her tiny frame in my arms, I realized that all of my fear, my anger, my worries . . . they were all lies. Lies I'd told myself because I thought that's what I deserved."

She breaks, unable to continue, silent tears streaming down her face. I take hold of her hand and squeeze. She squeezes back.

The weight in the room, the heaviness Catherine's words convey, it settles on us all. I read it on their faces, see it in their eyes. Most of us remember the pain, the grief, the heartache.

"Losing a child — regardless of how it happens — is never your fault." The words wrestled their way out of my soul.

"It's a hard truth to believe, trust me, I know," I say. "But it's the truth. We didn't lose our loved ones because of anything we did or said or even whispered in the middle of the night. They weren't taken from us because we're horrible people, because we need to be taught a lesson, because we don't deserve them . . ." My voice cracks as I think of my sister.

Catherine gives my hand another squeeze. She wipes the tears from her face and attempts a brave smile. "Nicole, I live with regret now," she says, once again focused on the woman across the room from her. "I regret not giving Trina every ounce of love I had, while I could. I regret not giving myself permission to love her, to dream of her future, to see her as her own person."

There's a pause before she stands and rushes across the circle to give Nicole a hug.

"Trina wasn't a replacement for Joshua. She couldn't steal the love I carried in my heart for him. I felt guilty for letting myself get pregnant, when I should have seen it as a gift," she says afterward, returning to her seat, setting her hand on top of her own stomach. A smile wreathes her face in joy.

No . . . my heart leaps with hope and joy as I watch her. She couldn't be . . .

"Catherine?"

She nods. "We have another chance. *I* have another chance."

The remainder of the session is full of congratulations, questions and Nicole herself finally able to smile.

I wait till the room is empty, things are cleaned up, and Monique is ready to leave when I stop her. "Care to join me for a cup of real coffee?"

"You read my mind."

With a promise to Anita to bring her back a cup, we head to The Mug Shot.

"Well, that session was . . . unexpected." Sometimes I have an idea of where our sessions will go, and sometimes I walk away completely surprised.

"Tell me about it. You were great, by the way." Monique reaches for the door to the café and holds it open. "I just have one question."

"Okay?" What is Monique going to ask?

"Do you truly believe what you said? That you aren't to blame for Jessica's disappearance?"

Why can't she leave well enough alone? Rather than answer, I head toward the counter where Marco waits with a bright smile.

"If you don't mind me saying so, you ladies look like you could use one of my cheesecakes." With his forearms planted on the top of the cooler where all his treats wait, he quirks his head toward Monique. "Especially you. I even made your favorite, hoping you'd pop in today."

Monique sidles up to the counter. "How did you know?"

The sparkle in Marco's eyes at Monique's teasing is contagious.

"Lemon for the tart one, so how about chocolate for the sweet one?" He sets two on a tray. "I'll bring the coffees over in a sec."

"Don't think I'm letting you off the hook," Monique says, using her *I-see-everything* social-worker voice as she drags me to our seats.

Of course she's not. I'd be surprised if she did.

"The easy answer is yes, I believe it." I wait till after Marco brings over our tray.

"I don't care for easy answers, you know that."

"I know. We've talked about this before. The easy answer is usually a lie, too, at least for me. It shadows the truth, and I'm tired of living in the shadows." I hold the hot cup in my hands, the mug burning its imprint into my palm.

"Shadows can mean a lot of things, Paige. How about you talk plain with me?"

Something seems off about Monique, but I'm not sure what. I'm trying to read her, but she's got a wall up. When we first met, Monique told me she's an open book with redacted pages.

"Shadows are fears, worries, masks we wear to hide ourselves, I guess. It means not being present as a parent or as a fiancé and that's causing some . . ." The ring of Monique's phone interrupts.

"Mind if I take this?" Monique holds up the screen to show that it's Pastor Jeremy. "I've been waiting for him to return my call."

I try not to pay too much attention while she talks, but the volume is turned up and I can hear portions of the conversation. It sounds like they'd been trying to get together to have a face to face talk about a situation that's come up in one of his home Bible study groups.

Probably something to do with Bryan Powers.

Monique takes a loud, noisy sip of her coffee after setting her phone back in her purse. "Sorry about that. We've been playing phone tag. He's going to come into the office in a bit."

"No worries. Did you want to head back, in case he comes sooner rather than later?"

It looks like Monique is going to say no but then changes her mind. "Sure, that's probably best. I can tackle some of the paperwork on my desk before he arrives."

I don't say anything, but I'm feeling a little left out. I shouldn't, because it's not like I have a monopoly on Jeremy. But the feeling is there.

If it's about Bryan, I should know, shouldn't I? And what if Bryan isn't the only one in his groups?

What if there's been a network right under our noses that Jeremy is only now noticing?

CHAPTER 36

DETECTIVE MERI AMBER

My bed is covered in random papers and notes and a thick file Detective Lindsay was kind enough to let me *borrow*. I'm meeting him in thirty minutes to hand it back to him.

I'll also be peppering him with questions.

I haven't been able to shake the overheard words from Monique.

I put feelers out about Michael Tinder onto my network of truckers, to see if anyone had something to share.

I got way more than I'd expected.

Michael Tinder is a long-haul trucker with solid fists and a soft heart. After his daughter went missing, Tinder went on a mission to educate fellow truckers about lot lizards — prostitutes who might actually be victims of sex trafficking.

His teaching methods often involved fists.

According to the file, Lindsay considers him a vital asset. Tinder alone has helped him rescue close to a few dozen victims, all underage, all kidnapped and sold into sex rings.

This doesn't surprise me. He's a man looking for his daughter. He has to see her face everywhere. If he can't save his own daughter, he'll save someone else's.

This is a man I can respect.

It also sounds like the man Monique assumes Rawlings is.

Throughout the file, I keep finding various initials. SJ. JH. CM. DJ. AR.

If Lindsay is using shorthand to conceal the identities of his informants, then I'm assuming AR stands for Andy Rawlings.

I'm not sure how I feel about this. The Rawlings I'm searching for sure as hell isn't an informant. He's not a nice guy who narcs on other truckers either. He's an asshole who hides for most of the year, only coming out in public for a few months at a time.

I think he's hunting during those months. I think he hunts until he finds a young girl and takes her for himself. What he does with her after that, I'm not sure. How many he has at one time, I don't know that either.

But I do know he's not a nice guy.

I hear voices outside my propped-open bedroom window. Detective Lindsay is out there talking with the owner of the bed and breakfast.

He's early.

I go through a folder on my computer, making sure all the scans I've taken of Lindsay's file are there. He probably won't like knowing I did that, but he also can't be surprised.

By the time I make it outside, he's alone.

"Did it help?" he asks as I hand the folder back.

"More than you know. I appreciate it."

"Took copies?" His lips barely twitch, but I see the smile there.

"A few."

I take it he appreciates my honesty because he gives me a nod before tossing the file through the open passenger window onto the seat.

"Go ahead," he says. "I figure you've got questions."

He figures?

"Why didn't you tell me you know Rawlings?" That's the main question on my list, the one that's been bothering me since I figured it out.

"You didn't ask."

I cross my arms.

"Do you know how many Andy Rawlings there are in the United States?"

"This morning there were a quarter of a million hits when I searched his name." I do this on a regular basis, just to see what pops up.

"Do you know how many of them are truck drivers?"

I wait for him to tell me, because he obviously wants to.

"Four hundred and twelve. At least a hundred of those are female. Another hundred who live around Colorado. Ninety are inmates in various prisons throughout the country. Forty-three have died in the last two years. Twenty-three are institutionalized."

Okay, so . . . he's obviously done his research.

"And how many have worked in one form or another for ALLS Transport?" I ask.

His shoulder lifts and he looks away.

Bingo.

"Why is Monique trying to cover for him?" That's another huge red flag in my book.

I really hope she's not dirty.

"Again, over four hundred truck drivers."

"And at least one hundred of them are female," I quote back. Yeah, yeah. I heard him the first time.

Another shrug.

"I noticed an awful lot of similarities between Monique's description of Rawlings and your notes on Michael Tinder."

He doesn't say anything and he should be saying something. Anything to explain the similarities.

"Is Tinder's reaction something you see in a lot of locals?" The moment I ask, I regret it. The one who remains silent is the one who holds the power.

I'm showing my hand too much.

"By locals, you mean local families who have children who are missing? Or by locals do you mean truck drivers?"

"The latter."

Lindsay sighs and sticks his hands in his pants pockets. "We've worked hard to educate local truckers in the area about possible child abduction and sex trafficking. It's a never-ending battle. You tend to notice the signs, sure."

He looks off into the distance. I see the emotional baggage this man has had to carry. It's there stamped across his features.

This life has been hard for him.

"There are three types of men we come across," Lindsay says. "Those who know what it's like to have a child stolen from them. Those who have families to go home to and are just putting in the time for the money. Then you have those who are stealing those children or having sex with them. It doesn't take much to see the signs."

"I get that Tinder is the type who wants to save everyone. What I don't get is Monique's firm stance on Rawlings."

Lindsay's lips tighten.

"Don't bother telling me there's a history there, or that it's need-to-know. If Rawlings is involved, and yes, I get you think it might not be my Rawlings, but it is, so if he's involved, I need to know."

He doesn't say anything. It takes a lot of effort to keep my mouth shut.

"How come you're not doing this?" He finally moves his mouth, but I'm not sure I'm understanding the words. "Why work in some small town precinct, handing out parking tickets and finding stolen property? Why aren't you in the FBI, or working on a task force like mine?"

Small town precinct? Handing out parking tickets? That's low. It's also not the answer I'm expecting to hear.

"Everyone's got to start out somewhere, right?"

His lips quirk. "True. But what's the end game? Where do you see yourself in a year? Five years? Ten years?"

I want to throw my hands up in the air but force them to remain at my sides. He sounds just like my father, who was always asking me what was next, telling me to keep my eye on the future, never relaxing in the present.

"How do you know I'm not aiming for more?" Stepping-stones. That's what I'd tell Dad. Put in my time, learn the right way, and this stepping-stone helps to create a firm foundation.

"Say the word. I've got room for someone like you on my team."

Whoa. I step back, taken off guard by that offer.

"Think about it. I've done my research on you. When you're ready to make a move, you let me know."

He walks away from me as I stand there, dumbfounded.

It's not until he's in his vehicle and backing away that I realize he never answered my questions.

CHAPTER 37

ANGEL

Angel's hands shook as she sat in Drew's pickup, drinking in the sights of civilization.

He'd finally agreed to take her shopping.

The trip was a quiet one. She took it all in, memorized every minuscule detail of their road trip so that she could dream about it night after night.

These trips were her sanity moments in her otherwise Groundhog Day life.

Drew surprised her about twenty minutes ago, telling her to put on a dress and get Sam ready to go shopping. He'd given her five minutes to get in the truck before he had it running, ready to go. She'd only needed three.

She had no idea where he was taking her — if it was to a new town or one they'd been to throughout the years. All she knew was that it was never the one close to her home, to her parents, where people might recognize her.

Once, they'd driven three hours, shopped for one, and then driven three hours back to the house. She was always on the hunt for someone she'd recognize. Sadly, she never saw anyone.

Drew drove down backroads and old country lanes sometimes covered in gravel. They'd passed a farmhouse here and there, fields with tractors and growing crops. She'd tried once to map out where they were, memorize turns and signs. But today, she had no clue which direction they'd gone or what town they were headed to.

Buzz-buzz-buzz.

Angel tore her gaze from the field of growing corn to find Drew tight-lipped.

"Grab my bag back there, will you? The keys for that are in the front pocket." He motioned toward the small duffle bag kept behind the seats.

Buzz-buzz-buzz.

Sam twisted out of the way so Angel could reach behind him.

"Just grab the keys," Drew barked, his hands tight on the wheel.

Drew never brought his phone into the house. He always kept it in his pickup truck, usually locked in the glove compartment. He'd run out to his truck a few times a day to check for any messages. Most of the time, those messages called him into work early.

So far, since he'd been home, they hadn't.

Drew pulled the truck over to the side of the road, dust billowing from the gravel. She fumbled with the keys, managing to get the compartment open before he pushed her hands out of the way. He grabbed the phone, slamming the compartment shut, pulling the keys with him as he jumped out of the truck, but not before she had a chance to see what else was in there.

A gun.

She knew he had one, she'd seen it before, had it pointed at her once. But Sam had never seen one, never been that close to one, and knowing it was there, so close, scared her.

Why did he have it in the truck with them?

Angel's free hand hovered over the door handle, the temptation to jump out strong. The idea of grabbing Sam, making a run for it to the farmhouse they'd recently passed flashed through her mind.

She gripped the handle and pulled Sam closer.

Drew, who had looked like he was about to turn his back on them, stopped, as if reading her mind. The glare he gave as he answered the call warned her not to do anything foolish.

His lips moved, but his voice was quiet enough that she couldn't hear him.

Her heart sank at the idea that they were going back to the farmhouse. So many thoughts ran through her head. How long would he be gone? Would they run out of food again? Would she be locked up in the ankle chain again?

Tight-lipped, Drew ended the call, running his hands through his hair, and stared up into the sky. He looked . . . frustrated?

She struggled to dampen her expectations. If it was indeed a call to return to work, they'd be returning back to her prison and she would need to fake a smile, not just for Sam's sake but for her own. Once, when she'd shown signs of disappointment before he'd left, he'd smacked her so hard she'd blacked out for almost an hour. Thankfully, that had been before Sam's birth.

"Change of plans," Drew spat out as he climbed back in. "Apparently my holidays have been cut short due to a driver calling in sick. Not sure how long I'll be gone."

Angel nodded, not saying a word.

"Don't worry, though, a promise is a promise. Plus you need food." He rubbed his hand over his face, pulling at his chin. "There's a town close by with a big supermarket. It has everything we'll need. Can't take all day, though. I need to head out in a few hours."

The breath Angel took in was shuttered, as if her lungs weren't sure they wanted to work properly.

"Make sure you get everything on that list, okay? We need to stock up those shelves at home, to make sure there's enough groceries for you and Sam." He spared her a glance as they drove down the road.

She dipped her chin toward her chest and pulled the list out from her sweater pocket. She couldn't believe they were still going, that he was still taking them. She had thought for sure he'd turn around and head back home.

Sam leaned into her, looked up and wrinkled his nose, their silent signal to each other that they were happy. She wrinkled her nose back and added a wink.

"Thank you," Angel said.

They turned a corner and drove past a sign indicating the next town was only thirty miles away.

"I need you to promise you'll stick by the rules, Angel. Okay? It won't just be you who pays the price." He dropped one hand off the steering wheel and patted Sam's knee.

He didn't need to say more.

"Don't worry," she said, infusing her voice with a smile, only for her son's sake. "It's a quick trip, we'll all stick together and no talking to strangers." She said this part to Sam, as if the reminder was for him alone.

It wasn't.

There were no worries about Sam talking to strangers. He didn't speak. Besides, what would he tell them? The life they lived, it was all he knew, which meant, for him, it was normal.

No, that rule was for her and her alone.

She'd broken it once. To retaliate, Drew had locked her in the closet for three days then kept her chained up for three months.

* * *

Angel was going to place Sam in the cart, but Drew insisted the boy was too big to be babied.

"You hold on to my hand tight, okay, Sammie?" Drew said as they walked across the semi-crowded parking lot.

They headed toward the entrance labeled Home, leaving the groceries for the end of their trip. Drew had set the ground rules once they'd pulled up to the big-box store.

"Pick out a comfy dress or two that you can grow into," he said, indicating her belly. "Then we'll get Sam some new pants and a top or two. Look on the sales rack first. If our boy here is good" — he tussled Sam's hair — "maybe we'll stop at the toy section."

Sam's eyes lit up, bright blue like a summer sky. That joy in his eyes, Angel would do anything to make sure it didn't go away. Even if it meant doing absolutely nothing about trying to save herself today.

She'd given up hope of ever escaping from Drew.

It didn't take her long to find the sales section. There were so many clothes she wished she could try on. She barely remembered the days when she would go shopping and try on outfits in the changing room.

Her son moved as if in a trance, taking in all the products in the store as if they were in a magical world.

Angel parked the cart off to the side, out of the way, and fingered the different items, enjoying the feel of the fabrics and daydreaming about what it'd be like to get dressed up again, really dressed up, in public.

She found a few dresses, held them up tight to her body, then put them back. She needed nondescript, ugly, boring dresses with room to stretch. With pockets if possible.

"Oh honey, don't buy those. Those colors wash you out." A female voice, off to the side, caught her off guard.

Startled, Angel glanced around for Drew and Sam. They were off a little in the distance, but Drew watched her.

Damn it.

She ignored the woman and went to move to another row of clothes, keeping her head down.

The woman followed.

"Here, how about this? This green will look so nice on you." A dress was pushed into her line of sight.

"Please leave me alone," Angel hissed, sneaking a peak toward Drew. He was headed toward her.

"Just take it, okay? It would look great on you."

Angel took the dress from the woman's hand. "Thanks."

"Everything okay? Oh, that's a nice dress." The smile on Drew's face might appear friendly, and the tone of his voice might come across as loving, but the hard edge in his gaze, along with the flare of his nostrils, warned her she walked on hot lava.

"Hi, sorry, I don't mean to intrude, but I noticed your wife was picking up some really drab dresses that didn't suit her at all." The woman now stood at Angel's side and would not shut up.

He reached for the dress Angel held. "Well, this is a nice color. Brings out your eyes, sweetheart." Again, his demeanor came across as deceptively normal. He dropped the dress in their cart. "Are you almost done?"

The woman beside her giggled, as if something funny had been said. "Her cart is empty, how could she be almost done?"

His lips tightened into a crooked semblance of a smile.

"Yep, I've got all I need," Angel forced herself to speak up. "Thanks again," she said, barely giving the unfamiliar woman a glance.

"What did she say to you?" The friendly facade he wore in front of the stranger disappeared the moment they walked away. His vice-like grip on her arm tightened when she didn't respond fast enough.

"Nothing. Just showed me the dress. I swear." She tried to pull her arm away, wanted to tell him his grip hurt, but she knew he'd only hold on tighter.

"Do you know her? Does she look familiar? I should have taken you straight home, I'm such a fool." He squeezed so hard he touched bone, making her cry out. She received a pinch on the underside of her arm for that.

Angel kept her head down as they walked through the children's clothing section. Drew, with Sam's help, picked out pants and a few tops, some new socks and underwear, and even two pairs of superhero pajamas that were on sale. While he remained friendly, upbeat, with a fixed smile on his face, she knew he was angry. It reflected off him in waves, heat from his fury scorching her until all she wanted to do was cry.

She remained tight-lipped, answered when spoken to and did her best to not show Sam how scared she was.

She was going to pay for that woman's gentleness. She knew it.

CHAPTER 38

Drew kept looking at his watch, his lips tightening, his movements hurried.

"Why don't you grab a book or two while I take Sam toy shopping," he finally said, completely surprising her. The books were on a single aisle, not far from the toys, which meant he could still keep an eye on her.

Angel stared at the books in front of her, overwhelmed by the selection. Was this a test? If she picked the wrong type of book, would he take it away? Deny it? She wasn't even sure what she liked anymore.

One by one, she picked up each book, enjoying the heavy feel in her hands, opening the pages to inhale the crisp, clean scent, turning it over to read the back copy.

Every so often, she'd turn and see him watching her. She couldn't see Sam, being too small to view over the chest-high shelves.

To her left was the craft section, with rows of stickers, yarn and knitting needles.

The woman from earlier stood there as well, just out of sight of Drew, but in clear view of Angel.

"I can help," the woman said. "Just say the word. I'll get rid of that bastard."

Angel dropped the book she held.

"I'm Ava. I saw how he held your arm. He's not a nice man. He deserves to be punished." The smile on Ava's face turned . . . sadistic.

Angel recognized that smile. A shiver ran over her body. She didn't dare respond, even though Drew was too far away to hear her. But he'd know if she spoke to anyone.

"I put a pen and paper in the women's bathroom, on top of the paper towel holder. Try to get in there, leave me your address. I'll save you, you and your son."

Angel didn't know who that woman was, or why she thought she could save her, but if life had taught her anything, it was that when an offer seemed too good to be true, it always was.

Always.

"Mommy, Mommy." Sam's voice was her anchor and had her turning. Her son ran up to her, holding a toy in his hands. Drew was right behind.

Hearing him call her name . . . there was nothing better. If that was the only word he ever said, she would forever be happy.

"Did you pick out a toy? Let me see." She gave her whole focus to her son, ignoring both the woman and Drew. Sam held out one of those superhero figurines from a coloring book Drew had brought home once. Same superhero as on the pajamas in the cart. "He's your favorite, isn't he?" she said.

While she oohed and aahed over the toy, Drew picked up one of the books she'd been looking at. "Find anything? This doesn't look too bad."

He held a Hannah Mary McKinnon novel titled *Sister Dear*.

"No, looks great. I couldn't really decide . . ." She casually looked around for that woman, but she was nowhere to be seen.

"Don't you want some books? They're on sale, grab another." He picked another, one with a bloody tulip on the cover, and held it out.

“Th . . . thanks,” she said, stuttering over the word. It was a test, it had to be. He was in a rush, she’d talked to a stranger . . . why would he let her buy two books and some dresses?

He reached for the cart, his fingers gripping the metal edge tight. “We need to grab those groceries and go. You have the list, right?” He took the cart from her, handing over Sam. Sam tugged on her hand until she looked down.

He was crossing his legs, doing a little dance.

Drew half paused in his step. “Seriously, kid?”

The bathroom was off to the right of them, just before they entered the food aisle.

“I’ll take him. I need to go too,” she said, rubbing her belly. Being pregnant meant her bladder felt full on a twenty-four seven basis.

They stopped at the crossroads in the aisles. For a brief second she thought Drew might continue, taking the grocery list from her and making her promise to meet him.

She should have known better.

“I’ll wait right here. Take too long and I’ll come in after you,” he warned.

Sam pulled her toward the bathroom doors, his need to pee quite evident.

The second they walked into the bathroom, she noticed the paper towel holder. The woman had asked for her address, but she didn’t know it. What could she tell her, though? The make of the truck? The license plate? Drew’s name? That she was kidnapped years ago?

The bathroom wasn’t empty. One of the stalls had a closed door.

For one brief second, Angel thought it might be Ava, waiting for her. She hesitated for only a second, but at Sam’s whimper, she walked past the closed stall and opened the handicapped stall door.

When they stepped out, there was an older woman standing at the sink, hands beneath the tap, washing off the soap she’d lathered.

"Well hello, young man," the woman said, her wrinkled face blooming into a smile.

Sam gave a soft smile.

Angel helped him climb up on a stool waiting beneath the counter. As they went through the motions of cleaning their hands, she noticed a poster on the wall.

It was a plain white sheet of paper with a blurred image of girl with hair in a ponytail. Beneath the image were words written in red.

ARE YOU SAFE? WE CAN HELP. STOP SEX TRAFFICKING.

Below that was a phone number for the CHILD hotline.

The woman noticed her looking at the poster. Their gaze locks together in the mirror.

"Do you need help, love?" the woman asked, her voice mouse quiet.

Time stood still for Angel. She'd waited for this moment for years. So. Many. Years. And yet, she was paralyzed. Everything inside of her screamed YES. HELP ME. But no words came out, she couldn't nod her head, blink or anything.

"Here, I have a phone. I can call for you." The woman riffled through the shoulder bag she carried.

"Mommy?" Sam must have noticed her tension. She forced her lungs to breathe, her lips to move.

"It's a shame what happens. Tell me your name." The woman seemed to sense Angel's fear and unease. "It's going to be okay," she said.

Angel licked her suddenly dry lips. A seed of hope, once squashed, stirred in her heart. After all these years, could her nightmare finally be over? Could she dare believe it?

"Honey, what name can I tell them?" The number had been dialed and together they heard it ringing.

Name . . . she had to give her name.

Did she give the one Drew gave her? Or the name her family would know her by — a name she hadn't uttered, or even thought of, for years. Why would she? That girl died a long time ago.

BANG BANG BANG.

All three jumped.

"Angel? What's taking so long?" Drew beat on the door again, his voice not hiding his anger and annoyance.

Angel reached for Sam's hand.

"Angel, that's your name?" the woman asked.

BANG BANG BANG.

"Don't make me come in there."

"Sam, we have to go." Angel gave her son's hand a gentle tug. "Coming," she almost yelled.

One hand on the door, Angel paused and looked over her shoulder. "Please help us," she whispered. The woman looked scared. Scared, nervous . . . but strong at the same time, with the way her hand remained steady and her chin notched upward.

Why couldn't she have that same strength?

In a store with so many people, she could stand her ground, not leave the bathroom, scream for someone to help. Drew would have to leave them, wouldn't he?

But there was no one around. The bathrooms were located at the back of the store, a store that didn't have a lot of people in it. He was right outside the door, a door that didn't have a lock. A door he could open with one shove of his hand. He'd barge in. He could knock the woman to the ground. Grab her, or worse, grab hold of their son and force her to follow him out of the store.

That's exactly what Drew would do. He'd focus on Sam, knowing their son was Angel's weakness.

"ANGEL." Drew's voice was so clear, as if his ear were pressed against the door. It edged open, as if he'd given it a shove, just like she'd expected him to.

She moved so she blocked his possible view of the woman, pulled Sam in front of her and opened the bathroom door just wide enough for them to pass through.

"What took so long?" The displeasure was enough to twist her stomach in knots.

“Sorry.” Angel rested her hands on Sam’s shoulders as they started to walk away.

In the background, through the open door, the ringing finally stopped and a voice came on the line.

“You’ve called the CHILD Helpline. How can I help you?”

CHAPTER 39

"You've called the CHILD Helpline. How can I help you?"

Drew heard the same words she had.

"What did you do?" For a brief moment his face paled, eyes widened with shock and he stared as if his world crumbled around him.

She didn't recognize him, not then, not like that. She'd never seen him scared. Angry, vengeful, sadistic, cold, yes. But scared? That was a look he preferred to see in her.

"What did you do?" he repeated, his words on a loop. He looked from her to Sam, to the front of the store, then back to her. "I . . ."

"Angel, help is coming," the older woman yelled out, her voice a battle horse, armed and prepared to fight for her.

Angel twisted, as if to run to the woman, but Drew blocked her with his arm.

His eyes narrowed as he stared at her. What did he see? The hope that flickered inside of her? The idea that freedom was soon to be hers? The knowledge that he held no control, not anymore, not over her.

Whatever it was that he saw, he didn't like it. That's when everything changed. Gone was the scared man. The one who stood before her was angry, furious, outraged that she would disobey him.

Drew stepped toward the woman, his fisted hand out, and Angel was more afraid of what he'd do to the kind old soul than what he'd do to her.

"Don't, please," she begged, her hand on his arm, as if that would stop him.

"Don't? You've got to be kidding me. You have no idea what you've done." His hand gripped her upper arm, his fingers clamped tight around her skin. He stormed down the aisle, dragging her with him.

"Sam. Now." Drew's lips were one straight white line, his voice deep, dark and scary.

Sam ran after them, his hand out, his fingers barely connecting with hers as she tried to pull back, to slow Drew down enough so she could hold onto her son.

Angel threw a desperate, pleading glance toward the woman, who followed, the phone still in her hand. She looked around the store for someone else to see them, to help them. There was no one. No store worker. No other customers. Especially no Ava, the woman who'd promised to save her.

He pulled her through the sliding doors and the alarm went off. "What the—" He looked at her, then Sam and then the toy their son still carried.

Drew tore the toy from Sam's tight hold and threw it back into the store.

Angel tripped over her feet and would have fallen flat on her face if Drew's grip wasn't so tight. He rushed them to the truck, opened the door and shoved her in, not caring how she landed. He tossed Sam inside, slamming the door closed. Angel barely moved her foot in time.

Large tears trailed down Sam's face, but he made no sound. He was scared, it was written all over him as he clutched her tightly. She didn't bother with seatbelts, she just held her son tight in her arms as Drew threw the truck into gear and tore out of the parking lot.

Angel's body shook.

The only thing keeping her together, helping her to remain strong, was the fact that the older woman had followed them out of the store, phone tight to her ear.

Drew was yelling. Swearing. His fingers worked the steering wheel, knuckles white from tension, but Angel heard nothing. She blocked out his anger. His fury. She stared out the window, off into the distance, praying she'd see flashing red lights that would indicate help was on its way.

Which was why she didn't notice Drew reaching into the back, behind their seats, or the hammer that he held, until it was too late.

PRESENT DAY

CHAPTER 40

PAISLEY VALLEY HOSPITAL
2:30 p.m.

It's been an hour. An hour of waiting that feels like a lifetime.

Something is wrong, I can feel it.

Monique has left the room three times in the past hour. Each time, the frown on her face deepened and she's less and less willing to look me in the eyes.

Something is very wrong.

Her focus is on her phone and often she'll end up mumbling something beneath her breath. There's been a few times she's jumped at the sound of her phone vibrating.

It's like she's waiting for someone to contact her but hopes they don't.

I wish I could talk. I wish I could ask her questions. I wish I could find out for myself if she's someone I can trust.

Because right now . . . right now, I don't.

Her phone rings. One glance at the screen and a smile of relief appears. She jumps from her chair and heads out of my room, again.

"Jeremy, where are you? Lindsay's been calling . . . What is going on? No, don't . . ." She looks over her shoulder at me and holds up her index finger.

Sure, she'll be back. Not like I'm going anywhere. I block out everything she is saying because none of it matters.

My eyes want to drift shut, my body begs for sleep, but not until my son appears. I need to know he's safe, okay, and here, with me.

I listen for noise. Any noise coming from the hallway. I want to hear the first steps of Sam coming to me.

I might lie here, broken, wrapped in bandages and sedated, but inside, I'm a coiled snake ready to attack if anything threatens my son. Every time Monique leaves me alone, I focus on lifting my arms, moving my body, even if it's just one wiggle of a finger.

I need to be ready for Drew. I need to be ready to protect my son, when he appears.

There's noise just outside my door. I tense. It's the nurse from earlier, the evil one. Why is she still on shift? Why is she still here?

She's going to come in and make me sleep again. What will she do to Sam when I'm not able to protect him?

I'm torn . . . I need my son here, but I need him safe as well.

I still don't know if I can trust Monique, but I have to alert her to the danger I'm in.

Moaning hurts just as much as speaking, but I raise the intensity of my moan until the door bursts open and Monique enters.

"Angel, what's wrong?" She tucks her phone into her back pocket and rushes toward me.

The nurse is behind her.

No. No no no no no. It's the only sound I can make. Please figure out what I'm saying. Please.

My gaze goes from Monique to the nurse and back to Monique. I shake my head, form a frown and continue to moan.

Monique looks behind her and sees the nurse.

"She's here to help," Monique says, her voice low enough not to be overheard.

I shake my head again.

"Angel, do you recognize her?"

Blink. Blink.

"Then how do you know she's not here to help? Has she done something? Said something."

Blink.

"What's going on?" The nurse's voice is harsh, with a hint of desperation. "Honestly, I'm starting to wonder if you are hindering my patient's care."

Blink. Blink.

Monique studies me. Her voice drops to a whisper. "What are you trying to tell me?"

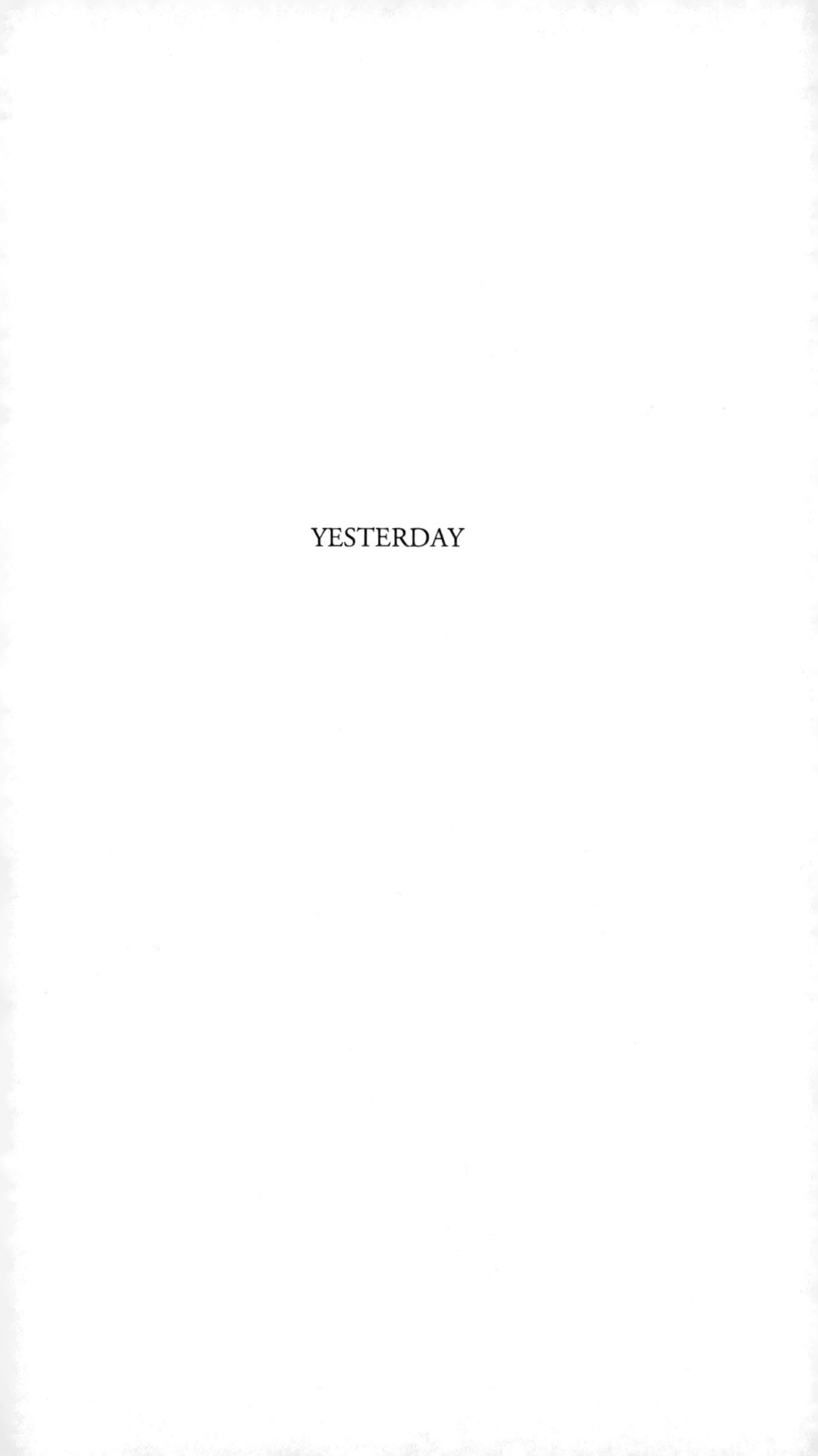

YESTERDAY

CHAPTER 41

PAIGE

I'd spent my morning running errands, visiting a total of twenty-two locations, a mixture of restaurants, grocery stores and truck stops updating our help posters.

Today's visits are a necessary part of getting the CHILD hotline in the faces of those who need help the most. We advertise on billboards, buses and online, but I've found it's the grassroots, in-your-face posters plastered in bathrooms that get the most attention.

I can't count how many times I've been on the other end of panic-stricken, rushed phone calls where someone needed help and they needed it fast.

We all take turns covering the hotline. Today, I'm on deck.

My cell phone pings. Jamie's been sending me messages all day. This one is a gif of a puppy waving a paw. I can't believe we're actually doing this.

Ready for tonight?

Am I ready for an overexcited boy meeting his new puppy? You bet I am. All I've done since getting back to my desk is look up puppy training tips online.

Rather than text, I give Jamie a call. I think he's even more excited than I am, truth be told.

"Do you think Charlie would like a blue or orange dog-bone name tag?" Jamie asks, not bothering to say hi.

"I thought we said orange. That's Flynn's favorite color."

"Right. Orange it is. I think we're done with supplies. We should be fine for pee pads and puppy toys too." Jamie's voice is full of that expected hope and excitement.

He says the dog is for Flynn, but I have a feeling it's as much for Jamie as it is for our son.

"I still can't believe we're doing this."

"I can't believe you agreed, to be honest." He chuckles, softening his words.

"I can't wait to see Flynn's face when—"

Ding ding.

The CHILD Helpline rings, the ding in my ear piercing.

"It's the hotline, gotta run." I hang up without giving Jamie a chance to say goodbye.

In the time it takes for the line to ring again, I've opened the program we use to log each call.

One breath. Two breaths. I've got this. The person on the other end of the phone call needs me to be calm.

"You've called the CHILD Helpline. How can I help you?"

No one answers, but in the background I hear pounding, hushed voices, with one raised in anger and then . . . nothing.

I repeat my greeting, making sure to keep my voice on an even keel while, inside, my heart races like I've run a marathon.

Again, no one answers.

The only sounds I hear are whispered mutterings, pounding on what sounds like a door, and a harsh voice.

"You've called the CHILD Helpline. How can I help you?" I speak slower this time.

There's more pounding, followed by an echoing cry. It sounds like a bathroom.

I document everything in the program, knowing it'll be added into the transcription of the call later.

"I'm not sure what is happening, but I am here," I say.

"Just . . . hello? I have a girl here with a child . . . one minute." The voice on the other line is older, with a slight shakiness to it.

"Angel, help is coming!"

Angel? I straighten in my chair.

"Ma'am?" I try not to yell. "Hello? Ma'am? Can you tell me what is happening please?"

There's hard breathing now. Like the woman is running.

"You have to help them." She's back on the line, her voice breathier now than before. "Sorry, I'm not as young as I used to be."

I resist the urge to tell the woman to hurry, to explain just how crucial every second is right now, but I shove every instinct to rush the woman and wait.

"I wanted to make sure I had as much information as you needed. It's a woman with a small child, a boy. I think the man is hurting them. She saw your poster, the one with the phone number, in the bathroom and asked for help."

My fingers tap-dance across the keyboard. "Did you say her name was Angel?" My gaze flies to the photo of Gabrielle tacked to my cubicle wall.

"Yes. That's what the man called her, and he's driving a green pickup truck. Ford. I have the license plate too. They just left, the poor thing."

"Ma'am . . . where are you?"

"Oh, that would be helpful, wouldn't it! I'm at Smart Shop in Tarrington, the one on the corner of Weston and Project. You should send someone, right? Do I have to stay?"

I bring up Detective Lindsay's number and wait for it to dial. "Yes, ma'am, if you wouldn't mind. I'm going to place you on hold right now, is that all right? I'm going to call the police and will be back shortly."

Without waiting for a response, I place her on hold. My leg bounces as Lindsay takes his time to pick up. The line rings and rings and rings until his voicemail comes on.

"It's Paige. I'm on the hotline today." I can't believe he didn't answer. "There's a woman at the Smart Shop, just on the edge of town, on the other line. She was approached by a woman named Angel, who asked her for help. I think it might be Gabrielle. The man she's with drives a green Ford pickup. And she has a young child with her, a boy." I pause, letting an idea coast into my head. He's going to hate it, but there's no way I'm putting the brakes on. "I'm going to go and wait with the woman. Call me as soon as you get this."

I can't believe I'm doing this.

My fingers tremble as I reconnect with the woman. I take down all the information I can get and remind her to wait.

I'm breaking every single protocol CHILD has in place, tearing up every single rule, but I don't care. I made a promise to the Manderas that I intend to keep.

Gabrielle has finally reached out for help.

I rush out of the office only to be stopped by Anita.

"Where are you going?"

"A call came in. It's Gabrielle. I couldn't reach Lindsay. Keep trying him, will you? I logged everything in today's file." I push open the door, not bothering to wait for Anita's reply.

"Wait, Paige, you can't do this." Anita is behind me. "Seriously, Paige, you have to stop."

"I can't. I'm just going to go stay with the woman who called it in. Until Lindsay arrives, okay? That's all, I promise."

Anita throws her hands up in the air in obvious exasperation. I understand, but it still doesn't stop me.

I know what I'm doing. I'm also aware of the ramifications. But none of that matters, not right now.

Gabrielle needs my help.

CHAPTER 42

"What do you think you are doing?" The anger in Lindsay's voice blasts through my speakers the moment I answer his call.

My fingers tighten their grip around the steering wheel as my foot pushes on the accelerator. Technically, I'm speeding. Hopefully I won't get pulled over.

I'm five minutes away from the store. I've made great time by taking a few shortcuts out of town, down the highway, and then a back road.

"Paige, you'd better answer me." Oh, he sounds angry. I can't help but wince.

"I'm heading to the store, I told you that already. Time is of the essence, right? Well, I don't want to leave the woman who called it in alone." My excuse is weak. I know, and by his snort, he knows it too.

"You didn't answer my call," I add.

"So you follow the protocol. Come on, Paige. You know better than this."

Yes, I know better. I get why he's upset and, truth be told, if someone else in the office did what I'm doing, I'd be one of the first to remind them about our rules . . . but I'm not them and personally, I don't care.

I. Do. Not. Care.

The need, the drive, the demand that I be the one to help the Manderas is overwhelming.

My mother gave up on Jess because I failed in finding her.

I'm not going to be the reason another family gives up.

"I'm just going to be with the woman until someone from your team arrives. Come on, Lindsay, what is wrong with that?"

I check the map on my phone. Smart Shop is close. One more shortcut and I'll be there in no time.

"What color was the truck? Did you get the license plate?" Lindsay's voice is clipped, tight, as if he can barely contain his frustration.

"It was a green . . . Ford," I say, just as a pickup truck goes past. "317 AMC . . ." I watch the truck pass by in the rearview mirror. "No way."

"What?"

I'm running on instinct now. I pull off to the side and do a quick U-turn. "I think I just passed it. Green Ford, same license plate, I think." My foot stomps down on the pedal, determined to catch up, to make sure.

"Stop. Paige, don't even think about it. I mean it. Do not follow that truck." Lindsay's voice rushes over the speakers.

"Why not? I should make sure it's the right truck, don't you think? I didn't get a good look at the driver or who was inside, but . . ."

My sole focus is that truck and getting close enough to make out the license plate. My heartbeat races, my chest aches from the steady drum, my hands sweat from the stress . . . What if Gabrielle is in that truck? And her son? Are they okay?

What if it isn't them? What if it's another girl who'd been taken from her home?

My mind races with so many scenarios, but in the end it doesn't matter. I'm here. I'm going to help.

I inch closer and closer until a car passes me on my left and snakes in between me and the truck.

"Damn it." I'm craning my neck to the left, tires following. I swerve too close to the white line and an oncoming car honks.

"I'm serious, Paige. You have no idea what you could be heading into. What if the driver has a gun? What if he's harmed that woman and child already?" The stress level in his voice rises high enough that it catches my attention.

For a second, just a second, my right foot releases from the gas pedal, my vehicle slowing until I realize I've left too much distance between myself and the truck.

I can't lose them.

No matter what Lindsay says.

"I won't get out of the car, okay? I'm just tailing to make sure it's the right one."

"For the love of . . ." He pauses and then I hear his siren.

"I can't believe I have to say this, to you of all people," Lindsay begins, almost shouting.

"Then don't say it," I shout back.

I sure as hell don't need a lecture, or a reminder that what I'm doing is stupid and careless. What I need is for him to tell me I'm doing the right thing, that we'll find Gabrielle, that we'll save her.

"What happened to meeting with the woman? Being there? Finding out more? That's more important than following a possible false lead, a truck you don't even know is the right one." Lindsay's voice is somewhat calmer now. Not much, but just a little.

"And you don't know it isn't."

"Let me do my job."

"If you'd done your job, this wouldn't be happening."

Silence.

Crap. I can't believe I just said that, to Lindsay, the man who has put his career on the line, time and time again, to help me and the families I work with.

"Lindsay, I'm . . ."

"Don't."

"But I . . ."

"Stop." The finality in his voice is all it takes. I crossed a line, we both know it, and eventually we'll have to deal with it, but not right now.

"Where are you?" he asks.

"Just passed the turnoff for the highway. I don't know if they went that way or not."

"Yeah, I know where you are. Pull back, Paige. I mean it."

"But . . . the truck?" I edge out a little to the left, over the solid white line, to see if I can catch a glimpse, then abruptly pull back at the sight of a semi barreling down the road. "Damn it, Lindsay. I can't see it. What if . . ."

"I've got units on the way. I don't need you involved, Paige. Not like this. Go back to the office and wait for my call, please. I need you there more than I need you on the road."

With lips crushed together, I groan in frustration. "Fine," I mutter, loud enough for him to hear. But I'm not going back to the office.

That's not where I'm needed.

"You're headed to the Manderas, aren't you?" Detective Lindsay reads my mind.

"Make sure you let me know if that woman can identify Gabrielle, please." I hang up, slamming my hand into the steering wheel with a slap.

What the hell just happened? What did I do?

I slow down to the speed limit and work on my breathing exercises. Inhale deep, hold, exhale, repeat. Eventually my chest stops hurting from the increased boom-boom, boom-boom of my heart.

Eventually I have to pull over to the side of the road and collect myself. The rush of the past half hour hits me and I start shaking.

I can't believe I did that. I'm going to be in so much trouble. I broke basically all the rules of handling the hotline. What if I just made things worse?

I can't believe I lost the truck. I try to still the memory in my head, visualizing the seconds it took to pass me.

Who was the driver? Was there someone in the passenger seat?

There's something niggling at the back of my head . . . something that seems familiar but I can't figure out what.

I don't know anyone who drives a beat-up old green pickup.

Breathe. In, out, in, out.

First things first. I need to call Jamie.

My hands shake as I hit the call button. He doesn't answer, so I leave him a message. I apologize profusely for possibly being late, for not being there to pick up the puppy, for everything and anything that pops in my head.

He's going to understand. He has to. He's not going to like that once again, I place my own family second, but what choice do I have?

If that was Jess rather than Gabrielle in that truck, I'd want to know every stone is being turned, every single piece of information looked into . . . I'd want to know that everything is being done to find my sister and that I'm not going to be left in the dark.

By going to the Manderas, that's exactly what I'm doing. Telling John and Liz that I'm there, right beside them, every step of the way.

CHAPTER 43

The first thing I do is stop at CHILD. I need to own up to my mistakes, face the consequences and pray for the best.

There's no action without reaction, as Dad used to say.

From the frown on Anita's face the moment I step through the front doors, I need to pray harder.

Lois is there, waiting for me.

Damn it.

After a verbal hand slap, a none-too-gentle reminder of the rules, followed by the suggestion to take a few days off, Anita waits for me.

I don't like the look on her face.

"I called Monique and she'll be waiting for you at John and Liz's. I tried Pastor Jeremy too but only got his voice mail. I think, if memory serves, he has that AA meeting he runs, followed by a men's Bible study, but I left him a message. Knowing him, he'll show up."

Normally Anita is an open book, all her emotions on display, not just on her face but in her voice too. Right now though, she's a blank page, as if she'd erased every single feeling and opinion.

I can't read her at all.

I already felt horrible for overreacting, for letting my emotions betray the process I know works so well. But this distance between Anita and myself . . . how she's pulling away from me, the guilt is so heavy.

"I'm sorry."

Anita's lips thin into a straight line. "Uh-huh."

According to Lois, by playing, or trying to be, a hero, I could have hurt any chance of bringing Gabrielle home. She's right.

"Maybe . . ." I sigh, "maybe I should just let Monique handle this."

That's taking the easy way out, one hundred percent.

Anita's lips contort into a mass resembling frustration, anger and irritation. "Oh no you don't," she says. "You don't get to make a rookie mistake and not try to fix it. You're better than that, Paige."

Ouch. "I screwed up."

Anita gives a half-chuckle, half-snort. "You think?" Her eye roll is epic. "You didn't just make a mistake, you made several. The first was leaving your post. Manning the Hotline, taking the information and passing it along, that was supposed to be your only priority. Today was your shift. What if another call had come through?"

My first instinct is to walk away from this interrogation.

"Don't even think about it," Anita warns, her finger wiggling between us. "Can you honestly tell me you were in the right frame of mind to take care of another call if one had come through?"

I don't need to respond. Anita does it for me.

"No, you weren't. And that wouldn't have been fair to that family, would it have? Seriously . . . rookie mistakes. You can't save everyone, and we all play a role, you know that."

There are so many objections I can give right now, they're sitting right there, on the edge of my tongue, but I swallow them back. Anita's right. So are Lois and Lindsay. Everything they've said is legit and justified.

They're upset with me, I get it. But no more than I am with myself.

Truth be told, I'm not upset. I'm furious. Furious and guilt-ridden, and sick to my stomach knowing how close I was and still I'd failed.

Failed. Plain and simple. How am I going to explain that to John and Liz? How do I look them in the eye and tell them I might have passed their daughter on the road, trailed her and then lost her?

I think it's the unknown that hurts the most, like a ball coiled in chains, heavy, massive and crushing. So many "what ifs" flash through my mind, play with my heart.

From the day Jess went missing, I've been on the sidelines, playing the waiting game. Waiting for the nightmare to end. Waiting for someone to find my sister. Waiting for life to return to normal. Then waiting for others to realize I was still there, still present, still hurting.

I still wait, but with a different outlook. Now I wait with others, understanding their impatience, their pain, their fears. I stay with them while they wait for someone else to provide information, to tell them if their loved ones are still alive.

Today, by a stroke of . . . luck maybe . . . I was in the position to do more than just be on the sidelines. I acted. I took the call, went to interview the witness and even passed Gabrielle . . . all moments that provided opportunity for action.

An opportunity I screwed up.

I try calling Jamie again, needing to hear his voice.

"Are you okay?" he says once he answers. "Do what you need to do. We'll be here when you get home." He doesn't sound upset. Or concerned. Or . . . anything actually. His voice is void of emotion. Damn it.

One more thing to add to my list of mess-ups for today.

"Jamie, I'm sorry. I really am. I'm on my way to John and Liz's and not sure how long I'll be."

The timing of everything now is dependent on Detective Lindsay and how long it takes him to track the vehicle.

"I already called about the pup." A thread of expectancy is woven through his voice.

I give a long, regretful sigh. There are times when my job, the passion and concern I carry for the families interfere with my own family life.

This is when my father would tell me I need to find a balance between priorities and boundaries.

"They said we could come anytime before nine tonight," Jamie continues, but this time there's a slight change to his voice, a softening.

"I really am sorry."

There's a brief pause, enough for me to feel even more uncomfortable than I already do.

"Flynn knows something's up," Jamie says. "Your mom told him not to go in her room today, so of course, that's exactly what he did."

"Of course he did." I can almost picture it too. He'd wait till Mom was busy doing something else, then he'd do the exact opposite of what he was told. He knows all her hiding spots.

"Right. Well, your mom had a bag of supplies she'd picked up for the puppy in her closet. I caught our son sneaking out of your mom's room with a bright smile on his face." Jamie starts to laugh, which has me chuckling as well.

I want to say more, but then I notice the time. "I'll make this work, I promise. Hopefully we hear from Lindsay soon, but if not, they know I'm only a phone call away."

"Do what you need to do." That time, when he says it, there's understanding there.

"Monique and Pastor Jeremy should be joining me, so it's not like I'll be alone." Which also means I might just be in the way. I don't tell Jamie that I'm supposed to be taking time off or just how much trouble I got into. I'll save that for later.

"PJ? He's at the hospital. Or was, at least."

"How do you know?"

"We were supposed to meet up for lunch today, but he canceled last minute. One of his small group members had emergency surgery and apparently is all alone."

"Which explains why he wasn't answering his phone earlier." Jeremy has a tendency to place his phone on silent when he's at the hospital.

"I'm sure Anita's been able to get a hold of him. I'll call when I'm leaving."

The first thing I notice when I pull into the Manderas' driveway is that I'm alone. Neither Monique nor Pastor Jeremy has arrived.

Liz is waiting for me, standing at her front window, holding one edge of the curtain back.

There's a sick feeling nestled in the pit of my stomach, churning, burning its way up my throat. It strengthens with each second that passes as Liz stands in that window, staring out at me.

How do I do this? How do I admit what I've done? I hope they can understand and forgive me.

John appears beside his wife. He's wrapped one arm around her and then beckons me in.

They know why I'm here. I know Anita would have told them, not just that there was a sighting but that Gabrielle called for help.

I also know they're going to have high expectations, believing we are close to bringing her home.

I doubt Anita would have explained how I'd broken protocol. She'll leave that up to me and I don't blame her. They deserve to know the truth and they deserve to hear it from me. I picture John's face when I explain my actions, when I tell him of my U-turn and stupid driving — he'll know. He'll know I tipped off Gabrielle's kidnapper.

He'll know I'm the one to blame if she's not found.

The front door opens, light spilling out onto their front porch.

I do the only thing I can. I brave a wide smile and struggle not to throw up in their front garden.

CHAPTER 44

ANGEL

The pain vibrated throughout her body, starting at the soles of her feet and ending in a band around her forehead. Every inch of her skin flamed with it, ached, burned, throbbed, hammered until the rhythm drowned out Sam's muffled cries.

She couldn't see him, but she felt him. Curled up tight around her. Every slight movement of his body against her chest and stomach ricocheted through her, like a pinball machine. Despite how painful it was, despite the tears that poured down her face, she held onto him as tight as she could, unable and unwilling to let go.

She didn't know where Drew was. She just knew he wasn't here, in the room with her. That was all that mattered. He wasn't here, which meant Sam was safe . . . for now.

The ferocity of his rage had been a shock.

She'd both seen and experienced his anger in the past. She knew what to expect with his rage. But today . . . today, the violence in his eyes, in the powerful kicks and punches of his legs and arms, spoke of death.

She'd never been more afraid for her life than she'd been today.

"Shhh." She tried to comfort Sam, but the simple hushing sound came out in a slur around her swollen tongue and lips. Drew's kicks had landed on her jaw a few times, along with her cheeks, nose and forehead.

She'd done everything she could to protect Sam from the brunt of Drew's anger. She'd wrapped herself around his tiny body, sheltering him as much as she could.

She might have shielded her son's body from the punishment, but not his soul. He wept like he was broken and that in turn, broke her.

Drew had driven home like a madman. The minute he noticed that one vehicle did a U-turn he became paranoid. He forced both her and Sam to crouch on the truck floor, the hammer he'd hit her with earlier, close by. While Sam shook like a leaf from being scared, she watched Drew.

His grip on the wheel tightened.

Sweat formed on his forehead.

He bit his lower lip until it bled.

His gaze darted back and forth from the driver's rear-view mirror to the side of the door.

They swerved, sped, passed other vehicles.

They made a few sharp turns, ones where the tires spun, gravel peppered the truck and they almost went into the ditch a few times.

When they'd made it back to the farmhouse, he'd dragged her from the truck to the ground, not letting her get a footing, her legs rubbed raw from the gravel.

She shouted for Sam to stay outside.

Drew threw her to the floor once they were in the house. She scrambled as fast as she could, half crawling on the floor, pushing herself forward with her shoes. Every inch was a victory, until she reached the main living area and looked behind her.

He arched over her, hunched like a monster from her childhood nightmares.

Words to beg for her freedom, for her safety, hovered on the edge of her tongue, but she knew they'd fall on deaf ears.

Kick. Punch. Guttural groans and grating cries. Her body a punching bag for the monster above. Her only thought to protect her children, to take the wrath, the rage, to be his focus. All for her children: the one outside and the one in her womb.

Then she heard the chilling sound that stopped everything.

Sam's scream.

Through slitted lids from swelling eyes, she caught the way her son launched at Drew, clinging to the leg raised in a kick.

She watched, helpless as he turned his body from her toward Sam.

She heard garbled threats no child should hear.

She screamed. With every ounce of energy left in her body, she screamed for Sam to run.

Not to her. From her. From him. From danger.

Sam ran toward her instead, curled up in front of her. His back exposed to the monster no longer recognizable.

Somehow, someway, she was able to move her arms to wrap around her son, cocooning him with her own body, protecting him from the man he knew as father.

That's when the kicking to her back began.

That's when she knew she could no longer protect the three of them.

She'd held on to a sliver of consciousness, until the stomping of Drew's footsteps across the kitchen floor, followed by the slam of the screen door, brought about a hush in the house.

She tried to comfort Sam, tell him they were okay, they were going to be okay, but the words wouldn't come.

CHAPTER 45

DETECTIVE MERI AMBER

I've been in Paisley Valley long enough to know that on the surface, it's too smooth.

The currents that flow beneath the facade, they're stronger than they should be, especially with headquarters like CHILD here.

I've done some research on Detective Lindsay and the team he surrounds himself with — primarily those he works with at CHILD.

His team reminds me of a basket of fresh-picked apples: sometimes you gotta look beyond the apples on the top, digging down deep, toward the bottom, to see if the batch is good or not. Who wants to buy a basket of apples when most of them are rotten?

Not saying Detective Lindsay is a bad apple. But this Bryan Powers dude was under his nose and he had no idea.

My finger taps on a notebook I've been scribbling in, trying to get my thoughts in order.

Something about Monique seems off to me. I looked into her, but there's nothing shouting *bad apple*. She's received some recommendations for acts of service, helped a lot of kids, and seems to be using her talents to help families now with CHILD.

There's something there, though. I know it. I can feel it.

The Tinders are straight-up good people. If the husband has a taste for buying girls, I can't see it. What I can see is him being an informant. One hundred percent.

Paige is one of those *trying-too-hard* types, she carries a lot on her shoulders. I get it. We're cut from the same cloth. We're both doing what we can to help others. If I were here longer, and under different circumstances, we'd probably get along.

I've spent most of the day digging as deep as I can to get some answers.

I believe I'm being fed a string of false information and all of it leads me back to the real identity of Rawlings.

That crap about how many Rawlingses there are doesn't add up, and I think Lindsay knows it. So why not be honest with me?

Because I'm not on his team. He doesn't know me from Eve and as far as he's concerned, the apple I'm offering is rotten to the core.

I get it.

Doesn't mean I'm going to stop digging, though.

In my notebook, I put a star beside Pastor Jeremy Rowland. He's in his late thirties, single and unattached. Everyone I've talked to loves him, thinks he's a great guy, and had absolutely nothing bad to say about him.

That's probably why he got the star. I don't trust people like him.

My phone pings with a new message. I'd put out some feelers back at home, requesting some background info on a few people, totally off the books. It was a long shot, but the worse that can happen is I get nothing.

I open the file that was sent and scan it. Nothing really stands out, which is disappointing. As expected, everyone on my list checks out. And then I get to the footnote and what I read there surprises me.

Go figure.

CHAPTER 46

PAIGE

The Manderas' house is full of photos. Every wall is plastered with smiling, happy faces of their children and their one grandchild.

Every time I visit, it seems like one or two new frames have been added to a wall or tabletop.

"You're looking for this one." Liz's voice is a little shaky as she takes my hand and leads me to the fireplace, picking up a photo of Debbie, their oldest daughter, and her three-year-old son, Jordan.

"I can't believe how old he's getting."

A real smile appears for Liz. "I know. We were planning on heading back down there in a few months, stay for a month or so . . ." She looks back to John. "That might change, though, now."

I give Liz a side squeeze, my main focus being on all the photos on the mantel. I almost feel a little guilty that I don't have this many of Flynn around the house. Or maybe that's a grandmother thing, but if that's the case . . . why doesn't Mom put up more?

No, that's not fair. Our fridge is covered in pictures Flynn draws for her. And . . . she has more photos of him on her phone than I do.

But here, there are so many. Not just of Liz and John, but of Debbie and her family. Gabrielle is there too, in the midst, a shadow of happier times.

She's the ghost of their past, a past revealing one hard truth: a family who hasn't moved on.

A part of me mourns for Gabrielle, imagining how she'll feel the moment she walks into the house and sees that life continued without her.

"Soon I hope to add Gabrielle and her son. I can't wait for those." The tremble in the older woman's voice fills the quiet between us. I almost take a step back, startled at how clearly Liz read my thoughts.

Discreetly, I check my phone to see if there are any updates. Nothing.

I swallow hard, pushing away the lingering self-reproach. If I hadn't gotten involved, if I hadn't tried to follow the truck, maybe, just maybe . . .

Maybe I wouldn't have scared the kidnapper off. Deep down I know he saw me weaving in and out, trying to pass, trying to stay close to him. I ran him off and, because of me, the likelihood of finding Gabrielle alive is minimal.

Ding-dong.

The three of us turn in unison toward the door, our collective breaths expanding until the room is full of hushed anticipation.

No one moves.

Ding-dong.

"I'll get that." John's voice is a little rough.

Liz reaches for my hand and squeezes tight.

I can't even imagine what is going through their heads right now.

John's gravelly voice is met with a softer, sweeter one. Monique is here.

I stay where I am, giving Liz time to be enfolded in Monique's hug. The two women speak to one another in hushed voices while John hovers, always within hand-holding distance of his wife.

"Paige, could we chat for a minute?" Monique asks after a bit.

My stomach drops like an anchor in the middle of a fishing expedition. Monique's smile disappears.

"I'll go make us some tea," Liz offers.

I follow Monique out the front door, closing it softly behind me. She continues down the front steps until she's a distance away. Dang it — that means she doesn't want John or Liz to overhear us.

Monique looks up into the evening sky, her hands jammed into the pockets of her light sweater.

I mirror her stance.

Do I start the conversation? Do I admit my screwup and save Monique from telling me how disappointed she is in me? Do I attempt to explain myself?

No. I stay silent.

I deserve whatever harsh judgment Monique tosses my way. I'm already neck deep in the mire, having slung enough dung my own way, what would one more shovel hurt? Especially from someone I admire.

"How are you doing?"

My mouth gapes open. How am I doing? Was that what she just said?

"I can't imagine what you're feeling right now. Today had to have been rough. What can I do to help?" There's no reproach in Monique's voice. No condemnation or judgment. Just . . . concern.

That throws me for a loop.

Tears well in my eyes and my lips tremble as I struggle to form words.

Monique steps toward me, arms reaching out. I step back.

A hug from her is the last thing I need right now. It'll send me over the edge and I'll be no good to John and Liz.

"Guilty as hell," I manage to croak. "So much guilt, it's a shackle around my neck, pulling me down into a grave I dug on my own."

Monique's features soften into a mixture of pity and understanding.

I hate that look. I don't need her pity.

"Go ahead," I say, "tell me how stupid I was to break protocol, that I did more harm than good, that I'm too involved and it's not healthy. There's nothing you can say that I haven't heard or said to myself."

I stare at the cracks in the walkway beneath our feet, cracks full of weeds powerful enough to destroy all the hard work the Manderas placed into building a welcoming path to their home.

Funny how weeds contain so much power.

"I'm sorry." Monique surprises me once again. "As soon as I heard, my heart went out to you, imagining what you must have felt. To take the call, to be so close . . . I think that was your first time, wasn't it?"

"That wasn't my first time taking a sighting call." She knows this.

"It was your first call for a family you've been taking care of for so many years."

Ahh. True. I let that sink in.

"I remember my first call. I was a wreck, felt utterly helpless." Monique shakes her head in memory. "But you weren't. You were in the right place at the right time. I understand why you did what you did. There's no reproach. No judgment."

There's a *but* there, I know it. I can feel it. So I wait, because I know Monique . . . she never shies away from the truth. Not with me at least, or when it comes to me.

She doesn't say it.

"Would you have done the same?" I ask, trying to keep the surprise from my voice. Please let her say yes. Please let her . . .

"Hell no."

So much for that.

My phone buzzes in my pocket and when I pull it out, I see it's Pastor Jeremy. It's about time. I hold it out for Monique to see before answering the call.

"Got your messages," he says. "Is everything okay?"

"I should be asking that about you. You're a hard man to track down."

"Yeah, sorry about that. You know I turn my phone off when I'm at the hospital, right?" He sounds hurried, rushed, his voice echoing slightly like he's speed walking down a hallway. He must still be at the hospital.

"Are you with John and Liz now?" he asks.

"We both just got here. Monique is with me."

"Ah, good. Okay, yeah, that's good." He sounds like he's trying to work out something in his head. "I'm not sure I can get away. I'll try, though. Hey, would you mind passing me to Monique?"

Without saying a word, I hand the phone over and watch intently as Monique gives Jeremy one-word answers to seemingly long questions.

"He says to keep him appraised if Lindsay calls, and that he'll call John and Liz as soon as he has a spare moment." Monique hands the phone back, concern bringing out the worry lines on her face.

"Did he sound okay to you?" I ask. I take a cursory look to make sure Lindsay hasn't tried to contact me during that call.

Still nothing. Why hasn't he called by now? He should have an update or something . . .

"Jeremy?" She shrugs. "He sounds fine. Busy, overwhelmed, like he's being pulled in too many directions, but . . . I think that's normal."

Really? She calls that normal? I can't shake the feeling I'm being left out of something, something I should know about. I hate being left in the dark.

Monique turns from me, obviously done with that direction of conversation. She stares at the house. "Have you thought about what you want to tell John and Liz? About today?"

Have I thought about it? What kind of question is that?

"Ladies? Tea is ready." Liz opens the door and calls us in.

John paces back and forth across the area rug as we enter. He's a powder keg and I'm holding the lighter. He wants details but he's being too polite and not demanding them.

I'm drawing this out and that's not fair.

"During lunch today, a call came into the call center." The only place to start is at the beginning.

"Lunch?" Liz carefully lowers her teacup. "That was hours ago."

Almost six hours now, to be exact.

"I took the call." I rub my forehead, my heart heavy with words I'm struggling to say. The truth is always the right call, the best way to handle situations, but how much of the truth, how much of my admission is helpful rather than hurtful?

That's what I'm struggling with.

John sits beside his wife, their hands clasped tight while I explain everything that happened, including how I'd trailed after the truck.

Both of them say nothing. They don't make a sound, they don't ask a question, they just . . . listen.

I can't stop looking at the photo of Gabrielle on the table behind Liz. She's watching me, Gabrielle. Judging. A ghost hovering, reaching across with foul fingers, waiting to be acknowledged.

"Gabrielle . . ." I pause, unable to break eye contact with the framed photo. "I . . ."

Knock-knock-knock.

Liz gasps from the unexpected interruption. John stands and rushes to the door.

It's Detective Lindsay. Thank God.

It's hard to hear what's being said between the two men, but from the slump in John's shoulders, it's not good.

Oh no.

"Paige, Monique, can I speak to you both for a moment?" Lindsay asks, his voice full of expectation and urgency.

He leads us out to the front porch and waits until John stops hovering.

"Please tell me you found the truck," I ask, not bothering to wait for him to speak first.

He holds up a hand, stopping me from saying more.

My fingers bunch together until they form a fist.

"We haven't located the truck, but I've got people on it. We'll find it, I'm sure of it. That's not why I'm here, though." He looks off into the distance.

"What is it?" Monique says the words I can't get past my throat.

"We've got a Jane Doe." He spits the words out of his mouth with enough force that I take a step back. He sounds . . . angry, aggravated, annoyed and . . . something else I can't place my finger on.

I am not going to ask if the woman is dead, if that's why he calls her a Jane Doe. A knot of unmistakable dread pieces together inside me.

Please don't let it be Gabrielle. If she's dead because of me . . .

"A driver spotted her on the side of the road just out of town and called it in. There's no identification" — he turns toward me as he says this — "but she's at the hospital."

I'm nodding, an instinctual response, but his words haven't quite registered.

"She has a son." He bomb-drops that info without saying more.

"A child." My inhale is sharp and hits the back of my throat. I glance over to the front window and catch the shadow of someone standing close.

I don't blame John.

"You think it's Gabrielle, don't you?" The words carried barely any weight on my breath, but they're loud enough to be heard.

No one moves. No one says a word. I barely even breathe.

Finally Lindsay nods.

A light streams out from the house as the door opens. Liz stands there, arms wrapped tight around her body.

"Have you found my daughter? Is that why you're here?"

CHAPTER 47

The red-and-white rotating light from a parked ambulance at the entrance of the emergency bay illuminates the muted gray walls of the hospital. John and Elizabeth are inside, along with Monique and Detective Lindsay.

I stay where I am. Outside. I told them to go ahead, that I'd catch up, but I wanted to check in with home first.

That's just an excuse.

The reality is, I'm too chicken to walk inside those doors.

I'm afraid to see Gabrielle. I'm afraid to look at the battered face of the woman I've been searching for and know that final beating is my fault.

"Do you need me there?" Jamie asks after I update him on what's happened. "Say the word . . . oh wait . . ." He stops before I hear a muffled conversation between him and Mom. "Sarah's says she's on her way, that Liz doesn't need to be alone right now. Guess that means I'll stay with Flynn."

I would really rather he be the one that came, but I understand why Mom insists it's her.

"You sound like you're outside," Jamie said. There's a slam, probably from the front screen door as he heads out onto the porch.

"Yep."

"How come? I thought you might have been inside, with the others?"

I can't answer.

"You should be there, Paige." He knows me so well. "If that really is Gabrielle, you need to be in there."

"I know, I just . . . can't. It's like my brain won't let my feet move, no matter how much my heart wants it."

"Why? What's stopping you?"

I stare up into the darkening sky, noticing the first twinkling of lights from the stars. "Me."

He makes a *hmmmm* type noise.

"I know, it's stupid." My one shoulder lifts in a shrug and I wait for him to agree.

He doesn't. In fact, he says nothing.

"For one . . . there's a part of me that is jealous." Gah, I really hate admitting this. "And a little bit resentful, that it's not Jess and I really, really wish it were. I know that makes me a bad person, but . . ."

"And the other reason?"

Leave it to Jamie to accept my ugly parts without hesitation.

"What if it is Gabrielle and she's seriously hurt? What if it's my fault that she was beaten and left for dead?"

I realize how ridiculous I sound the moment I speak these fears out.

Whoever it is in there — Gabrielle or someone else — at least that woman is alive. Battered, broken, but alive and that's what matters. I have to focus on that and only that.

I take a step forward, breaking away from the self-imagined cement I'd been stuck in.

"I'll text Mom what floor we're on and I'll let Liz know she's coming. Tell her to bring coffee. I doubt the cafeteria has fresh coffee at this time."

"I love you," Jamie says before we hang up. I say it back. but I'm not sure he heard.

There's a silence to the main floor of the hospital that I'm not used to, especially at this time of night. Marianne Kirby sits at the intake desk and motions me over.

"I can't believe it," she says, her hands fluttering as she speaks. "No one here can. What a week for you to go through."

I'm not sure if I'm supposed to smile or appear grim. Marianne is excited, and even those behind the desk with her all hold the same look. They all smile.

"Have you seen her?" I ask. "Any news?"

Marianne's fingers dance along a keyboard. "She's in surgery still." She looks like she's about to say more, but there are too many people around and anything said now would just be gossip fodder.

"I'm going to go wait with the family. Can you page Pastor Jeremy for me? Ask him to join us when he can?"

"Sure can. I haven't seen him, but that doesn't mean anything." Marianne scribbles something down on a notepad. "I'm about to head out on break, so I've left a note in case he calls in when I'm not around." The smile she gives is full of that same excitement from before. "I know the circumstances aren't the best, but my heart just feels full knowing the Manderas have their daughter back, you know?" Hand to chest, tears form in Marianne's eyes.

I swallow back a ball of emotion. I will not lose it right now. I will not lose it right now.

Once I do, the tears will never end.

Upstairs, my shoes squeak on the floor as I meet up with Monique who waits just outside the surgery waiting room.

"I was beginning to wonder," Monique says. "Everything okay?"

"Just had to take a breather."

Monique studies me as if trying to see the lie behind the words.

There's no lie.

Finally, Monique nods, appearing satisfied. "You know none of this is your fault, right? In fact, it might be because of you that Gabrielle was found."

I tear my gaze from Monique's and look around. I have a hard time with praise. Just like I have a hard time being here, in the hospital.

I don't think I'll ever like being here, no matter the reason.

Empty hall. Bare walls. Cold and sterile, with a cleaning smell I'll never get used to. I hate this floor. Hate these walls and doors and that waiting room, where everyone . . . waits.

The last time I'd been in that room was when my father was in surgery for his heart. A surgery he didn't survive.

It hurts to inhale. Hurts to breathe. Hurts to push the past behind and face the present.

Monique checks her phone, lips pursed. "You didn't see Pastor Jeremy at all, did you? I've sent him a few texts to let him know where we are. He has me on read but he's not responding."

I check my own phone in case he's texted me. "I asked Marianne to page him."

"Good call. He must be busy." She lets out a sigh, one that carries the weight of her disappointment.

"Mom's on her way." From the way Monique's brows lift, that surprises her.

"To support Liz," I add quickly, as clarification.

"I would think here, especially here" — she gestures around — "would be the last place she'd want to be."

My chest still aches from memories I've been trying to ignore since walking in here.

"Guess today is a day for surprises."

Give her time, she'll find herself again. Those had been Dad's words, words that may be coming true. There's a huge part of me that hopes this is the case, that maybe, just maybe there's a chance for us to heal as well.

By the time Mom arrives, with a tray full of coffees, I still haven't managed to step into the waiting room. It's silly, I know, allowing such a small area to hold so much sway, but . . . it's there, and I'm here, on the other side of the hallway, John by my side.

Him being here, with me, it reminds me of Dad. It's something he would have done. The ache for him intensifies, growing stronger until it crawls along my skin.

"John, I hope you don't mind me showing up." Mom gives his arm a squeeze. "I know Paige and Monique are here, but I thought Liz could use a bit more support, and you a good cup of coffee."

"Appreciate it." He lifts the to-go cup in a salute.

"How are you?" Mom asks after giving Liz a slight wave. "I can't imagine how you guys are holding up."

"I'm fine." John clears his throat. "I just . . . just want to see her. See for myself it's her." He swallows hard.

"Any news yet?" This time the question is directed to me. I give a small shake of my head.

The surgery wing door opens. A doctor walks out and heads toward us. The look on his face is grim, not giving any of us much hope.

Mom reaches for my hand and squeezes.

"Mr. Mandera? I'm Doctor Manuel. I apologize for making you wait, but we needed to confirm my patient's identity first."

"It's Gabrielle, isn't it?" Liz is there, in the doorway of the waiting room. "Please tell me that's my daughter."

Slowly, a fraction of an inch at a time, Dr Manuel's lips move in an upward motion until they resemble a smile.

"Yes, it's Gabrielle. She has several broken ribs, dislocated shoulder, a concussion and her body is badly bruised all over, but she'll be okay, physically."

"What about the boy?" John's voice breaks, his emotions teetering on the edge.

"Her son is okay as well. Some bruising on his skin from being manhandled, but he's okay. He's with her now. We've set them up in a room so they can be together. She asked for you."

Liz gasps. John pulls her into his arms and for a second neither one makes a sound.

A nurse appears and leads them away.

The rest of us hang back. The cries of reconnection fill the void between the three of us as we listen to the family reunion.

Everyone has tears.

Some reunions can be hard.

But after ten years, the only hard part about this reunion is having to stand on the sidelines.

Mom clasps her fisted hands tight to her chest as she stares at the partially closed door. Every feeling she's ever felt, every thought and yearning is there, clear as glass, on her face.

I watch as Mom gives herself the freedom to believe, even if just for a moment, that could be her in that room, seeing her own daughter after so many years. It's there in the whisper of her smile, in the trail of tears on her weathered skin, in the light of her gaze.

And then it's gone.

"I'll head home," she says, the words edged with sorrow. "I'll call Liz tomorrow, gather things for the little one. I think" — she glances my way — "we could use some of Flynn's clothes he's outgrown?"

Monique's the one who speaks up.

"That's a great idea, Sarah. How about I send a list home with Paige before she leaves? We also have supplies at the office that we can use for both Gabrielle and her son."

Monique's role now is to be a liaison between CHILD and the Manderas. She's the one who will be there for Gabrielle, provide support, get her the help that both she and her son will need in the coming days, weeks and even months.

Not me.

That hurts, but I have to push my own feelings to the side. This isn't about me. It's not even about Monique. It's about Gabrielle, it's about John and Elizabeth and it's about that little boy, too.

Mom hesitates, like she knows something's wrong. There is, but nothing she'd understand, not right now. I'll explain my mistakes later.

"Maybe one day it'll be our turn." The words, almost whispered, shock me more than I'll ever admit. Is she saying she's not giving up hope?

She turns and the sound of her footsteps echoes along the quiet hallway as she walks away.

"Honey, are you going to be okay?" Monique's gaze is full of pity and concern, two emotions I do not need right at that moment.

Am I okay? No. But, this moment isn't about me and I have to remember that.

"Do you mind if I stay for a bit? I know technically I shouldn't but . . ."

Monique looks like she's about to say something but stops when John appears at the door.

CHAPTER 48

"She wants to tell you what happened, while her son is sleeping. Come in." He opens the door and moves to give room for us to walk past.

I thought I was ready to see Gabrielle face to face. It's not my first time talking to a victim, listening to them retell their story, but it is the first time I feel personally responsible for what's happened to them.

I barely hold back my gasp when I step into the room.

Gabrielle is a mess. Her shaved head is wrapped in a bandage covering one ear. One eye is barely open, the other is swollen and circled in stitches. Her neck is covered in circular bruises, like she's been choked with a rope or chain.

"Honey," Elizabeth's hand hovers over Gabrielle's, not quite touching, but offering the same comfort. "This is Monique and Paige. Paige is the one who took the call, who alerted the police. She's the one who saved you."

Gabrielle turns my way. The look in her eye . . . it stops my heart for a moment. It's full of . . . nothing. No pain, no sadness, and especially no joy at being with her family again.

Despite her physical presence in the room, she's a shell, a ghost of the girl her parents remember.

"Hi, Gabrielle." I step close to the bed, my arms loose at my side. I glance over at the little boy asleep next to Gabrielle, the beds pushed close.

"Don't." The voice is low, guttural, with wisps of softness edged in.

I wince. Not from the word, but from the painful sound. I can't imagine what the woman lying there has been through.

"This is about me. Not my son, do you understand?" There's now an edge to Gabrielle's gaze, a sharpness in her voice.

"Of course." I turn my body so I'm completely focused on Gabrielle, honoring the woman's wishes.

"Gabrielle, do you mind if I record this?" Monique holds up her phone. "The only other person who will hear it is Detective Lindsay."

"Whatever."

Monique hits the record button on her phone and places it on the small table.

"I want to be clear about something," Gabrielle says, looking straight at me. "You didn't save me."

I force myself not to react. This woman deserves to be listened to.

"I wasn't saved. I was thrown away, like trash." Gabrielle's gaze is fixated on the blanket covering her body. Her body shivers, waves flowing from her shoulders down to her toes. Elizabeth immediately takes one of the blankets from the foot of the bed and unfolds it, covering her daughter with a gentleness full of love.

"You're not trash," Liz whispers.

"I'm useless, unwanted. Trash. He tried to kill me." Gabrielle swallows, pausing as she breathes through the pain. "But I don't live for myself anymore."

One breath. Two breaths. Gabrielle eventually raises her gaze. First to her father, then to her mother.

"He's a good boy. Hasn't been touched. I protected him, kept him safe." A fierceness shines through her eyes, her message clear and focused.

John nods, a deep dip of his head. A silent form of communication between father and daughter.

"I was grabbed, back then, something placed over my head so I couldn't see anything. Kept in a basement, in a room with other girls. Not many of them . . . they weren't all strong. Some died by suicide, some by the men who watched over us. Eventually, I was told if I wanted to be free, I had to earn my way out." She kept her head high, gaze steady, firm. She looks first to Monique, then to me.

"Yeah, I was sold for sex. That's what you want to hear, right?" The challenge is there.

My phone buzzes in my pocket. I ignore it. It buzzes again. Monique gives me a side eye.

"Sorry, excuse me," I whisper into the room as I turn slightly to see who is texting me.

What I read has me leaving the room without another word or glance.

I found her.

The number wasn't listed in my contacts, nor do I recognize it. But it's the next text that grabs my attention.

Come quick. I found your sister.

The next text was a shared location.

Who is this? I text back.

I glance around, my life completely shifted by two simple text messages. Life continues on as normal on the floor, nurses going from one room to another, a few doctors gathered together at the desk, their heads bowed, their attention focused on the charts in front of them.

Come quick.

Come quick? My sister is found?

My first instinct is to run as fast as I can to my car and drive to the location shared with me. But after today, and seeing Gabrielle, I've learned my lesson.

Before I take another step, I hit the phone icon and listen to the ring.

Ring. Ring. Ring.

Pick up. Pick up. Pick up.

"Paige?" The voice on the other end is hushed but familiar. I sigh with relief.

"Jeremy? Your number came up unlisted, what's going on?"

"I found your sister. Are you on your way? Please hurry." His voice is rushed and almost hard to make out.

"Did you call Lindsay? Is help on the way?"

"Yes, yes, just come, quick, please. I can't . . . I can't say more." He hangs up and the insistence in his voice, the rush of his words, they force me to run down the hall to the elevator.

I push the button and stare at the light indicator above the two doors. One is sitting on the L for Lobby. The other set of doors is at six, three floors above me. I hit the button again, my finger pressing once, twice, three times before I shove the phone into my purse and look around for the stairs.

I can stand here and wait for the aged elevator to finally make its way to me, or I can run down the stairs.

I replay Jeremy's words in my head. Something is off. Why hasn't Lindsay contacted me if he was called? Why was he so rushed?

I check the address and it's in the middle of nowhere.

My feet pound each step with a steady rhythm as I race down the stairs. Seven steps, turn, seven steps, now on the second floor.

Jeremy found my sister.

Another stair, another question, my mind racing as the need to know what's going on grows until it's all I can think about.

How did he find her?

Seven more steps, turn, now on the first floor.

My heart is racing, but I'm not sure if it's from rushing down these stairs or from the panic that's now the size of a grapefruit inside my lungs.

By the time I hit the lobby floor and pull the door open, my heart is racing so fast I'm almost dizzy.

I push my way through the crowded hallway and run to my car. Once I'm there, I remind myself to breathe and not be foolish.

First things first, I call Lindsay. He doesn't pick up.

"It's Paige. Jeremy just called and he found my sister. He told me to hurry. I'm sure you already know this but I wanted to let you know in case. He called from a different number than what I have listed. I'll send you the location. Please, please hurry." I end the call and then bring up Jamie's number.

He too doesn't answer. What is with people not answering my calls? I leave him a similar message as I drive down the streets and out to the highway, following the map directions.

The address is out in the middle of nowhere, about an hour away. What is going on? How did he find Jess?

I try to call him again, but it goes straight to voicemail with one of those automated messages coming up about the caller not being in service.

My fists pound the steering wheel in frustration. I pass the Paisley Valley welcome sign when my phone lights up with a call.

It's the same number Jeremy texted me from.

"I'm on my way," I say after hitting the speaker button.

"I sent you the wrong location. Where are you?" His voice is hushed.

"I just passed the town limits. The corn maze farm is up ahead."

"Good, good. Okay, take the second left after the maze. The one with the old truck stop. I'll stay on the line and direct you."

The one that's all boarded up? Why is he there?

"How did you find my sister? How do you know it's her?" I press down on the gas pedal, not caring about my speed, which feels way too slow.

"Turns out Bryan wasn't the only one in my Bible study group. I followed one of the other members here and came across a trade happening. I noticed Jess right away, she's your spitting image. You've got to hurry, though." There's a fumbling, then the sound of the phone dropping, followed by some yelling.

"Please tell me you called the police?"

I see the old stop ahead. The large parking lot has a few parked trailers, campers and other vehicles up for sale. But I don't see Jeremy's car or the police.

"Jeremy? Jeremy?" I'm yelling now.

"I'm here, I'm here. Sorry . . . almost got spotted."

"What? Are you in danger? Jeremy, what's going on? Why aren't the police there yet? I'm going to put you on hold and call Lindsay."

"Wait!" he yells out, stopping me. "Where are you? Is that you turning in?"

He can see me? Why can't I see him?

"Yes, I'm here. Where do I go?"

"Go around back. You'll see my car. Park there. I left the door open for you. But be quiet. They're parked over on the other side, close to the delivery bay, so you won't see them. I managed to get your sister away from them and she's with me, but she's in bad shape. Hurry, Paige."

I gun the car, taking the corner way too fast and almost fishtailing on the gravel. I see his car, just up ahead. I slam on the brakes once I'm beside him, shut the car off and throw open the door.

He's right. I don't see anyone else, but if what he says is true, then I'm not going to either. I can't believe he found my sister.

The door is left ajar just like he said. I slowly open it, wincing at the squeak.

It's as dark inside as it is outside.

"Jeremy?" I whisper the words, almost in a hiss. A hand grabs hold of my arm and I scream right before I'm slammed into someone's chest, my face pressed tight against their shirt.

Their hold is strong. The body I'm against is like steel. I struggle, desperate to get away, more scared than I've ever been. I'm suffocating, a hand against the back of my neck, fingers splayed against my skin, press hard, forcing my face tight to their chest, blocking all air.

I push. I kick. I attempt to scream but only get fabric in my mouth. I wedge my arms up, in front of me, palms out so I can push, but that doesn't work. There's something hard against my back, it's cold, solid, feels like a wall. I'm pressed against it, my arms now stuck between my body and whoever is holding me.

I can't breathe. I suck in air, but my mouth and nose are smushed tight.

I see lights, but they're behind my closed eyelids. I feel dizzy, woozy, my legs collapse, I can't breathe . . .

PRESENT DAY

CHAPTER 49

PAISLEY VALLEY HOSPITAL
3:00 p.m.

My son is here, in my arms, snuggled up as tight as he can be. One arm is wrapped around my waist, the other tight at my side. The weight of him hurts but it's a pain I'll happily bear.

We're alone. I listen as he sleeps, his body relaxed, and the tears I have been holding at bay tumble down my face with freedom.

He's safe.

Over and over I whisper how proud I am of him, for hiding, what a strong boy he was for remaining quiet, for staying safe.

He hasn't said a word, which doesn't worry me. The doctors say it could be a regression, but to give him time. He can have all the time in the world as far as I'm concerned.

When Monique returns, I can tell she's been crying.

She's carrying a tablet with her.

"I thought we would try something new. Since you can move your fingers, maybe you can type out some questions you have, or answer some of mine. It'll be slow but . . . better than blinking yes or no, right?" She attempts a brave smile.

I wish I could tell her she doesn't need to wear a mask for me. I'm the last person to judge her.

She positions the tablet beneath my fingers.

"Move your finger to the left or right so I know which letter you need, okay?"

Blink.

"First, I want you to know that the nurse from earlier won't be back. She left in a hurry and no one has been able to get in touch with her. But one of the officers did some digging and we believe she might be part of a sex trafficking ring here in Paisley Valley. I'm sure you're not familiar with anything that has been going on, but in the past week we've uncovered a cell and discovered a few surprises along the way. Your nurse has been added to the watch list."

I let a smile play with the corners of my lips. She's telling me that my son is safe, that I don't have to worry, and that's a good thing.

"There are also strict instructions that no one can enter your room after hours without an escort."

My smile grows.

"I would really like to contact your family, if that is okay with you."

I blink twice, but she doesn't notice. She's staring instead down at my fingers.

"I'm sure they would love to know you are safe and okay. I know you might believe otherwise, especially if you've been gone a long time, but that won't matter to them."

My smile disappears. I blink twice.

No.

Contacting my family is the last thing I want right now. They don't need this, my return, not right now.

"Can I ask why?"

What can I say that will convince her that I'm not the important one right now?

That's when it hits me. Sam, he's the one that matters. He's the only one that matters. Everything I've done since his birth has been to protect him. Which can only mean one thing.

It's a slow process, typing one letter at a time, but I do it.

I do it for Sam.

Find my sister.

Monique reads the words a few times before she looks at me.

"Who is your sister?"

I only need to type the first three letters of Paige's name before she gasps.

"Jessica?" Her hands cover her mouth in shock. "Are you Jessica?"

One slow nod and she drops into the chair beside me.

This wasn't the reaction I thought I'd get.

She stares at me, her head shaking, her mouth moving without words.

"Paige . . . Paige is your sister? She's been looking for you, did you know? She went out last night, because she got a call that you'd been found. Now we can't find her . . . You're Jessica . . ."

I don't know what else to say, what to do, so I stare at my son.

"Sam . . . he's beautiful," Monique says. "Paige has a son too, about the same age. His name is Flynn."

My sister has a son too? After so many years of pushing my family from my thoughts, of forcing them from my mind, of believing they considered me dead . . . I stare up at the ceiling, focusing on one small section, and stuff every single hope wanting to flare up, down.

I will not cry.

Monique pulls her phone out, types out a message.

"I'm letting Detective Lindsay know," she tells me.

Within seconds, her phone rings.

"She just told me. Yes, on the tablet . . . I know . . . Have you found Jeremy yet? Please tell me he . . . okay. Yes, I understand." She swallows hard before hanging up.

"Jessica, does the name Jeremy Rowland mean anything to you?"

Blink. Blink. I have no idea who that is.

She lets out a long breath. "Are you sure?"

Blink.

Her fingers send a message on her phone. Probably letting the cop know.

"The man who hurt you, who did this to you, out in that farmhouse, do you know his name?"

Blink.

If I tell, will they find him? If I tell, will we finally be safe?

Slowly I type out his name. Drew. The most vile name I know.

It takes her a bit to react. I watch as she inhales, holds her breath and slowly lets it out. She looks overwhelmed.

I then type out his last name. Rawlings.

Her eyes close. "Are you telling me it's Andrew Rawlings?" The name comes out in a whisper, like she can't believe what I just told her.

Andrew. I haven't heard that name in a long time. I hope never to hear it again.

CHAPTER 50

DETECTIVE MERI AMBER

Lindsay is wound up like a yo-yo and all it's going to take is one wrong word, action or even sound and he'll unstring.

"Tell me again." His demand is brusque.

I was on my way to the precinct when I saw him driving. I made a quick U-turn, honked like crazy and eventually got him pulled over into a parking lot.

We're now standing, between both our cars, his arms crisscrossed while I hold my notebook.

"It's all right here." I hand him what I wrote down, but he doesn't take it. He's focused on my face and I can tell he's trying to process what I've just told him.

"I don't have time for this, Amber. Paige has been missing for almost nineteen hours now."

And no one was out looking for her until ten hours ago, mainly because they all thought she'd been brought into the hospital. Talk about a clusterfuck.

"The man you know as Pastor Jeremy Rowland is really Andrew Jeremiah Rawlings, Jr. He was raised in Durham, a little over an hour away, a nowhere mining town" — I glance down at my notes — "by his grandmother, a Betty-Ann Rawlings, while his father, Andy, drove long haul."

"Andrew Rawlings?" Same question he asked me the last time too. How many times do I have to repeat the name?

"That's what I said."

A shadow of something I don't expect to see crosses his face. Betrayal. Over a name?

"So . . ." The word is drawled out. "He goes by his middle name and slightly changed his last. Legal?"

"I don't think so. In high school he was known as Drew Rawlings. Did some juvie, came out with a high school diploma and then made the change to Jeremy Rowland."

"Juvie?"

"Officially, records are sealed. Unofficially, he had a thing for petty theft."

Lindsay's head nods. "Got it. Keep going."

"Seems he got involved in a Bible study while in juvie, then kept at it when he got out. Bonded with the minister, saw him as a mentor. The guy travels to small towns and does home Bible study groups . . . sound familiar? He was the one who helped Jeremy get a theology diploma online. According to my partner, the minister is pretty chatty."

By now, Lindsay is rubbing the bridge of his nose.

"And your partner dug all this up for you?"

I can't tell if he's upset, surprised or happy for the information.

I give a slight shrug. "I've got a great team back home."

It goes without saying that whoever did the background check on Pastor Jeremy Rowland before he came on board to work with CHILD didn't look too far back.

"Didn't I tell you I'd look into Rawlings?" Now he's rubbing the whole of his face with the palm of his hand.

"Yeah, I'm not that great at letting things go. Sorry." Not really sorry, and I bet he knows that.

"So he changed his name . . . anything else?" There's a hidden fury intertwined with his words.

What am I missing?

"That's all we found. I figure it was a way to distance himself from his past. Other than that, he's an upstanding citizen and everyone loves him."

He snorts.

I'm totally missing something here.

I read through my notes again.

"I think his dad is the guy I'm looking for." I look in the direction of the hospital, where I want to head next. "My partner does too. He's put in a wellness request for the grandmother. The house is still in her name and there's no record of her death."

Lindsay leans his head back and arches his shoulders, resulting in a lot of loud cracks as he stretches.

His radio goes off and then his phone. He needs to be elsewhere and I'm only holding him up.

"Listen, I know this is low on your priority list right now. You need to find both Jeremy and Paige, I get it. But I think it's all tied together, in some sort of sick bow, that includes Paige's sister. I'd like to talk to her too, if that's okay."

When Lindsay doesn't respond, I take a step forward, ready to fight for this if needed.

"Jessica Fischer," he says, his tone stopping me from interrupting, "claims her abductor and abuser is none other than Drew Rawlings." The sigh he gives is deep, long and full of pain. "Otherwise, according to you, known as Pastor Jeremy Rowland."

Whoa. I didn't see that coming.

His radio goes off again. "Vehicle found, gray Hyundai Kona, back delivery bay of the old Pass Rite truck stop."

Lindsay straightens and grabs the radio. "Grey Kona? Plate ends in four-three-two?"

Crackle. "Yes, sir. Bay door wasn't closed properly."

"Damn it. I thought that place had been checked. Any word on the black ninety-four Ford Tempo?"

"Negative."

Lindsay whirls around and opens his door. "Coming?"

Am I coming? Hell, yes. I rush across and yank open the passenger door.

Nothing is said as he speeds out of the parking lot. His lights flare but the siren stays off as he makes his way of out town.

"How did I miss it?" He finally breaks the silence, his voice resembling the final echo in a mountain peak shout-out. "I had blinders on, but why?"

"You can't beat yourself up," I say. "Jessica might be mistaken, or, we've got the wrong guy. Pastor Jeremy—"

"His name is Drew," Lindsay interrupts, his voice ice cold and definite.

"He might be innocent when it comes to Paige." It's a weak argument, and I'm not sure why I'm offering it. I don't know the man and he doesn't deserve my support.

"They're twins," he says. "He's done with the one so he grabs the other? What I can't figure out is why? He had to know we'd find out, that she would tell someone about his call."

"How did you find Jessica?"

He rubs his face. "He texted Paige a location. It was in the middle of nowhere, about an hour away. That's when we found her. She was barely alive." He chokes up. This is hard for him.

I get that.

"I can't believe we didn't know it wasn't Paige. How could we not have known? He was there, at the hospital when she came in. No one wanted to give a positive identification till later, but he pointed out her tattoo. I should have looked. I should have noticed." He pounds the steering wheel with enough force that his radio shakes.

"You can't blame yourself."

"Like hell I can't."

I think about what he's just said. "What do you mean, he was there, at the hospital?" He wouldn't have dared . . . would he have?

"He was there. I don't know why. I had a uniform keep an eye on him because I wanted to find out what the hell happened, why he would call her and not me, and why he wasn't there at the farmhouse, but by the time I went to look for him, he'd disappeared."

There are so many holes in this story, I don't even know where to begin.

So I decide to start at the beginning and let Lindsay fill in what doesn't make sense.

A Jane Doe was brought into the hospital yesterday evening that was later identified as Gabrielle Mandera. Paige had received a phone call from Pastor Jeremy, aka Drew, somewhere between seven and eight o'clock. He tells her he's found Jessica and sends her the location. Paige then calls Lindsay, assuming he already knows. Lindsay doesn't answer the call, so Paige heads out.

Lindsay gets her message but the location she'd sent him wouldn't download. He tries to call her, but when she doesn't answer her phone, he goes into search-and-find mode. Thankfully Paige set her phone and computer to sync up, so all it took was Jamie to log into her laptop, forward the text messages to Lindsay and three hours later, they arrived at the farmhouse.

A woman was found in the main living room, broken, beaten and unconscious. She was airlifted to the hospital. Everyone assumed it was Paige. The good pastor was there and identified the tattoo on her wrist before somehow disappearing.

Now, no one can find him.

The woman brought into the hospital, the one they thought was Paige, is in fact her missing twin — Jessica Fischer. Not just that, but the man who held her hostage for years is the same man many people here in Paisley Valley consider a friend.

Then there's the nurse . . .

All the cockroaches are scurrying.

All of that means one thing: Paige is still missing.

"Why was he at the hospital?" Lindsay mutters.

I can think of several reasons. Guilt, assurance, curiosity . . . if he truly held Jessica Fischer captive for who knows how long, then he was testing his limits, to see what else he could get away with.

Or maybe he just wanted one last look.

One of the first things you learn as a cop is, most of the time, the perp is always a watcher when it comes to those first minutes on a scene.

"That the truck stop?" Stupid question since there are at least three squad cars with flashing lights surrounding the place.

"This place was checked earlier this afternoon. Either her car was missed or . . ." His lips tighten into a single line.

"Listen, I need you to do me a favor," he says, his hands tight around the steering wheel as he turns into the parking lot and drives around to the back.

"Anything. I know to stay in the background, but if there's something I can do . . ."

"Keep your eyes open. Anything seems off, or anyone . . ."

I know what's he asking. I also know how hard it is to ask for that kind of help. You never want to assume those you work with are dirty, but considering the week he's had, he's got to feel a bit off.

"You got it."

He pulls up beside some other cars and lumbers out of the car, his speed a lot slower than I'd expect from him. I stay in the car, just watching.

The delivery door is pulled up, revealing a car. Trunk and doors are open.

Someone approaches Lindsay, head shaking.

She's not in there.

I push my door open. Lindsay turns to me.

"What was that town called? The one he grew up in? Durham?"

"Yep." I know exactly what he's thinking.

CHAPTER 51

PAIGE
4:00 p.m.

I struggle to open my eyes. Every part of my body, from my eyelashes to the tips of my fingers feels heavy, like I'm weighed down by a blanket of bricks.

I'm lying on a mattress and my head aches. Things are hazy, blurry and unfamiliar. Where am I?

"You're safe." A familiar voice draws my attention.

I force my eyes open, blinking until things clear.

I'm in the middle of a room, and there's a cup of water on the floor to my side. The mattress I'm lying on is old, stained and smells . . . musty.

Pastor Jeremy sits against the wall in front of me, his knees pulled up close to his chest. His hair is disheveled, his head leaned back against the wall, his eyes are closed.

Feeling relief that I'm not alone, I try to sit up, but my ankles are bound together, along with my hands, with some sort of rope.

"Jeremy?" The words catch on my tongue, dry, rough and edged with a bittersweet aftertaste. I reach for the glass of water, my hold awkward as I bring it to my lips and take small sips.

"You're safe," he repeats. He won't look at me. Oh God, is he hurt? Has something happened?

"Are you okay?" The tremble in my voice is noticeable. I'm scared. I don't know where I am, why we are here, how we got here . . . my brain is fuzzy, a jumble of nonsense.

"What's the last thing you remember?" There's something . . . off about him.

"Were we drugged?" He must feel as bad as I do. How long has he been awake?

"You've been out for awhile. Feeling okay?" He eventually moves, rolling his head, stretching his back.

Feeling okay? No. My head is pounding, I feel like I've swallowed a cactus, and every single limb in my body moves like liquid metal — slow and heavy.

"Where are we?"

I think we're in a basement. The walls are gray, the only window is boarded up and there's a single light hanging above me. I twist around and see steps leading to a door. There's a metal shelving unit to the side with an assortment of packing boxes and cans.

"Jeremy, what's going on?" I wrestle to get into a seated position and that's when I realize my feet are not just tied together but they're anchored to a pipe in the ground.

"Jeremy?" I pull my legs, trying hard to not freak out but failing miserably.

"Jessica . . . where is my sister?" My words come out jumbled, tumbling over my sluggish tongue. My heart races as I struggle to make sense of what's going on.

"I'm sorry I've had to do this, Paige, I really am." He gives me one brief glance before looking away.

His words stop my struggling. "Do this?"

"I'm sure you're feeling a little dizzy. I had to drug you a few times to keep you under. Drink the water please, it'll help."

His voice . . . it's different. Deeper. Darker. Dangerous. The exact opposite of the Jeremy I know.

"You . . . drugged . . . me?"

"It was the only way to get you here." He says this so matter-of-fact, it scares me.

"Get me . . . where? Jeremy, where is my sister?" I have no idea what he is saying or why he's saying it, nothing is making sense.

"What do you remember?"

Remember? I . . . I remember being at the hospital. I remember his texts. I remember . . . he found my sister.

"Where is Jessica?" I try hard to swallow back my growing anxiety. I'm wound up, terrified, and I don't know why.

That's when I see it, resting by his feet. He has a gun.

He. Has. A. Gun.

"What have you done?" The words come out on the edge of my cry, my voice raised and laced with fear.

"I thought she was dead," he says. "I lost control." The air he lets out deflates his body. "I thought I could give her back, as a token. One for the other."

I tug at the rope, try to work my hands out, but it's tied pretty tight.

"Jeremy, please let me go," I beg.

He shakes his head. "I can't do that, Paige. I'm sorry."

He drops back to the floor and picks up the gun.

Everything in me stills. What do I do?

"Jeremy—"

"I thought I'd lost her and then I found her here, in the same spot you are right now. It was like God meant for us to be together. She was my gift." He turns the gun in his hands one way, then the other.

"I came here, to the place I swore I would never return to, because he said he was done. He swore he was. So I came." His gaze roams the room, and I see something resembling hatred settle into the sneer of his lips.

"He was antsy, rushed, like he couldn't wait for me to leave, even though we hadn't seen each other in years. That's when I knew. I knew he'd lied." His voice breaks. "When I saw her, she was barely alive and weighed like nothing. He let me take her, saying he couldn't do it. I think he was trying to tell me he couldn't kill her."

His gaze slides over to the shelving.

"He made me promise I'd take care of her."

He's scaring me. I'm trying so hard to remain still, to listen, to be docile.

He cocks his head. "Do you think you'll ever be able to forgive me? Do you think you'll ever be able to love me like she did?"

"Of course I love you. Why would I need to forgive you? For this?" I hold up my hands. "Just untie me, Jeremy. We'll figure everything out, I promise." His words play in my head, like puzzle pieces, shuffling to find their rightful place.

He glances over to the shelving. "There used to be fifteen boxes there."

I follow his gaze.

"I had to move them. Just in case they were ever found. I didn't want my Angel to be another box. I saved her. You might not agree with me, but I saved her."

"What angel?"

He points the gun toward me.

"Jeremy, where are we?" I need to get him talking. I need to figure out what's going on. I need him to stop talking in riddles.

"My childhood home."

"Why?"

He leans his head back against the wall, similar to the pose from earlier.

"This is where it all started. Seems fitting for it to end here."

My heart skips a few beats.

"Everything was perfect," he says. "Until yesterday. I should have turned around, taken her home. That was my mistake. Dad always said I'd make a mistake that would get me caught. Turns out he's right."

Turned around? Taken her home? Was he talking about Gabrielle? Is he confused?

"I saw you." His eyes open and he looks at me. "You passed me, on the road. I didn't think you saw me, I thought I got away, until you did that U-turn."

My breath catches in my throat as I inhale. That was him?

"You had Gabrielle?"

"What? No." A frown appears on his face. "That was a coincidence, her being found on the side of the road. I had nothing to do with Gabrielle." The way he says her name, it's with disgust.

"I wish you'd called me sooner. Then none of this would have happened. My Angel would still be mine. But I thought you saw me. I knew it was only a matter of time before Lindsay would find me. I thought I'd killed her. That stain would always be mine. I couldn't just leave them there. That's why I sent you the location. So you could find them."

Them? What is he talking about?

I shake my head, trying to clear it. More puzzle pieces have been added and I'm lost. I'm torn between staring at the gun and at his face.

"I thought I'd die without her and I contemplated taking my life" — he stares at the gun on the floor — "but I couldn't do that either. God would forgive me for being a killer, it says so in the Bible, but suicide? But how could I live without her? That's when I realized . . . I might not have my Angel, but you . . . you're an angel too."

Now he's staring at my wrist, the one with the tattoo.

What is he talking about? Who is this Angel if it's not Gabrielle?

It can't be my sister. He wouldn't do that. Bile rushes up my throat the longer he keeps his gaze focused on the angel wings inked into my skin.

"Your family would have one angel back. I could have the other." His smile stretches as a wistfulness enters his voice.

Has he gone crazy?

"I tried for so long to be good. I thought God would forgive me, that he'd let me have her because I did the right thing when I saved her. My father was going to kill her, but I saved her. She was my reward . . ."

"My sister" — it's hard to wrap my tongue around the words I need to say — "was your reward?" He can't be saying that, can he? "Is she . . . is my sister alive?" Has she been alive all these years and he knew? My whole body jerks backward as what he says hits me.

Oh God.

The smile on his face yanks my heart clear from my chest. His smile . . . it's not vindictive, it's not cynical or sinister. It's a sweet smile, a recognizable smile. It's one I see him give to others all the time. It's the smile that makes people trust him.

"Where is she? Where is Jess?" I struggle to free myself from the rope around my wrist, hating the coarse feel of it against my skin.

"At the hospital. Don't worry, your mom is probably there now. She's not alone. I saw them bring her in. And she's alive." He half turns away from me, his shoulders bowed. "I should have checked. All I've done is make mistakes. One after the other . . . all because I wanted to be nice. It was our anniversary and I wanted to do something nice for her. That was my first mistake."

Their anniversary? My stomach boils over and I'm throwing up. My head pounds, my throat is scorched from the bile and I wish I could block out his words.

He's talking about my sister like they had a relationship. How? I don't want to believe his words, I don't want to believe he could be that kind of man.

"Drink some water."

I reach for the glass of water, struggling to hold it with my hands tied so tight together, and drink half, the need to cleanse my mouth strong.

"Taking you wasn't a mistake, was it?" He directs the question to me, but I don't think he's expecting me to answer.

"I don't understand, Jeremy. When did you see her? Why did you send me the location to . . . where? Here?"

"Here? No, no. No one knows about here." His hands run though his hair in distress. "I sent you the text so they could find her. I knew eventually they'd find it on your phone, but by the time they did, we'd be long gone. No one knew you stopped at that old truck stop, though, right? How could they? I had you on the phone the whole time."

Any hopes of being found are squashed. My chest hurts as the air is syphoned out with his words.

"I waited until I knew they'd located her. You were drugged and would be out for a while, so I had time. Not much, because you had to tell Lindsay and Jamie I'd called, didn't you? Why did you have to do that? I thought you trusted me enough."

Trust? He's talking about trust? If I wasn't so scared, I'd be laughing. Tears billow in my eyes until the room swims in liquid. I blink them away. I don't know what to do or how to react but I do know I need to remain calm. Keep him talking.

Someone would eventually find me.

"I had some time to plan our getaway. I knew where we could go, even though going to him has always been a last resort for me. I swore I wanted nothing to do with my father after I rescued my Angel, but desperate times and all that. It was Jamie who told me they found a body at the farmhouse and that they thought it was you. They weren't sure where I was though, asked me to call him back." He *tsks* again. "That man of yours, he's a nice guy. A little too nice and a little too naive. Where did he think I was? Come on." He gives an eye roll and chuckles, while the tears continue to stream down my face at the thought of Jamie and Flynn and how scared they must be right now.

"Oh, don't worry. They still think you're alive. There's no way your sister is able to talk, not yet. With me being there, at the hospital, and identifying you, it gave us time to get away."

I search the room; there has to be something here to help me. A way out, a weapon I can use to protect myself. I can't trust him, this man I thought was my friend. My stomach rolls and turns with revulsion.

"Seeing her, though, that changed everything. I'm torn, Paige. So torn. You were in the back of the pickup, no one the wiser. If someone had looked in, they might have seen you behind my seat." His body deflates, leaving me really confused.

Who is this man?

"I thought about telling someone, of making up a story to explain why you'd been drugged. It's like I have two sides of me fighting against each other. Which one wins? The man who is more like my father than I want to admit, or the man who wanted to be better than him? I still don't know. I've already lost everything. I thought maybe you would . . . I don't know, be a replacement? My second chance? You once said you'd do anything, even give up your life, if it meant saving your sister. Did you mean it?"

I'd said that to him a long time ago, when I thought he was someone else, someone I could trust.

What is he asking of me? If I would willingly give myself to him in exchange for my sister? Is he delusional? Sick? Twisted? He has to be all those things. What kind of man can pretend to be kind and caring, all the while inserting himself into the family of the woman he . . . oh God, I can't even think of what he's done to her. To my sister.

My face is washed in tears. My sister is alive. She's alive and in the hospital.

And I'm . . . here. Kidnapped, bound and there's a gun in the room. Am I about to die? By a man I call friend?

"It was so easy to say she was you. She has the same tattoo, you know."

I look at the one on my wrist, the one he can't stop staring at.

"You . . . you showed me this design." The words taste bitter as I say them, they're chalky and full of disgust.

"I showed you your sister's wrist and you never knew."

I remember the day. My sister had been missing eight years. He showed me a photo one day, something he said he'd gotten online. I told him it was beautiful. Jessica and I used to say we'd get a matching tattoo when we were older, for our eighteenth birthday. We'd wanted to get angel wings with our birthdate written into the outline, because Dad called us his little angels in disguise.

He suggested I get the tattoo. He even forwarded me the photo.

"I hate you." The words fall off my tongue with no thought. It's a real, honest, feeling that's taken root in my heart. The more he speaks, the stronger the hatred.

"What is wrong with you?" The words continue to slip out, unintended.

He looks surprised at my question. "Wrong with me? You don't understand, do you? I found your sister on that same mattress. She was going to die if it weren't for me. I saved her." He pounded his chest with his free hand. "I. Saved. Her. You have no idea what my father is like. He's evil. An evil man with an evil heart."

"I don't care about your father."

"You should. You might meet him soon. He'll help me figure out this mess I've made for myself."

I tear my gaze from his.

"What are you going to do with me?" I'm so afraid he's not going to let me go.

"I don't know. When I found your sister, she was broken. You're not. I'll have to break you and I'm not sure I can." He shrugs, his tone uncertain. "All I keep doing is making mistakes. Maybe it's my subconscious tricking me, telling me it was time to turn myself in. I'd been so careful — no one knew about your sister, about me. Well, almost no one. Bryan knew and when he got arrested, I realized it was only a matter of time before he told about me."

He picks up the gun, holding it casually in his hand. Please don't let him point it toward me. Please, God. I can't look. I tear my gaze away and find myself staring down at the tattoo that has destroyed my life.

"I don't know what to do now, if I'm being honest. Keeping your sister . . . that was spur-of-the-moment. I was going to take her to the hospital, I was going to tell you, but then I couldn't. She filled something inside me, something I once thought broken. She's my Angel. I don't know what I'll do now, how I'm going to survive without her."

How can this be the same man I know? The same man I invited into our home? The same man I call friend? He's sick. He's disgusting. He's—

"Are you going to kill me?"

When I look up, the gun is once again aimed my way.

CHAPTER 52

DETECTIVE MERI AMBER

Lindsay has been nothing but a ball of tightly wound elastics ready to go off in different directions. The whole drive from Paisley Valley to this dinky nowhere town has been one question after another, followed by terse instructions to his team, followed by phone calls and text messages from Paige's family.

We've entered the silent phase, the phase just before all hell breaks loose, the phase where we internalize all thoughts and distractions and focus only on what's ahead.

Drew Rawlings' childhood home.

There's one lone police car sitting on the street, a sad attempt to barricade traffic.

"How did you find this again?"

"My team back at home did all the work," I remind him. Thank God they did. Not saying Lindsay's team couldn't have uncovered the house as well, but . . . considering they had no idea of the wolf masquerading as a gentle sheep farmer, it would have taken them far too long.

The house is run-down, old, a bungalow with a rotting front porch, weathered fence around the property and boarded up windows. There's an old shed located in the back and as we pull into the driveway, we see a green Ford pickup parked close to it.

Two other squad cars pull up to the building.

Lindsay gives me this look.

"I know, I know, stay in the background." Like I'm going to listen, but I get the need to have it be said.

I stay by the car and wait as they clear the shed and surrounding landscape.

I wait till they enter the house before I head toward the pickup.

I pull out gloves from a pocket and open the passenger side door.

His scent is what hits me first.

Grease, coffee and sweat.

A familiar scent from the first day when I'd arrived in Paisley Valley. I'd come out of the CHILD headquarters and bumped into someone. That someone must have been Drew Rawlings aka Pastor Jeremy.

What the hell? I was so close to him.

Keys are still in the ignition, bottle of water, half drunk, sits in the drink holder. A blanket, purse and needle are behind the seats, in the small cab.

He must have drugged her and hidden her back there, covered in a blanket, where no one would notice if he got stopped.

Where did he get the drugs? And what did he use?

A quick search finds a vial of ketamine, with a Paisley Valley Hospital sticker. He could have swiped it at any time he was in the hospital. From what I've been able to gather, he was there often.

A quick sweep through the glove compartment finds a box of bullets, napkins and a registration to Andrew Rawlings. I wonder if this is his father's vehicle or his. There are two bullets missing from the box.

Does Lindsay know he has a gun?

Someone comes out of the house and waves me over. "All clear, no sign of anyone inside."

No sign? Where are they then?

Lindsay is slamming through cupboard doors while barking out questions to anyone around them.

"We're missing something," he says when he finally notices me.

"What about the basement?"

"Nothing down there but dead mice and old canned goods. No one has lived here in years."

That doesn't make sense.

The truck is outside, with the keys still in the ignition. They have to be here.

"Mind if I take a look?"

"Yell if you find something." Lindsay leaves the kitchen and marches down the hallway to the bedrooms.

The house isn't very big. One floor, with a medium-size kitchen located in the back, a front living room, dining room and two bedrooms.

There's a long set of stairs leading down to the basement. A uniform is already down there, snapping photos. Looks like there's one bulb that hangs at the bottom of the stairs. The stairs creak beneath my feet and a shudder runs through my body, the feel of imagined spiders creeping over me.

I hate dank old basements.

Lindsay eventually joins me down here. "This feels off," I tell him. "Oh . . . I checked the truck. Box of bullets in the glove compartment with two shells missing." I follow him as he heads up the stairs and then out the side door.

He mutters something I can't hear, but I get the gist.

He motions me to follow him around the house. It's an older home, a cookie-cutter style from the early fifties.

"My grandma used to live in a house like this, when I was a kid. She always kicked us outside when we got too loud. We'd sometimes sneak back in through the wood chute," he says.

Wood chute? We head to the back of the house and he starts searching around the foundation.

"Got a window. All boarded up, like the others. This is where my grandpaps would toss down the wood and we kids would have to stack it. Paid us a dollar."

"You got paid for doing chores? Lucky."

He leaves my side and heads back into the house. I remain where I am. I hear my father's voice in my head: what's the scene telling you?

Rawlings' truck is here. Keys left in the ignition. No sign of anyone being in the house and there's no way he's hiding in the shed.

So where is he?

I shine my flashlight along the old dirty siding. There's one section that looks unsettled, there's a clear vertical line that's partially hidden by an old tree.

I step closer and hit something that looks like a rock with my foot. Then there's a swoosh sound and a hidden door opens.

I reach for my gun.

I hear Lindsay's voice off to the side.

There are steps leading down into a room. A room with an occupant in the middle of the floor, lying on a mattress.

Across from her is Drew Rawlings and the gun he points at Paige slowly edges up until it looks like it's going to point at me.

"Guess my decision has been made for me." His voice is hard to hear, along with the cry Paige utters.

What isn't hard to hear: the sound of a gunshot.

CHAPTER 53

PAISLEY VALLEY HOSPITAL
7:00 p.m.

My name is Jessica Fischer.

Not Angel. Not Sweetheart. Not Bitch or whore or dog.

I used to be called Jess. But that girl is dead and there will be no raising her from the grave, regardless of how miraculous my mother says my return is.

The man who gave me the name Angel, Drew Rawlings, will never hurt me or my son again. Those are the words Detective Lindsay is saying, words that I'm not sure I can believe.

Not yet.

My mother is here. She isn't saying much, crying a lot, and hovers way too close. She's not the woman I remember, but then, I'm not the girl she raised. I guess we've all changed.

My father is dead, only six months ago. I should feel sad, heartbroken that I missed him by mere months . . . but the truth is, I feel a little frozen inside, unsure of how I'm supposed to feel about any of this.

With one hand on the bed rail, my mother's grip is tight, knuckles white, and she is throwing question after question toward the tall detective.

He's answering as best he can.

His voice is smooth, his tone is commanding and my son can't keep his eyes off him. It probably helps that the man keeps looking at Sam and winking.

I've forgotten what it's like to have someone stand up for me. It's a nice feeling.

"Jessica." Detective Lindsay says my name, but it takes him a few times repeating it for me to realize he's talking to me. "I'm very sorry for everything that has happened. If there is anything I can do, I want you to know I'll do my best to make sure it happens."

I believe these words. He seems like a man of action, a man who likes to help others, others like me.

I give him a small smile and mouth *thank you.* I don't know what I need or what he can do for me.

"Jeremy . . . or whatever his name is, is going to rot in jail for what he's done, you promise?" My mother's voice shakes and I notice she's having a hard time looking at me. I don't blame her. I would have a hard time seeing myself in this bed too.

"Sarah, he will be paying for what he's done for a very long time. He's currently in surgery, but the shot in the knee has done a lot of damage." He pauses, looks my way, then down at the floor. "Not enough damage in my opinion," he mutters.

I want to know if there was an option to shoot him in the head and why that option wasn't taken, but I know I can't ask that.

Sam looks up at me. I can see the questions in his eyes and I wish I could answer them, but instead, I rest my head against his.

"Is there anything from the farmhouse you'd like me to retrieve? It's all evidence, but if there are any of Sam's toys? Or . . ."

Blink. Blink.

I want nothing from that farmhouse. I wish I could erase it completely from my head, except, to do that, I'd be erasing

Samuel and he's the only good that has come out of the last twelve years of my life.

I look to my mother and blink twice again.

Her fingers unwrap from around the bed rail and lightly touch mine, curling beneath the tips of my fingers.

"Sam will have more than enough new toys and clothes and anything else he needs," she says. There's something in her voice, something I recognize but I'm not sure how to process it or even if I want to. Her pitch is a little high, a little forced, like she's trying to make up for the years I was gone.

I wonder how long it will take her to realize she has nothing to make up for. That I'm not the same girl she raised. That mothering me isn't going to be an easy task.

I'm not sure she's up for it. I'm not sure I'm ready for it, either. I'm willing to try, though, and I hope she is too.

She's already told Sam about Flynn, my nephew. Having someone else to play with will be a good thing. I hope my family will be understanding towards my son's special needs, though. Not just his handicaps, but how he's been raised, what he's seen. Our . . . way of life has been so different from theirs.

"It's going to be okay."

Detective Lindsay looks at his phone, then excuses himself. The room feels emptier now.

Without his presence, there's an awkward silence in the room, punctured by my mother's sniffles and the scratch-scratch of Sam's crayon as he colors the cast on my arm.

I close my eyes, exhaustion hitting with a swift vengeance. One of the machines to my side beeps and I wait with expectation for that sweet rush of euphoria about to enter my body. I've been trying to stay awake, to wait for Paige, the sister I've missed with my whole being.

I don't think I can, though.

When I wake, even before opening my eyes, I know something is different.

Sam's not beside me. My eyes jerk open with panic only to see him curled up in the bed next to mine, blanket tucked tightly around him.

"You kept moaning in your sleep, so we moved him. I hope that's okay." The voice to my left is soft, cultured and oh so familiar.

My sister is beautiful. She looks as exhausted as I feel but braves a fearless smile that shines with love, happiness and pain.

Hi. I mouth the word, wishing I could speak.

"Hi."

One word and yet it's full of so many emotions.

I've missed you. I love you. Are you real? I'm so sorry.

So many things I want to say, so many things that will have to wait.

Both Monique and Detective Lindsay explained earlier what happened to her. How she'd been kidnapped and drugged, but other than that she looks fine. Did he rape her? Did he beat her? She looks fine, exhausted, but nothing is broken from what I can see.

She's the lucky one.

I'm still trying to process who Drew is or isn't. He's not a truck driver, like his father, but instead has been masquerading as a minister, a pastor my family has called friend for years.

How could they not know? How could they not see how evil he is? How could they be swayed by someone like him?

I'm not sure that's an answerable question, not right now at least.

Is this something we'll be able to work around? I hope so.

We stare at each other and I wish I could say the last twelve years disappeared, that the closeness we had is the same now, but I can't.

I don't know this woman. She sure as hell doesn't know me. We've lived such different lives, what do we have in common anymore?

"Sam is amazing," she says, reading my mind. She's doing what I can't — finding common ground. "He called you Momma earlier, while you slept. Just about melted my heart."

And there it is. We're both mothers. Mothers who will do anything and everything to protect our children. The way she looks at my son right now, for this reason alone, I know we'll be okay.

She glances at my wrist while covering her own. She's about to say something, but I stop her with a groan.

It's okay. I mouth. I know there's a story to her tattoo, just like there is to mine. It's a story we can rewrite together.

SIX MONTHS LATER

CHAPTER 54

DETECTIVE MERI AMBER
FCI SANDSTONE
(FEDERAL CORRECTIONAL INSTITUTION)

The prisoner enters the small interview room where I'm sitting, sipping a coffee. I pretend not to give him much attention, when in reality he's all I've been able to think about for the past six months.

Andrew Rawlings Jr. The one man who can answer so many of my questions.

Paige told me about the boxes he'd mentioned, boxes his father had kept as souvenirs. I believe one of those boxes has something to do with my sister.

For the past six months, he has refused to speak about his father or the house we found Paige in, until now. But he'll only speak to me.

Figures.

The man seated in front of me is different from the man I shot.

His wheelchair is locked and bolted to a lock in the ground. His wrists are chained to the arms of his chair. His right leg is swathed in a cast that starts mid-thigh and ends at his ankle.

"I'll never walk again because of you," he says as I take another sip of my coffee and finally look him in the eyes.

He lies. He'll walk again, but probably with the aid of a walker or a cane and never as well as before.

"The least you could do is apologize."

I take another sip as I consider his request. Apologize? What the hell for? For saving a life? For not ending his?

Detective Lindsay's voice is in my head. He's in the car, waiting for me outside. I think I'm going to take him up on his offer to join his team. I'd all but decided as I flew up here yesterday.

"Play nice, be nice," he said. "You'll get more if he thinks you're malleable. He's got nothing to lose, considering he got forty years with no parole."

"I'll get you a hand-carved cane as an apology gift for Christmas, will that work?" Oops, so much for following Lindsay's advice.

"I don't need any more gifts from you, but thanks for the offer." His tone is just as dry as mine.

"How is she?"

I'm not sure if he intended to ask this question or not. He seems just as surprised as I am.

"Sorry, forget I asked. How is my son, can you at least tell me that?"

I consider telling him where he can go and what he can do when he gets there, but Lindsay is right, I need to play nice.

"Sorry, I have no idea." This is the truth and I'm pretty sure he hears it loud and clear.

His head nods. "Yeah, I didn't think you would, but I figured it wouldn't hurt to ask. Sam is a good kid."

There is so much that I could say right now. He's a monster who doesn't deserve to know how the child he shares DNA with is doing. He's not his father and never will be.

"I'm told you're willing to talk about your father." I'm not here for idle chitchat. I didn't just fly up here for the hell of it.

"Andy Senior. He was a mean man. My best days growing up were when he was on the road." Drew heaves a lengthy sigh as he stares at his hands.

"Tell me about the room you kept Paige in." I only know what's on record, the things he mentioned in his testimony. That was his father's special room, one he was never allowed in as a child. The walls were soundproofed for a reason.

"I know you think I'm like my father, but I'm not."

Do I believe this? Considering they both led double lives and kept women captive, my answer would be yes, he's very much like his father. The only difference in my books is, one kept girls as prisoners and killed them after he got tired of them, and the other kept a girl as a prisoner and only tried to kill her when he thought he might get caught.

"My father was only ever in a good mood when he brought a new toy home," Drew continues, not waiting for my reply. "The first one I remember was when I was around seven or eight. He came home in the middle of the night, but the lights of his truck woke me up. I waited forever for him to come into the house, and when he didn't, I went out to greet him. Except, I saw him walking around to the back of the house, with someone in his arms. He never came in the house. Not that night."

Story time can be tricky. When you give someone enough space to tell their story, what often comes out is part truth, part exaggeration and part justification.

I need to listen to this story. I need to not just listen, but look past the words, try to view the memory, stage the scene in order to hear what's not being said.

Because if there's one thing I've come to realize about Andrew Rawlings Jr., it's that he knows how to craft the perfect lie in order to maintain his own truth.

I'm not here for just one person. This is more than finding out if Senior had my sister. This is about all the other victims.

Paige told us Drew mentioned fifteen boxes. That's fifteen possible victims.

Where are the boxes now? How big are they? What do they contain? Where are the bodies?

"I left as soon as I could. Most of my teenage life I was trying to leave, to get away from the monster. I even stole cars to do it. I was sixteen when I got caught an hour outside of town and was eventually sent to juvie. No one bothered to find out why I stole cars. They just saw a stupid teen making stupid mistakes."

"You could have told someone." There's no sympathy or understanding in my voice. There might be a hint of censure mixed in with an are-you-for-real exasperation. But this man gets no sympathy.

"I was more afraid of my father than the cops. No, the only way out was to get as far from my father as I could. Eventually I did. I changed my name and created a new life for myself."

He thinks moving an hour away from his childhood home was as far as he could go?

"Working with CHILD was my way of making up for what my father did. I know he stole girls. He picked them up while he was trucking, brought them home, and eventually killed them. I couldn't undo what he'd done, but I could help the families get through it."

I remain silent. He's giving me little tidbits of information while trying to exonerate himself. If I let him continue, I may just get more.

I need to remain patient.

He tilts his head to the side and purses his lips together. He's studying me. My face is a mask of indifference, so I'm not sure what he's searching for.

"You don't care about me, do you? You don't care why I saved Angel, why I couldn't give her up. You just care about my father and the boxes. Why?"

I can play nice. I can play nice. I can play nice.

"You weren't the only victim, Drew."

His eyes widen for one millisecond before something that looks like a smile tugs at the edges of his lips.

I just gave him what he wants the most. I acknowledged him as a victim.

"No, I wasn't his only one. But I saved his last victim. I saved her and there's nothing he can do about it."

Present tense. This is the first time he's talked about his father as if he were still alive. Until now, he's only ever spoken of Andrew Rawlings Sr. in past tense.

This has me leaning forward, fully intent on him and his upcoming answers. "Do you know where your father is?" There was no sign of him at the house. I keep getting updates of sightings, so I know he must be alive.

"Do you want to know about the boxes or not?" A cold, calculating, cunning look is all I see staring back at me.

I lean back, arms crossed, and wait.

"He likes to take one a year," Drew finally says. "I don't know what he does with them when he's done nor do I know how he kills them. What I can tell you is he only needs one girl a year to soothe the beast that rages inside him. He's good at hiding. He's good at covering his tracks. There's a reason you haven't found him."

His smile is bittersweet. I can't tell if he's proud of his father or not.

"I went home once for the holidays. My father swore up and down he'd stopped, that he was too old, that it was getting too hard. I believed him. He seemed antsy, though, like he couldn't wait for me to leave. So I did, then came back and found him in that room, with her."

"With Angel?"

He nods. "I . . . lost it. He lied and I believed him. I took her from him, I saved her."

I know all this. I didn't come all this way for this nonsense. The small room is starting to smell and it's not because of my coffee. Besides, between his confession to Paige and pleading guilty to kidnapping, forced imprisonment and sexual assault, I'm well aware of how he came to find Jessica Fischer and why he kept her.

Deep down, whether he wants to admit it or not, he's exactly like his father.

"I'm glad you saved her, Drew, I really am. Because of you, she's healing with her family, where she belongs. But that's not why I'm here."

His head whips up. "Where she belongs?" His mouth becomes a snarl, his true nature showing up.

His upper body tightens, his hands fist. When before he was ready to talk, to share his secrets, now he's not.

I've offended him.

Is this where I'm supposed to apologize? Lindsay would probably tell me to backtrack, remind me to play nice.

Damn it.

"The boxes?"

"What about them?" He's now adopting a tough-guy attitude, believing he holds all the cards. "You know, after I heard about your sister and how you're so interested in my father, I thought maybe I could help you. That maybe I could still be that guy . . ." He stops, offers up a few *tsk tsks*, all the while shaking his head.

"Be Jeremy again?" I ask, my voice noticeably softer.

"That's my true self."

I stuff my snort deep and thankfully he's none the wiser.

"What's in the boxes?" I ask. Our time is almost up and a bubble of frustration that's been sitting in my gut expands.

It takes him forever, but he finally lifts his hands, the handcuffs clinking against the chair, in a *who knows* gesture.

"They were locked and I didn't have a key. But they were also tagged, with names."

My heart skips about a million beats.

"What did they look like?"

"A square box, made out of wood. Something he put together himself, I think. He wrote the names on the front in black marker." He winces and leans forward. "They say my knee is always going to hurt."

If he's trying to make me feel guilty, it's not working. The only thing I feel guilty about is getting my hopes up that maybe, just maybe, he would cooperate with me.

"What did you do with them?"
"I buried them."

* * *

By the time I make it out to my car, where Lindsay waits, I'm seething.

"Well?" He puts down his phone and has a look of expectation, a look I'm soon going to squash.

"He's playing games."

There are so many names I want to call Andrew Rawlings Jr. right now. So many names that hover on the tip of my tongue, but I refuse to give him the energy he so clearly is craving.

"He gave me the location of five boxes. Seems he buried them all over. Each box is labeled, but he can't remember the names because he didn't want to know too much. Nor does he know what's inside the boxes." I don't believe him. I didn't believe him then, when he tried to sell me that BS and I don't believe him now, as I repeat it back to Lindsay.

"You think he knows?"

I snort. "Of course he knows. Come on. His father kidnaps and kills young women, keeps boxes for old times' sake and he doesn't know what's in them? Why would he hide them?"

"Did he say where his father is?"

I shake my head as I start the engine and put the vehicle in drive. "No. But he for sure knows. He was going to take Paige there, remember?"

Lindsay pats the file on his lap. "Yep, I remember."

"So what's the next step?"

As I pull away from the correctional facility where I hope Junior rots for the rest of his days, my hands grip the wheel a little too tightly.

"Now we go find those boxes."

THE END

EASTER EGG

Did you notice the easter egg I added to the story from my novel: THE PATIENT

HINT: While Angel was looking at dresses, a certain someone stopped to talk to her . . .

This is the second easter egg for this character. Did you notice her in THE PERFECT SECRET too?

THANK YOU!

To those in my Steena's Secret Society — my reader group on Facebook — THANK YOU for all your name suggestions, for all your plot help, for always being supportive exactly when I need it! You guys will notice I used your ideas everywhere in this book! A special thank you to Cecile Evans for reading this story so quickly at the last minute!

Thank you to my awesome ReaderTeam, for reading this book so quickly, sharing your thoughts, your passion, your praise for this story! No author publishes alone, and you, my Influencers, are part of my publishing team. Thank you, thank you, thank you! Kate Rock — thank you for your support, encouragement and help in spreading the word about this book!

Kelly Charron . . . you are my angel, my amazing friend and my cheerleader when I need it the most. Thank you for being the first person to read this book, for sharing your thoughts, encouragement and pushing me past my comfort zone.

Thank you to Jamie Fischer for your plot help at the beginning when I was piecing together this story, and especially for your suggestions when it came to Jamie and Flynn.

Thanks to the group at SouthTrail Hyundai who listened to me stress over plot ideas and characters and gave so many helpful ideas (specifically Ryan Daniels, Lexi Karns aka . . . Detective Meri Amber, Kylian Pomares and anyone else I missed).

But most of all, thank you to my family. To my daughters — it's a privilege and an honor to be your mother, to worry over you at night when you don't make it home for curfew or when I stalk your Instagram and Snapchat stories to see what you're up to (being a mother of adult daughters is HARD . . . check-in a little more, would you?). And to my husband: without you, I'm a shell of a woman surviving on cereal, toast and coffee. I love you babe, to the end of the line.

THE REASON FOR THIS BOOK

This story is one that's spoken to me for a few years now. It's a story that needs to be told for one simple reason: it's being lived by so many women and experienced by so many families all around the world. It's a story that happens here at home, and not just my home, but it's happening close to your home too.

There are many resources out there where we can educate ourselves on what to look for, how to protect our children, and how we can help those sold/forced into the sex trade industry. If able, please watch the movie TRAFFICKED starring Patrick Duffy and Ashley Judd.

Here are some online resources that can help you:

Canadian Human Trafficking: www.canadianhumantraffickinghotline.ca

Polaris Project: www.polarisproject.org

Human Trafficking Hotline: www.humantraffickinghotline.org

THE JOFFE BOOKS STORY

We began in 2014 when Jasper agreed to publish his mum's much-rejected romance novel and it became a bestseller.

Since then we've grown into the largest independent publisher in the UK. We're extremely proud to publish some of the very best writers in the world, including Joy Ellis, Faith Martin, Caro Ramsay, Helen Forrester, Simon Brett and Robert Goddard. Everyone at Joffe Books loves reading and we never forget that it all begins with the magic of an author telling a story.

We are proud to publish talented first-time authors, as well as established writers whose books we love introducing to a new generation of readers.

We won Trade Publisher of the Year at the Independent Publishing Awards in 2023. We have been shortlisted for Independent Publisher of the Year at the British Book Awards for the last four years, and were shortlisted for the Diversity and Inclusivity Award at the 2022 Independent Publishing Awards. In 2023 we were shortlisted for Publisher of the Year at the RNA Industry Awards.

We built this company with your help, and we love to hear from you, so please email us about absolutely anything bookish at feedback@joffebooks.com

If you want to receive free books every Friday and hear about all our new releases, join our mailing list: www.joffebooks.com/contact

And when you tell your friends about us, just remember: it's pronounced Joffe as in coffee or toffee!

ALSO BY STEENA HOLMES

STANDALONES
THE SISTER UNDER THE STAIRS

Made in the USA
Las Vegas, NV
21 March 2024